Juggling With Jelly

Mary Ann Pledge grew up in Devon. At Essex University she began singing and playing in a variety of rock bands. She lived in Barcelona and in Paris, where she taught English, but she returned to the allure of the Devon countryside to have her three daughters. There they remain with their extended menagerie. Her first novel, *Wading Through Jelly*, was published in 2006. She teaches part-time at Exeter University.

Juggling With Jelly

Mary Ann Pledge

Juggling With Jelly

(The sequel to *Wading Through Jelly*)

Olympia Publishers

www.olympiapublishers.com
OLYMPIA PAPERBACK EDITION

A CIP catalogue record for this title is
available from the British Library.

ISBN: 978-187897-046-5

This is a work of fiction. Any resemblance to real-life characters
would be entirely coincidental.

First Published in 2010

Olympia Publishers
60 Cannon Street
London
EC4N 6NP

Printed in Great Britain

To Arnold, for continuing to keep my feet on the ground
and my heart in the skies!

Acknowledgments

Many thanks to Mark Parkhouse, for his Antique knowledge and resources, to Nick Treble, consultant surgeon, for copious medical information and explanation, to Georgie and Charlie Cotton, for the Prosecco and fish pies, to Lizzie Wilson and BBC Radio Devon for their generous support, to Tory Cranfield for her jellies and to Pie, for his kind walks! Most of all, to my corking daughters, Annelisa, Miranda and Cissie – because they are!

Chapter One

A battered, but lovingly polished, pale pink Vauxhall Corsa ground into view, stopping sedately outside the old vicarage with an undignified clunk of the handbrake, propelling the incumbents violently forward. Susanna stepped demurely from the dilapidated driver's seat, which was adorned with a multi-coloured tapestry cushion to cover the holes where the sponge-work poked through, while Susanna's sister, Charlie, clambered out from the other side. Each looked strained and uncertain, glad that the other was there (though wild horses couldn't have extracted this admission!) A loud thud announced the hefty opening shove at the heavy, oak, side-door as the three sisters, inhabitants of the old house, tumbled through it to greet their friends. Ella, the eldest at sixteen, enthused politely at Susanna's 'new' car and Susanna smiled eagerly at finding a topic over which she could unwind:

"Isn't she amazing? I only passed my test on Friday and this is the first time I've tried driving in the little lanes."

"It was scary!" put in Charlie, mischievously: "We nearly ran down a deer."

"It jumped through the hedge at us," explained Susanna hurriedly, "And then a herd of cows!"

"We just drove round the corner and there they were. (*You are SO dead!*)" whispered Susanna, giving her sister a malevolent glare and shooting a quick look at Ella for reassurance, who raised her eyes to the heavens in empathy. Actually, she was thinking that Charlie was so like her own sister, Demelza, who was equally annoying, and at this thought she felt a little stab in her ribs:

"Why don't we take your car for a spin and you can show me what she can do!" she said quickly and Susanna agreed gratefully, mollified at the proffered gender to describe her beloved motor. She smoothed down her micro-skirt in preparation to leaping back into the intrepid jalopy.

This left Charlie, aged fourteen, hovering uncertainly amongst her best friend Demelza's younger sisters. Her skinny, athletic frame was made clearly visible by the expanse of midriff shown below her T-shirt; but what was not evident was the pumping whirli-wash within, at Susanna deserting her so soon. She had wanted to come, she had *asked* to come and her mother had thought it might help – but now she was here she was overtaken by paroxysms of shyness and nervousness in turns. Somehow sensing this, Poppy, the youngest, put her hand confidingly on Charlie's arm:

"I've got a poorly baby chick and it's living in the bottom of the Aga – want to see?"

"Cool," answered Charlie, with more enthusiasm than she felt, but relieved to have somewhere to go and something to do. She followed Poppy and Sophia (the one she thought of as the quieter, more bookish sister), into the relative cool of the house to a roomy kitchen, which was dominated by the Aga, from which came a series of high-pitched cheeps. Poppy gently eased the door to the bottom oven further open and drew out a damp and dilapidated shoebox, containing a tiny chick and an inverted jam lid of bread and milk. The chick was covered in a thin coating of golden feathers, through which could be seen the pink skin, stretched over a tiny pounding heart.

"You can hold her if you like," smiled Sophia timidly, hoping that this was what Charlie would like and that she wouldn't reply "*Gross!*" as Demelza might have.

"Her legs won't walk so we have to keep her warm in the oven until they get better – otherwise the mother hen might stand on her," explained Poppy, now displaying a confidence that Charlie would find this equally absorbing:

"*I* hope her legs never work so she can live in the bottom oven for ever!" she went on.

"I somehow think a *live* hen might find living in our oven a little too snug?" rejoined Sophia gravely.

"And Confusing!" Charlie stretched out her hands, the copious bracelets set dancing at the gesture, as her long fingers curled around the warm bundle, as light as air. She stroked the soft feathers and in giving comfort she felt comforted. Gradually, the angry acne bumps that she had earlier attempted so hard to conceal ceased to throb in her burning teenage face.

A scraping sound caught their attention as the French windows were expertly prized open by a Wellington clad foot belonging to Connie, the children's mother, her arms heavily burdened with logs.

She deftly hooked the door to behind her with the same foot, before shaking off each boot onto the mat and smiling her welcome. Charlie saw that she had lost weight from that day when she had last seen her and her face looked tired and gaunt, showing more lines, while shadows played beneath the smiling eyes where none had shown before. Connie's shiny, rebellious, tawny hair was the same sort of chaos though, pinned off her forehead by a blue china slide.

"Charlie, we're all so glad you've come!" Connie said warmly. *Were her eyes normally so shiny?* thought Charlie. "But where are Ella and Susanna? Have they deserted you already?" Charlie, still stroking the little chick, explained that they had taken Susanna's car for a spin. Connie nodded understandingly and excused herself:

"Let me lighten myself from this load a moment – they're wonderfully dry logs from last autumn's gales, and they go up like blazes."

Connie returned, scraping the moss absently from the front of her navy sweater and shrugging into a pair of worn Ugg boots, kindly donated by her brother, Jeremy. She hugged Charlie, thanking her again for coming, which Charlie was beginning to find embarrassing. Seeing this, Connie pulled herself together from the emotional inner jelly that she was experiencing so much these days and considered for a moment:

"It's lovely you're here: Demelza would be so pleased." She looked quickly at Charlie, who looked away. *That was the wrong thing to say,* thought Connie. She felt so dreadfully tired. She always seemed to find herself upsetting people or speaking her thoughts aloud unintentionally. It wasn't surprising that people had started to give her a wide berth! Why was dear Charlie here anyway? It was sweet of her to come, of course, but what did she want to do? Poor girl, she was obviously miserable, and it was unfeeling of Ella to have escaped with Susanna like that. Sophia and Poppy were so much better at making her feel at ease – perhaps she could also escape and leave Charlie to their ministrations? She got up and then changed her mind, chiding herself at her self-centredness. Looking around she was aware of an expectant pause, as all eyes fixed hopefully on her, the adult, to fill the void of conversation and to magically resume an unrestrained atmosphere of normality. She struggled to return to an equal wavelength:

"Just a thought, Charlie, but would you like to go up to *her* room?

It helps me sometimes, in a funny way, and Ella's developed some of Demelza's photos from her digital camera and of course you're in many of them. That is, perhaps you don't want…" she wavered, her new-found uncertainty rearing its unwanted self again,

"Oh I think I would!" answered Charlie, surprising herself in finding this to be true.

"Well go on up, you know the way, or would you like one of us to come with you?"

"No really, I'll be fine. I mean, it may be easier on my own." Sophia and Poppy exchanged glances of relief because this was proving unexpectedly difficult, and Charlie slid from the room. Connie called after her to come down when she was ready, but if they hadn't heard from her they would call her when it was supper time.

"I'll talk to her properly then," Connie promised herself, the familiar feeling of inadequacy reclaiming her.

Charlie ascended the green baize back stairs, turning right at the landing and opening the little rickety door, its white paint chipped and the area around the handle showing brown from numerous sticky hands. The smeary trail extended, hand-height, up a flight of steep narrow wooden stairs to the attic, which was tucked away under the gables on the second floor. The attic itself was divided by three stairs, one staircase opened onto the playroom, with its mixture of comfort for all ages in the way of sofas, a CD player, with the inevitable scattering of CDs and covers littering the surrounds, a dolls house, Duplo, and a vast and battered table-tennis table; the bats, weeping curled rubber, strewn carelessly on the dusty surface.

The other staircase led to Demelza's room, the door of which was generally welcomingly open, the scattering of clothes, more CDs, schoolwork and books, on general display from the landing. On this occasion, however, the door, which looked newly dented, was closed and when Charlie pushed it gingerly open, peering warily around the portal, she saw that the floor had been divested of its customary clutter, the books and CDs returned to their shelves, the schoolwork to the desk and her clothes into the unusually closed chest of drawers. Normally bursting forth from the drawers was a spillage of colourful clothing of every type and description. The pile of the carpet stood erect, the furrows of a Hoover noticeably visible, while the memorable stains of Coca-Cola and of the time they had sneaked in that lamb and it had whoops-ied everywhere, stood out in homely contrast to Charlie's eyes.

Charlie had always been rather envious of this room, as not only was it a geographical refuge, but it also gave those who approached it an enchanting feeling of entering a den, a magical Narnian wardrobe; for the ceiling was ablaze with streamers and curly-whirly, shiny, plastic strips that shifted gently in the draft from the dormer window, while the walk-in wardrobe itself was painted black, with phosphorescent silver streamers adorning the walls and luminous pictures that only emerged when you had got in and closed the door. Demelza had arranged her speakers in here and a small spotlight for when she actually wanted to see to do her homework. In spite of the apparent chaos in decor, everything was arranged carefully to maximise convenience and ease: the remote control for her sound system was situated for immediate waking access by her bed; its highly glossed headboard punctuated by more of the luminous stars that littered walls and ceiling to Torch up the Night! These words, borrowed from Dylan, were emblazoned across one wall. A solitary radiator bore a host of magnetic letters, depicting the feelings of the moment; anything from "Losers and geeks, unite and fight", as at this moment, to the words of pop songs: currently showing her number one favourite of all time: Plastic Max's I Feel Dangerous. The walls themselves were a mass of cuttings, displaying pop stars and teenage idols, their faces pouting, their jeans bulging provocatively and photographs – masses of them – mainly of herself and her friends and a few of her family. Some of the photos included humorous captions and comments, while others said enough by themselves.

Charlie had begun by feeling awkwardly intrusive at the prospect of being in this haven without her friend, but as she began to examine the photographs, she started to feel a fragile link with herself and a sense of belonging. She moved from photos of the school hockey team, Demelza's stick brandished rather over-enthusiastically, the mischievous grin belying, to those who knew her well, her feelings about being photographed in this situation. To be quite clear, "jolly brollysticks!" was written across the whole in biro. Then there was a picture of Demelza nursing her much prized cockerel, Ben, capturing an uncharacteristically namby-pamby expression on her face: "I called him Ben for short, but his surname is *the Bomb!"* she had explained proudly, arching her eyebrows quizzically to see if Charlie had understood and, she had to admit it *had* taken a moment or two before she was able to reward with the guffaw that her friend was awaiting, as she added that his Thai cousin was also called Ben: Ben Cock!

Charlie moved on to examine photos of herself, Demelza and Holly, dressed in some very tarty designer clothes that they had tried on in a shop, knowing full well that they could never have been able to afford them. Charlie smiled at the memory of the comments they had called loudly from the changing rooms, probably fooling no-one:

"I simply *can't* decide if this would go with my Prada stole! What do *you* think, Clarissa?"

"Ah yes – I can see that does suit – but perhaps a little on the cheap side? You wouldn't want to meet *everyone* wearing one you know!" They had lined up before the mirrors in the changing rooms pouting and sneering for the copious snaps that they took turns in taking, only to reproduce, accompanied by screams of mirth, on the computer screen later that day. Then Demelza would always drag her mother, Connie, in to see the photos of the antics that they had got up to, posing with security guards and bouncers, balancing along high walls by the river and so on. Charlie had felt quietly envious at the way Connie would gurgle with explosive laughter at their antics and never seem remotely perturbed at their behaviour – as her own mother would have been, had she told her, which she knew better than to do! Sometimes Connie would cook enormous dishes of pasta for them and the rest of the family and hang out with them for a time; but she was always busy and couldn't ever join them for long. This actually made them feel sorry when she had to return to other occupations, which included a band that she played in (*how cool was that?)* of which Charlie's own mother thoroughly disapproved, saying it was a terrible example to set her family. Charlie didn't argue at this, for she knew it was a waste of time; but she felt a stab of disloyalty at not standing up for someone who was – well sort of nearly a friend.

Here was a photo of Connie singing with the band. She was wearing a pair of tight jeans: something else that her mother said no woman over forty should do, but she looked cool with them tucked into high-heeled boots. The expression on her face was so absorbed, so completely detached from what you saw from day to day: the song must have really meant something to her. She wondered if it was love, sex or simply sheer rock and roll, for Connie's hair was streaming out behind her, presumably with the sway of her body, so she must have been giving the music a thing or two.

At the thought of love, Charlie's eyes fastened on the less familiar sight of Connie's man, Sebastian, whom she had only met a couple of times, but whom Demelza had pronounced as "quite cool and a definite improvement on *Psycho!"* There were no photos of 'Psycho', or Pete, as he was properly known, for beside Demelza disliking him, for no obvious reason that Charlie actually knew of, he and Connie had split up over what seemed to be quite a long period of time, with Connie attempting, as she would, to remain friends. Psycho had appeared to go along with this, but then he would push the boundaries and make Connie uncomfortable all over again. Charlie was rather hazy about what had happened between them to make the gentle Connie truly mad and Psycho to flee the country; but it was something awesomely awful, about which Ella knew, and she had told a little of this to Susanna, who wouldn't spill a *word* about it to Charlie, for fear of her telling Demelza which – let's face it – she would have done. Anyway, after the disgrace, Psycho had gone to Sri Lanka or somewhere and everyone had said good riddance!

Charlie examined Sebastian more closely: he was tall, much taller than Connie, and heavily built, with broad shoulders and a large head, the size of which was emphasised by the fact that it was a mixture of baldness and a Caesar number one and was therefore distinguished by being the same tanned colour all over, even peeping through the stubble on his chin. He was smiling directly and seemingly unabashed at the camera, with large, kind, amused, brown eyes that were creased at the corners; and she could just make out a small gold stud in one of his ears, rendering a somewhat piratical stance to his general appearance. His arm was tucked casually around Connie's shoulders and she was sort of leaning into him, looking up and laughing. Charlie suddenly found herself hoping that all would be alright there, for Connie looked so happy and relaxed in the photo, in contrast to the way she had seen her this afternoon.

If it could be believed, Connie and Sebastian had met under a table at a party, or so everyone said. He had taken a liking to the family dog, Tramp, who was getting very doddery, which meant that Connie took him everywhere with her so that he wouldn't be confused or lonely, as he might be if left alone or with others. Well that was what she always said, but Connie was so dippy about Tramp that it was probably just as much Connie who needed his company as a prop! Anyway she had taken him to this party at her cousin's in Kent and Sebastian had apparently asked her out for lunch while he was with Tramp, beneath the tablecloth!

Chapter Two

The day after that party, where Connie had met Sebastian, had been a stunning day, but she had felt thoroughly nervous – and if it hadn't been for her large and voluptuous cousin Boo, with whom she had been staying, she might have called the rendezvous off. She and Boo had tottered home from the party in the small hours, with Connie's guitarist friend, Ken. He and Connie had been a couple and in a band together years ago when she was a student: she had been studying classical music, while singing and playing in bands as a sideline. Ken's success had grown, taking him to different countries with bigger gigs and increasingly better known bands and he and Connie kept in touch only sporadically, but they renewed contact whenever it was geographically possible for her to attend any of his gigs. Recently, he and Connie had rekindled a short-lived romance, which had meant more to Ken than to her. He had written a melancholic song about his feelings and to everyone's delight and surprise, it had been taken up by a major record company and was beginning to do well as a single in the pop world, for it cashed in on his 'retro' image and timeless style, which had happily resurged into fashion, thanks to the leanings towards the likes of Kate Moss and Boy George.

Ken and Boo were obviously much taken with one another and they stayed up most of the night talking and canoodling on the sofa, where Ken eventually slept.

When Connie emerged, somewhat bleary-eyed, Boo was relieved:

"So you're going to meet your hunky dog-lover!" she said, her clear, twinkling blue eyes in contrast, giving no indication of having been up most of the night.

"Well, I don't know. Was I a bit rash? I mean, I *really* liked him – but we'd had a fair amount to drink and the whole thing was a bit surreal now I look back on it."

"Certainly does!" answered Boo with gusto, clearly relishing the notion, "But now's the time to discover the real man from below the table!"

"But that was *last night!* What's a nice man like that going to think of the likes of me: four children and an old mongrel down, agreeing so easily to a date from…?"

"From *above* the table?" Boo repeated. "You banged on relentlessly about him last night, how you felt he could 'see through' you – even through a hunk of polished pine complete with gingham cloth!"

"Did I?" asked Connie rather too innocently,

"You know perfectly well you did. *I'd* go for him myself if it wasn't that I…" she looked purposefully towards the sofa, where Ken's much tousled, dark hair protruded from the depths of a psychedelically coloured sleeping bag, his mouth hanging open in heavy slumber. Connie looked at the bundle that was Ken and laughed mischievously:

"I know what you're up to. You're trying to get rid of me! You don't care *where* I go or with whom so long as you can have some quality time with sleeping beauty!" Boo let out a squeal of indignation and her good natured peachy complexion split into a Simpson-esque grin!

"I confess I *do* fancy the idea of there just being the two of us here when he wakes up –" Boo's candour was always so refreshing, "but it's also true that I think there's no question about you're going out for lunch with that lovely man."

"He just wanted to see Tramp again – he only asked me out of politeness. Maybe I should let him take Tramp for a walk – well, more like a 'shuffle'. I could go to the pub in the village, out of your way and his. The trouble is…" at last she was warming to the subject, "I actually felt I liked him so much, which is silly after so little time and it's probably that I'm missing Mother and the children and getting all mixed up!" At the mention of Connie's mother, who had died very recently and with whom Connie had enjoyed the closest of bonds, Boo's voice softened a little and a gentler expression replaced the twinkle in her eye:

"But Connie *he's* the lucky one – and you know your mother would have told you not to be such a silly ass and to strike out and enjoy…"

"Go, Connie, *go!*" said a voice from the sofa. Ken was speaking with eyes still closed and Connie wondered how much of these admissions he had heard. "You obviously fancy him like crazy. After all he wasn't a werewolf, and what's wrong with a lunch to find out if he's still as hunky by the light of day?"

Propelled by this logic and eager to leave Ken to Boo's significant glances (Boo clearly suffered from none of her own scruples, Connie noticed enviously), Connie had hastily kissed each of them, grabbed her bags and Tramp and trundled out of the little cottage as fast as she could manage, calling that she would see them later, which was intended to remind them of this fact.

Now she stood in the picture-box splendour of the red brick Kent village and returned the lusty waves and rude gestures that Boo was making from her cottage window. She threw her bags into the car and walked slowly and companionably down the village street, with Tramp sniffing and raising his leg at every tree that marked the route, until they reached the well-manicured village green. Here, she shambled around the green with Tramp in tandem, jostling him along occasionally with the toe of her boot, musing excitedly and nervously at her actual prospective date, an amused half smile playing around her mouth. Examining her motives dispassionately, as was her wont, she knew that she had never intended *not* meeting Sebastian. She had just needed the support and encouragement, on which she could rely, from her generous cousin.

A series of beeps interrupted her reverie and she looked up to see a shiny olive green BMW, the driver definitely Sebastian, his face shaded by a floppy black felt hat and a pair of designer sunglasses, his gold ear-stud glinting in the sun. Connie's stomach lurched and she felt her cheeks flushing annoyingly, *like a stupid schoolgirl,* she thought, hoping that Sebastian's sunglasses would be kind enough to mask her crimson cheeks.

Sebastian was overjoyed to find Connie there on the green. He hadn't slept much, dreading the possibility that she might have taken fright in the cold light of day, made some excuse, sent a text – he had been there before – some simple reason to shrug her out of actually having *meant* what she had said last night: that she would see him again. However, his fears had been unfounded, for, on the contrary, she actually looked happy to see him and was smiling that lovely slightly lopsided smile that had so captivated him. He leapt out of his car; his long denim clad legs unfolding with surprising grace, and called out his greetings. He bent down over Tramp and made a fuss of him, lessening the awkwardness of the moment that they both suffered, and Connie joined in by gently stroking the smooth fur on

Tramp's head and behind the tufts on his ears.

"I'm so glad you made it," Sebastian began saying and Connie, not wishing to seem too much of a walkover, responded that Tramp had needed exercise and her cousin lived just down the road so she would probably have wound up here sooner or later in any case. As soon as she heard herself say this she regretted it, for she saw Sebastian looking slightly deflated: perhaps he didn't have quite the amount of confidence she had credited him with, and this was something with which she could empathise.

"I know a wonderful little pub restaurant quite near here," Sebastian was saying, "They're not at all ostentatious and are fine with dogs, providing they keep a low profile, which seems to be something on which we can depend!" He checked to see if Connie appeared offended but she laughed and he saw that Tramp had had enough of walking and was already slumped calmly and contentedly in the grass at Connie's feet. He absently accepted their caresses, the sun warming and playing sunbeams across his rusty-red coat, his silvered whiskers moving gently with his soft breathing, like water streamlining through the gills of a fish.

A discussion had ensued about transport. Connie suggested that she should follow Sebastian's car, but he found himself not wanting to be separated from her so soon and making ridiculous excuses, comparing the size and smoothness of the ride. Connie had asked about Tramp and Sebastian answered that naturally he was included. She looked at the immaculate car:

"Tramp's hairs would make a terrible mess," she explained apologetically and Sebastian, admiring her consideration toward what was – it had to be admitted – his pride and joy, said gallantly that it didn't matter at all and that he would collect every one of the hairs and keep them in a casket as unholy relics. He followed this smoothly with a master stroke:

"You may really need to hear my sound system. Everyone whose opinion I admire says it's the best!"

"Right: we're in!" responded Connie, opening the heavy door through which Tramp moved quite nimbly, before adjusting himself carefully, by shifting around until he had found a good place to settle, and then thumping his body down contentedly . His eyes closed again as he nestled against the warmth of the engine and Connie clambered around him, each long leg amassing a fine carpet of rusty hairs on either side of his shaggy bulk. Sebastian had thrown himself in on the other side of the great car and they sped off to the tune of Andrea Boccelli's rendering of Rossini's *Domine Deus*, to which Sebastian sang along lustily; although not especially *tunefully*, Connie couldn't help noticing: she liked the fact that he didn't seem to care, and envied his apparent lack of self consciousness.

They drew up at a large coaching inn, the upper third of its walls consisting of ornate terracotta tiles, in the Kentish fashion, while the lower part was painted starkly white. They approached it through an immaculately decorated garden, containing archways, fountains, little fishponds and what she couldn't help seeing as 'rather twee' trysting benches, which faced two ways. The garden was well stocked with roses and Connie found herself comparing the seamless glamour of this with the somewhat seedy beer gardens of Devon, with their bald grassless scars under heavy iron swings and climbing frames that kept the children amused and outside, while their parents seized at some sort of fleeting intimacy within. Here was neatness and elegance, here was Health and Safety and perhaps here also, were ruly children, who *sat* while waiting for the food to come, discussed issues quietly and intelligently, and listened to their elders and betters! Connie shook herself, remembering that right now children were nothing that should concern her for a change: she was *glad* at her own childrens' absence in this garden of herbaceous beauty, which should keep her mind from wondering whether they were behaving themselves for their father, Stuart – and if they weren't behaving, was he becoming angry, and if he was angry, were they missing her...?

They entered a low-ceilinged dining room, which was swathed in a stream of light, issuing across the floor from the latticed windows, which threw little squared patterns across the thick, plush carpet. The landlord of the pub was expecting them and it was clear that Sebastian had done his research in booking somewhere that dogs were welcome. They were ushered over to a table away from the others in the bow window, which was adorned with a cut glass vase of red roses, to which Sebastian nodded his approval. A large bowl of water was placed near Tramp's nose and the waitress asked if Tramp would be allowed a sausage, to which Connie consented. After his treat, Tramp settled into his favourite position, legs splayed inelegantly in the air, and Connie began to relish the rare thrill of being pampered: she sniffed the tight buds of the roses, which, in truth, smelt very little, since they were hothouse grown; but she pronounced them beautiful. Sebastian appeared to preen himself at this, saying that he was glad she approved of them and she could take them with her when they left. Connie realised, from his demeanour, that he must have actually ordered the roses and felt herself flush again with a mixture of embarrassment and delight at being in receipt of such consideration.

The menus arrived and they browsed through them, Sebastian being attentive towards her likes and dislikes and suggesting this or that accordingly. By the time the wine was produced, any traces of shyness had retreated, for their heads were close together, wrapped in the animated conversation of the night before: this time though, it could not be accused of being alcohol induced. When Sebastian was asked to taste the wine, he shook his head decidedly, and answered hurriedly:

"No, no: please *pour*!" continuing his previous sentence. The shared starter was enjoyed more for the coquetry of stealing the last prawn (smeared generously with what appeared to be an exotic form of garlic mayonnaise) than for the *haute cuisine* from which it had so painstakingly been made; and the delectability of the rest of the delightful meal passed them by also, in the haze of intimacy that was so rapidly stealing between them.

Sebastian asked Connie many questions regarding the children, her band and her job as a supply teacher and was enthralled by the different ways in which they seemed to touch her: her children were plainly both absorbing and adored, music seemed to be her passion, in equal dimensions of listening or taking part, while supply teaching seemed more a means to an end. He sensed, however, that she was actually fonder of some of the schools which she frequented regularly than she was prepared to admit, for she mentioned certain of the more colourful pupils with that sparkle in her eye, which, he had already noticed, only showed when she was amused or impassioned about something.

Sebastian, Connie learned, dealt in the antiques trade. At present he was after a refectory table for a special client, which he was finding an exciting challenge, for not only did it have to meet precise dimensions for the dining room it was intended, but there was a restriction on wood type and period:

"What about cost?" Connie had asked innocently, but Sebastian had smiled,

"If I get the piece right, they will have it regardless of cost. Some people have antiques sort of in the blood. They get this *must have* acquisitiveness, which isn't always pretty but it keeps me in socks."

"And you? Do you suffer from the *must have* syndrome?" Sebastian shifted a little in his seat.

"I think it might be true to say that I did have it when I started up, being surrounded by so much ageing splendour, but that's when you can get sold for a mug – and I certainly did many times: still do occasionally. People recognise that greedy look in your eye and you get done – and serve you right. Nowadays I'm content to be more *hands on,* and I follow my instincts, without getting so involved." Connie asked him if he had seen the series *Lovejoy.*

"I'm afraid I have been known by that title myself by certain so-called chums!"

"Are you anything like him?" she fished.

"Well, Lovejoy was just the wrong side of the law and I'm just within it. It doesn't make me perfect, but I don't swindle. "At least," he qualified, "not those who can't afford it – and I don't belong to any rings or anything that might put me behind bars. Disappointed?" Connie wasn't at all; on the contrary, she was impressed by his directness and relieved that he was fundamentally honest.

"But what happens when someone sells you something they think is run-of-the-mill and you actually *know* it has great worth?" she persisted,

"Sadly, that happens far less than we are led to believe; but those situations are what makes antiques so addictive: the *Ming* vase, used as an umbrella receptacle for generations, being sold with the jumble is what we all dream of – and if people are ignorant of what they're selling and ask a ridiculously low price, do you disabuse them of the notion and say 'Well actually Madam (not meaning to be sexist here, but it usually is a 'Madam') I'm afraid I can't give you a tenner for that – no! not even twenty: I'm talking about giving you a whole one thousand pounds since, with my knowledge, I know I can flog it for more!' It works the other way round too," he added hastily, "I've lost thousands on wrong hunches through the years, but now I'm a bit wiser and less impetuous than when I started in the business. I'm known in my field and people come to me with their requirements, knowing that I will make a profit but I won't rip them off out of hand. If, on the other hand, it is a little old lady with a teapot that's been in her family since she was a girl and she's loathe to part with it but needs the cash, it's another matter – I have a bit of a weakness there, I'm afraid."

"What happens then?" asked Connie, fascinated.

"One of two things: I ask to see her other bits and pieces at home that are less dear to her, and generally we can come up with something she sees as ghastly that will fetch a reasonable price, so she sells that instead and keeps the teapot!"

"You said there were *two* ways?"

"Well spotted." Sebastian was amazed and flattered in his own turn at Connie's obvious absorption at the minutiae of his business, but this answer, after the bluff exterior he had been attempting to give of his business acumen, was something of a give-away: "Well there are times when it's necessary to up the value for the sake of the feelings."

"Meaning? (Plain English would suit fine!)"

"Just that sometimes one doesn't like to disappoint and so one needs to give over the odds for the family treasure; rather than let them know that it might have spent better time on the rubbish heap than taking up good mantelpiece space all those years!" Connie was thrilled to find this humanitarian chink in Sebastian's apparently flourishing business and went on to tell him that, as a matter of fact, *she* had a teapot that... but Sebastian reminded her that *she* was neither little nor old and therefore wouldn't possibly qualify for his benevolence; in fact he would feel the need to rip her off big time!

The lunch passed distressingly quickly for them: Tramp continued to snooze, letting out the odd contented snort, which appeared to amuse the other diners; while Connie and Sebastian ate their three courses, absent-mindedly followed by coffee, which neither of them wanted to drink so much as to steal the extra time it would necessitate to make and take. Finally a waiter pushed the bill discretely at Sebastian and they looked around to find themselves the last there, while the long-suffering waiter waited agitatedly, anxious to glean what was left of his Sunday, away from the confines of the working environment. Sebastian reached into his pocket, producing a roll of notes, which made Connie feel a little awkward.

"I'm going halves," she insisted, drawing out her credit card. Sebastian pushed the card gently back into her Filofax.

"No. This was my idea so my treat!" he said firmly.

"But I've eaten half the meal and I believe in paying my dues," she replied, with equal vehemence. Sebastian turned his large chocolate eyes upon her:

"If you let me do this bill I'll let you do the next," he said craftily. Connie acquiesced with honour, secretly delighted that a future date had so easily been assumed.

"Ah, but the next one will be fish and chips!" she announced, as Sebastian presented her with the red roses, wrapped expertly by the waiter in a paper napkin.

As they walked to the car park, Tramp tottering behind, Sebastian slipped his arm companionably around her shoulders and told her that he couldn't remember when he had enjoyed a meal so much and they seemed already to be making a bad habit of being the last to leave.

"It's reluctance to part," Connie replied in that unsubtle, hit-the-nail-on-the-head way that Sebastian was already getting to know and enjoy. They drove back in a quieter mood, each accepting and savouring that something had begun between them: a small shoot had thrust its green head through the surface of the hard packed earth. Sebastian was wondering if he should kiss her on departure or whether he should save that up for the next time; resolving finally to simply go with the flow, as they seemed to have been doing effortlessly thus far.

Connie showed him where her car was parked, outside Boo's red-tiled Kentish cottage, and invited Sebastian in to meet Boo properly, having talked fondly about her at length and a little about Ken too, each of whom Sebastian had seen, but barely noticed at the party the night before. As they stepped across the little stepping stones that led to Boo's front door, they became aware of loud shrieks and high-pitched giggles, punctuating the stillness of the late afternoon and emanating from an upstairs window. Connie had noticed that Ken's car remained outside where he had left it the night before and now she could plainly hear what sounded like his voice, but very shrill and hysterical:

"No, no! *Anything* but that!" and then Boo's voice, excited and teasing, calling:

"*Tickle, tickle!*" Connie found herself suffering from a mixture of embarrassment because of Sebastian, and amusement because this really was a Boo special! However, just as she glanced at Sebastian to see how he was taking the uproar, a bright pink feather duster, the sort used for tricky cobwebs, came hurtling through the open window, heading directly for Sebastian, who leapt nimbly aside as it embedded itself, quivering on its bamboo handle, in the earth. In his haste at withdrawing Sebastian had stepped into a half submerged piece of corner stone and overbalanced into a rosebush.

Connie experienced one of those horrid moments to which she was prone, when she wished to appear all concern for the victim but was instead taken over by paroxysms of unshakable mirth! Sebastian extricated himself slowly, massaging the thorns from the seat of his hitherto impeccable jeans, now enhanced by a smattering of mud. Thankfully, he too was laughing:

"I suggest a tactical withdrawal!" he said in a hushed voice, not wishing to disturb the hilarity from the window above; however, the noise from the bedroom had now subsided somewhat and Connie had time to hope that neither passer by nor neighbour had been in earshot of the house of Boo recently.

"I'm so sorry!" gasped Connie, after she had regained some composure and they had escaped to the distance of the end of the garden path: "I did warn you about Boo, but I couldn't have anticipated that!"

"No indeed! You never once mentioned assault by feather duster," agreed Sebastian,

"And I really did want you to meet her!" persisted Connie, realising, to her disappointment, that she had now managed to miss the moment for prolonging the time with Sebastian.

"It seems she and your friend Ken are perhaps a little busy just now." This understatement was made while Sebastian continued to brush off mud and suck a finger which was bleeding from the harsh barbs of the rosebush, "Another time perhaps?" Connie nodded, but said she felt compelled to leave a note for Boo "for once she's finished," to explain leaving a day early and without saying goodbye. She delved into her cavernous handbag, complete with tissues, board markers and half-eaten doggie chews, and re-emerged brandishing a pen and a piece of torn paper, which had been the all-important list of staff to meet at Sophia's parents' evening.

Dear Boo, she wrote.

Just a quick not to say that due to the unforeseen circumstance of attack by feather duster, we have chosen to retreat with honour, in preference to dropping by for tea! Tramp says thank you and your

cats are delicious. Thanks for dragging me to the party – it's been the most wonderful weekend! Ring you soon – and love to your "ghastlies".

     And to you. And to Ken,   Sebastian and Connie cuz XXX

'Sebastian and Connie!' Writing their names together like that felt rather good and Connie nearly asked Sebastian to sign, but decided she had better not seem too cosy so soon. She showed Sebastian the note and explained that Boo always referred to her much loved children as her *ghastlies*, protesting that this was exactly what they were. In fact they were remarkably pleasant though in awe, perhaps, of their mother's exuberance.

Connie searched behind her automatically for Tramp as she prepared to bundle him into her car to head off a day earlier than intended, only to see him already parked on the scant pavement beside the car, his ancient peg like teeth gnawing happily through a myriad of bright pink feathers, the handle of the duster held neatly between both gnarled front paws! This was too much for Connie, who subsided into another uncontrollable fit of giggles.

"What?" asked Sebastian, enjoying his new friend's abandon, but Connie could do nothing but wave her arms about, pointing in Tramp's direction. At this Sebastian snorted with a deep gurgle of laughter too, as clouds of feathers scudded around Tramp's grey-whiskered head, resulting from the resounding sneeze that the plumes had engendered!

"I was about to ask him if he'd like to bring you back to my place instead – since your hostess seems a little on the pre-occupied side? What should be my interpretation of that sneeze noise he made?" Connie drew breath at last:

"He says it would depend on the quality of your feather dusters,"

"I think I can boast a thoroughly toothsome yellow variety!"

"He says yellow is his favourite."

"In that case, would he like to follow me in the westerly direction of London town?"

"Do you have a spare room?" This was Connie's modest attempt at explaining that she was not expecting to sleep with him – just in case he thought she was as much of a push-over as her cousin!

"Not so much a spare room – it's sort of taken up – but I have an infamously comfortable sofa!"

"Lead the way!" rejoined Connie, by way of acceptance, but before leaving entirely, Sebastian gently removed the remains of the mangled bamboo stick from Tramp's mouth, it's sides smeared in feather dye, and asked politely:

"May I?" before producing a small pocket knife, making an incision in the end and inserting Connie's note neatly into the cleft he'd made. He then skewered the whole remains, Red Indian style, into the lawn outside the sitting room window.

The niceties now over, Connie and Tramp had followed Sebastian's car (rather faster than the old Discovery was accustomed to going), affording her time on her own to reflect that this was not the sort of thing you were supposed to do with a comparative stranger, for, extraordinarily, they had only met the day before! However, in place of the shame or concern she told herself she should be feeling, she found herself wearing a silly secret grin of excitement, in anticipation of exacting more time with her new companion: *Thank you, Boo!* she thought.

Chapter Three

Getting into London on a Sunday evening was not plain sailing, but Connie stuck to Sebastian's car like a burr through the intricacies of side roads, traffic lights, slip roads and crossways until they eventually found themselves in a private car park in Chelsea. Sebastian indicated that Connie should park her car across the back of his; thereby not encroaching on another person's space, for people could become quite amazingly touchy over this sort of *faux pas*. He then led the way to a surprisingly quiet avenue, away from the hubbub of cars and buses, where birds could be heard amongst the abundance of cherry and lime trees that lined the road. A wrought iron gate opened onto a flight of steps, dividing the terrace of Victorian brick-clad houses from their basements, to which a further flight of steps descended. The basement, Sebastian explained, was his, for want of better words, 'showroom'. He fiddled with a number of well polished antique brass locks and finally threw the door open hospitably, through which Tramp clattered gratefully, a light flurry of pink feather parts still fluttering gently from his shaggy coat.

No sooner were they inside, than Sebastian dashed across the room to disable the alarm before clattering off to the kitchen in search of a bowl of water for Tramp. It arrived, a rather more elegant piece than that to which Tramp was accustomed, in the form of a pink and blue china pasta bowl. Sebastian apologised, explaining that he had difficulty in finding a receptacle not antique and Connie laughed saying that a washing-up bowl would have done equally well. She began to look around the room, which was a 'front room' knocked into what must have been the parlour, making it reasonably spacious for London standards. The space, however, could barely be appreciated, since there was a preponderance of elegant antique furniture spread around the sides, inserted into which stood a large worn leather sofa. Connie looked admiringly over beautiful French-polished finishes, with wood ranging from dark sixteenth century oak, engrained with the stains of time, to walnut veneers on delicately leggy Georgian occasional tables, their surfaces tipped neatly against the wall. There were piles of glossy magazines and brochures advertising antiques-fairs stacked on a sofa table, the further end of which supported a huge many coloured porcelain oriental lamp, which bathed the room in its soft glow. A television was seen to be peeking from an open cupboard door.

"I can't bear that evil eye gazing at me," Sebastian explained apologetically when he saw Connie looking at it curiously. A coffee mug sat on a mat on one of a pair of little round mahogany drinks tables next to the sofa, and a *chaise longue* stood at right-angles to the sofa. A decorative Victorian tiled fireplace took up part of one wall in which stood a convincing looking log fire flamed by gas, which Sebastian had hastily lit to add to the ambience, as he selected a timeless Eric Clapton album for the CD player. This, too, was discretely hidden amongst cupboard shelves, so that only four tiny speakers inserted in the walls paid respect to the twenty-first century. Connie felt the warmth of the gas-lit logs instantly and thought how unfair it was that her own genuine fires were only half as efficient and three times more trouble.

Having lapped up all he wanted from the pasta bowl, Tramp settled himself on the ruddy Turkish rug before the fire and Sebastian played the host, offering wine or tea. Connie felt she could murder a cup of tea but, anxious not to come across as a motherly stereotype, asked if she might have both. Sebastian, unfazed, soon arrived carrying a tray supporting a bottle of Merlot, some beautiful crystal glasses, two mugs of steaming Earl Grey tea and a large packet of oven crisps, such as Connie would never be able to buy, since they would have disappeared without due appreciation before ever she had got them home! She nuzzled into the cushions of the voluptuous leather sofa, the surface of which was cool to her touch, and grinned at the unexpectedly luxurious time she was suddenly having.

"Rather a mess, isn't it?" Sebastian observed.

"If you call this a mess!" Connie answered, mentally replacing piles of magazines for comics, delicate chinaware for toys, on which you could skid if you didn't look where you were going, and a lone used coffee mug for half a dozen crumb covered cereal bowls, the remains of the cereal glued fast to the sides. "No: I should call this delightfully ordered chaos!" Sebastian looked relieved:

"It's not to everyone's taste," he responded apologetically. "Many people – my mother included – despair, but these pieces," he threw his arms wide, indicating to the contents of the room, "are my much cherished favourites and from which I am too loathe to part. They have become my partners over the years."

"And they are lovely!" replied Connie truthfully. "There are quite a lot of bits at home which are antique, only because they have always been there and no one has ever seen reason to replace them. What I find hard though, is imagining that anyone ever *did* go out and buy some of our stuff and that once upon a time it was *new*. I sometimes wonder if my forebears considered it the only thing to buy old – *antiquey* old," she qualified.

They discussed the passions and idiosyncrasies of the antique world as they alternately munched, gulped and sipped their way through the contents of Sebastian's tray of goodies and he rose to fetch what he referred to as 'reinforcements'. Connie was amused to find another mug of steaming tea brought with the next bottle of wine and she explained that while she was actually capable of drinking one without the other, she might just as well have this next mug too, now that Sebastian had brought it – and to stop her from 'going too squiffy'. Sebastian was apologising again, this time for not using a teapot, which was because the only one he had was silver and would look 'a might ostentatious'. At the mention of silver, of which there seemed to be a sizeable amount, Connie's eyes caught on a photo in a silver frame of a lady with thick blonde natural ringlets and a round freckly face:

"Who's that?" she asked (the kind of question you asked on the second bottle, she told herself).

"My ex, Katy," he replied promptly. Connie apologised.

"She looks lovely: so when did you...?"

"Split up?" he pre-empted, "About six months ago. I think I became a bit much for her with my mess, my antique obsession and everything... Maybe that's why I've never married," he mused. "Anyway, we went our own ways with no particular hard feelings. Really its time to get rid of her," he added, striding across the room and picking up the frame, attempting to prise it open. "It's a nice frame though: Georgian." Connie began to remonstrate, but Sebastian was adamant:

"No, no. She's past her sell-by and must go forthwith!" with which the little photo came loose. Sebastian put it behind the carriage clock on the mantelpiece, which was out of time and adorned with dozens of yellowing, sagging invitations, past and future. He clearly was not short of friends:

"Oh dear!" he said, scrutinising a Hunt Ball ticket for the year 2004 "I suppose I'm not much good at throwing things away. *There!*" he propped everything back on the mantelpiece, "she's relegated to the mausoleum! And now how about poached eggs – my speciality,"

"I can't think of anything more apt!" answered Connie, wishing that she had some of their own best-in-the-world eggs, laid by her stalwart hens, Bashful and Bustle, to show off to this man who seemed to her to be adept at everything. Hastily she reburied thoughts of home, giving herself up to these precious present moments when she was free to be feckless.

She followed Sebastian into a cosy kitchen at the back, which smelt deliciously of furniture polish, for Sebastian made his own brand, which harboured many secret ingredients including, he said, quality boot polish, beeswax and linseed oil. The kitchen, with its scrubbed pine converted sewing-machine table, looked out onto a terrace, resplendent with huge terracotta pots of geraniums and stocks and which led, by way of a wrought iron spiral staircase, onto the garden below. The now floodlit garden was bordered, but evidently gleaned little natural light, so all the plants struggled upwards, thrusting their heads desperately over the tall fence. This afforded more privacy to the garden below them and Connie found herself being surprised at what nature could achieve, even in the heart of this metropolis. At the end of the garden there was a shed and Sebastian explained that this housed another of his small obsessions, which was his Harley-Davidson:

"It's a Heritage Springer!" he said, as if this explained everything. Connie found herself nodding her head wisely before asking facetiously:

"What's that? A kind of dog?" which led to Sebastian's spirited pronouncement on the particular attributes of the Springer: the springs and the force of the exhaust, hence the 'corking noise and vibration'. Connie found herself strangely captivated through his enthusiasm, and Sebastian promised that another time, when he was sober and the weather was warm, she could ride pillion.

The fact that the evening was now in the small hours passed them by, for each had become increasingly fascinated by the antipathy of one another's lifestyles. They were beginning to absorb the knowledge that this new relationship was both a necessity and a challenge, given their geographical restrictions, and Connie felt sadly that she must make it clear that it was very unusual for her to be this free; and that four children, her band and supply teaching generally absorbed all the time she had. Sebastian pointed out that he was not placed in quite so much demand and that he could visit her at weekends or when there was an antique show, a customer request, a car boot sale – in fact he would come anyway!

The sofa was as comfortable as promised and Connie discovered that the spare room, which Sebastian had described as occupied was indeed so, but by wall to ceiling furniture, rather than by human forms, as she had imagined. For some reason this information afforded a measure of relief, and after the warm and lingering caresses that each had been envisaging for some hours now, Sebastian relinquished her and toiled up to the loneliness of his four-poster.

Once safely ensconced, Sebastian began to think back on the excitement of the day's encounter with Connie, a gentle smile playing across his broad face. However, after a short time had elapsed, he let out a despairing sigh and clambered out again, wrapping himself in a huge (everything involving Sebastian had to be large!) felt dressing gown. He padded downstairs back to the sitting room and knocked on the door:

"Excuse me: are you asleep?" Connie was not asleep. It was cold in the place where Sebastian had been pressed against her and in any case, her mind was still mulling and revelling in the wonder of all that had passed between them in the last few hours:

"No – why?" she asked coyly.

"I'm missing you already. Do you mind if I come back?"

"No I don't: do!" she replied, letting out a contented little chuckle as she moved to her original place at the back of the sofa while Sebastian rolled himself dangerously onto the edge and held her tight in his arms for the remainder of the night.

That was how Connie and Sebastian began. At first he came down for the odd day when the children were all at school, or she visited him during the infrequent times that they spent with their father. When Connie deemed the time to be right, she asked him down to Devon for the weekend, when he could meet the children. He was very straight forward with them; not asserting himself or festooning them with presents for a quick sell (as seemed to be the procedure to which so many of Connie's friends' suitors seemed to adhere, when faced with similar situations: it was almost as though somewhere there was a manual entitled *HER Children – Recipe for Instant Hit*). Sebastian had come down on his Harley-Davidson and everyone had insisted on having a go as pillion. Connie had experienced this thrill a few times now and had regaled both children and friends with stories, trying to express the exhilaration the ride had provided. She adored each carefree moment, from throwing her leg expertly over the saddle after the ignition had sparked, and feeling the immense roar and throb of the engine beneath her as the wind whipped her hair to stringy threads from beneath the helmet and stung at her cheeks and nose, stealing the very breath from her lungs; to the moment when they returned, feeling inexplicably exhausted and without substance, in need of bikers' fodder, in the form of pies and mugs of strong tea. After this she invariably felt deliciously limp and satiated, the elements having ripped at her thoughts, her vitality, leaving only the rawness of being and she and Sebastian would snuggle up in the arms of the worn leather sofa and snooze contentedly for a while!

When riding pillion, Sebastian had insisted they all wore sunglasses in place of goggles, in accordance with the original Harley style – and the pimple helmet that he provided was hardly flattering either, resembling a button mushroom! He acquired the regulation leathers for Connie in Camden Town market; for apparently you couldn't be seen in anything that looked even vaguely new. They were stiff to walk in, cool to touch, but warm as toast between her and that buffeting wind. She found herself adopting a rolling John Wayne gait, which came naturally with the strictures of the leather that melded so accommodatingly when she was astride the bike but which dug and protested at any independent motion.

The children had negotiated their own turns as pillion, to be taken at a more sedate pace than his normal swash-buckling style allowed, down the lanes; the tall, weed-studded banks of which obliterated the view of the rich rolling rust-coloured turf of the Devon fields, then up the main road and back. Each found themselves both excited and trepidatious, but pronounced the whole as "so-oh! cool," which, in retrospect, it was – especially when you could tell your friends about it later! Sebastian gauged his speed by how tightly they held on around his waist: the tighter the clutch the slower he felt he should go. Demelza, however, had been something different:

"Faster, faster!" she had breathed as he emerged onto the main road.

"I've promised your mother to keep the speed down," he shouted back to the dumpy figure, eyes glistening behind over-large black sunglasses, which were sliding perilously down her nose. She took one hand away from Sebastian to steady them and he realised that this was someone who had little or no fear. He revved up on the straight and took the bike up to seventy, hoping that Demelza would enjoy the turn of speed,

"Wicked! *Faster, faster!*" she shouted gleefully into his ear, but, dutiful to Connie, he had resisted the temptation to show off, and returned her gently down the winding lanes, which were buttered so liberally with primroses, to the waiting family.

"Why are you called such a long-winded name?" she had asked as they bumbled around the potholes of the old Vicarage drive.

"Just am."

"I'll call you Sebbo, I think,"

"Then I'll call you Demo, I think,"

"What, as in '*demonstration*'?"

"No, as in '*demented!*'"

"Maybe I should call you Dad?" Sebastian was shaken and taken aback:

"But you've got one of those already." Demelza laughed:

"Ha – got you there! Just wanted to see how you'd react!" Relieved, but realising he must be careful not to underestimate this innocent looking youngster, Sebastian muttered what he saw as an inanity about her dad being a very lucky man. After he had said this, he considered that actually it might indeed be true and wondered where *he* might be, had he met Connie many years ago and they had... His musing was cut short as the thought transformed into the reality of Connie, her tawny chestnut hair caught up carelessly in a pretty blue and white china clasp, her mouth opened in some welcome, rendered inaudible over the roar of the engine, her bright eyes shining like the children around her. His stomach gave an unaccustomed lurch of excitement while a feeling of warmth stole through him: strange to feel like this over a lover and matriarch rolled into one. He held his hand out to steady Demelza as she leapt nimbly off, averting his eyes from the vast expanse of knicker-top escaping over her low-rise jeans.

"Cool! Thanks, Sebbo!" Demelza said casually as she alighted, afterwards telling Connie that they had gone *far* too slowly, while winking at Sebastian. He smiled back and the smile was for her, for her mother, and for this extraordinary other life that he was experiencing: the introduction to all those children had been a matter of private dread, in case he somehow 'got it wrong' by appearing gauche, had on the contrary become a gently buzzing breeze for all concerned. He allowed himself to be jostled into the cool of the porch, beneath the wreath of wisteria, for a family photograph, the bike taking the foreground, while they each wildly waved helmets, goggles, sunglasses, anything to show their involvement with the bike and one another.

Chapter Four

Charlie paused to look at a page torn from Demelza's school report, which had been inexpertly mounted and stuck on the wall with red drawing pins. It read:

Demelza can be entirely unquenchable, thus rendering her at times unteachable. This, in turn, distracts others in the class less able than herself.

Charlie flinched at this, remembering how the atmosphere had simmered when her own mother had subtly alluded to these same sentiments. Charlie had received a glowing report last term, which described in many ways her all round improvement, both in attitude and in academic results. Her mother was really trying to be nice, in a clumsy sort of way, when she had squeezed Charlie's shoulder whispering:

"Well *done, * Darling. I always said you were capable of so much more; if only *we know who* were not perpetually putting you off your stroke." Charlie had frozen in her mother's grasp and then, twisting out of it she had shouted:

"How *could* you?" and fled from the room. The better marks had been a betrayal and she might have to guard against them in future, she had told herself angrily. Demelza, however, had obviously thought her own reproving report of the previous term a hoot – and been allowed to stick it up on the wall! In truth Charlie *had* worked harder; but this was only due to the fact that she was bored without Demelza's notes and whispered comments at which to giggle; for there were times when she had been unable to contain her mischievous wit and distracted not merely Charlie, but the entire class. Once, in Biology Miss Cleaver had enthusiastically announced that they were going to study woodlice and Demelza had fired back "How lousy!" without so much as a pause! The class had erupted and Miss Cleaver had waited for the hubbub to die down before asking Demelza if she would care to entertain the class any further – or might it now be permissible to press on? She had said this with the merest hint of a twinkle, which had produced just the right effect for Demelza to apologise and explain that the comment had simply 'popped out' before she'd had time to filter it. On this occasion she had been quenched and with the apology accepted they had continued, with Demelza frowning in keen concentration at Miss Cleaver's every comment, making Charlie giggle at her serious face. The resultant homework on woodlice had produced an A* for Demelza, but Charlie, who had continued to smile inwardly for the remainder of the lesson, had scraped a C- and a 'See me'.

Outside school, Charlie had looked on with a mixture of pride, at being Demelza's friend, and envy at her apparently carefree home life, as she witnessed the muddy Discovery draw up at the bus stop, containing an assortment of sisters and that ancient dog, Tramp, sitting up beside Connie and dropping 'all hairs' over the front seat. The family were each dotty about him and would, unembarrassed, regularly *hug* the dog and one another – while Charlie's mother would *say* nothing, but wrinkle her nose, raising her eyebrows in what Charlie knew to be disgust.

~

Tramp's death, in spite of its obvious imminence, had shocked them all, and Charlie had been honoured by an invitation to his funeral: it was true that he had been doddery on his pins for some time, but he had seemed to take the state quite happily. This particular morning, however, Connie had called him to go for his customary elating walk and he had raised his head, tried to wobble onto his old, flat flipper feet, failed, and simply *looked* at Connie.

"All right, old boy," Connie had murmured, patting the soft down on his rust-coloured head: "I know." She had rung the vet, for she knew instinctively that the time they had all dreaded had finally come:

"It was just that look he gave me," she had explained, "I understood it: after all our time together I would, wouldn't I?"

Sebastian had arrived swiftly from somewhere and helped her to dig the grave where Tramp always used to lie, on the sun-warmed grass in a little dell near the front of the house, which was not directly obvious to the casual observer. They had then fetched the children and given them time to say goodbye to Tramp in their own way, which was when Demelza had urgently called Charlie for moral support.

"What a ridiculous amount of fuss over a mere dog!" Charlie's mother, Leticia, had said; but, shrunk from one of Charlie's most crushing glares, she had demurred. She had driven Charlie over, and told a tear-stained Connie – all over dirt from the grave digging: *"She hadn't even bothered to change!"* Leticia had remarked later disdainfully – that she was so sorry about the dog. Charlie had sighed relief that her mother had said the right thing and Connie had nodded, smiled wanly and thanked her. At this point the vets had arrived and Leticia had tactfully and hurriedly rocketed off up that 'frightful' pothole-ridden drive: "Why she doesn't do something about it is a total mystery!" she would say, and then wonder at herself as to why she always found the necessity to put Connie down in front of Charlie?

Connie had sat with Tramp on the grass outside the house, while the vets fired a barrage of seemingly unimportant questions relating to Tramp's remarkably untroubled physical history and the length of time they had owned him (for the children it was beyond all their lifetimes). After filling in the consent forms, which made Connie feel like judge and executioner rolled into one, they began a cursory examination of Tramp himself. The smell of disinfectant, however, seemed to revive an old familiar memory of dislike in the ancient dog and, to everyone's surprise and dismay he had struggled to his feet, barked, and tottered over to the car belonging to the vets. There, he carefully balanced on three legs – a feat he had been unable to achieve for some years past – and urinated a long, steady, steaming stream over its wheel, cleaning a shining stripe down its alloyed surface. Thus relieved, he had shambled back and thumped heavily down again beside Connie.

"Do you think he's better?" Poppy had asked, her face a ray of hope and wonder,

"He certainly couldn't have done that an hour ago," Connie answered inadequately, similarly nonplussed.

"This is not entirely uncommon," one of the vets was saying, "it's as though they sense what we're about to do and so disprove its validity."

"A sort of 'last stand'," Sebastian offered, looking gravely at Connie.

"Look, if you feel at all uncomfortable..." one of the vets had begun; her pretty, freckled face and short blonde bob giving away her youth. She was looking a little unsure herself, "we can always go away and come again when you're more sure..." She was becoming unprofessionally eager not to be the one to condemn this old stager herself, feeling an uncomfortable parallel with Pontius Pilot. Connie had hesitated, looking at Tramp and then at Sebastian:

"It's your decision, Connie," he said gently: "entirely yours – but I must say he does look tired." Connie looked again at Tramp, whose tongue was lolling pinkly out of his mouth, his sides moving imperceptibly in his return to dreamland, safe in the knowledge that his mistress was there, so no need for further exhausting displays of mistrust over that awful clean smell that had assailed his senses. Connie thought about the huge, heavy mantle of decision she had taken on when she had rung the vets: if she let them go she would only have to summon them again – and perhaps the next time Sebastian wouldn't be able to come. They would have to live with that grave gaping open and the children would be forced to go through their goodbyes again. Sebastian was right, Tramp did look tired and earlier he had been unable to walk: was it any kinder to wait for that to come about again?

Connie searched the faces and she could see that besides hope there was also a quiet acceptance that things were sad. By prolonging Tramp's life, he was not going to get better.

"Right, I think you'd all better go off to the trampoline," she had said gently, adding "I mean I'm not *telling* you to go – if anyone wants to stay until the end they can, but you've said your goodbyes..." The children wandered dejectedly around the corner, some stroking the old head gently, finally, but so as not to awaken him. Sebastian looked wretchedly at Connie.

"Do you think you could go with them too and make sure they're OK?" Sebastian felt inadequate and couldn't help feeling slightly hurt that she hadn't asked him to stay with her, rather than with the children:

"If you're sure you'll be all right?" he asked miserably, kissing the top of her head. Connie nodded. She had decided that she wanted to do this on her own. After all, how many times had Tramp sat up on the stairs waiting for her, suffered numerous journeys in the back of the car – rather than be separated in the comfort of home? He had lain beside her bed, accepted the namby-pamby hugs and tears to which few animals would have subjected themselves, such had been his devotion. This time it felt right that she showed a little of her own, by being there solely with him, without sharing or leaning on others.

Connie nodded to the vets and spoke briskly:

"If you have any further bureaucracy can we do it now because I'm sorry I won't want to talk afterwards?"

"I think everything is covered," the senior vet answered, glaring at the other, who seemed far too close to tears for her liking and would need to toughen up.

"The bill…?"

"We'll send it on."

"I did prepare a blank cheque which you could fill in later. It's here." She struggled clumsily with the pocket of her jeans.

"No it's OK: we'll send it."

"Right then – can we do it quickly and thank you," she gabbled, keeping her promise not to talk to them again as she proffered the worn pad of Tramp's paw, for them to administer their lethal dose…

From a long way away she heard the older vet explaining that they actually had to wait a little while afterwards to make sure that the injection had 'taken'. Once they were satisfied, they got up quietly and respectfully and Connie heard, above the footsteps receding across the gravel, a stifled sob, after which car doors slammed and the engine kicked in.

For a long time she sat there, Tramp's head warm in her lap, bird song and muted voices a distant blur. Sebastian had returned:

"Tell me when you're ready," was all he said and at last she struggled up, Tramp a dead weight in her arms.

"I can't step down into the grave with him," she muttered quietly, "he's too heavy."

"But I can," answered Sebastian, reverently relieving Connie of her precious burden and stepping down into the steep grave. "Facing the drive or the stables?" he asked.

"The drive I think." Sebastian turned slowly around and placed Tramp so that he was facing the way he would be when he arrived on his motorbike, wagging that absurd flag of a moth-eaten tail and showing the grinning stumps of his worn teeth. He stepped back out of the grave and told Connie that he would do the rest, but Connie was already shovelling, her head bent low, so that she couldn't see in.

When they had finished, Sebastian had called the children, who had elected to hold a memorial service. They had picked flowers and placed them around the grave.

"And now," said Demelza, tossing her head defiantly, "we must sing!"

"You're joking aren't you?" moaned Ella,

"Have some respect for the occasion!" reprimanded Sophia, but Connie said it seemed a great idea and asked for suggestions,

"I'll get my guitar if you promise not to laugh at the bum notes," suggested Sebastian, catching at the mood, and now that the idea had caught on they discussed what might be suitable while he fetched his nylon strung Hoffner classic and strummed a few chords.

"How about *Abide with me*: we had that at Grandma's funeral."

"No: it's too sad!"

"We *are* sad."

"But Tramp had such a happy life and he was so old, we should be glad he didn't die in pain." Connie winced inwardly at the thought of the needle as she had held Tramp's trusting paw, but she agreed with Demelza.

"It's not like we're going to sing *Glory, Glory What a Hell of a Way to Die!* or anything!" scoffed Demelza, receiving gasps of shocked disapproval,

"I know!" Poppy, who had remained strained and quiet, brightened: "How about *How Much is that Doggie in the Window!* Remember when we used to try to get Tramp to go *wuff wuff* in the right places?" It was agreed, to Charlie's amazement, that this was just right and they all began to sing it, first of all experimentally and in a subdued fashion, but as the absurdity of the words and the wuffs began to take shape they sang without restraint. After this, it was decided that everyone had to tell a Tramp story, beginning with Sebastian who told the company that he had met Tramp in an airport car park *before* he had clapped eyes on their mother and that it had been Tramp who had sort of played Cupid in his getting to know her at a subsequent party, and that, therefore, he would always be in Tramp's debt. Ella continued that Tramp had always been her hero since she was very tiny and had tried to stroke an Alsatian who had then snapped at her. Tramp, who was only collie size, had leapt to her defence, making the Alsatian wheel around and fix his slobbery jaws into Tramp's hairy neck, thus freeing and forgetting her! The owner had quickly called the Alsatian off and when they examined Tramp he was miraculously unharmed – while the Alsatian was choking, having swallowed a huge lump of Tramp's abundant fur! Everyone hummed approval at the demise of the Alsatian, resulting from messing with their hero.

"Something *I* will never forget," remarked Demelza wickedly, "is the smell of his farts... Not *ever!*" There were sounds of protestation, making Demelza the more emphatic: "But it's *true: you* all know it is!"

"Well you didn't sleep next to him!" retorted Connie "Sometimes I was barely able to breathe!" This admission released laughter that had been suspended at the lack of reverence in Demelza's truthful admission. "But they were all worth it," continued Connie loyally, not wishing to mock their beloved departed pet, however this provided more mirth. Sebastian had by this time produced wine and lemonade and each toasted Tramp with verve, their immediate sense of shock benumbed through shared recollections that could only serve to encourage smiles rather than tears. These continued until the sky darkened, the dew stole around them and the birds completed their own muted evensong.

Charlie attempted to explain later, to her mother's scornful questions, that actually she had never before been a part of such an uplifting display of courage, fun and good common sense in the face of tragedy!

"Ah well! You never listen to the wartime generation," sniffed her mother disparagingly, again disquieted by her daughter's quick and eloquent defence of that ramshackle clan: "*No wonder the husband buggered orff!*" she muttered, deliberately and annoyingly inaudible, a grim smile decorating her customarily impassive features.

Chapter Five

Charlie's gaze moved beyond the array of photographs, the banners, and the glitter: the display of sheer zest for life, and came to rest at the little dormer window. She rose from her perch, which was a large blue plastic blow-up chair. It was the sort her mother refused to acquire for her because she considered it took up too much space, which it did, and because it was vulgar, which it was. She and Demelza had spent ages hyper-ventilating in their efforts to blow the thing up but, they had felt, their efforts had been amply rewarded by its size and the very vulgarity her mother so despised. Charlie hovered by the window, willing herself in her resolve to look out. She drew a deep breath and forced herself to look down: directly below her she could see Susanna's car next to the grubby Discovery. (So she and Ella had returned, but not thought to find her. She was glad!) She glanced out at the hen run, beyond the fringe of shiny laurels, and saw Poppy and Sophia, who seemed to be acting as one these days, feeding the hens with scraps. They were all so lucky to have each other, their close-knit exterior a defence from the new world into which they had awoken. By pulling her head to the very corner of the window and squinting she could see it: the grass had not been cut there; so where relatively tame short grass, ideal for numerous games, had abounded, the paddock-cum-playfield was now a wilderness of thistles, docks and long grass. However, the trampoline could be seen peeking over the whole: a garish blue gaping mouth marking the middle; and the grass where the path made by running feet had led, was scarred a deeper green, and where the longer grasses had parted and refused to grow.

~

The fuss there had been over that trampoline! Demelza had seemed to want it most and had repeatedly begged Connie to provide them with one, naming every single acquaintance they had who possessed a similar item. Connie, reasonably, had demurred on the grounds that they were simply far too expensive – just because others could afford them didn't mean she could – and they should take a look around them and try being grateful for what they already had! Eventually the children had come up with a plan.

It was on a return school run and Poppy announced that she was busting to go to the loo, winding her legs impressively and dramatically around one another. Demelza had said nothing at first, but simply hissed:

"Sssssssss!" Poppy had wrapped her legs in an even tighter spaghetti knot and told her to be quiet.

"Sssssssssssssss!" continued Demelza.

"Demelza, leave her alone!" Connie had interjected from the front.

"I'm not sssaying a word!"

"You're teasing: stop it!"

"How can I be teasssing if I'm not ssssaying a word?"

"You know just what you're doing – talk about something interesting!"

"Think of *deserts!*" Sophia had tried, to help the suffering Poppy,

"What'sssssssssss interessssssssssting in desssssssertsssssssssss?" asked Demelza innocently. Here Ella began to snigger and even Sophia's loyalty wavered and her face twitched.

"Oh, Ella, *stop* it!" repeated Connie, only the twinkle in her eye, giving away feelings behind the stern façade. "Tell us about your day in school instead!"

"And you're *not* to make me laugh!" snorted Poppy, the attention she was receiving clearly not something that the youngest was resenting, in spite of her discomfort.

"We-ell," began Demelza slowly and deliberately: "we had Ssssscience at sssschool and I sssssat next to Sssssssarah on a ssssoft ssssseat…"

"There's no Sarah in your class and none of the seats are soft!" Ella rejoined matter-of-factly, unsure whether she should be demeaning herself this far by showing she was listening.

"Sssssso! My sssssssisssster sssssaysss I'm wrong!"

"Don't you mean sssssssilly?" put in Sophia before she could stop herself, clapping a hand over her mouth as she spoke and apologising to Poppy,

"Don't you mean sssssssssssssorry?" answered Poppy, to which they had all erupted into noisy laughter, Poppy now the loudest of all, as she clutched at herself and Connie had simply drawn into a gateway and said to Poppy: "Now just *go!*" and Poppy had gone sliding and giggling over the gate to do a pee in full view of them all, calling:

"Phew – that feels better – I bet you all want to go now!"

That was the trouble with Demelza, she had the ability to draw everyone into her mindset, and after a certain length of persistence on her part, and resistance from others, the spell of her clown's world infected most people that she touched – with the exception of the odd sour teacher, who, for some reason, really couldn't seem to fathom her: she never intended any malice, but was simply born with a perhaps over-developed sense of fun. There were times when she lacked the sensitivity to withdraw and hold back, resulting in frustration for others, but generally, as now, she succeeded in winning others round to join in the hilarity.

Demelza, flushed with her success in making a normal school run into one to remember with affection by all present, called her sisters up to her room, this room, to listen to what she called her 'cunning plan!'

"Right, who here would like to have a trampoline?" They had all answered in the affirmative, but Ella pointed out that they had been through all this many times with their mother and the answer had been *no,* on the grounds that she couldn't afford it.

"You've got to stop being so self-centred and start being realistic!" Ella had said smugly, the words tripping familiarly off her tongue.

"Look who's talking!" answered Demelza "Didn't I hear something about wanting a Ferrari when it came to your seventeenth birthday?"

"That's different!" Ella had snapped,

"Different because it would only be for you, different because it would be loads more expensive than a trampoline – or different because you wouldn't have had a single driving lesson, let alone passed your test?" enquired Demelza coolly. Ella was subdued for a moment and felt Poppy's gentle, comforting hand stroke her back.

"Well actually a trampoline would be really good exercise for getting toned, but there's no way Mum's going to give in."

"Aha! I think there might be if we are all decided that it is what we want more than anything. Sophia?" Sophia nodded, but looked disbelieving,

"Poppy?" Poppy's eyes shone in enthusiasm and hope as she nodded vigorously.

"Ella?"

"Like I said, she'll no way agree, but yes I'd *like* one – we could have trampoline parties with barbecues in the summer," Ella mused, sparkling at the thought, but then her features clouded at the unlikelihood of such an event ever taking place:

"So?" she looked at her younger sister wistfully, "How exactly do you propose effecting this miracle?" Her sarcasm was intended to mask the faith she had in her sister's greater creativity. Demelza savoured a dramatic pause as the attention and hope of all her sisters were focussed on her:

"What if none of us had a birthday present from her for a *whole year*? Or, even a Christmas present?" Sophia and Poppy looked horrified, but a glimmer of a smile played across Ella's face. "What if all that money that *would* have been spent on those presents, was pooled into one huge bumper present?" There was another pause, this time for admiration, as the younger children began to grasp what was being suggested: "Like a *trampoline* sized present?" Demelza finished, now unnecessarily, but milking her ingenuity for all it was worth, her hazel eyes dancing enthusiasm.

The children had united in their discussions as to exactly how to voice their proposal to their mother, although each was fairly confident that now they were onto a winner! Finally, they had trooped downstairs, where Connie was making a salad to go with the baked potatoes for supper.

"Mmm looks good!" smiled Poppy.

"Mmmmm – smells better!" Sophia added,

"Mmmmmmm!" joined Demelza and Ella,

"You sound like a swarm of bees – it's only baked potatoes. What do you want?" asked Connie, falling effortlessly into their plan.

"Funny you should say that!" Demelza replied significantly.

"Very, very funny actually!" went on Poppy. Connie stopped chopping, her attention properly caught now:

"Well come on, out with it!" she said, "Tell me what you've been hatching?"

"You know you can't afford a trampoline?" asked Ella unsubtly,

"Not that trampoline again! Yes, I know I can't – thank you for pointing that out."

"Please come and sit down," Demelza said smoothly, *most uncharacteristically,* thought Connie. *What ever would it be now?* She allowed herself to be led to the old pine rocking chair, which rested at the side of the Aga in the kitchen. Always an object to clamber around, there it stayed, nestling next to the warmth, its sagging faded cushions an invitation to all who relished a moment's time out. Connie sat down regally, only sorry that she was going to have to repeat the word 'no', just when all around her seemed comfortably harmonious.

"This is all very delicious! Well?" she couldn't help smiling, even in the face of imminent disaster, in reaction to the happy faces around her.

"We have thought of a way!"

"Go on then…"

Demelza began, to the tune of *John Lennon's* timeless idealistic classic *Imagine,* the lyrics of which Connie believed, the music of which she loved:

"Imagine there's no presents!" she sang in a lusty husky voice,

"It's easy if you try!" continued Sophia and Poppy, their hands extended in dismay,

"Not even for our birthdays!" continued Ella, her rich lustrous voice unconsciously eclipsing the others.

"Not even if we die!" They saw now by their mother's face that she hadn't yet understood but loved it nevertheless.

"Imagine all that money," went on Demelza,

"Sitting in the bank." Here Ella could no longer keep a straight face and let out a hiccup of mirth, which sent Poppy off.

"You-oo oo-oo-oo – you may say we are just dreamers," they chorused.

"But we'd like a trampoline!

"We hope some day you will buy one

"And if you do, you'll make our dream!"

Connie clapped delightedly at their ingenuity and made a quick calculation – she usually spent roughly fifty pounds per head per present, usually slightly more on the older ones, whose choices were more extravagant than the younger (who were more impressed by size than cost).

"OK – let me get this straight," she laughed: "no individual presents and a trampoline instead. No presents for how long?"

"We thought a year," answered Sophia. Over Christmas and

birthdays that would come to an incredible four hundred pounds: more than enough for a huge trampoline!

"And I get first bash?" Four heads nodded vigorously,

"How can I possibly refuse such a generous offer!" Demelza threw herself into the air with a loud whoop and the others followed her lead, leaping and hurling themselves at Connie, clapping one another with 'high fives', as though there were a trampoline ready assembled in the kitchen.

"A thoroughly cunning plan and wonderfully executed," continued Connie, after she had caught her breath, "And the most shamefully self-aggrandising words to the most brilliant idyll lyrics can convey! Let's have it again please!" The children formed a line and repeated the song, with more gusto this time, and Connie beamed:

"One more condition." The children looked up eagerly,

"I must be allowed to do small presents for each of you. I don't think I'd feel right not giving you any individual presents at Christmas and birthday – you know, little fun things?"

"Hmm," responded Demelza, "What do we think? Shall we allow her just a small pressie each?"

"I think we might cope with that," answered Ella in a mock doubtful voice, "Although perhaps *medium* might be the better compromise?" As they fooled and jigged around the kitchen, their suggestions becoming the more absurd every moment, Connie shrieked:

"Potatoes! How could I have forgotten them?" Diving at the Aga, she snatched out a baking tray containing five somewhat shrivelled and blackened potatoes.

"Oh!" exclaimed Connie, "Well I'm sure they'll taste better than they look – with lots of butter that is – and cheese!"

"And salt and pepper and anything that's unhealthy and disguises the taste of burnty," encouraged Demelza, looking at the smouldering pile.

"It's very hard to cook a potato badly," smiled Connie, not sure whether to seem rueful or proud, "but I do seem to be something of a master. Bread and butter!" she continued, "and plenty of this lovely salad, should disguise the burntyness a treat!"

"You're always saying that carbon's good for you and carbon is burnt stuff, isn't it?" Sophia put in helpfully and was confused by the response which, as far as she was concerned, was not funny in the slightest, so perhaps burnt stuff wasn't carbon and she'd got it wrong?

The family ate the 'burnty' meal with relish, the conversation, revolving around hopeful plans for the placing and execution of the trampoline's construction, which lasted well into the happy evening – and no one breathed a word about homework. That marked the conception of the trampoline.

Chapter Six

It had been Christmas – only last Christmas, incredibly, because time and children seemed to have grown immeasurably since then. Sebastian had come down on his motorbike on Christmas Eve, very cold because he had left his shopping in London so late – and then there were Christmas drinks to be dealt with in his favourite wine bar off Carnaby Street. The wind had penetrated the layers of leather and even the skin tight silk long johns, the essential trade secret of the serious biker for long winter journeys. His hands were frozen into their position on the chrome handlebars inside the fur-lined gloves; only his face remaining warm in the steam generated by the redoubtable visor, which formed a seal around his chin. He had alighted stiffly, thankful to have ended the journey; inwardly promising not to put himself through such a vigil again and in future to sail sensibly through the night in the radiated warmth of his car, the sound of the Stranglers pumping through him, willing him to remain awake.

Poppy had got to him first for she had refused to shut the shutters, positioning herself on the far side of the Christmas tree, so that she could see out onto the frozen lawn, where gesticulating trees stood starkly silhouetted against a deep starry sky. The needles from the Christmas tree tickled her back and broke off into her warm red sweater, endangering the whole into collapse, for, as of every year, it was overburdened with its own fruits of Christmas, consisting of homemade baubles from various school efforts from Christmases past, swathes of assorted tinsel, and magical glass icicles from the nearby Dartington crystal factory.

Poppy didn't notice the beauty of the tree or the night, for she was busy with her thoughts, not entirely happy ones, and willing Sebastian to hurry up and arrive to divert her from them. It was their first Christmas without Grandma, who would have arrived, panting huskily, in her Mini, bearing mounds of poorly wrapped parcels from used wrapping paper. "Always recycle pretty paper on family – it's *far* too lovely to throw away after just one use!" she would say, the thrift of war time never having worn off in such particulars.

Demelza's mother had been wildly busy as usual, scuttling mysteriously away upstairs to her bedroom for ages, with strict instructions not to disturb. They all knew that she was wrapping presents, although Poppy was unaware that these were Christmas stockings, being a firm believer in Mother Christmas. Indeed, it had felt odd to have bought the presents without the Cadbury's milk chocolate bar and the packet of Embassy cigarettes, of which Mother Christmas so heartily disapproved but provided anyway in Grandma's stocking! Meanwhile there had been the mistletoe from the apple tree to arrange in strategic places around the gothic archways of the corridor and bright sprigs of berry-bedecked holly to stick behind mirrors and over clocks. Demelza had been remonstrated against for sticking cotton wool on the windows because the glue was going to take forever to come off and anyway the shutters would hide it at night. The kitchen was its customary chaos, only worse, with piles of vegetables everywhere and the red cabbage already bubbling, its spicy pungency spilling into the atmosphere. Everyone, in fact, was going through the motions of their Christmas, but each was struggling with the shared knowledge that it wasn't like any Christmas they had experienced. Poppy gave way to a few confusing tears from her vantage point behind the tree – but then she heard it, unmistakably in the still night: the ever louder throb of the twin-forked engines that heralded Sebastian's arrival. This was to be his *first* Christmas with them and it must be good!

Flinging herself under the tree and rolling nimbly out of the way of its laden branches, Poppy ran to the heavy oak front door, dragging it open to be there at the house front to welcome him as he drew up. She just made it and Sebastian's heart leapt at the sight of the little figure, dancing her welcome for him, his harsh uncomfortable journey forgotten in the warmth of her smile. He hadn't known that children could do this to you – indeed he'd had slight reservations when first it was suggested that he join them, for they were so many and he was just him. (Did he really want to be further drawn into this shambolic life that entwined his girlfriend, Connie? Why did she have to be so 'all or nothing?') Here he had his answer irrefutably, as he lifted the little figure in her Christmassy outfit off the ground and the door scraped further open as the rest of them spilled out, all hugging and laughing and pulling him inside, where, they said, they had lit a roaring fire to thaw him out! He little guessed how *particularly* glad they all were to see him: a perfect diversion and break with the routine of the usual Christmas guest, making Grandma's absence less acute.

Connie was thrusting a glass of mulled wine into his chilled hands and when he pulled off his knee-length boots, Demelza had even dashed off to fetch his slippers! He had stood before the fire and glowed, both physically and metaphorically, as the firelight glanced and flickered on the fantastically ornamented tree on which, he noticed in disbelief, were displayed precariously, *real* candles that had clearly been used and not put there simply for decoration. Suddenly a sense of belonging took over, for they had become his closest friends, with whom he was now intertwined and really he loved them all, 'each and every one!' The realisation, after his laconic ruminations earlier, hit him with the same force as the mulled wine, which was filling his deflated veins and he let out a whoop like a schoolboy, grabbed Connie and whirled her around the room to the irreverent sound of Slade, thoughtfully put on by Ella, as he tunelessly intoned:

Merry Christmas Everybody's Havin' Fun!

Look to the future now it's only just beg-u-un.

To add to the frivolity, Uncle Jeremy's Christmas email gave details of his present, which was tickets for flights for all the family to visit his own family in Australia next Christmas. The news of this was met with incredulous excitement, even though there was a whole year to wait for the journey. In the midst of the leaping and cheering Poppy's face dropped, as she eyed Sebastian, who seemed to be appreciating the celebration as much as anyone:

"What about you? How will you have Christmas without us?"

"I won't," he answered shortly, adding quickly as he took in the crest-fallen faces: "That's if I'm allowed to get a ticket and come along?" This was met with more enthusiasm than ever – and assurances that Uncle Jeremy would love to welcome him! Connie nodded in agreement, warming further inside at Sebastian's easy assumption at being here a whole year ahead of this one. *Until the seas run dry,* was what her most secret self added wonderingly: perhaps, between them all, they had discovered a relationship that could be depended upon.

That was the beginning and later, much later, when all children had been banished to bed, Sebastian and Connie had gone out to the stable, equipped with supplies of mulled wine in a large soup thermos, and attempted to follow the instructions for the assembly of the huge trampoline, the effects of the wine dulling the sense of the complicated wording (surely a rather inadequate translation?) still further. In the end they had ignored the instructions and attempted to apply common sense, but here too, they had found themselves in short supply; and it took some time before they discovered that they were assembling the thing upside down! Eventually the cumbersome object had taken shape and they had lugged and shoved the completed article into the paddock for the morning. However, before taking themselves off for the well-earned rest they craved, they had not been able to resist clambering onto the huge, unwieldy thing, holding hands, and bouncing unevenly and perilously into the stars and back.

Chapter Seven

How everyone wished the trampoline had never been! They were all involved: the children for pursuing and persuading Connie to provide it, Connie for allowing herself to become persuaded and, most of all, Charlie, for her starring role in the whole tragic affair.

~

It had been one of those glorious days in early spring when every branch and blade of grass stood out stark and bare against the harsh sunlight refracted and filtered through the leafless trees. Charlie had arrived quite early and been directed to evict Demelza from her lair, from which could be heard the strains of heavy metal music, the bass reverberating to the floors below. Demelza was still in her (rather young but so *in-your-face*, thought Charlie) turquoise, spotted Viyella pyjamas, standing on her bed playing an air guitar, twanging at the imaginary strings impressively. She continued unabashed when Charlie let herself in:

"I was told to fetch you down for breakfast to provide peace from the 'infernal row'," quoted Charlie sternly, with what was intended to be a disparaging grin.

"What? Sorry? Can't hear you!" answered Demelza. It was impossible to guess if she was saying this deliberately or whether the answer was genuine, so Charlie attempted sign language, consisting of pointing to the loud speakers and then swiping a finger across her throat. She followed this up by hiding her body behind the door, leaving what looked like her disembodied head poking around the corner, after which she drew her hand disjointedly around her neck, which she appeared to pull after her. Demelza flicked at the remote and turned the volume down a fraction:

"I feel dangerous," she screeched with the music:

"I feel s-s-s-s-s so alive!" but now she jumped off the bed and got dressed in her regulation all weather skinny T-shirt and low rise tatty jeans, which were all over biro-ed names of cult heroes, the like of

which merely interested Connie, who could never quite identify if any of these were someone close to Demelza or admired from afar. Charlie rather despised her own 'chavvy' clothes with decent labels, bought fondly for her by her own mother, but she knew she was not up to the complication of explaining the merits of the preferred individualism of tat! She looked down sadly at her immaculate silver skate shoes, of which Demelza herself had declared envy, knowing, as Charlie saw it, that her friend was simply being generous, for how could she ever want anything that Charlie possessed, when presented with so much freedom just 'to be' with nothing to rebel against?

Eventually, leaving a long enough interval to prove that she was not giving in to popular demand, Demelza turned off the music and drifted downstairs with Charlie. Connie heaved a sigh of relief from the sanctuary of the airing cupboard below, as she became aware of just how silent the house could be for whole moments at a time – and this was one such hallowed moment, where she could almost hear the old mellowed stones of the house breathe their appreciation. She considered the plight of these very stones, which had lived in the splendid isolation of hillside and quarry, with little louder than the bleat of a curlew for thousands of years, to be so rudely ripped from their grassy home by industrious Victorian quarrymen and be subjected to the ordered chaos of a wall, through which they must conduct the current reverberations, now blasting inconceivably numerous decibels of electrical sound.

Connie was sorting through a quantity of baby-growers, dungarees and little jackets, which represented the baby and toddling years of each of her children. Many were hand-me-downs, of which Poppy was the most recent recipient. She allowed herself to wallow in the nostalgia of memories associated with the little garments, visualising all too easily how each of the children had looked – and even the occasions when some of them had been worn. A mixture of emotions induced smiles and tears in turn; smiles for the memories and at her private idiocy and tears at the knowledge that she had put these carefully away, as habit dictated, for a tomorrow of more children. She had never planned more babies, but the reality that she now forced herself to face was that the time had come to admit there actually wouldn't be any more inhabitants for these small cherished garments – at least, this was not strictly true, for the children were expecting a new sibling imminently and here Connie was, harbouring these now useless, but perfectly worthy, baby items, when a new relation might well be needful and appreciative of them. Again she checked herself: it was her ex-husband, Stuart, and his girlfriend Sue from Accounts, who were the excited parents-to-be, and it was they who might be glad of them for their baby. Indeed, Stuart had already expressed an interest in various baby necessities, such as the pram, the playpen and the Moses basket – and who could lay a better claim for them? She must resurrect these articles from the cellar and give them an airing before parting with them, but Connie was just beginning to see that she had started to face this task with unreasonable dread! She buried her nose in the absurdly fresh smelling towelling of the baby-growers and decided that she might as well get this job over and done with as, packing them reverently away, parting finally with each tiny thing, she stowed them into a large *Primark* bag with the intention of making them useful, by returning them once again to proper service.

Leticia, Charlie's mother, was differently employed, her rubber gloves twanged perfectly into position as she gave the kitchen surfaces the thrice over – *just in case,* because you never quite knew with germs! On the smoked-glass coffee table, which sparkled in spite of its cloudy exterior, there was a 'self help' book on parenting by John Cleese: Leticia had bought it on impulse and then questioned what had moved her, since what could someone who found the notion of parrots being dead funny (when they cost hundreds of pounds), and how could someone who did that ridiculous walk have any idea what she was going through? God knew, she had tried so hard: teenagers were supposed to be so clothes conscious, so she had taken Charlotte on a shopping spree to buy some delicious designer clothes, such as might make her friends envious, but Charlotte had turned her nose up at simply everything that was tasteful and chic, plumping in the end for some frightful things with the seams on the outside. She had commented that this looked like something from a charity shop and Charlotte had brightened at once telling her mother that this was a cool idea! Finally they had compromised on a pair of silver skate shoes which resembled boats, and were certainly expensive enough to be boats, but Charlotte had begged her mother to simply give her the money so that she herself could choose – however it was Charlotte's choice of which Leticia was most afraid!

When they were at home, Leticia attempted to indulge Charlotte by cooking all her favourites, but Charlotte claimed either to be 'full up' from some sandwich snack she'd made herself earlier, or that her taste buds had changed and she no longer liked what ever it was. Leticia would smile, tight lipped, and say:

"Never mind – just talk to your father and me then and have some grapes," but Charlotte would turn up her nose and say it was a waste of time sitting with them if she wasn't eating. If pressed further her voice would rise with threatened impatience exclaiming that, if Leticia really wanted to know, she didn't *want* to sit with them and didn't *like* family meals and – the jibe that really hurt – that they weren't a family anyway, since there were no other siblings, she and Susanna only being *half* sisters. To put it like that was so deliberately unkind – and the difficulty was that Susanna had never been anything other than easy going and Leticia had not given birth to her; while Charlotte was so wearingly at odds with everyone except Susanna (who was impossible to argue with because she always gave in, whether she agreed or not, just for an easy life) and Charlotte was Leticia's only natural child. She felt the failure of a parent who has tried everything and gained nothing.

Yet when she had dropped the surly Charlotte off at her friend Demelza's house, as she had today, Charlotte had been up early, when normally she claimed she couldn't rise before the afternoon. On arrival, there had been the usual galling transformation, when Charlotte had sprung out of the car, all smiles, calling "Goodbye Mummy!" Leticia would find herself pathetically grateful for being called 'Mummy' and in an unusually fond manner. This morning 'that Connie' had been there and Leticia had tried really hard not to look at her finger nails, for Connie had clearly been grubbing in that vegetable garden of theirs. She had asked her in for a coffee, but Leticia had known better than to accept such an offer! (As she suggested it, Connie had anticipated that for Leticia, she had better fetch one of the better mugs from the back of the shelf, which would mean surreptitiously cleaning off the fluff that would have congregated since its last venture!)

Leticia had tried not to mind when her daughter had hugged Connie, in her tatty wax jacket, but not hugged *her*; but the twinges of indignation, interspersed with a feeling of inadequacy, were strong and she knew she really shouldn't have reversed quite so fast and thrown up all that dust over the little gaggle of untidy children, who seemed to do nothing but grin annoyingly and wave, not understanding, or perhaps ignoring the fact that here was a bafflingly maddened mother! Letitia felt unable to cope with her feelings, for she wanted to stamp, to swear, not to mind and to cry – all at once. She felt frustrated at having to behave properly, as teenagers expected of their parents, instead of being allowed to let vent as they did. Moreover, where had 'behaving properly' got her? It was all so thoroughly unfair and now, on top of it all, she knew that she should feel glad! Glad that her daughter was safe in the country with nice people and having fun – so why did she feel so very miserable?

The door of the sideboard was ajar and she pounced to shut it and renew the symmetry; but she glimpsed the green glint of the gin bottle before she had reached the door. She looked at the closed door and then a naughty thought struck her and, fetching a hand-cut Dartington crystal glass and some tonic from the fridge, she re-opened the sideboard and fished out the gin, pouring herself a generous slug! Kicking the door to with the tip of her stiletto, she sat luxuriously on the perfectly fluffed up cushions of the sofa and flung off both stilettos, revealing coral painted toe nails within sheer tan stockings. She stretched out her toes gleefully from the confining shape of the shoes and propped them up on the gleaming coffee table, after which she tilted her glass towards the day.

"Sod you!" she said, and this felt so liberating that she repeated the toast and heard herself relaxing into a small, but none the less prevalent, laugh! Rapidly replenishing the glass, she began to wonder really what the big deal had been that morning, for surely Charlotte wasn't that bad: she wasn't pregnant or on drugs, and really that grotty old house that Charlotte thought was so very special, kept her away from the more serious allures, leaving Leticia to indulge in – well, to do this! One more invective before she finished this restoring glass then:

"Bugger!" she hollered, allowing herself the luxury of slipping into the natural Devon accent of her upbringing, before she had met Neville and he had so tactfully and kindly helped to hone and refine her honeyed brogue to something more fitting to her current station as wife of a chief executive. She thrilled and laughed naughtily at herself, openly this time:

"Bugger Oi!" she added, smacking the now empty glass down onto the coffee table and making the pot pourri dance in its container:

"Oi shell eff ter do this again some toime!" Leticia thought to herself, smiling conspiratorially.

Meanwhile, Demelza and Charlie had scrounged some bread and toasted it on the Aga, spreading the butter on the toast while still on the hot plate, to make it bubble; after which they slid out of the French windows of the kitchen and headed for the trampoline. Here they sat on the damp, taught surface, gently bobbing up and down as they ate their toast and put the world to rights. There was always so much to say, in spite of the service provided by Facebook only the previous night, through which all private communications between immediate friends were sent and received, it being silent – and a better protection from the adult world. There was that teacher, Miss Pringle (Pongle, as she was known) who Holly had said was totally minging because she'd confiscated her nose-stud and then at the end of the day, when Holly had asked for it back politely, Pongle couldn't find it. And then when Holly had put it to Pongle that she should therefore buy her a new one (*which she should!*) Pongle had given her a detention for being cheeky.

"There's *so* like completely no justice!"

"And it's so like *hypercritical* to ban nose-studs when most of the girls have got bellybutton bars *twice* as big as what Holly's nose-stud is: but there's no rule about that, just because they can't see them!"

"Yeah, but can you imagine if there *was* a bellybutton-bar check? It would be like *'Hello Demelza, now up with your blouse, let's check your tummy!'* Demelza spluttered her amusement:

"Yeah right: the pervs!" The two girls rolled around the trampoline, laughing and happy in their exclusive fourteen-year-old world, until Charlie stood up suddenly, spilling into Demelza as she did so and causing more amusement:

"D'you want to see what we did in gym club the other day? My mum still makes me go, because she's got some crazy idea the exercise'll make me hungry for one of her weird dinner-type things with fancy names like *Ragenough* and not be on my 'crash diet'. And I'm like: 'Who crashed?' 'What crashed?'"

"Go on: let's see a gym club demo fit for a *Done-enough* then!" Charlie jumped off the trampoline, her long legs splayed unconsciously athletically. Demelza, who was a good deal shorter and not gifted in this department, scrambled down after.

Charlie paced back from the trampoline impressively, counting her strides, after which she peeled away a section of the blue plastic safety covering around the circumference of the trampoline.

"We had two people on either side to help get us over, but I seemed to be able to do it anyway," Charlie explained modestly. She didn't want Demelza to think that she thought that anything she learnt at gym club was a big deal. In truth she enjoyed the sessions, but they sounded so very childish and sporty and she was afraid of seeming keen or *geeky*. She paced back and forth carefully another couple of times for now that she was committed to showing this privately to her friend, she wanted to get it right, but that other thing was taking over; her sporty side which she had been at pains to hide only moments ago. It was as if Demelza had subsided from the top of her list of priorities and this feat had taken her over, her body priming and straining to execute it perfectly.

After what seemed a bit too much deliberation for Demelza's short concentration span, her friend suddenly leapt forward, wearing a determined face that she barely recognised, as she approached the trampoline, put her hands on the bars, and sprang her long legs into the air. Up, up they soared, until her body was at full stretch upside-down, after which it curved gracefully, feet now first, following impetus and gravity and depositing her right way up as she let go her hold on the bar, to now be standing triumphantly, her hands by her sides, her composure complete; except for the give-away grin, which spread from ear to ear.

"Wow! That was amazing!" said Demelza, enraptured: "Do it again!" and Charlie, her confidence now restored in both her ability and in impressing her friend in a most exciting way, happily agreed, this time keeping both feet together and prolonging that upside down moment a little longer, before swinging them over and righting herself as before. Demelza looked at Charlie's stature and athletic build wistfully:

"Do you think you could teach me?" she asked. Charlie was thrilled, for here was something that her best friend, who could do anything, wanted to learn from her! She glowed inside as she assured her friend that she reckoned it would be easy.

As the morning progressed into afternoon and the shadows began to lengthen all too early, various members of the family turned out to see the impressive spectacle of Charlie's new trampoline trick, which she never tired of performing, with that ease and grace that bemuses those of average ability in the athletic field. As her self-confidence and self-esteem swelled, so did her performance; while Demelza continued to thunder after her up the well worn path to the trampoline, attempting to follow Charlie's anxiously called instructions. At times she hurled herself into the air, her posterior rising impressively, only for it to quiver and sink down defeated on the ground side of the trampoline and at others she arrived at the taking off point, grabbed the bar and refused, like a pony at a gymkhana; and all this to gales of laughter from the spectators, to whom Demelza bowed graciously:

"You know what I remind me of?" she asked the populace at large, "That time Holly told us about when she went to the disabled loo at school (you know, which is nicer because it's bigger), and there was no paper, so she up-ended and tried to dry off on the hand drier and she hadn't locked the door properly and Miss Spanner came in! *"Holly Stigmore: What ARE you doing!"* Demelza mimicked their teacher's understandable amazement to a guffawing audience. Before the ripples of laughter had completely subsided and while all eyes were still on her, Demelza's jaw set in determination: this was *her* trampoline, which had been *her* idea and she became determined that this time, *this* time, she was going to do that new trick if it killed her. She snorted theatrically and pawed the ground, to everyone's continued amusement, and then sped at the trampoline, ever accelerating until she caught the bar with her hands and, propelled by the speed, threw her stern into the air, up, up until she had got to the half way point with her legs, at last, directly over her. Demelza let out a yell of triumph, but at the same time her arms seemed incapable of holding up her weight and her body dove vertically, the springs of the trampoline parting neatly for her head then slamming viciously shut again at her neck, as the impetus of her feet and body swung on over to the awaiting expanse of the trampoline. As her body landed, there was a loud, dry crack where Demelza's neck had given in from the weight and the angle.

A blur of activity followed: Connie, dragging a sagging Moses basket from the cellar, full of mouldering nappies (which would need to go before anyone saw them) heard the hubbub and knew instantly, instinctively that this was not play. She dropped the basket and fled up the slate steps, wrenching at the door, which was closed in a vain attempt to keep the heat in on this January day. She flew to the trampoline at which, only moments ago, she had witnessed so much healthy entertainment and delight – particularly useful to that imp of a Demelza. Here, in the midst of a knot of children who were shrieking different instructions unintelligibly at one another, she found every parent's nightmare. It was her daughter's body lying limply, haphazardly across the trampoline, her lovely head trapped by the fierce springs that were keeping it in that grotesque position.

Chapter Eight

"Stop!" Connie found her throat dry and her voice hoarse, but its intensity penetrated through them all: "Call the ambulance and the fire brigade, Ella. I'll stay here – we mustn't move her. Go!" But Ella had already gone, her chest gripping her heart so tightly that she felt it burning. Never had she called 999: she'd always thought it would feel important and, it must be admitted, fun. However, now her fingers trembled so much and tears – she hadn't noticed those – slid into the dial as she waited five interminable rings to get through.

"Ambulance, police or fire brigade?"

"Both!" she had rasped in agitation.

Sophia had helped. She had quickly grabbed the 'phone from her eldest sister, knowing that, in spite of her fewer years, she would describe the problem more efficiently. Ella acquiesced dumbly and gratefully, as her memory blocked at the configuration of their familiar postcode, which her small sister, often referred to in derogatory terms as 'the bookworm,' was quietly supplying.

"Thanks: well done," murmured Ella, generous even in crisis, as Sophia threw down the receiver and shook with the emotion she had suppressed a moment earlier.

"They're on their way. We'd better tell Mummy." They ran back to find Connie with her arms supporting their sister's head, her thick mane of hair, like a thing apart, trailing in the mud below.

The ambulance seemed to take an eternity, though in reality it was only a few minutes, in spite of the lanes. The gravity of the situation had been recognised through the child's call. The paramedics had taken over at Demelza's head, but explained that they couldn't move her until the fire brigade arrived, because they couldn't budge the cruel springs that had so readily parted for her head when she had fallen. Suddenly, however, the fire people were here in the paddock with some severe looking callipers, which pulled back the springs with ease, not even breaking them. The family and Charlie watched intently, helplessly, while the paramedics did the routine job they were trained for with methodical dispassionate efficiency, as they fitted her head into what looked like a cage. All the while Demelza's normally lithe body remained rigid and inert, her bright, mischievous eyes now glazed and devoid of comprehension. As they completed their work, gently and adeptly manoeuvring Demelza onto a stretcher, an ashen faced Poppy asked the question that was in all their minds but which no one had been able to face.

"Is she *alive?*" After all, she reasoned, Grandma had died and Tramp had died, therefore those who were close to you were sadly not immune.

"Of *course* she is!" hissed Ella defiantly, but she joined the others in searching the paramedics' professional calm for their reaction to the question.

"She's breathing; but it's too early to say anything more definite until she's been properly examined at the hospital."

"You must try not to worry: worrying won't help her." Connie almost spat at this kindly intended advice, but she found Poppy's hand searching for the reassurance she couldn't give, thrusting trustingly into hers; her touch to Connie's dried out soul the only possible mutual comfort.

The family had marched behind the stretcher and Connie was reminded of the seemingly endless journey that she and her brother, Jeremy, had jointly made, only comparatively recently, behind their mother's coffin to the graveside.

There was only room for two in the ambulance, so Connie got in with Poppy, her youngest, telling a shaking Charlie to go home and Ella to look after Sophia (although it looked as though it should be the other way round, for Ella was sobbing uncontrollably while Sophia, a look of horror on her dry face, kept her arms about her).

Connie sat with Poppy to the side of the ambulance, out of the way, trying to answer the questions fired at her, concerning her daughter: her age, her doctor, and any allergies? Each question brought her back to herself with a jerk, for her mind was grappling and whirling with what she should do and Demelza, Demelza, Demelza...

With her mother gone, there was no one on whom to unload, and there was so much anguish to share and sob over! Suddenly, amongst the screaming in her head she knew and searched for her mobile, only to be reminded that she couldn't use it in the ambulance. They were using a phone of their own, however, and it was now that she heard confirmed what she had privately dreaded:

"Suspected severance of the spinal cord..."

"I need that 'phone a moment – please!" she called desperately, the words vomiting from her in a torrent. Without speaking the paramedic looked up briefly and handed it to her.

"Stuart!" she intoned at the answering message: "you need to come now!" When her mother had asked urgently for the phone, Poppy was expecting to hear a frantic conversation with Sebastian. When she heard her father's name, however, part of her was pleased that he was coming; while the other was the more scared by the gravity of the situation impelling her mother to call him – and not Sebastian. She dropped her confused and burning little head into her grubby hands.

~

"Dahling!" Leticia drawled "I can't make out a *word* you're saying! Let's get Daddy to put you down for elocution lessons next term." She continued eagerly, since, for once, Charlotte was not actually arguing back. "That should do it... *Actually it helped me!*" she whispered, thinking how very sporting she was being, in confiding this little nugget of her past to her daughter, but the child appeared to be unimpressed and crying, in fact she seemed quite upset: *What had she said this time?* Letitia suppressed a small, but eloquently swallowed hiccup and didn't feel exasperated.

"Dahling – only an idea! If elocution lessons upset you that much there are *other ways!*" However, even to Leticia's befuddled brain (*she'd been having a teeny nap: that was why*) there seemed some urgency in the child's disjointed sobs. Eventually Leticia was persuaded, much against her will, to come at once – which was really inconvenient. Normally Leticia was crying out to be wanted by her only blood daughter – and the best she could hope for if there was a 'phone call during the day, was a request from Charlotte to prolong her time away and stay the night! Now – just when she was actually *enjoying* time out on her own, here was Charlotte wailing like a banshee that she wanted to be taken home immediately!

The stilettos had come off again and had to be retrieved from either side of the waste paper basket, *(how on earth did they get there?)* Then it was necessary to repair her make-up, for her mascara looked smudged and her foundation had ceased to be founded on anything above chin level: indeed her whole face appeared to have slipped! She had dabbed and painted deftly, relieved that at least this interruption had prevented the disaster of Neville catching her thus compromised.

Her face restored, Leticia slid into the confines of her Saab convertible, but fumbled slightly as the keys refused to go directly into the ignition.

"Blast!" muttered Leticia demurely and had another shot: this time they entered perfectly, but an almost imperceptible lurch took place as she negotiated first gear. She considered for a moment and an unusually impish grin split the tautness of her foundation:

"I think I must be tight!" she said to herself, as she attempted to replay the number of visits she had needed to make to the sideboard. Another discrete hiccup produced itself, as if from nowhere, to confirm her suspicions. Well, actually it had been fun: great fun, and really quite liberating! She wasn't sure what had prompted such a diversion from the norm, when she had been alone in the middle of the day – and of course she wouldn't repeat it, but no harm done. It had been a 'proper job' in fact, she thought, her sub-conscious launching into her natural Devon vernacular that wouldn't do at all.

Arriving at Connie's house, having carefully negotiated the frightful drive with success, she had very unfortunately taken off some of the gate post; but it wasn't worth demeaning herself to explain that she hadn't realised the posts were quite so close together, because nobody seemed to care anyway! *Extraordinary family,* she thought as Charlotte flung herself into the car, giving her mother the unexpected hug she had been craving for the past year. It was a shame that Charlotte was so *damp,* however, thought Leticia; at the same time mentally assessing the damage done to the car by Connie's stupid gateposts and wondering when she could decently extricate herself before the salty tears ruined her Cashmere. She patted Charlotte's back experimentally, which seemed to make the child cling tighter and spoke gently in her ear about getting her home, lovely cups of tea and a nice hot bath – after which she ran out of epithets. Leticia wondered where Connie was; for she usually rushed out to greet her. Up in that grubby garden more than likely – and what about Charlotte's bosom friend, Demelza? One would expect her to at least wave Charlotte off? Then it dawned on Leticia, and stroking Charlotte's beautiful, bright blonde hair, in the way that she had longed but not dared to do, she whispered soothingly, grateful that there had been no reference to the gin on her breath:

"Darling – it's nothing: tiffs blow over, you know!" Leticia felt bad about this remark later, once she understood what had happened, but how was she to know? Charlotte had wrenched herself free from Leticia's arms and screamed at her – actually *screamed* – and Leticia, much shaken, had driven off in a cloud of dust, almost scraping the other gate post in her hurry as she flew over the potholes (a far more successful way of dealing with them, she was discovering). Finally, with the help of internal play back, she was able to reassemble Charlotte's actual words:

"A *tiff?* She may be dead and I got her to do it!"

Chapter Nine

Stuart was holding his mobile in one hand and the steering wheel in the other, forgetting the 'hands free' mechanism that he always used – not that he was law abiding or anything, but that he would never risk a fine:

"Sorry Darling: I simply can't be at the birthing class – not this evening... of course you can go on your own... Well I should know about the breathing bit: it's not like I haven't done it four times before... Sorry, Shoogy: I know it's different this time I didn't mean... Look you've got to understand –" Here he began to shout at her (*why did pregnant women have to be so particularly dense?*)

"My daughter's in hospital and it sounds really bad. Sometimes other things have to take precedence over you... Well if that's what you really think I'm best off out of it: see you when I see you!" He slammed the mobile onto the seat beside him. *How could she be so self-centred?* But women who were pregnant *were* well, pretty self-obsessed, which past experience had taught. This made him think uncomfortably of Connie again: their past and their restrained present. Tonight she had called him desperately, actually needing him to be there. For *herself* it seemed, as well as for Demelza: and it must be admitted that it felt good after all this time, and all her great show of independence, that when the chips were down...What a cock-up he'd made – they'd made – over his childrens' lives! Now here he was, shouting again, this time at Sue, when her only crime, from her perspective, was to crave his presence at a birthing class! He relocated the mobile and dialled Sue, but only got her answer message. She must have switched it off:

"Look, sorry! I'm really agitated about Demelza and I can't think about anything else. Have a good class," he said, replacing the mobile more gently. That was what the therapist had told him: *Confront your anger. If it does let you down, explain and apologise: don't pretend it didn't happen. Gradually you will become the controller and not be controlled by its ferocity.* Stuart began to feel better about himself, which was important, as he sped through the traffic lights before

Brigstow Hospital and came to a halt outside Accident and Emergency, where a green uniformed official told him that he couldn't park there as it was reserved for ambulances. Stuart swore at him, but the recipient seemed completely unperturbed by the display, so there was no option but to screech off onto a verge, still in a 'no parking' zone, but this time out of anyone's way.

Stuart barged through the heavy swing doors to Accident and Emergency, scattering a handful of people, nursing their own injuries, who stood back without objection, each registering the panic on his face. He shouted at the calm receptionist, demanding the whereabouts of his daughter. She responded gently, which made Stuart angrier, for he felt she did not understand the particular urgency of his own situation. Actually, the receptionist felt enormous sympathy for this aerated young man, because she had witnessed the state of his daughter when she had come in and been issued directly to Intensive Care. She instructed him on how to find his way to Intensive Care and Stuart had begun to run before she had finished her sentence.

As he eventually belted into the Intensive care area, skidding to a stop at the desk, he became suddenly aware of the order and quiet surrounding him, which both sobered him and halted his instinct to yell. Instead he pulled himself together and asked to see his daughter, Demelza, and was told by a kindly looking nurse in a lilac uniform that Demelza was being examined at present and if he would like to wait in the waiting room she would bring someone in to see him just as soon as they knew anything.

"Is she going to be alright?" he asked submissively, recognising and respecting her seniority in the situation.

"We can't give any assurances at this stage, but we'll let you know as soon as her examination is completed," she repeated to the dazed and unusually deflated Stuart. "Let me show you the way to the waiting room. Your wife and another daughter are there already and perhaps I can get you all a cup of tea." At that moment there was no one Stuart wished to see more than the erstwhile wife he had divorced with such vehemence. As he pushed open the jolly pink door he rushed into her arms, stroking her hair and mumbling incoherently about the time that his journey had taken.

"Well you're here – that's the main thing," crooned Connie and the strange thing was that he was a true comfort to her, too. Poppy was somewhere, a part of the strange embrace. She couldn't really remember her parents showing affection for each other, even in those far off days before her father had inexplicably left them. It felt both reassuring and disturbing all at the same time: reassuring because really she loved them both and it felt good to see them looking like 'proper' parents, but disturbing because it somehow highlighted the gravity of Demelza's injury – and then, far away, there was a small bell in her head that sounded *Sebastian.* She was very close to him and even though this was her mother and father she was seeing in embrace; she felt discomfort on his behalf…

~

Sebastian had been very excited when he received Connie's call, for he was on the path of what might prove to be quite a find in the collectors' world of Victorian portrait figures. These consisted of various series' of figures depicting the news of the day, in the realms of theatre, the circus, royalty, famous politicians, criminals, equestrians or war heroes. When a portrait of the famous, or indeed infamous, person was obtained, it would be copied onto Staffordshire pottery – but the figure would be only as exact as the artist's original depiction in the portrait. The face of the figure, therefore, was an amalgam of impressions executed between artist and potter; the final miniature possibly being more recognisable by the title than any real-life resemblance. The figures were pleasant enough set singly on a mantelpiece, and for this reason collectors still remained so often thwarted and frustrated; for it was through collection of *complete* sets or couples, that the true value lay. The Crimean war saw the heyday for such media figures, but in this case Sebastian was searching for a historical portrait figure entitled King William III. He had already acquired its partner, which stood about nine inches high and was well coloured (instead of a mere gilt and white, as were so many.) King William, prince of Orange, was wearing a glorious hat with a plume, a flamboyant riding jacket and breeches with knee-high black boots. He was sitting astride a horse facing left, holding a document conspicuously (possibly one of the treaties drawn with Sweden, Spain and various German princes in order to set up the coalition against Louis XIV in 1681), and the inscription, *William III* was written in gilt beneath the figure. The figure he sought had a plate number already reserved for it, in spite of the fact that its existence was unknown, and was almost identical to its partner, which held the preceding plate number. To the expert eye, however, there were minor differences, especially in the tilt of the head, and he, Sebastian, a known expert in this field, had received a definite tip off!

Sebastian's entrance into the unpromising looking barn in Radstock, near Bath, was studiously unhurried and casual. There was an immediate aroma of damp wood and decaying linen, the accustomed hallmark of many a good repository for antiques. The barn was large and contained a heater which could have joined fellow antiques itself, so ancient and inefficient was it. Tables, hung with faded velvet draperies, groaned with goodies, ranging from Victorian rose-budded porcelain potties to tiny silver thimbles, their shape disfigured and scratched with the genuine use of generations for whom needlework was a prerequisite for accomplished women. On the uneven stone walls drooped a number of somewhat jaded, moth-eaten looking standards, used for rallying the cavalry and under which a faded notice read 'Raise the standard of revolt!'

What revolting standards! smiled Sebastian to himself, for this was his natural environment, where he could feel himself coming alive and positively tingling with awe at being surrounded by the means of so much history surviving in today's world of computer science. He was a known figure at these fairs and he recognised various fellow misfits, taking similar refuge and glory in a past world. Some shuffled and tipped hats, others raised a furtive eyebrow, in much the same manner as they might later place their all-important bids. To the outward eye it would be hard to guess that within these furtive, unassuming, cadaverous looking people there lurked razor sharp wits and judgement, the linings of their worn wax jackets a bulging home to several rolls of notes of high denomination. After the auction was over, the atmosphere would change and over pipes and cups of warming tea this unlikely band of high-flying anoraks would hobnob with one another, discussing who had made a steal, who had been sold for a mug; but also genuine interest at one another's finds and deals. Now, however, they each observed restraint, for the stakes were high and they needed to rely on judgement and instinct over what an item was worth to them and how they could best sell it on. Certain items were an antique trader's delight, but not saleable to the average punter and, like Sebastian, their homes bulged with their unmarketable like.

Sebastian's trained eye had taken in what he was searching for, and he casually picked up various other attractive items from the table that would fetch a fair price, while all the time assessing the little figure, *King William III.* In a moment he would put down the little gold and bright blue Crown Derby watering can showered with tiny flowers, with feigned reluctance. Then would be his moment! Others would be watching where he was looking, to check if there was anything that they had missed, so he would need to be quick but casual: he replaced the watering can gently and carefully and then, willing himself not to seem eager and to assume the expression of indifference that they all attempted to wear, he watched his large hand seemingly detach from his body and extend across the patched green baize towards the figure. He would have to examine it: nothing was certain until not only the diagnosis, but the price was paid – and he had already taken in one or two dealers in Staffordshire pottery who were, in all probability, after the same thing!

As his fingers curled around the figure, his mobile 'phone hammered out the tune of the cancan! Several heads looked up and he cursed inwardly while gently, casually, replacing his find. He bet everyone important had spotted him now. All he could do was withdraw to a place a distance away to answer his ill-timed caller, which he noticed, without the usual delight at seeing her name emblazoned across the screen, was Connie:

"Good job I'm dotty about you," he began "You have no idea –"

"Can you come?" Connie interrupted him, her voice barely recognisable.

"I suppose later – that would be lovely," he was slow to fathom, so far removed had he been by his beloved world of Victoriana, but a certain urgency was filtering through from this other track, which was his life outside: his salvation from obsession.

"What's wrong? What's happened?" he tried again.

"Demelza!" she stuttered.

"Oh no!" he answered, her panic now penetrating his own calm, as his stomach lurched uncomfortably and he felt the taste of that BLT sandwich he had eaten for lunch turn sour in his mouth.

"Yes: Sebastian she's broken her neck and they don't know –" she was speaking in little hiccups – "they don't know if... and Stuart's looking after Poppy... she shouldn't be seeing me like this."

"But she's alive?" He had to know.

"She is but they don't know…" She repeated, unable to continue. She didn't have to.

"I'm coming," answered Sebastian: "I'm coming now," and after checking the details of the hospital he strode out of the barn and jumped into his car, revving away over the bumpy turf.

"So t'wadden the original then." A rakish looking gentleman, who sported a trilby complete with jay's feather, muttered confidentially from the side of his mouth to his partner in business as they witnessed Sebastian's swift departure.

"Couldn't have bin."

"Ee must've got a tip: you don't reckon he've gawn to that sale down the road?"

"Hmm. Capricious old bugger – trying to turn us off the scent! Better see I s'pose." The two gentlemen looked surreptitiously behind them, checking that they were not being watched, and then shuffled off hurriedly. Following their exit, an atmosphere of unease fell amongst the selection of professional buyers, as each began to question their own judgement in staying in what had at first glimpse appeared to be a promising venue. Quietly, subtly, still more prospective buyers raised eyebrows, much in the manner they might adopt for a bid, and sidled off to the other sale down the road, while the disappointed vendors made mental notes not to return here next year.

Chapter Ten

Sebastian's mind raced to match his driving as he sped down the M5. Demelza: his 'Demmy'! She was the one who had first made him feel a true part of the family, with her cheeky humour and zest for speed: here, he was thinking of the occasions when she rode pillion on his bike. He had known a changing moment, a before and after, when not just Connie, but her whole family in some small way – and perhaps this sounded cheesy – had become a part of *him,* and he accepted them as an entity, a welcomed entity, which made him feel as though he mattered to someone other than himself and his ancient possessions. When dear old Tramp had passed on he hadn't simply wanted to help, he had found himself actually sharing their grief for that extraordinary mangy old thing that used to run its head affectionately under your foot, if it extended casually from the duvet, in a gesture of simple devotion and adoration. (He *had* been somewhat taken aback when first he sampled this gesture, but with it another proof had emerged that he belonged within the household.) He cared and shared, and now Demelza: as he had understood it, a broken neck meant death! He felt his ample stomach constrict at this thought, a thought which he decided to jettison here and now as too mammoth to deal with.

Sebastian now attempted to swerve his ruminations to his beloved William III portrait figure, which he had held in his hand for a precious moment, but not long enough to check the signs: that tilt of the head, the paint; how near and now how far! He had been looking out for that particular piece for some years now, knowing it to be officially missing. Apparently the potter had included a slight stoop as a hint of authenticity, for it was known that William was a hunchback and asthmatic (not so appealing for his fifteen-year-old bride, Mary, who had wept for two days at the prospect of their marriage, but who, once reconciled, proved to be a successful match). Sebastian expected himself to be excruciatingly frustrated at being thus foiled from at least examining what could have been one of his most challenging, and potentially lucrative, finds; but instead he found himself numbed at the irrelevance of the thought. He tried repeatedly to exercise his brain into its customary pastime of historical process, as he drilled his mind through the life of William III, his war with France resulting in the rank of Admiral-General, his victory and popularity as Protestant champion in Europe, his setting up the Grand Alliance in Europe and his devastation at the eventual death of his 'good wife' Queen Mary from smallpox, when she was but thirty-three. Here Sebastian faltered again: Demelza was but fourteen! He would have to cope better than this when he saw Connie, for she would need his shoulder; however, she had Stuart – and he was already there! This meant that she had called Stuart some time before she had called him. An unwelcome dart of resentfulness sped at him and then, mercifully, carried on through the other side; for of course Stuart, as the father, had a natural and formal right to be informed and to be present. It was strange how at times he fancied his own importance as greater than it surely could be – and yet, the children had each indicated to him in their different ways that they assumed his own presence, expecting him to be there with them and their mother, 'as bees in one hive'.

Eventually he arrived at the automatic barrier of Brigstow Hospital and snatched his ticket from the machine. This hospital car park, which now housed the frail Demelza, was the place where Connie told him she had been when she received the news of her mother's death. This was also the place where each of her children had been born, Stuart would have been present then, too, and now the normally thoroughly equable Sebastian experienced a short stab of envy. Being father to those children: how stunningly brilliant must that have felt to have produced them, and through that wonderful woman! He hated himself for the relief he felt at the fact, not that her relationship with Stuart had gone wrong, but that the going wrong had given him the chance to know her and to become 'special'.

Slamming the car door to and sprinting briskly across the car park with surprising speed and agility for someone of his size, weighed down by a cumbersome full-length navy cashmere coat and supporting, miraculously still, the soft black felt hat, that had seen newer days (*never better,* Connie had insisted) but that melded perfectly to the contours of his head, he was the second to arrive at Casualty and ask for Demelza Sharland.

Sebastian explained that he was not a relative, but that Demelza was a very special friend, and as he said this he heard his voice wobble annoyingly. He was told to go to the waiting room where Demelza's parents were. As he opened the door, Connie had flung herself at him. She didn't appear to be crying; probably because Poppy was there, but he could feel her poor skinny body shaking uncontrollably as she gabbled at him incoherently. Poppy had been sitting in what he presumed to be Stuart's lap; out of which she scrambled and came over demurely, her face white and shrunken from crying, all its habitual pink softness pinched out of it. He bent down to her height and held her close for a moment, but then Stuart left his chair hurriedly and stepped across the small room, his hand extended. Sebastian had never expected to shake that hand, for he had perceived enough to feel a strong disliking for this person he had never met.

"Sebastian, I presume," Stuart said, unnecessarily, his face forcing a smile: "It was so kind of you to come." *Kind!* As though there would have been any situation where he *wouldn't* have come; however, Stuart was an overwrought father and Sebastian had put him in, if anything, an even worse position by enforcing some necessity for social niceties, to which he was coping as best he could. He grabbed the hand and wrung it; oblivious to the discomfort on Stuart's face from the unintended pressure exerted.

"Pleased to meet you," Sebastian heard himself, to his horror, saying; but thankfully no one seemed to notice the inappropriateness: "I'm so sorry it had to be like this," he went on hopelessly.

"I know. And I was supposed to be at Sue's antenatal class!" Stuart answered miserably,

"My God! How inconvenient," foundered Sebastian, in an abortive attempt to reach the wavelength and surf through the small talk that only the banality of a hospital waiting room could excuse. Sebastian was having difficulty imagining his Connie, for this was how he found himself thinking of her, ever having anything much to do with this weasel. However, perhaps he could discern through the short beard a sort of 'Noel Edmunds style' charm and brashness that might be appealing, generally to those harbouring a low IQ! Stuart, for his part, was thinking down parallel lines: this guy was enormous! He dwarfed everyone in the room, which included him. He bet he couldn't dance for toffee though. So what would he do to Connie's music? She liked movers and shakers, like himself. And that coat!

Never mind the obvious quality: it looked more like a nightie!

Connie and Poppy were too miserable to register the male juxtapositioning in finding mutual conversable ground outside the pressing immediate situation, beyond which neither were really able to concentrate. However, saving the conversationalists from wading further in their discomfort, there was an interruption as the door flew open and a middle-aged, bespectacled consultant strode in. Everyone sprang apart and the consultant felt the familiar riveting of attention from all in the little room. He shook hands with Stuart, who introduced himself immediately as Demelza's father, lest there be any doubt; Connie being with that grizzly chinned elephant, whose large dark eyes kept filling with tears, he noted.

"How is she?" In his practised way the consultant carefully avoided giving what might prove false hope:

"I'm afraid she's very poorly," he answered candidly, "We've examined her thoroughly and checked her level of feeling. She's in what is known as 'spinal shock', which means that at present she is deeply unconscious – but also that she's in no pain." He took a brief look at the stricken mother as he said this. The job never felt any easier and it was always worse when there was a child involved. "As we thought, she's broken a part of her neck – cervical C6 in fact (that's the particular vertebra that is broken) which causes difficulty with the nerve supply to the lungs."

"Sorry. Lungs, does this mean she can't breathe?" put in Stuart, and the others gasped at his directness, while similarly craning for the answer.

"It does mean that it's hard for her to breathe. We're doing all we can to help her of course, and with your permission, we need to operate as soon as possible."

"Sorry but how? On what? I mean what exactly *are* you doing?" Stuart's exacting questions echoed the thoughts of all those around him.

"Well, I was going to say that from the x-rays we can see the dislocation: one vertebra has slipped forward and squeezed the nerves, which is why she's having the difficulty with breathing. We'll endeavour to reduce it with skull traction, but first we must operate to set the traction up."

"*Reduce?* What do you mean reduce?" Stuart, a natural pedant at the best of times, was grappling at the familiar words used to represent the unfamiliar.

"*Stuart!*" breathed Connie. "Give him time to explain."

"Sorry: we'll attempt to pull the vertebra back towards its original position, which will, in turn, hopefully, reduce the pressure on the nerves. We will also remove any crushed bone that's still floating around there. We've also noticed that she's evidently received a bit of a blow to the head, which probably occurred as she hit the bar of the trampoline, so we'll need to investigate the damage from that and patch it up too. The point is, because she's a minor, I'll need one of your signatures for the op. which, as I said, we need to do very quickly" Stuart and Connie sprang forward. Stuart had already produced a pen from his breast pocket.

"The nurse will do the paperwork with you. I'm going to be taking part in the operation myself so now we'll get her prepped and off we'll go." He shot a brief tight smile, intended to instil confidence, across his otherwise impassive features before diving, with some relief, for the exit to get scrubbed up. Stuart lunged at the nurse to shake her hand and introduce himself again. When she called him Mr Sharland he replied confidentially "No, no: Stuart, Stuart," as though this was a matter of vast importance to the situation.

Sebastian sat with Poppy while the paperwork was going on and asked her if she would like to try on his hat. Stuart raised his eyes to the ceiling when he heard this, but Poppy, perhaps to make Sebastian feel better, meekly complied and adjusted the felt around her small head to make it look like a bonnet. She squeezed Sebastian's hand and smiled up at him:

"*She'll be OK,*" she whispered, "I just know." At this small child helping him through *his* trauma regarding her own sister, Sebastian felt the traitor tears well up in earnest and splash down his cheeks. If he reached for a handkerchief and dabbed he would be drawing attention to them, but if he didn't he would look the more ridiculous, for he was the non-relation: he should be helping, supporting. He decided to blow his nose, as discretely as possible, at the same time surreptitiously staunching the flow. Connie looked over to him to exchange a glance and took in his discomfort for the first time. She also noticed Poppy, whom she had forgotten temporarily in her anxiety. She looked wretched and Connie realised that it had perhaps been a wrong decision not to leave her at home with her sisters. Everything had been so split-second though, not something to which she was ever particularly adept. She made up her mind now, however, thinking at last of Ella and Sophia, who would be desperate for news. She went over to Sebastian, hugging him and Poppy again, and summoned the last of her practical reserves:

"Darling, can you do something for me?"

"Anything!" he answered eagerly.

"Would you take Poppy home. This isn't right for her – and would you look after the others and explain? I don't know when I'll get back and there's school tomorrow and everything and it may be best that they go... But you were in the middle of something weren't you? Wasn't it your William III quest?"

"Yes of course I'll do it. I can take them to school and remind me – *who* was William III?" asked Sebastian, to give himself time to think of a suitable reply that wouldn't bother her. Connie gave a tired smile at Sebastian's vain attempt at humour but persisted.

"No – you said you thought you'd found...?" Sebastian gave a quick glance in Stuart's direction. Was that intrigue he had fleetingly read, or was it his own paranoia, making him forever cautious where antiques were concerned. Anyway, what was there to tell? Suddenly it was all so boring.

"Wrong William," he answered briefly. "And now, young lady," he made another attempt at heartiness "Let's get you home, via the ice cream department at the Deli."

Poppy was glad enough to go and leave this sad place, but she hadn't really taken in that it would be without Demelza. Past visits to Casualty had resulted in their being put back together, the pain stopping and everyone going home in a taxi; which was rather exciting. The enormity of the situation loomed in on her as she smiled bravely and seized Sebastian's hand (his other was being pumped again by her father), ready to go.

"And supper!" Connie had wailed after them. "They may have forgotten to eat!"

Chapter Eleven

Poppy and Sebastian arrived back at the house, encumbered by a large hamper. Sebastian had realised that they may well be on their own for some time, and he had no idea what was in the larder. Not being a fan of the supermarket system, he didn't know his way around them, so they had bought arrays of delicious and impractical delicacies from the Brigstow delicatessen. It was as well, for Ella had sat herself in front of the computer, telling all her friends on MSN Messenger what had befallen her sister, while Sophia had tried to use the unusual quiet to read; but for once her bookishness deserted her and the print danced before her eyes, leaving her completely unaware of what she had read the page before. They welcomed Sebastian and Poppy dramatically, desperate for news of their sister. When they had seen her coming away from the trampoline on that stretcher, with 'all things' over her face to deliver oxygen and stuff, they had known it was serious and not just Demelza's customary horsing around. No, this time she had really done it – but surely Mum would be home?

Sebastian told them as gently as he could. He had been willing himself to resist giving vent to tears in front of the children and found, to his relief, that in this situation he was able to rise above them pretty much; but after he had explained about the implications of the operation he added:

"I'm sure she'll be OK," and Poppy had piped up:

"Actually the doctor didn't say she would be: he said she was very poorly and couldn't breathe much – it was only *me* that said she'd be OK because I had this feeling – at the time…" She trailed off unhelpfully, and Sebastian was forced to acquiesce grimly. Connie had said to him you should always be straight with children so they knew where they were, and here he had been, stringing them along with what amounted only to everyone's fervent hope, rather than any concrete knowledge. Even the surgeon hadn't known.

He unwrapped the glorious parcels of sun-dried tomatoes, pâtés, crusty loaves and elderflower cordial; spreading the goodies anyhow across the broad, scrubbed pine kitchen table, while Sophia selected knives and spoons. They dug in, not bothering with the niceties of plates. The activity of feasting cleared the air and the feeling of full stomachs cheered them a little. After sweeping the crumb-scattered floor (this had always been Tramp's job), Sebastian told them, a little shyly, that it was probably now time for bed, that they must remember school in the morning when, he hoped, they might have better news from the hospital. He was surprised how the children meekly accepted his authority, but then reasoned that it would have been left to Demelza to make the cracks and complaints and without her there was a shift in emphasis to the family structure.

Ella came down again, to find Sebastian hopelessly staring into an empty grate, since he hadn't bothered with the fire on which Connie would have insisted. He was ruminating on whether he should or shouldn't 'phone the hospital, whether Connie would want to hear from him or simply not want to talk, or if she had managed to snatch some sleep, from which he would hate to awaken her.

"I didn't want to alarm the others," Ella said sadly, "but was there anything you didn't tell us? She's not going to die, is she?"

"They said that they'd do everything," he answered, in as reassuring a manner as he could muster, "And I don't think they would operate if there wasn't a good chance." Then, remembering his foiled attempt at an optimistic half truth earlier he went on:

"They didn't know, Ella. They just didn't seem to know."

"Thank you," said Ella, as she laid her head briefly against his and awkwardly kissed the top of his shaven head, before scampering to the confines of her bedroom to place her own head beneath the duvet and roar, like the child she wasn't supposed to be any more, for her pest of a sister.

Sebastian rummaged in the larder for a glass of wine, cogitating on all the frazzled happenings of that dreadful day: he wondered again if he should or should not telephone Connie? Surely if there was any news, good or bad, she would call him anyway – and supposing, in the unlikely event that she'd managed to grab a bit of a doze – well then it would be terrible to awaken her into the awfulness of reality. He convinced himself that a call would be pure selfishness and desisted; reliving instead his feelings of astonishment at the touching way she had remembered his foray after William III on that day. In spite of all that had since happened she had asked how he had got on, understanding like no one else he had known, how much his subject and that little piece had meant to him – and without resentment or ridicule. He felt immensely proud to be able to do something, to show dear, ravaged Connie that he could; and that he cared – and because it entailed her children it would mean a lot to her anyway. Well he had better turn in: who knew? She might need him in the night and then there was his first school run to wake up for. He must set the alarm early enough to wake the children and for them to have their breakfast. This would take him two seconds, but girls were a different breed: how much time would they need for their ablutions and such like?

As Sebastian juggled these wonderings around what was appearing to be his most inadequate brain, he climbed the stairs to Connie's bedroom, empty of Connie, feeling very alone and horribly wide awake. He switched on the bedside light, preferring its yellow glow to the harshness of the one overhead, and drew the heavy velvet curtains. His shadow danced across the primrose wall, the brown stencils of grapevines standing out in subdued silhouette. The French polish of the sprawling, mahogany chest of drawers, adorned with pictures of him and of the children at various ages and stages, winked at him. Demelza was amongst them, of course, in mid leap-frog over her friend Charlie, both of them mud spattered and dressed in some sort of extraordinary leopard fancy dress, which, judging by the look on their and the onlookers faces, was seen with much merriment. They liked to dress thus wildly when they went to the shops as a dare, the more outrageous the better, their grins giving away the satisfaction derived from the ability to shock.

Sebastian was sorry there wasn't that Tramp to patter after him and sink down exhausted and snoring on the worn sheepskin beside the bed. Connie's brush and comb lay haphazardly on the dressing table, a trail of fine chestnut hairs cob-webbing the bristles. Of course, he should pack a bag of such items for her tomorrow: a change of clothes too. He felt in her top drawer, which was already half open, (thankfully, as opening it himself would feel the more invasive), for what he assumed would be underwear, discovering not merely what he sought but amongst an assortment of letters and photographs, a bible also. She had never mentioned being at all religious, but he hoped that her religion would help her now, where he couldn't. He would say nothing, but simply enclose it in the bag. Should he check the girls? Connie always did that before she turned in. Would they want him to? He was *in loco parentis* so perhaps he should.

From the light of the corridor, Sebastian saw that Poppy was in an exhausted sleep in her little bunk, her small face pale and shadowed, her eyelashes stuck together from the copious tears and a lack of washing. He felt the desire to kiss her on the nose, but shied against the impulse in case he should awaken her. Sophia's light was still on and Sebastian tapped very gently on the door (which she appreciated, since everyone normally barged in, not considering her old enough for the courtesy of knocking). She was sitting up in bed attempting still to read and she hastily shoved the Jacqueline Wilson book under her covers, but not before Sebastian had noticed:

"I know it's rather young for my reading age," she explained, "but Mummy says she always reads children's books when she's worried or upset, because they're comforting."

"Sounds an excellent plan," answered Sebastian, never having read any Jacqueline Wilson anyway and thinking that this was another thing he hadn't known about Connie; she was perhaps a more vulnerable person than she liked to let on.

Ella was next, and Sebastian wondered if a visit to a sixteen-year-old might be too invasive: but if he left her out, might she feel somehow marginalised? There was no light showing beneath the door, so he knocked very gently, feeling somewhat foolish, and was grateful when there was no reply. He tiptoed away, safe in the knowledge that he had done his bit anyway and he now faced a bedroom empty of Connie and Tramp, where he clambered dolefully under the multi-coloured counterpane on Connie's bed, the words of a past pop song sprang unbidden into his head:

The bed's too big without you...Without you!

Meanwhile, Ella was holding her breath beneath the bedclothes, willing Sebastian to go away before she could let out another stifled sob.

Chapter Twelve

Rowan was scurrying down the stark corridors of the hospital in Exeter. She was absurdly over-laden with a cargo of dummy newborn babies and some strangely heavy pinafores. These were for her antenatal class, with the thirty-four to thirty-eight week mothers-to-be and their partners. The pinafores had large pockets all along the front, into which two-stone weights were to be added, for the men to carry around in front of them. She took a certain sadistic pleasure in making the men dress in the pinnies and parade ridiculously around the room carrying these weights, in order for them to experience first hand the beached whale sensation, suffered perpetually by their dear pregnant partners. She smiled to herself at the thought of strapping Stuart, the ex-husband of her best friend Connie, and now partner to a very dolly looking pregnant girlfriend, Sue, who worked in the accounts department in his firm.

Sue was obviously not entirely at ease with him, and Rowan remembered that although Connie had said nothing about her husband's behaviour when they were married, she had always been slightly subdued around him: almost fearful, in case she might say the wrong thing and allow others to witness his easy irritation perhaps. It was just a feeling, but she had seen that when Connie was no longer in his presence, she had appeared to regain the free spirit of the effervescent character she truly was – and nowadays, post-Stuart, there was no stopping her! She hoped that Sue was not similarly deflated by him, for her astute eye thought it might have detected the beginnings of a submissiveness towards Stuart too, which, given time, might offer him the tyrannical edge. She had noticed Sue try pitifully hard at the simplest of exercises in the hopes, perhaps, of winning his approval – and he had seemed to try to look involved where, with Connie, he had left all that side to her. Maybe the effort was paying off and he would handle things far better this time. Sue had evidently invested heavily in some trendy skin-tight maternity wear, designed to specifically emphasise the bulge, in contrast to the smocks and dungarees that the more comfortable mothers waddled placidly around in. This made her stand out as sweetly young and fluffy. Rowan prided herself in her professionalism, but Stuart suffered no such qualms from a parental perspective. His annoyingly facetious observations seemed calculated at times to deliberately undermine her, and Rowan felt these to be barely excusable, considering this was actually the fifth birth that he was to sire. Perhaps, though, this was the very crux of the problem, since no one could tell him anything in which he didn't already have first-hand experience. Rowan was reliably informed, however, that he had never before attended any ante-natal classes! Thus she felt it incumbent on herself, for Connie's sake as much as for Sue, to labour the labour and 'talk up' the biological side. In this way she could demonstrate that there were things he had yet to learn in order to be useful to Sue – and to realise how little he had understood the needs of his ex-wife during her various pregnancies. Selecting a cheeky, pale pink checked affair with lacy straps, reserved especially for those fathers displaying an overdose of testosterone, Rowan was looking forward to this particular class and later to filling Connie in with the details over a glass of something strengthening back at Connie's.

Sue was fed up. She knew she shouldn't be, but she couldn't help it. She was really sorry about Stuart's daughter, Demelza, of course, but why now? Why today, when there were the breathing exercises to practise together! And didn't Stuart just *have* to point out that he'd been through all this four whole times before? It was all very well for him, but this was her first baby and she could do with his input and his understanding that although this may be number five for him, it was unique for *them* – and for the little person she had carried for the past eight months. She had been glad about the baby for she had always wanted to settle down and have one, preferably with the likes of Stuart, who offered the security of being in a senior position at work but, if she had to be honest, it had all come a bit soon. And then Stuart's reaction was really quite shocking, for he had grasped his head in his hands (which was not awfully becoming because it made that thin, baldy place on the top of his head which she tried not to notice, very visible to her indeed), and he had said something like "Oh Christ, not again!" He later denied this; but she had heard him alright and it wasn't the sort of thing you forgot. After that he excused himself by saying it was the shock. Well the shock she could understand: it was one for her, too, but did he have to say the 'again' bit? It was as though all babies were the same, no matter who bore them, and she had wanted to feel special and clever and to have made the father ecstatically happy! She bet he had been nicer about *his* first daughter, Ella, the photo of whom sat smugly smiling on his desk. She bet that he danced Connie around the room, gave her flowers and chocolates, and came to all her antenatal classes without even having to be reminded.

Then there was the pram! It had been one of those treasured Saturday mornings when they lazed in bed, making love, talking, reading the papers and drinking tea; while agreeing that these lie-ins together were becoming numbered (due to the imminence of the baby), and they must make the most of them, when Sue had made the suggestion that it was about time they chose a pram and a cradle and what about this afternoon for a trip to *Mothercare* or the like? Stuart had answered that he had already 'fixed' that and gone on perusing the Business section of the paper. Sue had asked him what he meant and he had answered that he already had them – and indeed many more of such items; he had reeled off a list including baby clothes, the bath, the changing mat and in fact a Moses basket, 'for this was more practical than a cradle and could be carried more easily'.

"You mean your other babies' cast-offs?" Sue had been horrified, but Stuart answered without concern that these things tended to be pretty expensive and what was the point when they already possessed them?

"*You*! You already do, but *I* – my baby – doesn't."

"But Connie doesn't mind," he'd answered patiently and this had made Sue more exasperated still:

"So you've asked *her* and forgotten to mention it to *me*: that's just great!" Stuart began to see that he had perhaps been a little on the tactless side:

"It's pure economics," he blustered, "You, of all people should understand… All these things cost money – big money and I should know! I've already paid for them once. Why sting myself for a double ticket when it can be avoided?"

"What do you mean *I should understand*?"

"Well, you work in Accounts and you're great with figures. In fact you have a *great*, great figure!" he simpered, attempting to stroke her soothingly and finding thin air where her body had been, for she had heaved herself away from his touch:

"*Some* people might think – some people *might* think beyond economics when talking about their own new baby." Her voice began to tremble, "And putting my baby in some other baby's stuff, which they've puked and poo-ed in – it's plain disgusting! Anyway, what if your *ex-wife* doesn't want to part with the stuff? After all I bet *she* was allowed to buy them new."

"Like I said, she doesn't mind. And they were for my first babies – which in any case are relations. She's hardly going to need them again: I mean she's in her forties," Stuart put in smartly, in an attempt to mollify,

"Her age has nothing to do with it," Sue had snapped, surprising herself that she was taking Connie's side when normally a subtle put down aimed at Connie did her good, "they're her things for *her* children, and not *my* relations, let me remind you… and I hate it that you've discussed taking something so personal as a cradle too!"

"*Moses basket.*"

"Moses basket, without even consulting me: our baby's mother! I was really looking forward to choosing, say, one of those sort of three-wheeler things or…"

"I think you'll find that the three-wheelers are actually *buggies*!"

"Buggies, prams, Moses baskets: bugger them all! I just wanted to choose our own with the money *my* mum's giving *me* for *my* baby." Stuart didn't even score the obviously proffered point by pointing out that the baby was actually theirs, but that by the same token the Moses basket was therefore technically *his*. He thought these things and was proud of his restraint in not taunting her with them. He had seen Sue's distress and although he still felt it was a fuss over nothing, he wanted to pacify her: he didn't like it when she got mad and she looked so hugely sad, all puffed up and pink in her tent of a nightdress, which produced in him a quickly smothered desire to tweak her nose! After all, if her mother really was helping out with the costs then what did it matter (although surely the money could be better spent on what they *hadn't* got?) He wondered about school fees… He took her in his arms, to which she, a little too readily he thought, gracefully submitted:

"It's okay, Shoogie, darling," (this was his corruption of 'Sugar' and it usually went down well), "we'll get the things you feel strongly about and ask Connie for the rest."

"Don't actually want *any* of them," Sue had responded quietly, under her breath, and Stuart pretended not to have heard. She felt somehow as though she had let herself down and made a fool of herself, so getting her own way in essence carried with it none of the triumph she might have hoped to feel. Instead she had felt oddly deflated.

Now here she was at the antenatal class and instead of the ecstatic charge, which seemed to fire most of the other mothers, she felt depressed and incapable of carrying off this birthing thing at all. The more Sue wallowed, swollen and sad, at the injustice of her lot, the more miserable she felt – and what made it worse was that when she arrived, everyone else not only seemed jovial, with caring, sharing partners; but each immediately asked after Stuart! They were too tactful to ask where he was – no – they simply asked *how* he was, as though *his* well-being was an issue and not hers! Rowan, the midwife who ran the class, was firmly sympathetic: she knew her mums, and recognised the first timer, over anxious to conquer the rigours of baby bearing, bottom lip quivering ready for a bout of despairing, humiliating tears. Rowan knew enough about Stuart too, and assumed he was skiving. She immediately asked if she could partner Sue and whether she could help with a breathing demonstration through the stages of labour. Sue was at once eager, for she had read much about this in the baby book her sister had given her and had practised the panting repeatedly, which had seemed to irritate Stuart, so she had kept it for mainly solitary moments. She thumped down – she could be as ungainly as she liked now – on the floor with Rowan crouching behind her, supporting her arms and back.

"Ladies, enjoy the support he gives you," Rowan called, as all the women moved carefully into position on the floor, their partners anxiously attending to their every move. "Now lean back into him, relax… and breathe: in through the nose – and out through the mouth. That's right, this is the first stage and we're trying to keep things slow and relaxed for you and baby. OK now here comes a contraction - breathe through it, increasing your speed… now *pant* - and relax. Good! Well done boys and well done ladies." Sue brightened at the praise. Now that she had a partner – and was doing the demonstration too – she felt in control again. She was still sorry Stuart couldn't be there but she realised it wasn't devastating. She said as much to the lovely, unflappable woman-of-the-world, Rowan:

"If Stuart's daughter hadn't had that accident today he could have watched you and me: I think he could still learn a thing or two…" Rowan whirled around. She, too had been disappointed he hadn't made it, but for a different reason which concerned the pink pinnie – suddenly she was all attention:

"Stuart's daughter: who do you mean?" she asked, rather sharply. Sue fluffed importantly at being the one to impart the rather shocking news:

"The second one. She fell off the trampoline or something?"

"You mean Demelza? Oh no, how bad is it?"

"Pretty bad, actually! She may have broken her neck!" Sue answered importantly, with the conspiratorial voice that befitted being the bearer of tragic news worth discussing – and she knew it first! Rowan gasped:

"What about Connie? Is she OK?" (*Silly question!*) "My God, she'll be in pieces… I'm sorry, but she's one of my best friends: I must ring the hospital and find out if there's any news…" Sue had not expected this reaction, Rowan's tact and professionalism having hidden, until now, the depths of her friendship with Stuart's ex-wife – and of course Stuart hadn't been over-anxious to emphasise it either. She had interpreted that certain distance between them to mean that they were merely acquaintances – and now her midwife was claiming best friend status with her partner's ex!

Rowan instructed the class to get on with their breathing practice while she raced out and made an urgent phone call. Utterly deflated, Sue sat in the middle of the floor, partner free now and feeling stupid. She supposed, wrongly, that since Connie and Rowan were such great friends, Rowan would have learned things about Stuart, unfair things – and only one side. The whole small town situation was simply too invidious for words: it bordered, in fact, on the incestuous! One of the fathers asked her if she was OK and she said she did feel a little shaky actually, so he gallantly hauled her onto her feet so that she could sit on one of those inadequately small and hard seats: great for pregnant mothers! Rowan would be in directly and Sue would make it clear to her that she was disgruntled, for really none of this was her fault and yet, for some obscure reason, she seemed to be the one on whom the 'lot was falling'. Beginning to feel thoroughly nauseous now she began thinking through square roots, a pastime she had utilised for many years when in fraught situations, designed to concentrate the mind and bring down the blood pressure.

Chapter Thirteen

Connie and Stuart sat side by side on the uncomfortable upright chairs of the waiting room for what seemed an eternity. While they were in such enforced close proximity, they attempted to use the time by discussing the affairs of the other children, from the subject of Ella's GCSEs, for which she was supposed to be working only wasn't, to Sophia's vast and varied reading repertoire, resulting in her covering subjects over which they would have hoped that, at twelve, she should be *less* knowledgeable. Each tried to throw themselves whole heartedly into discussion, while at the same time listening for the tiniest sound indicating the approach of a medic with news of their daughter. The conversation drifted into the past when they had been together and the children had been equally shared: presents, games, laughter and tears were remembered fondly, as each tried for the sake of the other, to show some involvement in what they were saying and to remember the times as good. Their differences were for the moment forgotten and they found themselves extraordinarily grateful for the other's presence, both for comfort, and understanding that the level of hurt and anguish was meted out equally and most cruelly between the two of them: the creators of the child who was fighting for very breath only a few doors away. Connie was missing her mother's calm, practical presence: that war-time generation had been forced to learn stoicism from an early age and Connie wanted to feel it rubbing off on her. She missed, too, the feeling of having her own parent to grieve and worry, as she was doing, but over *herself*, a parent's child also, as well as for her grandchild. She knew she couldn't share this with Stuart, who had moved on to the subject of ever-escalating school fees...

At last footsteps could be clearly heard along the quiet corridor. They hesitated outside and then entered and Connie and Stuart sprang from their seats simultaneously, all the strains of the night showing plainly on their features.

"*How is she?*" they asked, their words thick in their throats, as the nurse in faded turquoise responded quickly:

"Mr Sharland?"

"Yes – and this is my wife," Stuart's answer had been out of habit. He had momentarily forgotten the chasm that divided them; their new chapters and partners having become suspended through the inextinguishable bond of parenthood, where they shared an eternal partnership through, not so much the good times; but the bad ones – and not so much health, but sickness. He shrugged apologetically at Connie for the mistake, which she hadn't noticed,

"There's an urgent phone call for you Mr Sharland." Connie followed Stuart and the nurse into the corridor, both looking puzzled, for surely almost no one knew they were here – and those who did, would hardly call him on the hospital 'phone just now. The nurse indicated the desk which housed the telephone and instructed Stuart not to be long. Still dazed and frowning he lifted the receiver:

"Stuart Sharland?"

"Mr Sharland, this is Devon and Exeter Hospital. Were you expecting to come here today?" Stuart's tired mind grappled back to what seemed an age ago:

"Yes, for my girlfriend's antenatal class... I couldn't." He had forgotten Sue's very existence temporarily. The voice cut in:

"Your wife has gone into premature labour."

"What? But she's less than eight months! Couldn't it be one of those Braxton Hicks things?" Stuart grappled rather crossly. He simply wasn't prepared for this. He had other pressing things weighing him down and, like many men, he never was good at dealing with more than one issue at a time.

"Mr Sharland there's no doubt about it: your wife is in labour and she needs you with her now. She says never mind about packing the bag for her, just come!"

"Oh. Thank you. You see my daughter's very ill..."

"I'm very sorry to hear that – but, Mr Sharland, nothing alters the fact that you are needed here by your wife and baby immediately!" The authoritative tone left Stuart extraordinarily defeated and he mumbled submissively:

"Right, right. I'll see what I can do," and replaced the receiver. He turned to Connie, who had picked up the gist of what had happened:

"Oh God!" he said, and then, "Oh shit!"

They returned to the waiting room, Stuart cursing and grumbling and asking what he should do by turns.

"The answer is simple," answered Connie, "you have to go."

"But I can't! I can't leave Demelza like this – she's my daughter! God, I didn't know how much I cared."

"But Sue is giving birth to another daughter – or son – right now!"

"Son, actually. It's not the same! She's giving life, while Demelza might be, might be…" Connie now felt torn by her own feelings:

"Well it's your decision. But I think you have to think of Sue: she'll be desperate to have you there, goading her on in your inimitable way" she ventured the glimpse of a smile. "To be giving birth alone – when it's her first too."

"And last!" put in Stuart firmly,

"To her first and last baby – even more so if it's the only – and the father isn't there – I don't think I could have done it." For a moment Stuart felt absurdly touched at the implication of his own importance at their childrens' births – Connie had never actually articulated this before. However, one of the very births to which she was referring was Demelza's: how could he then desert Demelza at a point where that very life was in danger?

"But it's the situation: I *would* be there! She knows I would be. She'll understand. She has to."

"Well I hope she does!" retorted Connie, part of her relieved at his apparent decision to stay, another appalled for Sue, who must at this moment be struggling without the partner whom really she couldn't know that well. Her mind reeled on, reliving memories of giving birth, with the eager voice of this stranger beside her – then her nearest, her dearest – willing her on! Finally a logical thought swept through her tired brain:

"This is Demelza's sibling you're missing the birth of: Demelza's. Perhaps you should go – I don't know – sort of *for* her."

"Nice one! See if you can make me any more wretched, will you?" sneered Stuart viciously. Connie cowered mentally, as she was meant to, and as she had so often in that other remote chapter of her life when they were a part of one another, locked into a hermetically sealed family unit. He had always hated interference, she knew that: and this time it was not without reason. She should have known better than to try.

"Sorry," she muttered mechanically, as she always had; miserably knowing that it was her who had managed to stupidly set him off – and all through the thoughtlessness of the tiniest straw of an ill-judged emission. Through Sebastian, she had grown out of that necessary wariness, she told herself; that sifting and guarding every small spontaneous whim or passing quip. Silence was the answer – to let him work out in his own mind what he would do. However, to her surprise, he spoke:

"Sorry," he muttered, in his own turn, almost inaudibly,

"Don't worry. We both know that was nothing for you! You are under massive pressure and I interfered." To Connie's further surprise, Stuart began to sob.

"Stop it. Stop being so bloody reasonable: I'm doing it again, aren't I? And the worst thing is, I've started doing it to Sue now, too!" Connie remained silent, but, timidly, she put out her hand, a gesture of Poppy's, and gently stroked the back of his boiling neck. His sobs subsided as he succumbed to the comfort of Connie's cool touch, but the anguish stayed. They had been good together, everyone had said, surely they had been a strong combination – yet here they were, divorced, living separate lives and feeling closer to one another at this moment than many people ever were – more, perhaps, than they had a right to. As Stuart pulled himself back together, Connie moved away again, sensing something from Stuart for which she had no desire. For her, the stroking hand had been a natural animal reaction to soothe and comfort, such as she would extend towards anybody; but because this was Stuart, with whom she had once shared one life, her touch had been a mistaken impulse. She had just had a quick reminding glimpse at the cowering person she had necessarily been and felt no answering desire to return there.

"Don't stop doing that," Stuart sighed, but Connie sat quietly motionless, rather wishing she had not given way to that fleeting lost moment, and he moved into a mode of self-castigation, one to which she was also familiar:

"I really want things to work with Sue and me," he protested, as though Connie had suggested anything other, "but I've started flaring up! I want this baby to have everything I didn't give the others. I do miss them, you know, more than you'd ever guess. More than I'd ever have guessed. You know – lots of the time the children just used to annoy me and I spent the time wishing they weren't there – not wishing them *away* exactly, but just not wanting to have them under my nose, or for them to take up our time together. And now that they're *not...*" Stuart trailed off, fearing the return of further unmanly tears, his head in his hands. Connie said that she had seen that this was the case, thinking, wistfully, that it was a shame he hadn't felt these sorts of emotions about them when they shared the same roof. Suddenly the Joni Mitchell line, *Don't it always seem to go that you don't know what you've got 'til it's gone,* echoed sadly through her head. Meanwhile Stuart had made his decision:

"So I'm not going. I'll go when I've seen Demelza but I can't go until then. I have to be here for *her.*"

"OK," Connie answered submissively, "OK."

More painful, sleepless hours later a young surgeon, sporting a jaunty stripy bandana, a white coat and trainers put his head apologetically around the door of the little waiting room, where Stuart and Connie were slumped, mesmerised into silent misery. Once again they shot into life in an instant, scanning his face for news. The surgeon was careful about his facial expression: it didn't do to look jolly when people were dragged through the harrowing process of powerlessly waiting, as it could be interpreted as hopeful. On the other hand a very grave face made them the more anxious. Thus, keeping his handsome features to a non-committal placidity, he spoke evenly and, he hoped, in a kindly tone; for they both looked utterly ravaged, poor things:

"Well. We're done for the time being. We've patched up the head injury: a glancing blow it seems, so hopefully no lasting damage, but a certain amount of concussion seems to have resulted... but I think the main operation in reduction has so far been a success."

By this, he meant the patient had not died, which was a very real possibility (and there had been one or two rather hairy moments he need not mention, when paddles had been necessary, during surgery).

"How is she?"

"What exactly did you do?" The words tumbled from them both.

"She's still very poorly but we've made her more comfortable. I must warn you that she won't look all that good when you see her, but you mustn't be alarmed. We've patched up the fracture, but you see we've had to screw two bolts into her head and put the neck into continuous skull traction to keep it in the correct position for healing to take place." The casual mention of bolts drove the icicles in Connie's stomach to a still more bilious high:

"Can we see her now?" interrupted Connie. It was ridiculous, she felt, to have to seek permission to see her own daughter who must need her by her side.

"Of course you may – but you need to understand that she is at present very deeply unconscious in what's known as 'spinal shock'. The next few days are extremely crucial and we have to monitor her blood pressure continually to make sure it doesn't drop." They could see by his face, without needing to ask that this would be very threatening if it did. "Obviously she can't perform any normal functions by herself, so she has an oxygen mask to help with breathing, a drip feed tube and a catheter attached to her bladder. I'm telling you this first because it can be quite a shock seeing your daughter in this state, and it's important for you to understand what's being done, beforehand, and why." Connie nodded briefly:

"You're very kind, but can we see her now?" she asked again, not attempting to conceal her impatience.

"Of course, please follow me," answered the surgeon, trying not to feel aggrieved at being cheated from giving a more in depth analysis in describing the stringent lengths necessitated by this most interesting case, over which he had officiated. He padded ahead of them down the familiar long, echoing, lifeless corridor and asked a plump, fresh-faced nurse to take Mr and Mrs Sharland to Intensive Care.

It was a relief to escape the confines of the entrapping waiting room and step out into the greater space of the corridor, where the only sign of life appeared to be ward orderlies shifting trolleys containing grey faced people, either still sleeping from their operations, or drowsy from their pre-meds. At last they arrived at Intensive Care.

~

Stuart and Connie had been warned what to expect; but nothing could have prepared them for the reality. Their super-active daughter looked like someone else's daughter not theirs, as she lay wasted and inert, apparently screwed onto the spinal bed. Tubes seemed to have wound themselves, spaghetti like, into so many parts of her body and it was on these that she was depending for survival, as they sucked their way into her mouth, her nose, her finger and her bladder. Her beautiful birds-nest of hair was hidden from view by what looked like a white bath-hat, while her mouth gobbled, necessarily and grotesquely open, to accommodate the tube that breathed. The air mattress on which she lay was to prevent her getting bedsores they were told (the very idea of Demelza being in one position long enough was hard enough to take in on its own!) and it let out a gentle huffing, puffing sound into the quiet, ordered room, where everything was white: the walls, the sheets, Demelza's gown – the very floor, demonstrating starkly its blinding cleanliness. Demelza's tanned skin was now free from the spattered dirt of the paddock and reflected a dull yellow, while her face showed a pallor Connie had never before witnessed on a live person. One thing was dominant and incessant; and this was the high pitched pip-pip-pip demonstrating, in a way that had become reassuring, Demelza's continuing life.

Connie fought back the nausea she was experiencing from the beating butterflies that had invaded her stomach and churned her insides to water, as she picked her way around the bed to the side where surely there should be a free hand that needed to be held - that she needed to hold. She found it; floppy, cool and dry and as she pressed it and kissed it, in the knowledge that this was her precious tomboy daughter, there was no answering response. She had half expected the roguish mischief that was unique to Demelza to find its way somehow even into this situation, to hear her giggle and exclaim that this truly was a poser, wasn't it, Mother dear? She chafed at the hand in order to try to find at least some warmth in answer, but the hand remained as cool as before and Connie was suddenly reminded of her visit to her mother at the mortuary and how that hand had been blanched, devoid suddenly of its familiar freckles and withered as that of an Autumn leaf. Again she realised that there was really one person whom she truly needed to see, above and beyond Sebastian and her other dear children, and that this was an impossibility. She needed to tell her mother, for her mother to take on the shock, the incredulity and to understand her suffering completely. Her mother, who would somehow seek to reveal a less bleak side, would comfort through her words, her presence. Connie, who had felt she had been handling the bereavement so well, now realised that before it had manifested itself as a dull ache, missing the laughs, the interest at the *minutiae* of the children's idiosyncrasies (about which no one else would be genuinely bothered). This had been hard, but there had been her brother, Jeremy, with whom she shared the loss – and her own children, who needed comfort over the sudden absence of their beloved Grandma. Now there was, she reminded herself, the kind and wonderful Sebastian both to be there and to listen to her ceaseless attempts to conjure up the caustic, bizarre banter, peculiar to herself and her mother: the endless toasts over anything, from cups of tea to her aunt and uncle's rhubarb wine:

"*Yur'z to us.*"

"*None like us! Oi looks towards you.*"

"*Oi bows accordin'!*" Their repetition of this piece of Devon rhetoric may have served as an irritant to some, but to them it never ceased to amuse!

Stuart felt drowned in exasperation: used to being pro-active, he was suffering severely from feelings of inadequacy. He had seen Connie's sweet open face taking on an expression of utter devastation, to which his own feelings were too full to cope. Somehow he had messed up further with her, by giving away to raw emotions, including anger and tears, and confiding things with which he would have preferred her not to be acquainted – and then accidentally calling her his wife! His way of coping with situations with which he actually couldn't deal was to bluff and pretend and to this end he had taken on a lengthy conversation – well more of a monologue really – with one of the nurses attending his daughter. The nurse was helping keep Demelza's head and trunk in place to prevent twisting when they turned her, but she appeared to be attending earnestly to the uninformed babble that was gushing from him, regarding his understanding of neck injuries. Finally he had allowed the poor nurse to back off and had asked for paper, which she returned with quietly and efficiently. He left the room himself, for he felt stifled and couldn't think properly in there, with the constant bustle around someone whom he knew to be his daughter on that sighing white bed. He whipped a pen from his jacket pocket: Demelza had called him a 'chav' for its distinctive Burberry label. He hadn't been certain of the meaning of the word, but had been exasperated at her laughing at a smart garment that was both tasteful and expensive. Moreover, he was pretty certain he looked damned good in it too! He held the pen poised over the sheet of paper, wondering what on earth he should put to Demelza for when she awoke:

Dear Demelza, he began, but then he decided that 'dear' was too formal so he asked for more paper. The nurse brought him a whole sheaf this time, which was understanding of her: letters were not his thing. Connie had written them when they were married and other than that there was his secretary for the niceties. *Darling,* he began this time; *By the time you read this you will hopefully be feeling a whole lot better.* He paused, trying to think of a suitably encouraging fatherly remark, hoping fervently that all this was to be very temporary and the letter would prove unnecessary for he would ring up and they would chat, as usual, after which inspiration struck: *By then you should have a baby brother and I will bring him to see his lovely big sister Demelza, who gave us all such a scare! That is why I must leave now – for his birth – but I will be back soon!*

Lots of love and get well quick so you can hold him, Stuart.

Stuart returned the pen to his pocket and scanned through his note for Demelza. Somehow it seemed inadequate, yet the message was there. He had paused rather sadly before scribbling his name at the bottom. What misplaced vanity had pushed him into insisting the children call him by his first name, and not 'Dad', like everyone else? At the time he had felt the title to be too ageing, too average, too much like dumbing himself down to the ranks of the unremarkable. He felt good when his two-year-olds had lisped out his name, for he was a modern man – a shade different to the norm: it made people think twice. Yet now, when it mattered, he wished away the pomposity that had prompted this step, for he felt it would be far more special to be Demelza's dad: the one and only. Ah well, what was done was done, but he wished this feeling of inadequacy that seemed to be haunting him would go away. He felt superfluous to requirements, for everything had its own order and management without his input. He was the father and yet he felt dispensable. He was at his best when he felt needed and he could rise to an occasion: hadn't he dropped everything when he heard about Demelza? However now he simply grimaced in his discomfort as he handed the note to the nurse, together with the unused paper, asking her to give it to Demelza when she awoke. The nurse felt both glad at his confidence and sad at the thought that it was almost certainly misplaced, as she pocketed it. Stuart steeled himself and popped his head again around the door of Intensive Care to take his leave of Connie, but she was sitting slumped in a chair next to their daughter, holding her hand, apparently asleep.

"Got to go to Sue now," he called, with a jauntiness he did not feel at all, "See you soon – and please keep in touch," he added pleadingly, because he felt that there was nothing he could actually contribute here at all, whereas, he brightened at the thought, he could arrive in the nick of time for Sue and she would be so relieved, because she truly needed him – and then his new baby would be born!

He would protect and nurture this baby like none before, he assured himself, as the doors swung to behind him and he was able to turn his back on all that suffering, and feel vital again! His feet propelled him down the echoing corridor in answer to the upturn in his demeanour, as he sprinted for the stairs in preference to waiting for the lift; the harrowing, sleepless night shaken off in the exuberance of an imminent newborn – his first son! On the ground floor everyone stood back dramatically as he belted past, thinking, if they thought at all, that he would be subject to an accident or emergency. At last he reached his car, carelessly parked on the verge of the 'No Parking' zone, as he had left it, what seemed days ago. There was a notice stuck to his windscreen pointing out the obvious, but the tone was kindly, the perpetrator of the note probably guessing that a car like this would not be parked in such a manner or place without an emergency of some sort. Stuart scraped at the mark the note had made with his thumbnail and swung into the driving seat, turning the ignition without bothering to fasten his seat belt. However, no answering thrum was to be heard from the engine; only an annoying clicking sound of the key being turned. He tried again and yet again repeatedly, losing his temper with it and cursing as he pulled the leaver to release the bonnet, which revealed nothing amiss. He attempted to turn it over again, but with no result. Slamming the bonnet down hard and swearing furiously he strode back to the hospital, barging heavily this time past the mass of lost looking people at Reception, as he made his way back to Intensive Care. All again was ordered, quiet and professional as he clattered to the room where his daughter lay lifelessly, at the mercy of machines and his ex-wife lay inert beside her. Connie looked up as he strode in, seeing immediately by his manner that something had occurred to annoy him, but too weary to care much.

"What?" she asked weakly and uncomprehendingly.

"Bloody battery's flat! Arrived in such a hurry, I must have left the lights on and not noticed the warning sounds." Poor Stuart: this was the kind of inadequacy that *Connie* had irritated him with, for how was it ever possible to make such mistakes? This, then was how it happened, how it felt: totally wiped out and incredulous at your own stupidity. What could highlight his ineptitude more? He wanted to kick something!

"Oh no," Connie was sympathising tiredly (not carping as he would have done). "Do you want to take mine?" Stuart thought of the dirty old Discovery that once they had bought together and it had been (incredible to think of now) new! New, pristine and shiny!

"That's very kind of you –" he began, "but then I shall have to get it back to you and I should really spend some time –" Connie's tired brain caught on:

"Yes of course," she answered, thinking women's thoughts concerning birth, babies and the necessity for Stuart's arrival as soon as possible. "Had I better take you to Exeter then?"

"Well, *could* you?" he asked politely: "I know you want to be here, but it's less than an hour down the link road and if we go now, you can be back before Demelza wakes up. Then I can use Sue's car because she won't be going anywhere, and get someone out with a new battery for mine?" Connie could see the logic in Stuart's reasoning and the need for speed; but she hated leaving her daughter like this. She knew there was nothing practical that she could do, however; while Sue must be desperate by now.

"Right then," she answered: "We'd better get going."

Chapter Fourteen

Rowan, normally calm and sensible within her profession (her life outside it demonstrating the antithesis), felt torn and exhausted through helplessly witnessing the two lives impinging across mutual territory. First there was Sue, her charge, going through her first labour alone. Sue was understandably scared by the intensity of the pain, as the waves of contraction seared through her already tense body. However, she was also horribly vulnerable, for she knew her partner so little, and was hurt and angry at his absence – when surely all proper fathers would unquestionably have chosen their partner's side. *If he had intended to come, Stuart would have been there by now – and he hasn't even 'phoned,* thought Rowan in disgust as she meanwhile attempted to reassure the distraught young woman, by suggesting all manner of reasons for the odious Stuart to be inexplicably held up on the road. The obvious answer – that he had decided to stay with Demelza – although uppermost in both Rowan and Sue's thoughts, was not voiced. And Connie? Rowan felt confusingly glad for her friend that Stuart had decided to stay and support his second child, thereby not leaving *her* alone! Connie wouldn't have forced him to stay, so it must have been his decision. Sue had begun to rail at him, which was not unusual when women gave birth and their partners knew rationally that it was simply a reaction to the extreme pain. Perhaps, psychologically, their ranting was designed to demonstrate to their partners the magnitude of their suffering, which was forgotten and laughed off after the sound of that first magically piercing cry that triggered an immediate response: that of an all-enveloping, unconditional, animal love!

"That's it: have a good swear at him if it helps!" Rowan's professionalism had returned with the urgency of the job in hand: "I've heard it all before." *Mind if I join you?* was what she was actually thinking. "You don't need Stuart when you've got me!" she laughed wickedly, hoping to lighten the atmosphere. *Steady on, Rowan,* she told herself sternly; *you don't know this woman or want to be out of a job!*

Beyond her professionalism, Rowan was beginning to experience an unexpected empathy with this young mother: she was accustomed to seeing couples united in the act of birth giving, where scores were settled in their mutual ecstasy at the accomplishment of what they had created. Their delight and subsequent mutual adoration was a joy to behold! She would return to her flat alone, tired but buzzing from another job well accomplished, and try not to notice the silence: the echoing clang of the front door, the ticking clock and the dishes in the sink where she had left them when the call had come through. The call illustrated how desperately she was needed in her professional life, but the unsociable hours encroached and invaded any chance of a personal life of her own; and this was perhaps why she seemed to swoop rather too obviously on potential partners, usually resulting in scaring them off! She squeezed single Sue's hand tighter, before gently extracting it to examine how things were going:

"Come on Sue: I can see its little head – loads of hair – you're eight centimetres now and you'll be pushing soon! You're really doing so well!" Sue's strangled moan was hard to interpret, being a cross between relief at the imminence of pushing at last and exasperation at the slowness of dilation but, as she felt the cool damp cloth draw across her burning temples again, she registered that Rowan thought she was doing well and a tiny ray of pride rippled through her pain-wracked body.

It had taken Connie and Stuart the best part of an hour, during which they covered the more barren, gorse blotched, windswept reaches of Witheridge and Rackenford moors, dissected by the cruel ravages of the commuter-friendly North Devon link road. The earth of mid-Devon gleamed yet more ruddily red, as they had neared Tiverton and at last the outskirts of Exeter; at which point their tense, tired silence was interrupted by the sound of Stuart's mobile. Hoping it would be news of Sue and that he could assure her that he was nearly there, Stuart answered it excitedly.

"Oh," he said. "I see. Thanks… thanks very much." There was no warmth in his voice.

"What was that?" asked Connie,

"It was Rowan. To say the baby's arrived already and it's a girl.

Strange: I could have sworn I saw its tackle on the scan."

"Sometimes the cord looks sort of similar I think," answered Connie, after which she experienced a double take: "But you've got a new baby: that's wonderful!" She spoke with forced enthusiasm as an unexpected twist of envy knotted through her at the thought of a newborn. Stuart didn't seem to share any feeling of excitement:

"I *so* nearly made it," he exclaimed, angry and deflated: "if it hadn't been for that flat battery or the fact that your clapped out old car won't go above forty on a hill!" Connie knew better than to expostulate, as she witnessed Stuart's anguish, punctuated by his deliberately banging his head against the window as she drove over the hospital speed bumps at too great a speed. Nursing his head and cursing – he looked so crest-fallen – there were too many disasters to deal with as far as he was concerned. As the car came to a standstill for him to get out, he was suddenly filled with remorse:

"Oh God, I'm sorry. I've been a bastard again, haven't I? You never wanted to come – of course you didn't. And you just did it without a murmur. Look: why don't you come in and see the babe, eh? You know you want to," he pleaded. He wanted to make things up: they had been so close and he didn't want to close the lid on it again over a crass spurt of exasperation.

"Oh for goodness sake, Stuart," said Connie crossly: "You've just missed your new daughter's birth, do you honestly think Sue will want to see me right now? You have a lot of catching up to do." As she said this she thought, wistfully, how magical it would be to hold the baby in her arms and blot out the rest of her world in exchange for a world that was new. Stuart saw the fleeting indecision in her face and tried again, but Connie demurred. The fact was that he was rather dreading facing Sue's wrath at his absence, and their mutual disappointment at her not providing him with his first son, as they had expected. Connie's presence might defuse things, but now he saw a way:

"Right then: I'll go in and see Sue and I'll see how she feels. You stay here for five minutes and if she agrees, then I'll call you."

Connie was desperately tired. She had turned off the engine as they sat absurdly arguing while Stuart's new baby grew older only a floor away.

"Well I may do; see how Sue feels," she prevaricated, anxious to be finally rid of him; for they hadn't spent this much time together in years and everything was becoming too much: she felt the need to cry coming on and she didn't want the comfort of Stuart's arms around her when Sue was up there and who knew? She might look out of the window and get the wrong idea... after all Stuart should be tearing in, taking three steps at a time! Connie mumbled her agreement hurriedly, intending to drive away directly he had gone, while Stuart, briefly mollified, ambled off muttering:

"That puts paid to calling him Stuart Junior too!"

Connie's shoulders shook as the convulsions of confused tears rent her narrow body. Meanwhile upstairs, Sue was sitting up expectantly in her hard hospital bed, holding her newborn. She had been cross: well, furious really, and resentful at Stuart's absence. However, from the moment when her baby had been handed to her, all brick faced, in a tiny white gown which was swaddled tightly by a cellular blanket, she simply couldn't wipe the silly grin from her face or wait to show Stuart! She had managed the whole thing without him, all by herself, and this was something Connie had never accomplished! The instant that Rowan had told her in, it had to be said, a slightly amused or bemused voice, that it was a girl, she had known that this, too, was actually exactly what she had wanted all along. It was a pity that the pram she had finally been allowed to buy was all done out in blue, but maybe they could exchange it? She had attempted to feed the little thing, but it hadn't seemed remotely interested, which Rowan said was usual with *prems*. Instead it had nestled into the damp heat of her body, which had been freshly and deliciously washed clean from the sweat of labour, and slept: contented as a new kitten.

At last a refreshingly uncertain looking Stuart came through the doors – and all Sue could do was to beam at him! He saw the little white bundle with a halo of sticky, dark hair spiking rebelliously from its red crown, and Sue's serene smile, and felt the tears pour down his grateful cheeks! He felt somehow undone and eternally in awe of this sweet young girl who held his baby, smiling beatifically, her cheeks a matching burning pink, as a result of her recent production. His heart felt as though it was running over and all the blistering misery of the past twenty-four hours seemed extinguished by a bright sun, which shone through all the grey uncertainty. He held them both, his partner and his baby, and attempted to explain why, how, that he was so very sorry – but all Sue could do was hush him, tell him it was alright now, like in the song, and go on smiling! He had never seen her properly without make-up, for she was normally assiduous in going to the bathroom first and titivating; so he had not properly appreciated until now how adorably young and beautiful she was in her halo of happiness. He had so successfully blotted everything out that it was some time before he remembered Connie in the car outside. He didn't need her any more, but he did want someone close to admire his new daughter. Wondering how Sue would take it, he extricated himself a little and explained to Sue that he had thought this might cheer Connie up:

"I haven't even done my hair," answered Sue, quickly fingering the bright blonde mop: "I must look a right fright."

"You look the most unutterably ravishing thing in the world!" he exclaimed and Sue giggled, which was an unfamiliar feeling – but then so was everything!

"Oh bring her up then!" said Sue, with a willingness which was genuine "She'll just have to take me as I am!"

Connie was called by such a buoyant Stuart that she was unable to resist his insistence, for he said that Sue was dying to see her. *I doubt that,* she thought, but his enthusiasm had rubbed off, so she climbed wearily out of the car, rubbing the residual tear stains surreptitiously from her cheeks and chin, and feeling the weight of her misery dragging her down as she followed Stuart slowly and in her own time; for this time he had skipped away up the stairs. She found the Maternity Ward, hearing first the tiny and unmistakeable yowls of the newborns: their cries designed to penetrate the urgency of their demands on the hugeness of the world which had opened to welcome them. She saw Sue and Stuart, a happy cosy family entwined amongst one another and almost bolted back in the direction from which she had come, so intrusive and awkward did she feel. However, they had spotted her and called her over. Connie began to congratulate them, while chiding herself for not having thought to buy some flowers from the moth-eaten collection downstairs, wondering how she could be interrupting their privacy, and hating herself for feeling so old and envious at Sue's delighted youthful bloom. However, those feelings just as suddenly left her, to be replaced by a faded delight at their obvious contentment.

"Excuse my hair," Sue fussed,

"Excuse mine then!" Connie rejoined, for it stood at even further odds from her face than usual. At this they all laughed and Connie took the ends in her fingers and held them out further still.

"We thought she was a *he!*" continued Sue, amazed at the way that she seemed to be taking the initiative and everyone seemed to defer to her.

"Girls are best," answered Connie emphatically, "Well I suppose I *would* think that," she went on, hoping that the reference to the number of girls that she and Stuart had produced wouldn't in anyway belittle Sue's obvious feeling of achievement.

"I've got a blue pram," explained Sue, hoping in her turn that Connie wasn't going to be offended that she had hoped for a boy and hadn't waited for *her* pram,

"Be careful who you say that to: people will tell you that it will come in useful *next* time and that really used to hack me off!" Stuart, realising that the two girls, as he thought of them, were getting on OK, shambled off in search of tea, while Sue asked Connie touchingly, if she would like to hold the baby.

"May I?" beamed Connie, gently stretching out her arms to gather the little bundle to her, and Sue answered that actually she wanted her to.

"You know," Connie began, as she rocked the infant ever so slightly, "you know Stuart *really* did want to be with you for the birth. It was just that he was sort of caught up with all that was going on – and then we thought the operation would take less time than it did –"

"And he can never make his mind up about anything so he went with the flow!"

"You know him so well… *and* because he's a man!"

"And useless."

"Totally, totally!"

"I don't know how you coped with him all those years?" Sue was fishing.

"I didn't – that was the problem. But, you know, his heart's in the right place –"

"Most of the time."

"Yes, most of the time – we are talking about Stuart here!" Again they laughed easily, conspiratorially, but Connie sensed there was an underlying serious note to Sue's euphoric mood, which she didn't want to dampen: perhaps this was a case for seizing the moment:

"I think, from what I can gather, that Stuart wants to make things better with you," she said carefully. "I was wrong for him – although I didn't really realise that because I was always so busy with the children: too busy, probably. He cares much more deeply for you I think – and he truly wants to get it right."

"But he gets so angry sometimes. Did he get angry with you, or is it that I'm too…"

"Well he did – but *you* are fine! You are right for him. He knows that."

She didn't want to say that he had more or less said this to her earlier, because Connie neither wanted to break his confidence or admit that such an intimate conversation had taken place between her and Stuart; however, she was now having the same conversation, more or less identically, and this time with Sue. Surely this was a good omen that they were both of a similar mind and willing things to succeed between them?

"It's not really you that he gets angry with, it's more likely himself: I can see he adores you – and your gorgeous baby!" Sue's grin, which had waned a little during the more intense moments of the conversation, lit the room again:

"Do you think so?"

"Certainly do!" Sue pressed Connie's hand for she couldn't speak: to hear this from Connie's lips in particular, her cup was in danger of running over!

Stuart re-entered the room triumphantly, bearing a tray with three dark green cups containing orange-coloured hospital tea. He saw his partner and ex-wife laughing comfortably together and became instantly alarmed because he didn't feel it would do for them to get *too* close:

"Now I hope you're not talking about me?" he asked, in what was intended as an affable tone, but his anxiety showed. Connie and Sue both laughed in response, which was disconcerting, and Sue asked:

"What do *you* think?" He answered, uncomfortably, that he didn't quite know what to think:

"Ah! That's what we suspected all along!" smiled Connie, and he felt so high from his new fatherhood that he joined the merriment and, lifting the baby from Connie's arms, said:

"Hi: I'm Daddy!" and this was the first time out of five babies that he had ever used that word. Connie said that she must get back, and Sue and Stuart were genuinely sorry to see her depart. Stuart saw her to the door.

"That was truly marvellous; I was pretty much in pieces and now I feel I can keep going!" confided Connie.

"Me too: restored, so to speak."

"Yes, quite a bit. But Sue too: she's lovely!" Connie enthused. "Really lovely," she added.

"She is," responded Stuart with enthusiasm, especially delighted that this had come from Connie, *"But the baby's so like Demelza!"* he had added.

"I know - I saw that too!" she had responded, as her stomach returned to its roller coaster ride and the pendulum swung from the newborn to her fourteen-year-old.

Chapter Fifteen

Dearest Connie-cuz,

Where have you been, you naughty girl?! Doing everything you shouldn't do, I hope? I've been trying to call, but didn't want to leave a message because I want to get your reaction. So this means pick up the phone and stop messing directly you get this: orders! OK? I – that is we – I repeat WE... (geddit?) that is I mean Ken and I... Can you guess? You won't believe it! We're GETTING MARRIED!!!!!!!! Oh yes! I kid you not etc. World's honour! And I know you'll remind me concerning my embarrassing thing about saving myself for David Cassidy, but he's simply not available and Ken's the very next best thing!

Next, I know that you'll remind me about all the things that went wrong in my own debacle of an erstwhile hmmm 'marriage thingy'. That, though, was not marriage – I now know – that was sin against humanity; although really it couldn't have been, for I do have my dear ghastlies – who I rang at Cheltenham Ladies to inform and really – I have to say – they were just super about it! (Alright, so Samantha might have refrained from telling me that I was past it and Jules actually shouldn't have said that she'd have preferred it if I was after a PROPER rock star with dosh, like Ozzy Osbourne (I reminded her, witheringly, that I didn't DO married men!)) But after I didn't hang up and they had stopped their fearful sniggering, they really did seem quite taken with the idea and were talking what dresses they wouldn't wear as bridesmaids before ever I'd thought I might have any!

It's all just taken my breath away! Ken says he's amazed at himself, wanting genuinely to settle down at last and he says that all his musician friends are teasing him rotten, for – as you know – he does have a really long history with women. But I think this is good, because if it's taken him this long to find someone he wants to marry then that PROVES I must be pretty special to him... Now I know you had those flings with him yourself and I'll forgive you because it was through you, of course, that we met – but paws off from now on! (Only joking: I know you wouldn't now – with or without the lovely

Sebastian – and I know Ken wouldn't... would he?) (And what of Sebastian? All blooming wonderful, I hope?)

Anyway, I digress a little: we would both like you to be my 'best woman', of course! I haven't decided on the theme for the wedding, but I'll keep you posted.

Don't know if you're aware, but that song Ken wrote for you, after you'd split up and before we'd started up, is doing rather well because it's just entering the charts and I keep hearing it being played all over the place. I feel a bit funny about it, it being called 'Connie's Song' and not MINE, but I'm cool, because it's just timing really. It couldn't be better timing for my ghastlies though because it gives them something to brag about at school... So mostly things are simply buzzing and I can't w8 (as we say!) to hear what you make of it all. Ring, ring, ring quick!

Loads of love. Cuzzywuz,

Boo XXXXOOOOO

Boo eased herself away from the keyboard and snatched the warm sheet from the printer: snail-mail it would have to be, since Connie hadn't appeared to go on-line to answer her emails requesting she answer the 'phone. She re-read it and heaved a large sigh of contentment, scribbling her name and extra kisses at the bottom of the page as she did so. She was thinking about Ken again and as soon as she did, she caught a silly smile curling her lips gently upwards, her luscious stomach, which was reducing in size alarmingly, churning. Normally she would have been happy to shed a few pounds, but Ken said he didn't want to lose any of her! It had to be true, though, that love made you lose weight, for she'd been eating like a hound – and then there were the frequent boxes of heart-shaped chocolates, wrapped in red foil and ribbons that were even beginning to make the postman smirk! Yes, love was a many splendoured thing and she and Ken were wallowing in its thrall.

Ken was touring all over the place in order to augment the cash they had put by for a bumper wedding; Boo's family having stated firmly and fairly that they had stood her first wedding, and marriage was supposed to be for ever, so they were not paying for subsequent ones.

Each night Ken and Boo would perform a particular ritual which they referred to as 'candles'. This consisted of each of them lighting a candle and thinking deeply of the other while sitting in the lotus position – or as near as they could get to it – at a pre-arranged time. They would stare into the flickering brightness, knowing that, how ever far away the other might be, they were singing a telepathic tune together, side by side. Boo had given Ken a snowstorm, such as she had owned when she was a child, which he would shake in vigorous fascination and watch in naive wonderment as the flakes refused to respond to the frenzied stirring but drift slowly, lazily, happily around the little golden Swiss chalet at the bottom. This, Boo had told him, represented their home; in which time was suspended and in which they, and the falling flakes, were together. Ken couldn't believe how much comfort he derived from this simple glass dome, but at 'candles' he gazed and communed with Boo, longing for her, yet so very happy, in the certain telepathic knowledge that she was out there feeling the same for him at this very second.

Nothing outside seemed to touch the lovers in the same way. Boo now rose above the teenage angst of her children, while Ken found the blunders made by his agent, or any incompetence from other session musicians, entirely comical. He was not treading on the same ground as them, for the fire in his heart illuminated his new rosy world, making everything on which it shone strangely distant and unimportant. He found himself appreciating the syrupy love-filled lyrics of the songs he sang with his bands in a new and exciting way: and his guitar breaks seemed to reach realms previously unexplored. He was further amazed that he had lost his propensity for flirting, which had always been a habitual, if only a playful, part of him. In fact, he barely noticed other people, be they male or female, so pre-occupied was he. However, when he did, his inner vision of the voluptuous Boo clouded any appreciation he might have felt; and this inhibited him from his usual affably delivered teasing remarks, that most girls seemed to enjoy and some to reciprocate. Furthermore, if anyone did manage to penetrate his rose-filled vision by indicating a playful interest in him, he merely told them, with pride, that he was 'flattered but taken!' He *was* flattered, it was true – a leopard didn't entirely change its spots – but willingly turning down such suggestions was entirely new to his existence and he revelled in what had so simply taken him over! It was true that he had been somewhat cut up when he had seen the futility of his relationship with Connie, and it had been from this that his increasingly successful song 'Connie's Elegy' had emanated. From that moment he had glimpsed the attraction, perhaps, of a less complicated and more grounded existence, and wondered for the first time if it wasn't possible to somehow amalgamate that with the hedonism of his life on the road as a session musician. However, he had become convinced that this relationship with his old friend had served to prep him for tumbling headlong for her wonderful cousin, Boo; the like of whom he had never known. Connie had been the step necessary to reach the diving board – and the waters were *so cool!*

Ken had felt some trepidation when Boo had announced that he must visit his future stepchildren: not only were they described by her as bolshi teenagers and *ghastly,* but there was the Dad bit. In his chequered career as man about town he had never been near women much involved with children – and in fact he had never met Connie's mob; indeed it was really because of their needs that things with her had fallen apart. Now, however, he had amazed himself because he felt it simply *didn't matter* in the scheme of things. He had necessarily had quite a bit to do with would-be teenage rocksters, behind stage after shows, and been gently amused by their earnestness and dedication. Also it was so easy to enthral them, by demonstrating some of the best known fast guitar licks – the slow ones didn't impress – some of which he could even do with his teeth, or behind his back, in the tradition of the erstwhile stars. In fact these were actually so simple to pull off, since he had the quick ear of the session musician and little fazed him, yet it was always a buzz to see them lapping up the moment, his musical abilities later to be broadcast by them as legendary. This time, however, things were very different and he was sitting meekly beside Boo, without the prop of his guitar, heading towards a school which was incredibly known as *Cheltenham Ladies College* – and that said without so much as a flicker of a grin!

The road to Gloucester had not been an easy one and, as they tackled the sporadic mayhem caused by traffic lights, Boo ran through some of the rather more alarming traits he might encounter with Jules and Samantha. Jules was apparently frightfully acquisitive and if she were to ask him if he might slip her a crisp twenty at a quiet moment, he must decline. Likewise, if she asked him how much he earned he should remind her that it was actually none of her business. Here he had protested, saying that this would sound rude and he didn't want to start on the wrong foot.

"You have no idea!" Boo had answered firmly, "She would be testing you out and if you give in with your usual grace and charm she will walk all over you!" Ken didn't like the sound of this very much, but suggested a softer approach:

"How about 'I'm not really sure I'm afraid' (because, of course, I'm not). 'I don't have a salary. It all depends on how many gigs and for whom'."

"Say that, say that! It's perfect: you're answering the question but not feeding her prying, calculating mind with detail! However, if she asks how much per *actual gig*, well *then* I think you'd be entitled to tell her to mind her own. Oh dear!" she went on, taking a bend at a pace to set them both reeling, their seat belts straining at the leashes: "I'm not painting much of a picture, am I? But you see I don't want you to expect too much and be disappointed – then I'd feel dreadful!" Boo giggled a little self-consciously. "And now I realise I'd better warn you about Samantha... there are two particular things she's very passionate about, the first being fashion."

"That sounds OK to me," answered Ken easily, relieved that here there were no instructions to follow,

"I think you'd better see her first before you say that – she's been in an awful lot of trouble with Miss Toot (isn't that the most killing name?), who seems to have absolutely *no* sense of humour whatsoever. Samantha likes to express herself – you know – like *I* do!" She wiggled seductively in the bucket seat of the car and purred. "The trouble is the school has all these rules: they can only dye their hair in their *natural colour spectrum* – can you imagine?" She shook her pink locks defiantly: "I mean who on earth would want to dye their hair within its *normal* colour? I'm totally with Samantha on that one and I told Miss Toot too! (*That* didn't go down too well, I thought for one awful moment she was going to expel me as a parent!) And then there are silly things about the uniform: Samantha only tries to make a statement and maybe if they ignored her for a week she'd get bored and become less extreme."

"Like what?" asked Ken, becoming intrigued,

"Well you know, the usual things that all girls do with hitching up their skirts – but then she also likes laddered tights, which she's forever being told to change, and tattoos – which are *actually* only henna. I bought them for her for Christmas but I never thought she'd put them up her arms in school – they're really punky symbols; rather fun, actually," she chuckled, narrowly missing a pedestrian, who was wavering undecidedly at a crossing. "And then there's excessive jewellery – her ears are like sieves, and she's always putting in new holes everywhere: Miss Toot would have a fit if she knew the half; but there's this perpetual battle over her nose stud and tongue bar, not to mention going beyond the regulation one earring per ear!" Ken was beginning to look forward to this particular interview:

"But you said there were *two* things about Samantha – dare I ask what the other is; a penchant for navel art?"

"Actually, she *has* got a bellybutton stud. But there is: she's passionate about playing the cello."

"I should have thought that was something to hail rather than decry?" (He was standing up for these prospective step-revellers before even meeting them, his mind running on cello and guitar duets – not impossible and a cello always added depth to rock music).

"She likes to play it in the shortest of micro skirts with stockings! Its pure exhibitionism I've told her!" she shrilled over Ken's outburst of laughter "And if she does it, you *mustn't look!* I always try to look totally bored, because I think that might unnerve her – hasn't so far though," she admitted, joining the laughter, for suddenly it did seem killingly funny!

Soon, still rippling amusement and Boo breaking off every now and then to reprimand and say that it *wasn't funny*, they were negotiating the driveway of a large, stone, meandering building – which seemed like a cross between a castle and a church, thought Ken nervously. Boo came to a screeching halt at the car park, and they both shot forward in their seats. They began the brisk walk towards the school and soon noticed a lady walking purposely towards them, waving genteelly. Impeccable deportment served to give the impression of her gliding over the ground. She was dressed smartly yet discretely in a tailored jacket, long skirt and brogues and at her throat was a chiffon scarf, neatly knotted and tucked into her blouse. On closer inspection it became obvious that the lady was quite young, which had not been apparent from further away due, in part, to the sensible shoes and generally controlled demeanour. Now Miss Toot – for it was she – was extending a long white hand, complete with a flawlessly French polished manicure:

"Ms Boothroyde! Lovely to see you!" Boo extended her own hand, rings and red varnished nails glimmering,

"Boo to you, Miss Toot – how nice – I was only just telling my fiancé all about you!" she trilled demurely, her face deadpan, with only the twinkle in her eye belying her amusement at the coincidence of Miss Toot being the first person from the whole school for them to clap eyes upon.

"Ah – the pop star! We've heard *much!*" Somehow her tone appeared to convey that it had been *too* much. Boo turned to Ken to introduce him properly, but he had reversed himself and could be seen heading rapidly back to the car:

"I think he may have forgotten his handkerchief!" Boo explained smoothly with attempted composure, for she didn't want to let the side down any further. Ken, meanwhile, was basking in relief at his back being turned for a moment and, having spluttered his amusement and agitation, he turned straight faced to brandish an umbrella at Boo and Miss Toot:

"Here it is!" he called triumphantly, "Knew it was somewhere!" It was a sunny day.

Miss Toot waved a Queen Mother flutter, before retiring to discuss the finer points of a memo she intended to circulate, to be entitled 'Uniform and Taste', for Ms Boothroyde's nail and hair combination had provoked one or two pointers not yet covered. Boo, however, seemed to have disappeared between two hearty looking girls in school uniform, both taller than her but with less girth, one lugging a cello, her hair an unlikely flame red, in bottle-brush bunches, which stood at right-angles from her head; the other less remarkable but with their mother's milk and roses complexion, dazzingly free from teenage spots. Ken could feel goose pimples rising on his skin at this sight and at what it represented to him, as he strode back towards them, using the umbrella as a prop for walking – for suddenly he felt intimidated and bashful in the presence of these ladies: the girls were so much more grown-up looking than the verbal impression he had received. Not quite children at all! To make matters worse, a melée of girls stood at a distance behind them, each watching and shoving one another. He put his hand up to his flowing hair self-consciously and threw it off his shoulders – it seemed that *he* was the subject of their gaze and not Boo and he wondered uneasily if his discomfort was so discernable and whether it was quite necessary for them to peer in that disarming way. After what seemed an interminable interval of tact, he finished loitering and hurried to join Boo and be introduced: he needn't have worried about their reception for they were extremely welcoming, pumping his hand enthusiastically:

"I've brought my cello!" Samantha was telling him unnecessarily, "because I hoped there might be a chance for me to play to you and you could tell me what you think. I mean you can be quite candid! I've been doing that Karl Jenkins Benedictus thing from *Fanfare for the Common Man*. Some people say the cello part would sound better as a saxophone, but I think it's really cool the way it is. Do You?" Ken was thankful that she had picked a piece he actually knew, and he was able to agree with conviction, (while with difficulty steering his attention from the stocking tops which peeped from below her school skirt.)

"Apparently he – Karl Jenkins – once belonged to a band called 'Soft Machine Turns You On'. Wicked name, don't you think? Do you know him?" Ken answered that he hadn't had that particular pleasure but he certainly knew the music of the band Soft Machine, even though it was slightly before his time it was music that endured, like the Beatles.

"Do you know Paul McCartney?" The insatiable Samantha was demanding,

"No, not really, though I get to know about him through some of the guys in the bands. I've played for George Harrison though – in his last gig."

"Cool. What was he like?" Ken didn't want to disappoint with his answers, but there was so little to say about the big gigs, when everyone kept their distance between rehearsal and performance.

"Well he seemed really nice – quiet and sort of self-contained – and very polite – he thanked me after the show," he added, sensing the need to 'up' the association.

"How much did he pay you?" Jules wanted to know and Boo glanced warningly at him. His prepared speech went out of his head in the heat of the moment and he muffed it:

"I actually can't remember," he answered inadequately, for the next question was:

"Well *roughly* how much?"

"In fact he didn't pay me at all!" He'd got it now: "It was a charity thing in aid of the third world: you might have seen it. It was televised." Before Jules was able to ask what he might have been paid *if* he had been paid, the gaggle of girls who had been watching pressed in closely.

"These are some of the girls in my year and they're all dying to be introduced!" Samantha shrilled importantly, and Ken began to understand the reason for their previous stares. It wasn't often that anyone knew who he was – or that he received celebrity status, since his job as a session guitarist only occurred on stage, when he came alive under the lights, after which, chameleon like, he reverted to his life of anonymity. The girls were introduced one by one, shyly asking if he knew who ever happened to be top of their own chart and if he did, which of their songs he liked best and if they were nice people away from the razzmatazz. He began to relax and quite enjoy their reverence and, it had to be admitted, their utter gorgeousness in spite of their school uniforms; which hadn't served to make them look part of a well-oiled machine so much as chic and appealing: their blouses provocatively too small, their kilts hitched somehow to make the most of their shapely legs and behinds, and their pony-tails as sleek as paint! The icing on the cake was to see Jules and Samantha's obvious delight at their connection with him. Really things couldn't have turned out easier and Boo was looking like a peacock; for it hadn't occurred to him until now, that this moment had been a little nerve wracking for her to contemplate too.

"Is it right you've got a single out right now?" one of the girls was asking.

"Unusually for me – yes," Ken answered, thinking how opportune the single had turned out to be, "although I think it's somewhere around number forty!" This was a pretence at modesty, when actually he was delighted at its reaching this number and would still be satisfied if it climbed no farther.

"Oo how exciting," another cooed and went on innocently: "Isn't it about an ex – who is actually Jules and Samantha's aunt?" *Those girls had certainly done their fair share of broadcasting about their mother's new fiancé.* He hoped this wasn't about to prove embarrassing and shot a glance at Boo, who answered happily:

"Well yes and no: Connie and Ken did have a brief fling – not that it's any of your business," she winked as she made this mock admonishment, but it also hit home because the girl coloured, "But she's my cousin, so their first cousin once removed, to be exact, and we remain staunch allies!" A girl with the velvet, honeyed skin of mixed race pressed up to him, producing from her blazer pocket a piece of paper and a Parker pen.

"Do you mind if I ask you for your autograph?" she asked politely, as the others giggled and shoved one another, producing scraps of paper of their own.

"I'll turn my back so you can lean on me," offered Jules proprietorialy.

"Mightn't the ink go through on your blazer?" asked another.

"Doubt it – and if it does, it'll be a memento."

"For you and Miss Toot!" suggested Boo naughtily and the girls giggled again at a parent's disloyalty to the school system.

"Right – what shall we say? Two pounds an autograph?" asked Jules.

"*Jules!*" admonished Boo in brusque reproach,

"Only joking," Jules answered hastily, sensing the inappropriacy of her suggestion,

"She wasn't," returned Samantha evenly.

Once all papers were signed, and questions answered to the best of Ken's ability, his confidence was more than restored and he took over the wheel to take Boo and the girls out to tea at a little place he used to know in Cheltenham,

"Mostly I know all the dives, but I hope this place will prove an exception."

"Oh no! Can't we go to a *Greasy Spoon* and eat fried egg sandwiches with brown sauce and mugs of tea?" Ken was beginning to warm towards the girls already:

"It mightn't go with a cello recital?" Ken answered, attempting to gauge the mood.

"No it will be far more fun!" Jules responded and everyone seemed in agreement:

"Right, *Greasy Spoon* it is, if we can find one... but no grassing to Miss Toot, or she'll think I'm a worse influence than your mother!"

"Well up hers then!" pronounced Samantha resoundingly.

"*Samantha!*" spluttered Boo, her indignation unconvincing.

"I'm only expressing the general consensus: Ken's the best influence we've seen in ages," Boo thought of the legions of unsuitable boyfriends to whom she had attempted to introduce her children and realised, deliciously, smugly, that they were right! *I can't wait to tell Connie!* she thought ecstatically.

Chapter Sixteen

Connie had spent three days at the hospital, feeling thoroughly helpless and fearful, for Demelza had made not one single independent movement in that time. One consultant had assured her that Demelza had retained 'reasonable anal tone', for which she was supposed to be grateful because this was the only positive sign.

Sebastian had brought in changes of clothes, books and washing things and also some favourite CDs of Demelza's, which the staff said sometimes helped re-awaken people into consciousness. It had given Demelza's sisters a job for her on which to focus, and they had discussed her taste in music without once mentioning the words gross or rank. The results were a selection of heavy metal with a smattering of Queen (to everyone's relief), and top of the list was the screeched lyric of *Plastic Max's* latest single:

I feel dangerous… I feel ssss so alive!

The hospital staff had been somewhat taken aback by the pitch of the lead vocalist, *Baz Tard,* not to say the macabre and horribly inappropriate lyrics; but they had shown good grace and humour and Connie felt that it was an improvement on the silence and order of before. Normally she banned this particular CD in the car because she said she couldn't bear the screeching sound, making the excuse that it could result in her driving up the proverbial lamp post or, more likely, whacking into an unfortunate farm animal. Now, however, it made her feel nostalgic for the tearaway daughter that had so suddenly deserted, and the angry angst-ridden sounds of rebellion made her hopeful; as though Demelza, with her appalling musical leanings, were still asserting her will amongst them. It was true that the volume was very much below what Demelza would have considered listenable, but perhaps this, too, might drive her into the frustration of telling them that it should be 'well turned up'.

Connie sat beside Demelza willing her with all her being to move or show some sign of recognition. She prayed, making deals with God if only he would spare Demelza. The nurses brought her sandwiches at first, but after a while they were instructed to remind Mrs Sharland to go to the canteen. This was not as mean as it sounded, for the consultants were worried by her appearance and her obsessive vigil, encouraging her to take a break and go home.

At the end of three days of watching her daughter being constantly monitored and checked for signs of recovery a kindly looking, elderly consultant indicated that Connie should follow him into a side room. Connie followed fearfully, knowing that no improvement had been made, or it would have been mentioned and rejoiced over in front of Demelza.

"Mrs Sharland, Demelza is still not responding to treatment, as you can see, but you are aware that we are examining her constantly for clots and should anything occur, good or bad, we would contact you immediately. You really need to go home and get some proper rest: you are clearly exhausted."

"I know I should, but I keep thinking I want to be there for when she wakes up and I can't bear to leave her."

"Mrs Sharland," he wanted to put this as delicately as he possibly could, and he wished that truth and tact could be easier companions in his line of work, "this could be a long process – and your being here or there is not actually going to make a difference to your daughter regaining consciousness at this stage. Anyway, if she does wake up, you won't be good for much in the exhausted state that you're clearly in."

Connie began to waver, knowing he was right, but her tired mind couldn't quite overcome the illogical maternal pull that had prevented her leaving.

"But I thought just being here and talking to her might stimulate her into wakefulness – like the music, which you say can be beneficial?" she wheedled, her hands picking nervously at invisible particles in the air,

"Mrs Sharland, I must insist," the consultant continued authoritatively, "Think of your other daughters: they need your reassurance. Your little girl looked very distraught the other day – and little wonder. She's had her sister removed from every day life and not only that, she has barely seen her mother since it happened!" This was playing the guilt card he knew. Cruel perhaps, but worth it if it proved effective. A different refraction shot through Connie's perspective as she realised just how much she had left up to Sebastian who'd *said* he was coping, *well he would do, wouldn't he?* Yet all the time her other daughters were attempting to cope with the void Demelza had left – and without their mother.

Stuart had popped his head around the door once since the first night, vainly trying to hide the beatific buoyancy that the birth of his new daughter and new chapter had produced. It was true he had rung a few times, but the new life had claimed him and he was unwilling to spend any more time away from Sue, to make up, as much as he could, for missing the birth. He needed to demonstrate to Sue his commitment to her and to baby Fifi. A fluffy blanket of exhaustion was settling all around Connie and suddenly she knew that the consultant was right, that at present she was barely coping and no use to anyone and that what she had put aside was her need to be home with her other children to share their trauma.

"I think I've been selfish and short-sighted," she said simply: "Sorry: I'm off." The consultant was a little taken aback at such a swift change of heart, but he heaved a sigh of relief: *Women!* He thought to himself, *unfathomable, bless 'em!*

She returned to the room where Demelza lay and whispered in her ear what should have been a little tickly message:

"Right Darling: I'm getting really sleepy and I think your sisters may need me at home. That doesn't mean we won't all be thinking of you all the time – but now, you know, I need to be with them: you've been getting far too much limelight and will become impossibly spoilt if this is allowed to go on! I'll leave you with all the most awful of your music that you love... You know, I'm just beginning to possibly see why you like it – so it must definitely be time for me to go! How un-cool would it be to have a Mum who's into your own bands? Enough to make you start to enjoy Country and Western I bet! Maybe I'll bring in some Tammy Wynette to rouse you from your torpor! Love from us all – and from Stuart. He's called and he wrote you that note I read you, so he must be thinking of you loads too. Now you've given us all enough of a scare, so come back to us soon when we both wake up again. Bye, darling."

Connie gathered her possessions and, thanking the nurses, walked quietly away, the tears sliding down her faded cheeks.

"Get a taxi. You mustn't drive in your state," a well-meaning staff nurse called after her, but this fell on deaf ears as Connie sought her car and drove the bumpety road home.

The first thing that filtered through Connie's tired brain was that the daffodils had come out, dotting splashes of brightness down the overgrown verges of the drive, putting the drab, grey rain-filled potholes in relief. They had been tight buds when she had left, with only the snowdrops daring to rear their delicate heads as a bid for survival amidst the February depths. She jerked open the rusted iron latch of the side door, to afford entry for herself and her battered holdall, reversing herself to butt it to with her behind. As the door slotted back into place, her senses were assailed by the damp, churchy, toasty smell of home, while the mud-spattered terracotta tiles of the passage illustrated a trail of use from un-wiped feet of all sizes. It was strange for her not to have been immediately discovered, as would have happened if Tramp had been there to clatter fussily towards her, his flag tail swirling so emphatically from side to side that it impeded progress. She called out, but her voice was drowned by loud music from upstairs. She paused, taking in the all-enveloping homeliness of the sounds, the smells, and the chaos – there was a trail of trainers and schoolwork up the back stairs and a blazer hung rakishly from a banister. She waited for the familiar course of tears to subside before announcing her arrival. A tuneless, droning hum came from the direction of the kitchen, only the muttered lyric a giveaway to the intended tune, which was that of Norah Jones' *Don't Know Why*. She pushed the door slowly open and there stood Sebastian, resplendent in a pinny far too small for both his girth and stature. He glanced up from his assembly of smoked eel pâté on melba toast, both straight from the delicatessen, and his face lit up! It was the visible delight on his face that did for Connie this time, as more tears eased their way down her strained face, over which she appeared to have lost all control. He held her very close, sensing that this moment of sheer joy at her presence must be met with restraint, due to the missing child; but he could enfold her, which was everything she wanted at that moment and they hugged and hugged, the now waif-like Connie barely able to breathe, in the pressure and enormity of Sebastian and his vast embrace.

Another shove at the door and Sophia was with them, her book actually flung aside as the arms of the tangle of her mother and Sebastian extended to include her. Soon she was gone, to report Connie's return to the others. In even less time they had all returned, again with nothing to say, no customary peels of joy, that had emanated more from Demelza than anyone else – just a silent, tightening, clinging warmth of closeness and empathy.

"We've missed you so much," began Poppy unnecessarily.

"I promised myself I wouldn't cry in front of you and now look at me!" began Connie, attempting a smile, which had faltered and failed. However, each of them was returning tear for tear and smile for smile. They sensed that their mother – who, with her gaunt, pale face, barely looked like their mother at present – wasn't really herself because of what had happened to Demelza. Demelza was one of them: an integral *part* of their shared DNA.

Sophia broke the introspection with a speedily delivered monologue:

"Tonight for 'starters' we're having smoked eel pâté, which I chose myself, and after that there's fresh tortellini in a wild mushroom sauce with basil and parmesan. Then yesterday was scallops in a white wine sauce with rosti potatoes: all you have to do is heat them up and it's all done! And then for pudding we've discovered a wicked banana and black treacle ice cream. Sebastian, you promised we could have it again... could it be tonight and Mummy can try it? That's if there's enough. Can we?" Sophia finished, breathlessly pink. Connie realised that permission lay with Sebastian and not her and he looked a little sheepish:

"Whatever your mum would like," he answered and then, facing Connie, he smiled apologetically, "That was all a bit of a give away – but cooking for four isn't really my forté and that Deli in Brigstow has been a God send! I'm sorry everything has been so pre-packed though!"

"You called that ice cream totally health free! But I've been helping him loads, haven't I, Sebastian?" Sophia was evidently very comfortable with Sebastian *in loco parentis*, Connie thought, feeling slightly odd, for she felt the smallest twinge at being quite so easily replaceable.

"And the washing!" Sebastian was saying: "I've had to do it every day and even then I've never quite caught up – and then there's the school run! I don't know how people hold down jobs at the same time as this parenting lark!" He caught Connie's eye as he said this, wishing he had chosen his words more carefully, but she was smiling.

"Perhaps that's why we mess up so much," she answered comfortably. "Thank goodness you were able to take the time off and be here when we all needed you so much: I do hope you've all thanked him loads!" They evidently hadn't, and chorused their thanks now, which embarrassed him:

"It was a very tiny thing in comparison to what you were dealing with and I'd rather do it without thanks," he said in a slightly offended tone, making Connie sense that her exhaustion was somehow sending her out of kilter with reality. Indeed, she felt as though she was floating and that she didn't really belong anywhere.

"Guess what?" Poppy interrupted excitedly, her eyes rounded in wonder: Bustle and Bashful have started laying again! Their combs were getting really red and floppy and I thought it would be any time now and I was right! Look!" Poppy opened her chubby round hand to show a dark, brown freckly egg, not too dissimilar in marking to the hand.

"And I bet you found Bustle's egg in a hollow under the yew tree, just outside the hen run?"

"Exactly there!" answered Poppy, glowing at her mother's shared knowledge,

"She's been doing that for years and I don't know where she gets out or how she gets back in." Connie's enthusiasm was muted but genuine, for here was an indicator of longer days and warmer nights.

Meanwhile Ella had laid the table without being asked and smearings of smoked eel pâté on Melba toast disappeared rapidly, after which Sophia raced to the oven to fish out the little packs of main course, which were hidden in large Aga pots. She kept stealing quick glances at her mother to see how impressed she was at all the helping and cooking she had been doing and, once again, Connie felt overawed at her home having altered so much in so short a time. To her senses it felt like a weary year from when they had all last sat down at a haphazard meal, cooked by herself, at this table, instead of a few days.

When every delicious scraping had been scooped up and the banana and black treacle ice cream was but a memory sustained by the sweet caramel taste that lingered on the tongue, the family continued to sit on at the long pine refectory table, from whence chairs were usually scraped back rapidly at the close of the last mouth-full. Sebastian had taken Connie's hand in his own as he sat beside her, chafing it into warmth and communication, but it felt almost lifeless – and much as Demelza's did, where she lay back in the hospital. Poppy brought Connie the 'phone and dialled the number which she had by heart. They all sat silently as Connie was put through to Intensive Care and it was clear from her expression and her responses that there had been no change. After she had returned the 'phone, Sebastian broke the silence:

"Now – would you like a cup of tea, or a night cap?" he asked, the wheels of his large dark eyes intent on Connie, like an imploring animal, wanting so much to find the thing that he could do to please.

"You know what I'd like the most?" Connie asked rhetorically, "A hot bath with smelly oils in *and* a cup of tea!" Children leapt up in all directions to put the kettle on, find aromatic oils left over from Christmas, and run the bath. Connie felt the attention and pampering were undeserved, but exactly what she needed – and if she had the energy she would revel and make the most of the novelty! As it was, she sat back on her cushions and allowed things to be done, only rising from her chair once she was assured that the hot steamy cup of tea that she was bearing matched the pungent bath that awaited her. Sebastian had balanced clean towels over the radiator and turned on the electric blanket, thus Connie's aching body was able to be suffused in warmth, the hot oils having seeped into the pores of her drawn skin.

Wrapped in her soft, Viyella dressing gown, Connie snuggled into bed, spreading her limbs in the way she had longed to do over the last few days, across sheets, warmed by the luxury of an electric blanket, while leaving the children's bedtimes in Sebastian's evidently capable hands. However, on the point of closing her heavy eyelids at last, Ella bustled into her room and shoved the door to behind her.

"Ella! You've barely said a word: I can see you're finding it really hard. I'm not coping any better myself," Connie admitted. Ella shifted uncomfortably and Connie indicated for her to sit beside her on the bed, while Ella mumbled agreement.

"I would find it harder, wouldn't I?" she said finally and inadequately.

"Why's that?"

"Well I was always arguing with her, wasn't I?"

"But Ella; you are her closest sibling in age. It's natural that you argue – if annoying at times!" she admitted. She focussed on Ella and saw that she was close to tears:

"Ella – tell me," she said, her voice gentle but devoid of emotion.

She desperately needed sleep, but that would be impossible while Ella looked as troubled as this.

"I pushed her into doing that stupid thing that broke her neck – it was me!"

"Ella, what do you mean?" Connie was sitting upright again. "The whole thing was a ghastly, awful accident. It was no one's fault!"

"You have no idea. No one has – that's the trouble. I'm the reason it happened."

"Ella tell me," Connie coaxed.

"You will be angry," Ella warned, while Connie murmured that she doubted it, her intrigue getting the better of her exhaustion for the moment. Ella heaved a quick sigh, indicating that she was ready to get what ever it could be off her chest:

"Well *on* that day – you remember Charlie came round?"

"Yes of course,"

"Well, before she came, Demelza – I'm sorry, Mum – but, well she was being fairly, like, insufferable. I wish I hadn't felt like that, but I did then. She was playing that minging *Plastic Max* CD *again* really loudly, so I couldn't hear my own stuff properly because hers was actually still louder than my own! I was trying to practise and then I just gave up and yelled at her. She couldn't hear me even when I banged on the door, so I went in and she was still in bed – in her pyjamas, like she'd just woken up. I started yelling at her, but all she did was turn the volume up even louder and go: *Sorry! I can't hear you!* That made me even angrier..."

"It would me," Connie put in, as yet unable to find anything unusual having taken place: "I know how it feels too."

"Well I went on yelling and she just went on laughing and making faces, going 'Oo I'm *so* scared!' all sarcastically and I backed off and slammed the door as hard as I could, which she probably couldn't hear because of her row, so then I turned and kicked it and I'm sorry but a piece of sort of carving stuff broke off the door with my shoe – but of course she wouldn't have noticed that either."

"*I'll* notice though: what a pity that bit of wood has lived all these years and it took one cross moment of our generation to spoil it. You're going to have to learn to curb that temper of yours, Ella, life won't get any easier and you can't take out everything that's excruciatingly infuriating with the sole of your foot! But it's really such a small thing in the scheme of things," she went on, relaxed now that she understood what had bothered Ella and to know that it wasn't dreadful.

"I haven't told you yet!" wailed Ella, more exasperated still, "Just let me tell you and don't butt in, or I never will!" she threatened. Connie apologised: life was getting back to normal and this was the old Ella, teenage angst to the fore and on the very edge of lashing out. She had not displayed this trait so badly since before her beloved grandmother had died, the tragic event having somehow triggered a hitherto unknown consideration and kindness to others. (Ella had come to Connie's rescue at the funeral, by singing the song that Connie was supposed to sing when she had seen that her mother was overcome.) Since then, Connie had gradually begun to appreciate the deep change in her and to rely on her eldest as being generally calm and wiser in understanding her siblings. It was true that Ella and Demelza argued infuriatingly at times, but there was nothing in this beyond tedium. Ella sighed dramatically and began speaking deliberately slowly and quietly, so that Connie had to strain everything to pick up what was being said, for if she were to ask, she feared Ella's renewed wrath!

"As I said - Charlie - turned - up - and - I -was - still - completely - fuming - with - Demelza. No matter what I said, she and Charlie laughed and said I was a saddo and stuff like that." Connie could imagine how humiliating this 'two against oneship' must have been, but she remained resolutely silent.

"Well they went off and played on the trampoline and Demelza was like: 'See what *my* friend can do!' and Charlie kept doing that trick so kind of gracefully. I told Demelza – I told her – quietly, you know, so that Charlie couldn't hear – I said '*Right you sad little loser, SHE may be able to do it but you know what? YOU never will because you're too stupid, too short and too FAT!*' She said it was just puppy fat and I said that by her age it was *doggie* fat, so she was a fat dog then, by her own admission. I knew I'd touched a nerve at last, but she turned and sort of sneered at me and said 'Just you wait – you'll see – I'll be doing it by the end of the day and THEN you'll have to say sorry!' And I went 'Oh I would – but that's never going to happen, is it? In fact I'll *bet* you you'll never do it – and *then* you'll have to say sorry and beg *to me* Fat Dog!*'" Ella had begun to cry and her voice had risen in pitch as she heaved the damning words off her chest, "and all the time, Mum, she was laughing, but it was a challenge, a bet: the sort of thing she loves. I was so hoping she wouldn't be able to do it – and *she* was so determined to do it right to humiliate me into saying sorry. It was all going to be a huge joke for her and I wish it had been – I *so* wish it had!" Ella crumpled beside Connie and sobbed, while Connie stroked her back in an attempt to comfort, but just now, Ella was inconsolable:

"Those were the last things we said to each other and really it was all because she made me so mad that she had the accident."

"Hold on Ella," Connie said at last, "Let's take one thing at a time. First of all, do you think its right that Demelza blasts the house out with her music over everyone else's?"

"Well now I wish she would. I don't care any more. It's not really anything I can get wound up about."

"I know what you mean. When they were playing some of that awful blood-curdling screeching *Baz Tard* – aptly named, I must say – for her in the hospital, I felt almost nostalgic. But the fact remains that it *was* very selfish of Demelza to put her sounds and needs over everyone else's – and it's inconsiderate." Connie had caught herself speaking of Demelza in the past and had changed tense mid-sentence, hoping that Ella hadn't noticed: "Just because she's not at all well doesn't change her into some sort of saint! She will always be our bubbly, over-buoyant Demelza." As she heard herself use the phrase 'over-buoyant', Connie's mind flipped from *that* Demelza to the one inert and spread on the hospital bed, and she had to check herself. "So please don't start blaming yourself for a perfectly natural reaction," she hurried on. "Which – let's face it – was *words* and not the violence you've had recourse to in the past. Just words: a taunt, which we both know she would have been able to handle. Maybe you only said it because you knew she could take it?"

"Oh, like I was thinking anything other than to bring her down a peg!"

"OK, you meant to wound her. She'd been pig-headed – but you would *never* have told her to go and break her neck!"

"Well I might – but I wouldn't have meant it," answered Ella with candour and the faintest glimmer of humour; for she was beginning to see what her mother was driving at and her heart was starting to feel lighter. Connie was pressing home her advantage now:

"Can you imagine how many times I've cursed myself for buying that bloody trampoline?" Ella had rarely heard her mother swear before and looked at her in disbelief, both for the language and at the absurdity of its meaning.

"But we begged you to! You only bought it because we all wanted it so badly – especially Demelza. It was all her idea – she planned our proposal!" This was a thought for both of them.

"Well there you are! Demelza wanted the thing so badly, that she put in the lion's share of the plans when you all came to me singing that song and suggesting that the money for all your Christmas presents and birthdays should be combined towards it. If *I'd* had a crystal ball I should have answered *'Never',* just as if you'd had one you would never have challenged her to do that stunt!" Ella wound her arms around her mother in a rare and demonstrative hug.

"You don't think she'll blame me then?"

"Not a chance."

"I wish we hadn't spent so much time in our lives bickering!"

"I wish too – but it wouldn't be very natural amongst siblings, would it? I mean you should have seen Uncle Jeremy and me! And when I played my progressive rock music, as we pretentiously called it then, it didn't turn up as loud as it does now or I'm sure I would have cranked it! As it was, Grandma and Grandpa used to get so cheesed with it and say 'Do you call *that* music?' and I'd think *What prats – what the blob else d'you think it is!"*

"You thought that about Grandma?"

"Oh you bet! I'm sorry to say we didn't always see eye to eye. And I look back now, rather in the way you were just now, and think what a waste all that angst was too. But we came out at the end as close as can be, as you know." Connie was wistful for an instant, as it occurred to her that there was a possibility that with Demelza there might not be an end from which to emerge, swan-like into the sunshine; that she might remain frozen in the zenith of exuberant teenagehood. She shook herself out of that space and noticed that this thought had not affected Ella, for she was gently smiling at the notion of her mother and her grandmother having teenage rows and at the fact that she could think of her sister now with sadness, but not with dread. She had not wanted to visit, but now she did: she wanted to tell her things, to apologise for being a pig, remind her that she wasn't so saintly herself though and to please wake up now… and if she did, she would argue no more. Her sigh was less heart-rending this time as she mused:

"It just seems we've wasted so much time."

"There's a lifetime more time – it's never wasted."

"Do you think Demelza's going to get better then?" asked Ella, her eyes locked with Connie's.

"I daren't answer that – but if you think of all the people that you know in the whole world, who would you think would be most likely to fight the odds?"

"Demelza," her sister answered simply and without hesitation.

"That's exactly who I think too."

~

Sebastian locked and bolted all the outer doors, safely tipped up the logs of the roaring fire vertically (that he had puffed into a frenzy especially, thinking that they might retire there after supper) and turned off all the lights and computer and television standbys. The wide oak staircase creaked complainingly at each tread as he ascended the stairs, where he noticed with pleasure that Connie's bedroom light was still on for him. How he had longed for her presence in the austereness of the large oak bed, from which he would gaze at the ochred walls, stencilled with bunches of drooping grapes, imagining Connie up a step ladder laboriously painting in the luscious blooms, while the swaying branches of the ancient lime tree thrummed majestically outside. He pushed the door open gently and tiptoed in, his eyes swivelling straight to the bed in which Connie lay, her lips slightly apart and her chestnut hair all across the pillow. Beside her, however, lay Ella in her mother's arms, her glossy head turned towards him, the shadows beneath her darkly fringed eyelashes telling a similar tale of anxiety and tiredness to her mother. Both of them were lightly snoring and snuffling, resultant from too many tears. He backed out again quietly and turned out the light. Hating himself for the overwhelming feeling of disappointment, he made his way to the spare room.

Chapter Seventeen

It was the pungent aroma of fresh coffee that finally aroused Connie and she opened her eyes to see Sebastian looking at her quizzically and bearing a vast tray of breakfast, which included the much hallowed eggs from Bustle and Bashful and marmite soldiers. She sat up hastily:

"The children – where are they? What time is it?"

"They were despatched to school some time ago. Even Ella managed to creep out without waking you and it's now around midday!" This meant Sebastian had got on with the school run in spite of Connie being at home to do it, which was not something she was used to or relished. She began to push back the covers prior to getting up:

"Demelza! I've left her on her own. I must get over there."

"I've rung the hospital and explained that you were still sleeping and they said 'Good'. They said that you should not hurry and take everything easy. Demelza's the same and they're playing her Jack Johnson compilation this morning. So please relax and eat this special breakfast," he said, deftly fluffing up the pillows behind her and settling her comfortably back as he put down the heavy Butler's tray, which he had found to his delight at the back of the cleaning cupboard. He lowered himself gingerly beside it, keeping an eye on the silver coffee pot (another find – Georgian, with bone handles, in need of much love and polish, which he had willingly administered before clearing out the cobwebs from its inside and warming it for its first outing in many years). Connie looked gleefully at the splendid array, complete with snowy damask napkins in also newly polished silver napkin rings, bearing initials carved to mark past christenings.

"Sebastian," she said, delightedly dipping a marmite soldier into the yolk of the brown, freckly, boiled egg,

"What?" he answered eagerly.

"Please never lose touch with your feminine side!" This was not quite the compliment he was preening himself to receive and was precisely what he enjoyed in Connie. They both laughed – probably for longer than it actually amused them, because the sensation of laughing together had been missing for so long. The tension, at least for the moment, had broken as Sebastian persuaded Connie that she was definitely in need of another bath, after which she must condescend to his taking her to the hospital in person. She agreed dumbly to this and to his bringing the other children in later to see Demelza and to pick her up again.

~

This was to be the rough pattern of things over the next few weeks. A number of surgeons visited Demelza and checked for the development of inflammation higher up her neck, which might stop her spinal cord from functioning properly, and, in turn, her breathing. She continued to wear the ugly plastic elephantine oxygen mask; to ease her breathing, and her blood pressure was observed repeatedly, in case of it dropping. In fact none of the situations they dreaded had occurred, but neither had she come out of spinal shock. Two weeks had passed and Demelza simply hadn't changed. Connie never actually heard the word 'paralysis', even when the team turned her, so very militarily, while she lay riveted and stiffer than the mattress on which she lay. Somehow, though, the word repeated itself around and around her head. Once, Connie had asked James, who was both her friend and doctor. He had turned up to visit them both and after his examination of Demelza had begun to advise Connie to take care of her own health:

"You're used to loads of exercise and fresh air and here you are all cooped up. You wouldn't be that much use to Demelza if she were capable of coming home right now – harsh words, Connie, I know, but someone's got to get through to you that you can't spend every moment in here." There was something in the way he'd mentioned *if* Demelza were capable, that made Connie look beyond the immediacy of the need for Demelza to regain consciousness:

"When she wakes up, will she be able to move?" Connie asked James levelly. It was harder with a friend, especially when you knew the family, and James was aware he had to meet Connie's green eyes.

"We can't rule out that part of her may be paralysed," he answered, "and the longer she's unconscious the more we worry."

Connie reeled! This was not at all what she was expecting to hear from gentle James, sharer of New Year's Eves on Bideford bridge, tennis partner, carer of her babies and children's ailments, drinker of copious amounts of beer: how could he say this?

"I see," Connie answered evenly: "I'm rather sorry I asked you." James didn't look as wounded as he might; he simply looked sorry and gloomy. He didn't apologise or retract anything either, but went on looking sympathetic, muttering about how lucky she was to have that marvellous big chap, and what was his name again? *Sebastian's* support.

Connie felt as though she were removed from reality. When she was amongst her family, it seemed that she was in another room, that people could see through her, over her, under her – for her existence was all connected to one spinal bed that punctured her mind, her thoughts; wherever they happened to be. Her concentration was consequently woefully impaired and she failed to notice when people spoke to her – and when she did, she instantly forgot what they had just said. The contents of the peanut butter jars at home disappeared rapidly, as she absent-mindedly scooped finger-fulls of the comforting mixture into her mouth, never conscious of having even selected a jar from the cupboard! Each day after the school run, she went to sit beside Demelza and would mutter endlessly into her ear: only at these times did she feel real and able to sustain the monologue. She would prattle on about anything, in much the same way as Poppy did, when she picked her up from school;

Today I went shopping with Ella. She needed new tights – in fact everyone does, and I got some for you, too. Well you'll need them when you're out of here. (I wonder if you'll have grown?) We had lunch at that salad bar that you like and we had smoothies: mine was called a 'flu buster' – what about that for a revolting name! But it seemed like a good idea, because it wouldn't be great if I got flu and breathed all vile germs over you. Then we went to Miriam's and there were these gorgeous trousers I thought I could wear with the band – they're a bit too loud for ordinary wear. Well I wish I'd thought to go to the loo at the salad bar: I think that when I took my jeans off it must have triggered a message... I got the new trousers on and I would have been OK if I hadn't sneezed! Well of course I had to buy the trousers then – which is really annoying because they were too small!

Connie was so wound up in her story that she found herself shaking with laughter at the admission: *Now when you come to, there's a lot of secrets you'll have to keep,* she added. *And do it soon. I'm going to have to return to a bit of the dreaded supply teaching because, with all this skiving, we'll be running out of dosh!*

Connie was following a stream of consciousness, but she always felt that somewhere her words were being fed into Demelza's psyche and there would be a time when she would answer her with a giggle and everything would fall back into place. When Sebastian brought the children to visit, they had become more inured to the sight of their supine, sleeping sister; however, Poppy found it very hard to accept that Demelza was being fed through her wrist and not her mouth. She would gaze at the little tube and ask what if they were feeding Demelza something she didn't like, like mushrooms for instance. Her face puckered at somehow having made everyone smile when actually it was a serious question.

"I know – I'm her sister – and she hates mushrooms." Poppy continued insistently, "I know because she gives hers to me – she says they're like slugs! Supposing she gets forced them and can't spit them out? We should tell the nurses."

"Demelza would be laughing at that," answered Ella, not unkindly, "It's all glucose stuff, to give her energy to wake up – no mushrooms at all." Poppy looked relieved:

"You sure? Then why doesn't the glucose stuff work?"

~

The life of the Sharland family began to take on a pattern, with Connie spending the days at Demelza's side, Sebastian fetching the children and bringing them in to visit, after which they would leave her and drive home, subdued, to carry out the evening's routine of homework and supper, without Demelza.

One evening Sebastian remained outside for some time, re-entering the kitchen, his arms sagging with a vast quantity of mature logs, from the chestnut tree that had fallen some years previously. During its lifetime its long green fingered leaves and polished chestnuts had given joy and succour to generations, but even after it had fallen victim to the gales, which were supposed to be a sign of climate change, it continued to afford appreciation this time through transmitting heat, provided by its dense limbs.

"That took a while!" said Connie, eyeing the quantity of logs while realising that she could only have managed half the load Sebastian's capacity afforded, "But now I see why." Sebastian looked pleased:

"That wasn't what took the time. I'd figured out where that Bustle was getting out and I've sorted it. I never knew hens could fly, but she can! I watched her and she was getting through a little gap between the top of the gate and under the netting roof. My, what a bird! Anyway, now I've put up some wire in the gap so she will be relegated to laying within the henhouse from now on." He looked up at Connie, expecting to see appreciation, but saw none. He knew Connie was pretty much independent, but it was these kinds of jobs for which she seemed to have a blind spot, or saw them simply as not important enough to warrant the time. It felt good to make these small differences and improve the order just a modicum. He hugged the logs to the Aran sweater he had taken to wearing (a present from his mother which had lain unworn in his drawer for some considerable time, as somehow inappropriately dated for his suburban life), and hovered uncertainly; then crossed the room without further comment from anyone. As he reached the door he heard her say quietly to no one in particular:

"What harm was there? She's been flying out for years." Sebastian didn't answer the obvious, which was that for a start it was safer. He realised that just now Connie was so particularly fraught over Demelza that she could absorb little else. He heaved his burden higher and shambled through the door.

"Why did you say that – you've hurt his feelings now?" demanded Poppy.

"Bustle will be distraught; so she probably won't lay any eggs now anyway," continued Connie, by way of explanation.

"But he was only trying to be kind and help," put in Sophia, also siding with Sebastian. Connie knew they were right: why hadn't she laughed and explained to Sebastian, teased him and called him a townie? How was it that she was complicating every simple thing? She seemed to have lost her capacity to engage in anything, for it felt as though a heavy blanket had descended between herself and her sensibilities. However, this new attitude had certainly aided her teaching in her more obstreperous classes.

~

She had walked into the classroom, her arms heavy with the register and reference books, while the children were still cramming their cards, models and sticker albums into their drawers. Before she had even reached her desk, she had heard a voice behind her register her presence and groan "*Oh no!*" That was all – and probably it wasn't so much personal as voicing the thought that their every-day class teacher, who knew them and their routine, was to be absent. Here was someone who represented strangeness, and who knew none of them, come unwelcome to supplant and this big difference to the school day unsettled some people. However, Connie whirled round to face the child from whom the words had come. He was tall for his age and had very obviously died blonde hair. Connie glared at him:

"Did *you* say that?" He took in the flinty green eyes and shifted his own gaze to his scuffed Doc Martin boots:

"Yup."

The class had stopped their occupations and watched coolly, glad it wasn't them but glad, too, of the spectacle.

"I'm sorry?" Connie's tone of voice was strangely menacing, as she made out that she couldn't quite take his meaning,

"Yes, Miss. Sorry, Miss," he muttered sullenly.

"I wonder how *you'd* feel if someone spoke like that about you as soon as you appeared in the morning?" *She was scary. What did she want him to say now?*

"I wouldn'."

"Wooden, wooden what?"

"Loike it," he mumbled, humiliated. The class had begun to snigger at him and what was worse was that he could feel stupid tears pricking his eyelids and his nose was running. Connie noticed this and told him hastily to sit down. He grabbed a class reader and slumped behind it, longing for the moment when he felt people would no longer be looking and he could wipe things on his sleeve. Connie would have pointed out that the book was actually upside down, thereby easing the tension for him and for the rest of the class, but somehow she felt ashamed and went on to read through the register to a hushed room.

Much more work than usual was carried out that day and no other pupil thought to cross her, which made the day refreshingly easy and peaceful. However, neither did anyone sidle up to tell her whose guinea pig had died, who was going swimming afterwards, or whose birthday was next week. Her sole communication had been that of imparting knowledge: this was how she had witnessed proper teachers keep control – had she crossed a threshold? She drove home strangely disquieted.

Chapter Eighteen

Dearest Boo,

I'm sorry I haven't immediately responded to your amazingly wonderful news but that doesn't mean I'm not over the moon for you!

Demelza's had a most terrible accident. She broke her neck on our trampoline and we've been waiting and waiting for her to come to. I would have rung you straight off, you know, but it's so stupid – once I start talking about it – and of course I can't really think of anything else – I start to wobble and flounder and I have to ring off in a hurry!

But you and Ken! I'm so very happy for you both and even though I've been so miserably out of touch, I want you to keep us up with everything!

I know we both talked a great deal about the pitfalls of marriage, but we've said so many things over the years which we'd have sworn to at the time and we may now mellow over in retrospect – without each other and the alcohol egging us on... I do now still think all those things – but only if you're married to the WRONG person! I've known both of you most of my life and know, as much as anyone can, that each of you is wickedly perfectly right for one another and it's great that you found out. And I'd simply love to be your Matron (Silence in the dorm, please!) It will be a positive honour, and I'm exceedingly flattered you're trusting me with such an office. Who's the Best Man, by the way: you know he's not meant to be married (and you will be, so you'll have to keep paws at bay!) Is he famous? How about that crooner, James Blunt, singing 'You're Beautiful' as you sign the register? (Just a helpful hint.)

You kindly mentioned my fling(s) with Ken, and I think I can honestly tell you that though they were certainly fun-(ny!) there was nothing remotely lasting between us, such as you contemplate. So fear not-- I think you are his first and – I assume – his last sort of committed relationship. So congratulations – you are boldly going etc.

You've probably heard, via the grapevine, that lucky old Stuart has been blessed with another daughter – with Sue from accounts.

Through a bizarre situation I was practically in on the birth and have to say that both babe and Sue were just wonderful – any wistful feelings I MIGHT have been harbouring melted on meeting. I'd never met Sue properly before and imagined her to be your archetypal money-minded accountant type, but she's rather sweet and sensitive and doting – on both the daughter and the father. (Lucky Stuart again. How is it that whenever he falls in the dung heap he comes up smelling of honeysuckle?) If I say she can't be very bright, that would include me, too, for my own history, wouldn't it? So I won't – I'll just say it's a rum old world instead... (And how could she? He? I???)

And now to (still) better things – you asked after the hunky Sebastian and I must say he's been amazingly supportive. In fact he's really held things together and I can't think how we could have coped without him. We've all depended on him and he's very fond of Demelza of course. Our barn is starting to bristle with antiques as he 'dabbles', as he puts it, during the day. Nevertheless, he'll soon have to get back to his base, from which his main dealing takes place. I'm back at work some days (dosh, dosh, dosh!) and can do the school runs around Demelza if I need to.

Sorry if I've sounded down beat: not my intention, since I'm right over the moon for you both,

Hugs all round – and one on the nose for Ken. (We keep hearing his single on the radio – it must be doing well. It shouldn't have my name on it I know, because it was only a tiny space when I happened to be there – but I can't help rather enjoying the vicarious adulation! Heh heh!)

> *Oodles of lerve,*
> *Connie XXXXXXX*

Connie wrote this as she sat beside Demelza. At times she chuckled slightly and whispered what she had thought or written, to her daughter. She had been allowed to help in turning Demelza to the counts of three, and this was the only movement that took place, other than the incessant changing and checking of tubes and monitors. Now that the sound system with Demelza's personal favourites was installed, the order was less pronounced and, indeed, some of the younger nurses clearly enjoyed hearing their sort of music during working hours and would argue with one another which track they felt that Demelza preferred today. When the consultants and their entourage of eager yet deferential junior housemen, swept into the little room to do their daily examination of her progress, Connie was ushered out. It was an ideal opportunity for the students to give their personal diagnoses under the watchful eye of their consultant mentors. On this particular occasion Connie was called in, and one of the house-women; an earnest young lady, wearing black rimmed spectacles over which she peered, her hair somehow swept behind in an old fashioned bun, altogether disguising her youth, was singled out to address Connie, the anxious mother of the patient:

"Mrs Sharland, we've examined your daughter and we believe that she is ready to breathe on her own, without the aid of the oxygen mask." The pinched face broke out now into a beautiful smile, "This is a small, but significant, step forward!" These were the first encouraging words, in terms of progress, that Connie had heard and she accepted them gratefully, but it was swiftly succeeded by a greedy desire for more:

"Does this mean she won't be paralysed if she's breathing for herself? Does it mean she'll come to?" *Don't push it!* She told herself. The hood of professionalism had replaced the smile on the young woman. She flashed a quick, quizzical glance at the consultant, who nodded almost imperceptibly, encouraging her to continue:

"Well we can't be sure yet – there are no definite signs – but perhaps…" she faltered, catching this time a very faint shake of the head. How many times had they had drilled into them not to give false hope – or indeed anything that might mislead friends and relatives to accuse them at a later date of having given a wrong diagnosis? She felt so sorry for this mother, who was hanging on her every word (not a thing to which she was used and it made one feel authoritative, as if one knew more, simply because one knew more than them!) She corrected herself:

"Let's take one thing at a time," she back-tracked awkwardly – *that poor woman could see she was hedging too:* "As I said," she continued, "this is a significant improvement and let's hope – *but not assume* –" the consultant was nodding again now, "that it's the first of many. Anyway, once she's breathing for herself we will be able to operate to remove the bolts, which will make her look much more normal." She finished in a rush, relieved that her explanation was over, realising too, that there was so very much more to this job than swatting up on your medical knowledge.

The journey home was a jollier affair. The children were all sure that this was a sign: Demelza looked so much more like herself without that awful thing over her face – she seemed to be more engaged with the world they all inhabited and had returned to their own side of the fence:

"Won't be long now!" said Poppy faithfully, but Sebastian noticed that Connie, while pleased with the improvement, did not share in this conjecture.

"I think," said Connie, "I think, for me anyway – and any of you who'd like to join me – that it's time for spiritual intervention!"

"Can I invent something too?" asked Poppy, enthusiastically,

"I mean I think we should go to church. I've been praying for Demelza to get better, but that may not be enough. I think I actually need to visit God's house and have a word with him there."

"Cor blimey!" said Ella,

"Ella that is short for 'God blind me' and we could do without that sort of disaster on top of everything else."

"I'll definitely come," said Sophia, "It'll be like when we went with Grandma and she used to sing the octave below."

"And she wouldn't sing *Onward Christian Soldiers* because she said it was a contradiction," put in Ella. "Count me out."

"No one *has* to come: it's got to be that you would like to."

"Well I'd like to as well," Poppy said supportively, "and then we will make a miracle!"

When they entered the porch, its thickly entwined branches of wisteria blotting out what little light they were getting from the new moon, Connie fumbled with the lock. She felt something under her feet and bent to pick it up: it was a parcel of some sort and seemed to smell of fish.

"Yuck! What's this?" she said, bringing it into the light of the now dimly lit front hall. As she held up the crumpled brown paper a fish slid out and then another. She scooped them off the floor and brought the parcel into the kitchen to examine it properly. There were five fine brown trout, glistening with freshness, without a mark of a hook on them:

"These must have been tickled," remarked Connie,

"That's not the first food parcel we've had," said Sebastian, "I hadn't thought to mention it, but there have been beetroot, onions and even parsnips: but never fish before. Where do they come from?"

"Rivers," responded Ella in a bored tone.

"It's country people," answered Sophia patiently; "They bring things that they've grown, when people have illnesses. They don't like to get seen, but they'll know us and know when we're all out and pop the goods round then."

"That's so kind! I wish we knew who they were, so we could thank them."

"That's the whole point," Connie explained, "They don't want to be thanked. You just know that someone's been digging or poaching recently and were thinking of you."

"But have *you* ever done anything like that with ailing neighbours?"

"Not with food – we don't usually have much to spare – but I do it with flowers when someone's relative has died and they're at the funeral. I just pop a bunch by the door or in the knocker so that there's one bunch of flowers after the funeral that's solely for them – the survivors. But it would be very embarrassing to be caught. In fact, if we ever do spot anybody dropping round a kindly package, we must look the other way... And now! Who likes gutting?" she asked with relish, as she brandished a gleaming kitchen knife.

They were interrupted by the phone ringing it's familiar Big Ben tones and Sebastian fielded it, as had become his wont, since this saved Connie from what she called her wobbly calls, when she had to explain or give an update on Demelza.

"Ah Cake!" he exclaimed, looking quizzically at Connie to gauge her reaction. Cake was the drummer in Connie's band: he said he was gay, but chose celibacy to avoid hassles, with which he felt unable to deal. He had no mobile, there being a payphone in the meagre flat that he shared with his other Buddhist friends and anyway, he had long ago ditched his possessions to go to Thailand and become an unofficial trainee Buddhist monk, the details of which were somewhat sketchy. However, after four years his grandmother had come over, finding him much emaciated, alone, and in a befuddled emotional state through lack of sustenance. She had eventually managed to persuade him to relinquish his begging bowl and return home with her. He conceded to her calling him by his original name of Samuel, but to everyone else he only answered to the name of his reincarnation, Cake, which had been chosen for him because it was the thing he found the most difficult to give up when he took his

Buddhist calling more seriously. He would acquire a cake and then give it up both gladly and longingly to the small effigy of Buddha, in front of which he would meditate, hungry, his sense of smell for the cake heightened by the hunger.

Being aware of Cake's financial predicament and that he would normally leave one of the other band members to call her, Connie knew it must be something important. She mouthed to Sebastian to tell Cake that she would call him back straight away on the pay phone and he relayed the message and hurriedly rang off. Connie dialled 14713 immediately, as promised, and after the initial questions – none of which concerned Demelza – Cake said the other band members had been doing some thinking.

"If you want to replace me in the band, I completely understand," Connie pre-empted, "I know I've made you miss gigs, first when my mum died and now with Demelza."

"Actually it's not that exactly…"

"But I think maybe you should – I'll miss the band like crazy, but it's yours and Nigel's livelihood – of course Andy has his own job-generated income, but I feel wretched about you two and at present, with things the way they are, I simply can't be relied on…" she finished bravely, anxious to get it all out.

"Connie – the band wouldn't be the band without you. None of us want to get rid of you but, like, Nigel and I think we may have worked out a solution." Nigel was something of a recluse when he wasn't playing the guitar for the band, preferring his cottage, vegetable garden and animals to human company. When he played, he could transport himself into another garden, that of music, and the spell would hold him only for as long as the music lasted; after which his sole intent would be to scurry through dismantling the gear and escape after it into the van, to roll another cigarette, evade interrogations, and wait for the other band members. He was blessed with extraordinarily good looks, which fascinated a number of beings from both genders, but of which he was both disinterested and unaware.

"Well what we thought was – a bit the opposite of losing anyone in the band. We thought maybe we should get in a keyboard player who can do lead vocals. The keyboard would be a new dimension like, and the singing could be extra harmonies while you're there – but they could do your lead vocal when you need to be with your family." Connie was touched by the mixture of straight forwardness and tact of his delivery. There was a pause before she answered.

"Cake, that's brilliant! Then you could keep gigging, but I could come in when I'm ready." Cake had been cranking himself up for this call all day. He had risen at midday (which was pretty early for him. He didn't like to contend with too much day time because he said it did his head in) for he could sleep no longer, with such an important task to perform. Yet he had waited until after six to be sure Connie was at home and to make the call cheaper. Now he felt a surge of relief that she had taken it as he and Nigel had hoped:

"We thought you'd like a keyboard," now he was clearly preening,

"Mm, and the more harmonies the better. Have you thought about an advert?"

"We thought we'd run the whole thing by you first and we don't want to put you to any trouble, so maybe Andy could put the ad in the Gazette?"

"I'm sure he would – and, Cake, please may I be at the audition? It's really important we all like both the music and the person." Cake glowed! She was showing her commitment after all, without probably noticing it.

"Yeah, for definite. What we could do is audition all the dross on the first one and then make a short list for you to listen to at the deciding audition: that would save you an evening." He had thought this one out too: it had come to him immediately after his meditation, when everything stood out clearly for a while, before the humdrum of everyday existence intervened to smear his outlook. Connie was overwhelmed by Cake's consideration and thanked him, promising to speak to Andy (who would go along with anything because the band, for him – instead of being the hub of his existence, as it was for Cake – was the outlet from his occupation with things legal, and very much an amusing diversion from defending the sometimes indefensible). The responsibility for placing the advertisement would probably finally fall with his already overworked secretary, but at any rate Andy could be relied on to get the job done. Now the situation with the band was clarified and she didn't have to lose her place in it, she felt another burden removed from her shoulders.

"Cake: you've been a hero. Thank you so much for everything." Cake felt the heat of the sin of pride sear through his sarong and didn't quite know how to reply.

"Sorted," he said at last, "Goodbye," and beaming, he hung up and hurriedly took his confusion into the privacy of his small room, lest any of his flatmates should see him looking so elated and he would have to explain. Once inside his room he fell to his knees before his Buddha, and offered thanks for the guidance he had received in helping a friend. A friend who had seemed to understand his darker moments, without interfering, and for whom he felt a strong affection. He had done something positive in her hour of need and it felt so good. The room began to turn from white to blue before his practised eyes, but his smile remained undimmed.

Chapter Nineteen

Poppy stood behind Connie's chair as she sat slipping the skins off the beetroots. She was holding them in newspaper, in an effort to save her hands from the red dye, but they kept escaping and scudding across the table, leaving a rouged stain across the stripped pine:

"You can see why people used beetroot for dying clothes in years gone by," Connie mused, as she surveyed her stained hands and table.

"Why did they want to dye things?" asked Poppy, genuinely interested.

"Because it made more exciting colours than what they had, I suppose. I mean the things they made out of jute and stuff would have probably been a sort of grey."

"Why didn't they like grey colour?"

"Maybe because it seemed sort of dull, washed out, non-descript?" she offered.

"But *you* don't mind it in your hair?" Connie looked up aghast:

"What do you mean? *My* hair's not grey – or it wasn't the last time I looked!"

"No, but there *are* some little grey curly ones in your parting – I think they're *pretty*," she added, a fraction too quickly. Connie had whirled across to the mirror and pulled her head into tortoise like contortions in an effort to see what Poppy had referred to. She shrugged and gave up:

"*I* can't see any – are you sure?" She returned to the table and Poppy yanked a spiralling short grey hair from the crown of her mother's head.

"Ow – that hurt!" protested Connie: "Let's have a look," she added. Poppy held out her hand and, sure enough, there was a little silvery corkscrew!

"Ohhh," Connie wailed, "I don't think I'm ready for this – are there any more?"

"Quite a few," answered Poppy simply.

"Right, I think you'd better pull them out then…"

"You didn't like it before: you said 'ow'!"

"No, but this time I'm prepared: weed away!" Poppy set to work loyally, saying that probably the invasion of grey was just something to do with Demelza and once she was better they would all grow back coppery again. In a short time a modest pile of the little grey corkscrews had sprung on the table.

"Maybe you should try some beetroot dye," suggested Sophia who, until this moment had been apparently totally absorbed in her book.

"I'm quite happy the way I am thank you very much," responded Connie, untruthfully and with an attempt at hauteur; however, she was having surprising difficulty in absorbing the notion that after forty odd years of the auburn hair that she had taken for granted as God given, she had come to the moment in her life when her hair had decided, unbidden, to change. She had never given the matter much thought and if she had, she would have expected not to mind; for surely this was only the wiles of Mother Nature guiding her through the patterns of life? However, while walking, talking, growing and puberty were all signs of growing up, this hair business – and people had always said nice things about the colour of her hair (not that she had paid much attention to them at the time!) this was a first sign of growing *down,* and she found herself feeling oddly disconcerted! She shrugged, there were far more important items on her worry list than to bother about a morsel of grey hair, and sang *Que Serra Serra* pointedly, loudly, as she resumed her attempts with the beetroot.

Sebastian, meanwhile, was in the midst of an animated conversation on his mobile, the subject evidently was what he referred to as 'elderly junk' which, properly translated, meant *Antiques.*

"Well, thanks for letting me know anyway. I'll settle up with you when I see you at the Midsummer Norton sale... What time does it start? ... Two. OK I'll meet you at the Mount Pleasant at – what shall we say? Twelve thirty-ish? ... Look it's not your problem – it's me – I just haven't been on the ball lately. See you then. Bye." He snapped his little mobile shut (the dial so minute it was hard to imagine hands his size negotiating it), while tunelessly humming that song he didn't even like, but which his subconscious had picked up a moment ago: *Que Sera Sera.*

Connie had heard enough of his conversation to realise not only that things hadn't gone to plan, but also that the reason was almost certainly connected with Sebastian's presence in her family. However, when she quizzed him about it he answered that it was nothing, just 'elderly junk business' and she didn't have sufficient energy to pursue it. Actually, the call had been to confirm that the Victorian portrait figure *had* been the one that Sebastian was after. It had not sold at Radstock when Sebastian had hurried off at the news of Demelza's accident (which was curious, because there had been many people he had recognised there who were in the know and he had expected some competitive bidding). Anyway, it had been withdrawn, due to its not reaching the reserve price. This much Sebastian had already gleaned, from the inner circle of antiques traders (one or two of whom, knowing where his interests lay, scouted unofficially for him). However, this latest call was a confirmed report that the William III piece was thought to have been authenticated and bought by a third party, unknown in the trade and therefore possibly a private collector? If this was the case, the new owner would not only be harder to trace, but also less likely to wish to relinquish, if collecting were a hobby and passion and not a livelihood. Had the person owned the partner to the piece, Sebastian would have felt reasonably satiated; for justice would have been served in terms of the pieces being fairly reunited. However, now his own piece was worth far less and its sense of promise was lost, through being devoid of its pair. The only course left to him would have been to discover and approach the new owner directly and offer to buy the piece; or failing that for them to buy his. With his life so inextricably bound up with chores in Devon, Sebastian knew that he must draw a line under this particular goose chase. He had asked his informant to continue to keep him informed if there was any definite confirmation of its whereabouts and told himself he didn't mind so very much, for this was a confirmation of the fact that he now had other priorities, which, for the first time in his life, took precedence. He thought briefly of his previous girlfriend, Katy, a confirmed night life-ing spinster, who was totally against increasing the population – she would be both astonished and probably hurt, that anyone could steer Sebastian from his tiresome 'treks after tat!'

Lurking behind the 'new improved' Sebastian, however, there still sometimes nestled a small yearning to cut free and follow his William III quest – and a heaviness at heart that he must abandon it; in spite of knowing that on this occasion it was the right thing to do. He wanted to hug Connie, to explain that this showed how very highly he prized her and his relationship with her family – his family, sort of – but the worst of it was that these days she wouldn't be able to take it in the manner he meant and she might push him away, when what he truly wanted more than anything else was to feel she needed him.

Sebastian muttered that he had a few final improvements to do to the refectory table, which he had at last managed to procure from a farm in South Molton. It answered to all the proportions his client had demanded and was of a good, solid, dark oak; but there was a slight burnish at one end, probably due to a knocked over candle, which had reduced his buying price conveniently. What remained for him to do was to minutely shave off the burnished part, thereby regrettably losing the many years worth of patina, built up with the whole, from being repeatedly polished to show it off to its greatest advantage. Next he would have to bring the surface up to match that of the otherwise virtually blemish free table, by dint of his trade-secret potions (the pungent, but by no means unpleasant, smell of which had assailed Connie's nostrils on entering Sebastian's house in Chelsea for the first time). After the precision work, the job required much elbow grease, which was precisely what Sebastian felt he was in need.

Sebastian climbed the rickety ladder from within the ramshackle barn, which already housed a white elephant's assortment of bicycles, garden tools, logs, flowerpots, grain sacks for the chickens and toys. The floor of the loft, however, had never been used other than to store hay; so Sebastian had dragged the bales to one end, hurling them into a loose stack, repaired the dodgier floor boards and opened up the far end to receive his antique furniture. It served as an ideal work base, and the children, fascinated by the noises of hammering or plane-ing, would clamber up and watch; whereupon they would soon be thrown a rag and instructed to polish until they could see their reflections. Ella, having been once caught when she and her latest boyfriend had visited in the hopes of privacy, had felt her street credibility much reduced by the cheery invitation from Sebastian asking them if they had 'come to sponge?'

Procuring the table from the farm had proved to be none too simple. Sebastian's brief had been that it was in the farmhouse and, if he was satisfied with it, he would have to remove it himself. This was something to which he was practised and unfazed; however, he had not been prepared for the fact that the farmhouse appeared to have been built *around* the table – and there was no door big enough from which to exit it. The new owner was keen to get an 'up to date Formica': a far more practical option, as a replacement, and was on the verge of chopping the old oak table into pieces before the news trickled down to Sebastian. Sebastian had not been able to believe how perfect it was in every detail and had begged them to wait just a little longer still for their new kitchen to be erected while he found suitable tools for dismantling the legs and base from the top. This he had managed to do, eventually taking it out to the car in three sections and strapping them to the roof. The owners had been thrilled and amused at getting rid of 'thicky there piss of ol' junk an' then geddin' *paid* for 'un on top!' Once Sebastian was safely around the corner with the old junk, they had celebrated with two glasses of their best homemade scrumpy, declaring this to be the best day's work they had seen in ages; while Sebastian had driven carefully back along the testing, windy lanes from South Molton whistling, and feeling a small twist of guilt at the paucity of the sum they had asked for – given what it would fetch once renovated. He had clients who had been pestering him for such a find for many months and they would be delighted: they knew Sebastian could be trusted to understand their precise requirements and had been content to wait until he could mirror them exactly. However, everyone was to be satisfied with their own price and acquisition and this was one of the buzzes that never diminished for Sebastian: the chase, the find and the outcome when everyone involved in the chain felt they had profited.

Sebastian set about 'hot waxing' the affected part, which was a procedure Demelza had never ceased to find fascinating, since it involved the use of a blow lamp to warm and 'texturise' the area, swiftly followed by the vigorous application of a stick of beeswax. Next, he began to gradually create a matching patina, through larding in generous scrapings of his secret formula with much gusto, varying the proportions of turpentine and boot polish for colour tone, until eventually the whole length of the table looked like glass, its toffeed lustre seeming almost edible. Each time he promised himself this was the final coat, he found he needed to apply just one more, but finally – spent, but with spirits restored, he rang his clients to arrange delivery the next day.

Chapter Twenty

Neville, Leticia's husband, was finding himself surrounded by chaos and he was displeased. It was most unfortunate that the poor Sharland girl, the scruffy one his daughter Charlotte hung around with, had suffered the most frightful accident; but it was annoying that something removed from his own family should have so much of an impact on their own already busy existence. Charlotte was upset – that was understandable, they were close friends after all – but it should not result in her becoming impossible to live with. She apparently blamed herself for the whole sorry escapade because she had taught Demelza the particular flip that had caused the devastation. Well, the answer was obvious: first, why had the mother given them a trampoline; a piece of equipment known to cause statistically more accidents in the home than any other, and second: the girl shouldn't have attempted to copy Charlotte, who's abilities for gymnastics were, as far as he was given to understand, legendary. Why had Demelza assumed she could do anything that Charlotte could? Without Demelza's, it must be admitted, demon influence (she was likeable, yes! but she had far too much energy of the wrong sort). Charlotte had come to her senses and put in some proper work at school, coming up with grades more realistic for successful GCSE results. Susanna, his daughter by his first wife, had attained straight 'A' stars and had been rewarded with a car for her seventeenth birthday. She had passed her driving test three weeks later: these were attainments necessary if one was to get on in life and Charlotte should by now begin to set her goals in sensible order.

Instead, she was storming around the normally ordered home like a churlish little teenage zombie, and one couldn't get a civil word from her. This, in turn, had somehow affected Leticia, who ranged from icy to raging in moments, after that more often than not taking to her bed early with a headache! She was sleeping too much and was still exhausted in the mornings, so he had persuaded her to get some of those jollying pills that she took from time to time – Prozak, that was it – which made life more bearable for everyone; but now she said she had been refused them on one ground or another. She still looked immaculately groomed and coiffeured, but sometimes she seemed quite fired up, her eyes all glistening, and not quite as deferential as he had become accustomed. Indeed, if he didn't know her better, he might almost think she was laughing at him! At other times she looked sort of glassy and lacking fibre. Then there were the terrible rows she was having with Charlotte, from which he kept well clear. He had been unable to ignore the volume, however, of some of the vile things they were flinging verbally at one another.

"Really," he had said to Leticia in exasperation, "You should rise above the things she says: what can she say or do to touch *us*?" It was truly too bad of her to behave in this odd way when he considered the long road Leticia had covered since he had spotted her, a pretty little assistant at Dartington Crystal. She had been fine to look at, but once she had opened her mouth, he had realised that she suffered from a God-forsaken Devonshire accent, which gave away her lowly origins.

Leticia had been so pitifully proud of her job and the fact that her grandfather had been one of the key glass-blowers in the factory. The industry was considered to be a part of her family, she had said, 'in the blood', and he, Neville, had been at such patient pains to point out tactfully that, if she were to marry him and be a mother to his Susanna (whose own mother had so tragically died of septicaemia in childbirth), then there would be no need to work again. She could keep house and there was a Daily to do all the household chores: the housework, the shopping and so on. It had taken Leticia a surprising amount of persuasion and time to understand that her life would become one of leisure, and therefore amazingly changed, like Cinderella's – and he was to be the fairy Godmother, she had said gratefully, when at last she had understood the enormous benefits of what he was so magnanimously offering!

She had delighted in the new wardrobe Neville had provided for her, which was fitting for a wife of someone of his station; but he had said there was one more little thing she must do for him. By this time she was utterly hooked and dependent on his generosity, his daughter, Susanna, being an easily contented child who just needed indulging – and because there was nothing else to do, indulge her she did; and with none of the ill effects about which they had been warned. The 'little thing', then, that he required was for her to attend elocution lessons, to rid herself of those dreadful vowels and crisp up some of those missing consonants. Leticia went willingly, realising that there was much she had been content with before which, on objective reflection, could not now be acceptable. Thus, she gratefully and humbly accepted Neville's present of private lessons until she was able to stun her family by walking in one day, Eliza Dolittle like, and remarking that she and Neville felt that their new home was in want of 'a naice discreetful par*kay* to en*harnce* the floowah area'. Her brothers had fallen about laughing, her father had looked dazed but proud at what a *proper lady* his daughter had become, but her mother had looked worried:

"I 'ope you don't come to luke down on uz. Uz may be simple, but uz knaws how to enjoy ourzelves and you've never known what tiz to want."

This was true Leticia had assured her, but Neville was to be her husband now and she must do what she could to please him.

"What's wrong with how you wuz Oi'd loike ter knaw," her mother had persisted, and Leticia began, privately, to wonder for a moment also – but she was so caught up with her new life with her fairy Godmother that she brushed away her mother's concerns:

"Anyone would think you weren't pleased for me, after all Neville's done!" she protested, to which her mother had shaken her head and muttered:

"There! Tiz started already, Maiden." Her father had given her a hug and told her mother not to be such a silly old bat, whereupon she had retaliated by calling him a 'no good Dicky-no-drawers!' at which the warm home humour of former times was restored and they all joined the laughing and teasing, between mouthfuls of mother's best 'licky pie'.

"Bugger: Oi s'pose tiz to be called 'Lake Pay' from now on," commented one of Leticia's brothers and they all began to guffaw anew, with Leticia uneasily unable to refrain from joining in.

Her mother had indeed been right – it wasn't that Leticia never visited her little home cottage where everything was normal, but gradually, as her life of holidays abroad, hunt balls, dinner parties, (where she *ate* the lobsters that once she would have caught in the deep rock pools far out on Abbotsham cliffs), she felt alienated from the easy home banter, and she made sure that her few visits were when Neville was away.

Her family couldn't understand the need for her children to be attending private schools and made little attempt to conceal their bemusement – with the result that Leticia kept Susanna and Charlotte as much out of the way as possible, *to avoid awkwardness*, she told herself. However, had she ever allowed a moment to reflect or analyse her present much spoilt existence, she might have noticed that she had never enjoyed what her father referred to as a 'proper belly laugh', of which they used to share daily and make the walls of the little cottage ring with honest merriment; when she would rock backward and forward in her chair, incapable of speech, doubled up over some daft thing one of her brothers had said. Well, she thought, she *had* bettered herself as she and Neville had intended, and that was the price you paid: small really, when all was said and done.

Chapter Twenty-one

When Sunday arrived, Connie eschewed her usual delicious laze in bed with the papers; instead making an English breakfast with eggs and bacon for any who were up and ready to be church goers. There had been a time when all the children attended Sunday school at the local church, but Ella had felt too old to continue, and weekends with their father contributed to a lack of continuity and commitment. Connie suffered occasional pangs of conscience about this to begin with; but the delights of returning from gigs with the band on a Saturday night without having to drag herself out of bed to the church the next day, coupled with the children's indifference to whether they attended the event or not, won the vote for sloth and the sanctity of choice for Sundays.

Poppy and Sophia scooped up the runny yolks of Bashful and company with wedges of fried bread, and Sebastian had bought a bottle of brown sauce to top just such an occasion. He explained that he would be busy with the delivery of the refectory table, the freight of which, this time, was going to need much careful cosseting, beginning with the copious binding of bubble-wrap, rugs, rags and old towels, to resist any rain and buffetings en route. Connie was aware both that this job must be done, but also that the timing had been chosen to get him out of the churchgoing, where she would have appreciated his moral support. She tipped more eggs onto his plate, the enamel blistering from the piping heat of the Aga, and dropped the sizzling dish in his place with a thud, saying nothing.

Ella was the only one indulging in a teenage world of the fuggy duvet as Sebastian, armed with a multitude of washed out rags, headed for the barn and Connie, Sophia and Poppy set out across the fields for the short walk to church. Connie imagined how well worn this track must have been in the days when their house had been residence to the vicar and his family; at how many times a day he had toiled to and from 'work', sometimes his young family trailing raggedly behind him, as Connie's was now, and his wife, responsible for the flowers and the brass rota, upstanding community member and chairwoman of the Women's Institute, taking up the rear. The track was now a disused public footpath, a mere stain across a stubbly field, soon to be ploughed and sewn.

They entered the church hurriedly, the cessation of the tolling of the bell giving away the fact that they were late. As they clattered through the door, a sidesman sprang up to provide them with dank looking hymn and prayer books and all eyes of those already seated swivelled around in curiosity to view the new arrivals. Connie looked up with a practised eye, to locate the placing of the ceiling heaters, under which you could toast to the point of discomfort, while all around remained uncomfortably frozen. The sidesman, Mr Oaks, gave a hushed greeting, happy at the swelling number in the congregation, and ushered them to one of several empty pews. They shuffled in sideways, there not being the space between the polished oak benches and the sticking out shelves of the prayer racks to walk any other way than crabwise. They shifted the hassocks off their hooks and sat down briefly, before the organ music began and the vicar entered, flushed from his speedy drive from his previous parish of Tawstock. He had been aware that he was overrunning on his sermon but was feeling particularly lucid, indulging in the lust of good delivery which, when in its grip, was hard to break from. He hitched up his cassock and stepped out a modicum faster than was common, to the tune of *Fight the Good Fight*, taking in as he swept past his congregation, the Sharland family: so sad about the daughter, what was her name? He had made a note of it because he was going to pray for her anyway, as in previous weeks, but it was one of those names that was hard to remember. Annoying that the scrap of paper on which it and the other names of elderly or infirm in the parish for whom they would pray, was in his trouser pocket; for it would hardly be seemly to hitch up his cassock to find it. It meant he would have to dive into the vestry to rescue it, taking up yet more time. He would have to pray again for patience and ask forgiveness for the sin of pride, which had been responsible ultimately for this state of affairs: but not yet, for he knew he could get through the notices at a cracking rate and gain a couple of valuable minutes to shorten this service before the final one of the morning at Horwood.

The church door clanged again and hurried footsteps could be heard, resting at the Sharland pew.

"Budge up!" Ella whispered to her sisters. Connie leaned over in surprise:

"But Ella! I thought you weren't coming?"

"If church is going to get Demelza better, then, like I want to be blamed if it doesn't work!" Connie, touched at her twisted logic, tried to squeeze Ella's hand (a mass of metal rings and bracelets) before she had hastily snatched it away.

~

On leaving the church, Connie attempted a 'last in first out' principle, in order to avoid kindly welcomes and questions from well-intentioned parishioners. They had all prayed hard for Demelza and been embarrassed but pleased when the vicar had included Demelza by name in the prayers for the sick. Poppy had dug Sophia in the ribs and Sophia had frowned horribly at her and said fiercely:

"*Pray!*" to which Poppy had humbly bowed her head, pressed her hands together and done just that. Now they were trying not to look as if they were actually sprinting through the grave yard, having first shaken the vicar's hand and thanked him for the service. Sitting still for an hour had given them all the fidgets and they were glad to be off. However, as they left the graveyard Connie hesitated:

"You go on," she instructed "I'll catch you up back at the house." Still feeling the freedom experienced after confinement, and the smug, cleansing feeling of having done something entirely altruistic, they didn't bother to question but galloped away, through the kissing gate and over the fields towards home.

"Why d'you s'pose she wanted to go back? We didn't leave anything," Poppy asked her sisters,

"Maybe she decided she should talk to people after all, but she was sparing us?" supplied Sophia generously.

"Doubt it," replied Ella: "There's Grandma's grave, you know, and she so won't want to make a thing of it, so we shan't say anything." This was an order, to which the others agreed.

"I miss Grandma more when we need her, don't you?" sighed Poppy, skipping a little to keep up.

"Like she could have done anything about this!" rejoined Ella, completely missing the chance to mock the nonsensical.

"You never know – she may have special powers from beyond the grave," retorted Sophia, to which Ella made ghostly noises.

"Well you *do* never know," Sophia persisted: "Suppose, for example, you get three wishes after you're dead..."

"If she did she would have used them up by now trying to find Grandpa in heaven because it's got to be really crowded up there," sighed Poppy solemnly, enjoying being involved in this macabre discussion, over which she had pondered much since Grandma's death, but feared asking anyone in case of making them either scoff or sad.

"She must have joined the Red Cross then," answered Ella, with a superior smile.

Ella was in fact right. Connie had lurked in the lee of the kissing gate until the rest of the congregation had dispersed. It was chilly, and they felt the call for the attentions to the Sunday roast. Thus, after a few hasty greetings and a brief chat with the vicar – who had looked wistful at the speed at which the Sharland family had managed to exit – they followed the vicar's car, which led the short procession at an almost unseemly pace, out of the car park and away to the warmth of their Sunday homes, where the smell of roast meat was just beginning to tickle the atmosphere.

Connie walked around to the side of the churchyard, where the wild daffodils and primroses were at their thickest, buttering the long grass in their sunny splendour. Here was Mary, Connie's mother's grave, a small mound already dusted with a smattering of bolder weeds and dark green leaves, which were all that remained of the crocuses and lilies-of-the-valley that Connie and Sophia had planted when the grave was fresher. There was as yet no gravestone, for the earth needed to settle after its disturbance. Connie stood before it, a gaunt figure, hunched against the spring breeze and felt strangely calm. Before she knew what she was doing she had begun talking, in much the same way as she had used to when on the telephone to her mother, where she would recount, in a stream of consciousness, what had happened that day:

"You really shouldn't have left us *then*," she muttered. "What timing! It's a cop out – having to try to manage all this on my own – and I'm *not* you know! Managing that is... And I wish so much you'd met my new man, Sebastian. I just know you'd like him: you'd probably say he's got a bit of a screw loose like me - but it takes one to know one! The children like him and he's kind – but me! I can't remember how it feels to be me any more, except I know it's not like this. And I can't be bothered with things or people. I'm just there, that's all – boring and – and I don't *laugh!* I need you to be there and feel sorry for *me* and make me laugh and tell me it'll all be OK – when really we have no assurances at all – but I need you to tell me all the same and then *I'll believe you.*" The words were spilling out of Connie at the speed of thought and she broke off with a short hollow laugh, continuing aloud:

"I can't believe I'm doing this: talking to a grave! I thought they only did this on *Eastenders* and *Forrest Gump!* How sad is this?" She laughed again: an old familiar feeling, lacking restraint this time: "Wow! If anyone caught me doing this I'd be carted off to the funny farm which – I've always sneakily thought – might just be a bit of a holiday!" She knew she ought to return now, to make a pile of sandwiches and then visit Demelza, with any of those who wanted to join her; however, she was finding this visit strangely comforting and therapeutic:

"I've got to go now so I shall have to say *Oi looks towards you,* like we always did when we were doing our Devon toasts over a 'snifter'. And now you reply: *I bows accordin'. Yur'z to us,* and I say, *I say: None like us!* ... None like us at all," she added ruefully, amazed that she found herself smiling and feeling some of the uplift she got from the company her mother had provided above ground.

Connie backed away from the small mound reluctantly and waved a silly hand, before turning to see she was no longer the sole living member of the populace in the graveyard, for an elderly man was bending stiffly over a well sunken grave, which was immaculately adorned with primulas. He was changing the flowers in the pot at the head of the grave, but he looked up at Connie and nodded. She reddened:

"I'm sorry about the chat – I must have got a bit carried away," she stammered, feeling very foolish.

"What d'you mean? This be the only place *Oi* get to talk to the Missus, so there's always so much to ketch up with: looks like tiz the same for you," he said, indicating towards Mary's grave over his shoulder. "If we've got to start *apologisin'* it's going to be a purty pass!" Connie nodded her agreement and he continued:

"'Twon't be long, as Nature would hev it, before I spends my whole gurt future back with the missus in this yur piece of earth. So I keeps it nice for us both because it will be home, instead of back there

166

in the village. Now you: you've got plenty more times to puff over, but me!" He thrust his hand deep into a capacious pocket in his wax jacket, bringing out a paper containing some rather grubby looking sandwiches, from which he took a bite, "Oi hev lunch out with the missus yur any time I need company and then," here he tapped the side of his nose and positively twinkled at Connie, "Then I have me pipe of baccy. Missus always said I had to smoke the dratted thing outside and so I do! Right yur after our lunch! And 'er can't scold back!" To prove his words he felt in another pocket and brought out a briar pipe, which he waved at her delightedly, laughing at his own mischief:

"Now, I don't s'pose you'd like a sandwich?" he asked, "only you look as though you could do with one." Connie couldn't resist him – although she might have preferred to resist the sandwich, which was corned beef and mustard, enveloped in very thickly buttered white bread. He had a surprisingly abundant crop of white curly hair, which stood up from his round, weather-beaten face, much like the stalk of a turnip; perched on top of which was a greasy green cap. His milky, cornflower blue, eyes reminded Connie of Tramp's; and they shone out of a multitude of seams and crinkles, appearing to miss nothing. When he smiled, Connie saw that his teeth had given out rather earlier than he, for the front ones were ground into an arch, which perfectly fitted the pipe that he was now drawing on. The aromatic scent of pipe tobacco, redolent of grandfathers, enwreathed them:

"I hadn't thought about coming here today," Connie ventured, "but now, you know, I'm so glad that I did – and that I met you."

"Joe's the name," He held out a huge, hard, creased hand, almost the size of a dinner plate, the result of years of coarse farm work, which Connie took, her own hand completely hidden by its magnitude.

"Connie Sharland," she answered warmly.

"Oh I know who *you* are, Maid!" he replied, "And about your hard times of late. But I'm sure your liddle maiden'll get better d'reckly, in 'er own time, and 'er'll zoon be 'urtlin' round the village again… and if you need anything meantimes, just you let me knaw: carrots, teddies, beets, swedes – I gottem all." Here he appeared to close up again and, with a flash of intuition, Connie realised that she was probably confronting one of the kind donors of vegetables and poached fish. She squeezed his hand, but it was doubtful that he felt it, and muttered that she 'didn't realise', while he looked away shiftily, sensing he may have said too much. She finished the sandwich and thanked him profusely, saying that she hoped they would meet again soon:

"Not in that gurt big bugger that you drive I 'ope," he answered, "or I'll be alongside the missus before tea time!" They both laughed again and Connie returned across the fields her steps feeling marginally lighter.

Chapter Twenty-two

Hi Jeremy,

Thanks so much for all the supportive texts etc. and sorry to have replied to so few. Hope to bring you up to date with this email.

Hope Jenny and the boys are all OK, but I have to state what must be the obvious. That being, that clearly we won't be able to make the holiday with you all in Australia while Demelza's like this. We're all horribly disappointed – and I know Demelza will give me hell when she wakes up, but I've cancelled the tickets for now and we WILL come – but not this year. I'm so sorry: why do I always feel as though I've let you down? (Don't dare answer that!) As it is, I'm having difficulty in envisaging Boo's wedding without D, but when (ever?!) I'm realistic, I know that if she comes to tomorrow, it would still take ages of hospital and therapy before she will be allowed home, let alone off on a jolly. (And talking of therapy, I'm wondering seriously if I should succumb? Would it make everything better? No! But would it make me more tolerant of everything/one else??? In which case... I hear tell la-la land is actually a pleasant place for a visit...) These are only thoughts, you know, and who better to voice them to.

Does that bring you up to date? Not quite – the absence of Tramp has resulted in the ducks getting bolder and coming right up to the French windows, looking in and knocking with their beaks. We can't leave the door open or they waddle right in and whoopsy all over the floor. I never realised Tramp's powers of dissuasion, because, during his final years, he would have barely seen or smelt them!

Once again – so, so very sorry; but I've known inside for a while that it can't be done. All disappointed big time but trying (ha!) to be philosophical – whole thing makes me miss Mother the more, but thank mother earth for you!

Trucks of love,

Lil Sis

After Connie had sent her email she wished she had told Jeremy of her encounter with Joe after the visit to their mother's grave, for Jeremy had never lost interest in local colour, even though his home life had been Australian for a considerable time. As usual, she thought: I was 'me, me, me!' Preparing to exit from her messages, Connie noticed a new one in her inbox while she had been sending. It was from Leticia, and began formally enough with regard to her sorrow for the family at this most difficult time, after which it continued in a tone quite different to that which might have been expected from Leticia:

I know you must be kept busy, what with hospital and so on but please could you come and see me urgently? Sorry to ask, but it's urgent you see – or believe me I wouldn't. So please give me a ring when you get this and I can be over in fifteen minutes.

Yours affec.

Leticia

Certain things about the email struck Connie as odd; the affected formality that was typical (who else signed themselves *Yours affec.* for goodness sake?) but it appeared to be mixed with something more genuine, which was a down to earth and repetitive call for attention. Wondering what could possibly merit such urgency, Connie had a gut feeling that she should respond at once and she reached for the phone.

Leticia answered the telephone at the first ring, which was not what she had learned to do. Normally she left it three or four rings in order to seem occupied, and to give the impression that she had actually had to move herself to reach the receiver. Her voice didn't manage to mask her relief at hearing Connie's either. Connie asked if anything was the matter and Leticia answered that she was afraid there was and that she couldn't really speak about it over the phone because it was delicate. Connie took the hint and asked if Leticia would like to come over, but was pleased to hear that this wouldn't be possible (since the house was in the usual mess and Leticia had made her aware that this was something she found somewhat abhorrent). Instead Leticia invited Connie over for 'a small sherry'; this delivered with a shrill laugh, for it was 'that time of day, wasn't it?' The mention of sherry gave Connie a quick stab of memory of her mother's 'snifters'.

"That sounds like just what I need!" she answered, perhaps over heartily, *and I suppose I shall have to change into something less disreputable* she thought, as she put the phone down, saying she would be right over.

~

As she negotiated the smooth curve of the drive, sweeping past perfectly manicured lawns she noticed one of Ella's cast off boyfriends tending what looked like a weed free flower bed, Connie considered that the difference between this drive and her own was so marked that she could well understand Leticia's distain directed at having to drop her Charlie off to play with Demelza – and her intrigue was the greater over what had prompted Leticia's urgent request. She had always refused Connie's attempts at hospitality and left the house without coming in, probably for fear of dirtying her famous stilettos. The drive finished in a circular sweep, the inside of which resembled a roundabout in preparation for the annual contest for 'Devon in Bloom' so busting was it with fountains and topiary. Leticia had once again put protocol aside for, instead of waiting behind the front door for it to ring and then counting to ten, she opened it at the first sound of the car and dashed down the brick steps to welcome Connie, tripping over in her haste. By dint of grabbing at a life-sized statue of *Venus de Milo,* she managed to steady herself from the ignominy of hitting the ground, and quite graciously extend her other hand in formal welcome.

"Do come in and have a drink!" she gushed, and as Connie's eye fell on the open gin bottle she added, unnecessarily, "I must confess to having started!" Connie said that there had been the mention of sherry and she hadn't had one for ages and needed the excuse to see if it tasted just the same, like *Winnie-the-Pooh* and the honey. At this reference Leticia seemed a little blank, but hastened away for the decanter – another cut-glass treasure from Dartington crystal – and sherry glasses. She returned with a tray, bearing the sherry, glasses – there must clearly have been another bottle in the kitchen, for Leticia's glass was replenished – and some tasty looking nibbles. These, Connie attempted to eat slowly, for not only were they delicious, they also gave her something to do with her hands: she appeared to be the only one bothering with them, however. Leticia produced more, and Connie asked her to put them out of reach for she was such a pig with nibbles and, to Connie's disappointment, Leticia obeyed.

"I'm sure you're wondering why I've summonsed you so greedily," drawled Leticia, "but I have to confess that I have a confession to make: please accept this little envelope." She pushed a slim, cream vellum envelope across the table at Connie, who opened it in bewilderment, to discover a cheque made out to her for three hundred pounds.

"What on earth is this for?" asked Connie in disbelief, pushing it back across the table.

"Your gatepost! I'm sure you must have known it was me. I reversed rather too quickly and - as luck would have it... I know I should have stopped, but I panicked and fled, which was too stupid! Neville was furious over the damage to the car, of course, and I have to beg you not to tell him because I'm afraid I didn't mention doing any other damage!" The grandness of the gesture had become hidden by a genuine semblance of fear and pleading, which Connie found disconcerting, particularly in comparison with Leticia's habitual ebullience. "Then there's been all this frightful stuff with your daughter and I didn't like to intrude, so I apologise profusely and please accept..." Connie began to giggle:

"Leticia I hadn't really thought *who* might have knocked it over – it could just as easily have been *me*, with the way I drive. Please don't think about it any more and please keep the money because I had no immediate plans for fixing it in any case."

"I insist! Keep the money and then whenever you do want to fix it, there it will be: I won't want to go through this again!" Connie could see this, but protested that it was too much.

"Oh I doubt that very much: they all -" she gestured wildly in the direction of Carl, who had stopped for a cigarette and was waving wildly at Connie through the window, who returned the gesture with equal enthusiasm, stopping abruptly as she became aware again of Leticia's eagerness to make amends, "They all charge completely ludicrous prices. The sum is realistic, I assure you."

"Well, if it truly makes you feel better about it –" Connie's hand slid back across the table to retrieve the cheque that she had hurriedly deposited there, thinking that actually, since she was doing so little teaching, she could do with it while Leticia wouldn't notice its absence: but for living rather than replacing gateposts!

"Oh I *do* feel better *thank* you. I think this calls for a small replenishment, don't you?"

"Not for me: I'll be under the table if I drink at this time of day." Again, Leticia's expression stopped her.

"But go on – just a sniff!" Connie continued smoothly, to which Leticia leapt up eagerly to re-charge (this time she joined Connie with a sherry, which she slewed into her gin glass) and, once accomplished, smiled beatifically at Connie:

"Now you don't realise, but a little tot or two is probably actually exactly what you need..." Leticia was beginning to slur: "and you won't know either that your daughter's demise has had its effect on many of us."

Connie's brow furrowed, in an effort to follow the conversation, which seemed to be sliding away from them both.

"You see my Charlotte – she has barely spoken to me since – oh she has *yelled!* She has sworn: she has told me how much she hates me... but *speaking*, telling me what she's done today – the little things, you know – not a word!"

"I'm so sorry – we're all so fond of Charlie – Charlotte. She must be deeply upset if she treats you like that. Teenagers can be complete pigs sometimes – I should know. But how can you be sure it's connected to Demelza? Mightn't there be some other reason – or just general angst against the world?" Connie managed to refrain from adding her standard post-script 'who ever he may be', realising that Leticia was too wound up, even if she had taken it in, to be amused.

"Well when it – the accident – happened, she said it had all been her fault. That if she hadn't shown Demelza the move, nothing would have happened!"

"But that's like blaming your swimming coach when you fall in the pool!"

"I know, I know!" Leticia wailed, "I have tried so hard to explain that to her, *sensitively,* but each time I try to comfort her I seem to make it even worse and she gets angrier. She truly frightens me!" Leticia took another slurp at her sherry, while Connie attempted to assuage Leticia's obvious anxiety with platitudes:

"You will not be the first parent to get blamed when anything goes wrong in your teenager's life."

"But forgotten when anything goes right! It's so unfair and, you know –" she leaned towards Connie confidentially, wagging a finger bedecked with Neville's diamond encrusted rings: "you know she's *driving me to drink!*" Connie, rather unsuccessfully, feigned surprise:

"Ah – is the drinking a new thing? I don't know you that well and I thought perhaps…"

"Never touched a drop! Well, that is to say, not before Neville got home. Now I can't wait to get him out of the house because it's the only time I enjoy myself." Leticia was making a sound half way between a laugh and a whimper: "Driven to drink! That's a good one when you think about it – that's what happened to your gatepost! Driven *into* by drink!"

"Oh I *see* - so that's how it happened! Oh Leticia: how awful things must have been!"

"Lettuce!"

"What did you say?"

"*Lettuce!* That's my name – Lettuce – but no one is allowed to know. Neville had it changed for me by deed poll. He said it sounded too much like a vegetable and no one would take me seriously. Even my family in Torrington are supposed not to call me by it – so they don't call me anything!" Connie smiled kindly at her:

"Well *I* think Lettuce is a lovely name – in fact I like it far better than Leticia: Leticia sounds to me more like a sneeze!" Leticia looked up sharply and Connie immediately realised she had over-stepped the mark, but couldn't retract what she had said. There was a short and awkward silence before Leticia continued slowly and with some effort, crinkling the foundation on her brow in her efforts to get this correct:

"So you really ought to say – you *really* ought to say *'Bless you!'* (D'you see? 'Leticia?' *'Bless you!')"* Leticia cackled with sudden laughter, with which Connie joined, still puzzled by Neville and his snobbery, but relieved that Leticia had seen a funny side to her remark after all. Soon, however, Leticia had returned to confidential mode and, having extracted a promise from Connie that she would never, ever, tell anyone about 'Lettuce' she continued to tell her very much more than she had dared tell anyone about her comfortable life with her family in Torrington and the down side of Neville's courses in 'betterment'. In the relief of confiding the feelings that had remained repressed within for so long, her natural Devon brogue eased its way into her speech. Connie listened sadly, feeling somewhat ashamed at how easily she had misjudged and dismissed the lonely Leticia, avoiding her where possible in fear of causing derision over her unkempt appearance.

Leticia talked herself into a sobriety of sorts and Connie found herself offering to have 'the little tinker, Charlotte', over for a chat, to see if she couldn't manage to help her see Demelza's accident as a calamity over whom no one could be held responsible. Connie told Leticia of her own and Ella's self-recriminations with regard to the cause of the accident – after which she asked a question to which she was pretty sure she knew the answer:

"By the way, does your Charlotte smoke?"

"I say! I should think not; she's only fourteen remember. Of course Susanna wouldn't smoke anyway – but then she's Neville's daughter and not mine." She seemed almost sad that Susanna didn't smoke, for that would represent something that Neville's deceased and perfect first wife's child had embarked upon that wasn't sweetly lovely! The fact that all the childhood problems appeared to emanate from Charlotte, the child that she herself had begat, made her feel the more inadequate.

"Well Ella's been smoking since she was thirteen – she's lied about it, but I know she still does it. When I first found out, I took away the cigarettes, but she only bought more – or cadged them off those who could afford them even less. Now we have a sort of agreement that it is not mentioned as long as it happens out of sight and smell of the rest of us – which means it's confined to the great outdoors."

"My dear, how frightful for you!"

"Well I certainly don't like it, but you sort of learn to live with it, hoping she'll give up before she does too much damage to herself; hoping the others won't follow suit; accepting that there are things over which, once our children reach a certain age and they remain our responsibility, we don't have that same power of persuasion."

"Or veto."

"So I think what I'm trying to say is sometimes there's little point in trying and we have to save the really mega exasperation for only the truly dangerous or unkind – and accept that by the mid-teens we can no longer fix anything!"

"I can see what you mean, I think, but I sometimes wish that Neville had divorced his first wife and that she was still around, rather than feeling I'm competing with an angel! Doesn't that sound dreadful though: I'm sure I don't know what I'm saying, but here! I'm amazed at your Ella: who would have thought one of your happy little troop would step so defiantly out of line!"

"Leticia, you simply have no idea! I bet masses of the 'perfect' parents you see around you probably have mega spats behind closed doors with teenage angst and egos – far worse than Charlie: be thankful if it isn't Susanna as well... In any case, where did you smoke when you were thirteen? ... I had it easy! My mother smoked like the proverbial chimney, so she couldn't pick up the smell and there were fags in little silver boxes parked all around the place!" Leticia gasped and giggled, declaring that she had never – well hardly ever (and only if you counted Denzil Dapp's pipe, which had smelt rather manly, actually, but tasted dreadful). No, she had almost never smoked in her entire life!

"D'you know, you have made me feel a whole lot better!" pronounced Letitia emphatically.

"Knowing we're a whole lot worse than your children?"

"Well yes: I thought it was only me receiving the sort of treatment I get from Charlotte – and then Susanna has always behaved like a little adult, so I've never had any practise in step-mothering really. She's a naturally good Daddy's girl and pleasant to live with. I mean we get on – who couldn't? But there's not that 'bond' that there might be if we'd been through anything a little tricky together."

"Count yourself lucky then. There are lots of us abused parents around – and loyalty forbids us from mentioning it! But, Leticia, I really must go – I have to get some outdoor chores done with the hens, before I do the school run and visit Demelza."

"Oh I'm so sorry I've kept you so long... Just before you go though, promise me you won't be offended but I've thought of a little treat I'd love to give you."

"I make it a rule never to be offended by treats," answered Connie with a grin. Leticia rose to her feet, staggering slightly, and proceeded to hide the evidence of the empty sherry bottle at the bottom of the rubbish container and to scrub ardently at the glasses, the one exhibiting a heavily engrained give-away smear of deep red lipstick. Leticia's explanation came out in a rush:

"I have a beautician who visits me twice a week. I could ask her to call and do you a facial – and your hair too! She does everything and it might help to pick you up in the way this stuff," here she gave another exuberant rub to the lipstick smudged glass, expertly holding the crystal up against the light as she did so and making dazzling rainbows dance about the room, "does for me!" Connie began to protest:

"God, do I look *that* awful? The children were only saying that I'm going grey!"

"Well *I* have it all done as a matter of routine and you'll feel wonderful afterwards!" Connie privately doubted this. "And I can only notice the grey now I'm standing up and looking down into your hair – it's only a little," she added reassuringly, "but she'll fix it! Please say yes – look at it as a way of my saying thank you for our little chat – *and not a word about Lettuce!"*

"But you've already given me a cheque this morning," answered Connie, beginning to waiver.

"Please don't mention that subject either," answered Leticia ruefully, and Connie found herself once again giving in, as a card was thrust into her hand, showing the name and credentials of the 'All Round Travelling Beauty Salon'.

"Now that is settled and the evidence is hidden, it's time for my nap!" said Leticia mischievously: "That way I can look all refreshed when they return home and Neville doesn't suspect a thing! (I'm *so* big on strong mints.) Toodleloo: and do have Charlotte nice and soon – for as long as you like!" Letitia made a magnanimous gesture as she kicked off her stilettos, throwing herself into the luxury of the sofa cushions, while Connie hurried out waving wildly at the recumbent form.

Connie raced into the chaos of her own kitchen to find Sebastian unblocking the sink from the detritus of vegetable peelings, orange pips and cat nibbles. His face lit up at the sight of her and he opened his arms for a welcoming hug. Connie nuzzled up against his moss-coloured ribbed jumper, enjoying the texture against her skin. Things had become so fraught that there had been little time for shows of affection, but he pulled back:

"What's this? Do I detect a spot of alcohol before the sun's over the yard arm?" he teased.

"Hmm – as a matter of fact quite a lot spot – and I do feel a little tiddly which, if I were a lady of leisure, I would now sleep off so as to fool you all!" Sebastian laughed uneasily:

"So you've just been drink driving."

"Only a *little* way – just around the lanes – I won't tell if you don't!" she laughed.

"What about the school run? What if you were to have an accident after you'd picked up the children?"

"Sebastian! Don't be so melodramatic: the alcohol will have all washed away by then!" She tried to pull him back towards her, but he resisted.

"Well it would only take a small miscalculation and you'd have more children in hospital – you'd hardly be laughing then!" Connie reeled, hurt at Sebastian's astuteness at how best to wound her, but all she said was:

"Don't be such a wuss – you should know better: you know I'd never put the children in danger!"

"I wonder how many people have said that?" rejoined Sebastian reasonably; "Connie, I know you're really hard hit, but you need to watch yourself." Connie was stung by the truth in his words but was unwilling to admit it. She was exhausted, overwrought and still a little tipsy, and before she knew it she had spat back a vitriolic reply:

"It's amazing how we survived all that time before you came along to tell me, so eloquently, where I'm going wrong!" Sebastian turned on his heel and walked out of the kitchen, leaving the contents of the sink in a pile on the draining board. With a churning stomach, Connie heard his bike revving up before it disappeared around the bend in the drive.

Chapter Twenty-three

Connie had kept her promise to Leticia, and Charlie was now upstairs in Demelza's room – it had seemed the most natural place for her to be, for this was where Charlie and Demelza had always escaped for hour after secret hour. Connie found that she was on her third finger-full of Crunchy peanut butter, into which she frequently found herself having involuntarily dived for comfort fodder. She withdrew her finger slowly, savouring the oily taste, as she munched and mused: she had taken in how awkward Charlie had seemed on her arrival, and wondered if she had really wanted to come, or whether her new friend Leticia had goaded her into it. There was another reason: she wasn't sure how capable she was of the task of talking to Charlie, given her own topsy-turvy behaviour of late, and she needed time to consider how best to tackle another mother's daughter. Another mother who hadn't been capable of talking to her daughter herself: the upshot of which had resulted in her hitting the bottle!

"I'll have to have a go at this for Leticia's sake," she had told herself severely, with which resolve she was now mounting the narrow staircase leading to the attic rooms, which included Demelza's bedroom. She had only once set foot in it since the accident, to clean it, but every familiar object had brought with it so much sadness that she had not returned.

Connie knocked gently:

"May I come in?"

"Of course." Charlie had been sitting on the bed, a scattering of photographs around her, staring into space until she heard Connie's knock, at which she had straightened herself and looked politely and enquiringly towards the door.

"Are you OK?" Connie asked, looking for signs of stress on Charlie's spot infested face. (This was an on-going problem to which Charlie was subject. Leticia had dragged her along to a number of dermatologists until Charlie had rebelled, refusing further treatment and lecturing her mother witheringly on the subject of adolescence, hormones and nosiness).

"Are *you* OK?" she rejoined and Connie was torn between interpreting this retort as exaggeration or concern. Plumping for the latter, she decided to answer the question as candidly as she could:

"Well sometimes I am, but at others I react unpleasantly all over the place. I've always been the hippy, peace mongering sort, but since Demelza, I snap easily without warning – and I find myself being unkind and inconsiderate to those I care the most about."

"I know where you're coming from. I've been really minging too. Like everyone's going on about my work being better since Demelza, but it's only because there's nothing else to do. Last week I did this really good project – it took me ages – and then when Mum started on about how *wonderful* it was that *now* I was attaining my potential, I ripped it all up just to spite her because I just knew where she was heading again."

"Don't you think she might have been speaking the truth – about your work being better I mean?"

"Well maybe – but please don't even think about sticking up for her. She's always had it in for Demelza." (She refrained from adding Connie's name too, but sensed that this was understood.)

"But – I know I'm in dreadful danger of sounding school marmy here – how can ripping your work up help anyone? Surely if your work's better, then that can't be anything but good?"

"Well actually I saved it, so I *can* reproduce it if I feel like it, but Mum doesn't know that and she's fuming! Every time I mention Demelza she bangs on about the *good* things that result and it makes me mad. Of *course* there aren't any *good* things – none at all. She's got no idea how I feel about the whole thing. I've never been back to that gym, by the way, and that annoys her too, because she says I've got so much *potential* that I could be a star. As if! And she simply won't listen when I've tried to explain that it was the stupid gym – well that's where I learned that move – if it hadn't been for that, Demelza would be here now and we'd be messing around together." Following this diatribe Charlie hung her head to hide the water in her eyes. Connie was somewhat taken aback by the venom in the easy going Charlie's voice, and she began to see that Leticia's description of her daughter's feelings had been no exaggeration.

"What would Demelza have said if you'd told her you didn't want to play on the trampoline because it might be dangerous?" Connie asked slowly,

"She'd have called me a wuss and gone on it without me," was Charlie's knee-jerk response.

"And what if you'd refused to show her your new move because she might have an accident and hurt herself?" Connie continued.

"She'd have gone on and on until I gave in."

"So. She would have played on the trampoline anyway, with or without you. And she would have forced you to show her the move... What if you'd told her not to try to do it because you're a better gymnast and she would be unable?"

"She'd have taken no notice, and done it anyway I s'pose."

"So who chose to do the move resulting in the accident? You?"

"Demelza – Mrs Sharland you're just being clever," this was definitely not meant as a compliment, "if it wasn't my fault, it still doesn't excuse Mum whingeing on about us," Charlie faltered, confused by the fact that she had just, for the first time, acknowledged that the accident had possibly not been her own fault. She felt a mixture of relief and disloyalty for admitting that it might actually have been the responsibility of her friend.

"Don't you think your mother might be trying to say all the things I've just said, but fear of putting her foot in it and having her head bitten off may have made it come out differently?"

"Maybe," Charlie answered grudgingly. Connie pressed her advantage:

"I think she must be distraught that for some perverse reason you want to take the blame for the whole sorry incident with my daughter, when she can see you're wrong. And then you taunt and put her down each time she attempts to help you. I feel very sorry for her indeed." Charlie wished she had a handkerchief, for she needed desperately to blow her nose. However, she wasn't going to give Connie the satisfaction of seeing her cry: not after she'd sided with her mother, which was typical of the conspiracy of adults. She would have expected sympathy from Connie, who had always seemed approachably different and with whom she had always actually got along, enjoying the contrast of her Bohemian lifestyle in comparison to that at home. Thinking about what she had said hurt though, because she began to wish she hadn't been quite so harsh with and about her mother: she had deserved some of it, but that bit Connie had said about her mother being afraid to speak in case it came out wrong and she, Charlie, got mad at her – that struck an unpleasant chord,

181

.

making her feel positively demonic! And *why* had she piled it all on her mother? After all, her father never even attempted to become involved in her imperfect life, yet she had never bothered to take it out on him! Was it because she knew her mother really cared; which meant her spitefulness would hit home – and taking it out on another somehow off-loaded her own misery?

Charlie's nose became unbearably uncomfortable and she had to allow herself a loud and undignified sniff, at which Connie produced a tissue from her sleeve and apologised for its being a little grubby. That was enough; Charlie fell into Connie's arms and hugged her as she hadn't hugged her own mother in years.

"Thank you," she spluttered.

"I usually have a spare somewhere around," answered Connie, deliberately misunderstanding Charlie.

They were interrupted by wild screams and Connie ran to the door to discover the reason: Poppy was thundering up towards her:

"It's Ken! You've got to see! He's on telly now and he's *singing your song!*" Having successfully delivered the message she turned and galloped downwards, taking two steps at a time and leaping several towards the bottom of each staircase. Connie turned to Charlie, whose grief seemed to have been curbed with the news:

"This I must see! Come on!" she urged and Charlie found herself clattering downstairs behind Connie's measured bounds, the angst of the previous moments apparently forgotten.

As they rushed into the playroom, panting slightly, the family and Charlie's sister, Susanna, were excitedly gathered around the television, on which Ken was displayed, mid-screen, perched on a high stool with his guitar slung across his lap. He was crooning into the microphone, his large eyes looking appositely baleful as he murmured Connie's name in the chorus. Ella dug her mother in the ribs and giggled in delight. Ken had reached the point where he played a soulful guitar break, executed with his usual aplomb. He left the stool to swing the guitar gently, feelingly, across his pelvis; while the assembled crowd around him cheered and moved with the rhythm, vying for the camera.

"Poser!" exclaimed Ella to Susanna, who nodded her head in agreement. At the front of the crowd they became aware of a large, loudly dressed lady on whom the cameras had zoomed in:

"*Boo!*" they all shouted at once as Boo, for it was indeed her, began a captivating hip swinging shimmy; her arms aloft, her lips parted in a pout for the camera – of which she was clearly aware and milking for all she was worth!

"Dear Boo! You could rely on her to find the limelight!" Connie called delightedly as they watched Boo unhurriedly turn her back and give the camera a saucy waggle of her deliciously ample *derriere*! The family squealed and thumped each other, each trying to blot out the exultation Demelza would have derived from this scene. The cameras eventually panned back from the crowd to their performer showing Ken's final cadenza as he slumped dramatically over his guitar in apparent misery as he repeated Connie's name, muffled by the cheer that arose from the rapturous crowd.

The door had been gently pushed open and Sebastian had entered, unnoticed amongst the excitement, but now it was over, he spoke:

"I hate him," he said vehemently and everyone laughed. Connie was relieved beyond measure at his safe return.

"You'll have to get over him by their wedding," Ella pointed out facetiously.

"He was really only joking," Sophia explained hastily to a shocked Poppy. "Weren't you?" she added, just to be sure.

"Yes – I love him!" he answered. "In fact I don't think I could have played all that any more eloquently myself!" He hummed the chorus loudly and tunelessly and Poppy, reassured, asked when her mother was going to 'phone Ken and Boo to tell them that they were brilliant.

"I'll ring them later," answered Connie, not entirely enthusiastically because she knew the call would involve questions regarding the wedding, about which she felt a reluctance to talk: while she knew that one of their number would necessarily be absent, it was something with which she had not quite come to terms.

"Later…" she repeated as Sebastian returned with a bottle of wine and some glasses:

"I think your mother and I had better join Ella and Susanna in a drink to celebrate your mother's fame!" he announced.

"I'll drink to that excuse!" retorted Connie.

"But *I* certainly can't because I'm driving," pointed out Susanna primly, trying, unsuccessfully to hide the pride she felt at being able to deliver such a sophisticated line. *Let's hope her mother follows her example,* thought Connie, grinning to herself, *for the sake of all our gateposts!*

Chapter Twenty-four

The beautician arrived promptly, dressed in a short white nylon overall, her hair coiffed into a no-nonsense knot on the back of her head. Her face was the orange colour associated with the over-use of fake tan, her makeup severe and her smell professional and pungent. She carried a large case and asked Connie what she wanted to have done, to which she answered that she didn't know.

"Well there's facials, hair-do, waxing..." Connie made a face:

"Definitely no waxing please – I'll be good... I actually haven't got much time: what's the quickest?" The young lady sighed audibly, *who did this woman think she was, making out that she wanted the session to be as short as possible, when her lovely regular lady, Mrs Leason, had kindly stumped up for the work – and she could see why! This woman looked a right mess and in need of 'the works' in her professional opinion!*

"How about a nice facial to start with to relax you – and then perhaps we could do something with your hair?" *She would say that,* thought Connie, and gave in gracefully.

"A nice facial sounds perfect." At this point Poppy had wandered in and asked politely if she could watch the proceedings; to which the lady had answered quite firmly that this was Mummy's special time, when she would need to go on a relaxing journey, without the distractions of her charming family. Poppy had then asked how far she was going.

"Poppy I'm not *actually* going anywhere: we're going to pretend that I'm going on holiday – somewhere lovely – while this kind lady does a facial."

"Then why can't I go on the pretend journey too?"

"Well – if you're very quiet, I don't see why you couldn't watch anyway?" Connie looked questioningly at the lady, who was shaking her head vigorously:

"What Mummy will be undergoing will be lovely to her but rather boring for you: it looks as though you have lots to do here. Why don't you draw a picture of Mummy on her nice relaxing journey?" Poppy began to ask how the lady knew that she would be bored or how she knew that the journey was going to be nice – especially without her *own* presence; but the lady was obviously more used to children than it at first appeared, because she had produced some shiny looking paper from a capacious suitcase and handed it to her. The surface of the paper was tactile and calling to be drawn on in bright colours, so Poppy, mollified, trotted out of the kitchen and the lady was able to continue her analysis of Connie's needs, unhampered:

"What sort of facial would Madam like? Here's my list – and you don't need to take any notice of the prices because you're all inclusive." Connie ran her eye down the list of exotic treatments and made a show of great interest, returning more subtly to the time theme, but on this occasion more tactfully:

"The 'Deep Heat Treat!' sounds fine: how long must that take you? And 'Get Down to Basics' – I suppose that's just something of a wash?" Gradually, by dint of asking questions over the techniques used, she continued down the list and worked out the one that sounded the quickest and led the way to her bedroom, legging the stairs as fast as she could in order to get there faster and throw piles of clothes from the repository of the armchair into the wardrobe and kick shoes under the bed. The lady popped her suitcase on the now free armchair and took command. Slotting a small CD player into the electrical socket, relaxing distant jungle sounds began to pump their weary way around the room.

Connie gave herself up entirely to the experience and began to revel in being pampered: the whiteness of the towels, placed lovingly beneath her throbbing head; the warmth of the cleansing water and the contrasting coolness of the balmy lotions that were massaged so gently and caressingly into her temples; while the aroma of soothing pungent therapeutic oils dipped and swirled into her psyche. By the finish, Connie felt cosseted, lulled and completely enslaved by this lady in white, who had so professionally transformed the evening. Her skin felt zingy and smooth and her eyes had ceased to be sore: she stretched like a contented cat, not wanting to allow the rest of the world back into her consciousness.

The lady felt satisfied that this client, who seemed at first to be one of the more awkward customers (the sort that fretted about time, when a skill and art form were being perfected), had succumbed to the effects of her facial massage and as she deftly removed the bandana which held Connie's mess of hair from her forehead, she asked if this would be all. Connie answered through loose lips swathed in layers of waxy substance, that it wouldn't for she would like a hairdo next.

The lady was relieved about the hair, not merely for reasons of finance, but because the unruliness of the hair deflected from the becoming glow of her handiwork with the complexion:

"I would suggest a trim to get rid of those fly-away ends and a treatment to rejuvenate the follicles," she said, enjoying, as she always did, the sound of her professional advice.

"Actually I'd like you to get rid of the grey in my hair," explained Connie simply. The lady ran a practised eye over Connie's head:

"In fact, with your colour, it's what we call *pepper and salt,* Madam," she corrected.

"Then I want the salt out please – and just keep the pepper,"

"I'd have to do the whole head – and your discoloration's only about two percent and in the parting."

"Two per cent! That's loads: take it out, salts n' all with what ever means you like!" answered Connie quickly and decisively.

"Well your chestnut is very individual and hard to match exactly – but I would think if I put on a 'semi', it should do the trick."

"I'm in your capable hands – fire away, and we'll see if the others notice any difference. Hopefully they'll just think the grey – the *salt* – has been shaken out."

The lady mixed up a black sticky concoction in a white enamel bowl and daubed it all over Connie's head by means of what looked like a pastry brush. Next she placed a plastic cap over the top and announced that they must leave it for twenty minutes.

"Would Madam like me to do anything else while we're waiting – a manicure perhaps?" the lady asked, looking away from Connie's nails, which she felt were in dire need of cleaning, conditioning and several layers of polish, but Connie declined, explaining that she spent so much time doing outdoor things that the polish would chip in no time at all, and then they would look worse – especially when she played the flute. She then began to explain about her band and as she did so, she wondered how they had got on with the auditions, resolving to ring Cake once the evening's transformation was complete.

The twenty minutes was taken up with the compromise of her nails being soaked in oils, deep cleaned and evenly filed; after which they trooped to the bathroom, where, clad in a pair of latex gloves, the lady washed and conditioned Connie's hair, before wrapping it in a towel and leading her back to the bedroom to dry it. Connie perched on the edge of the bed, her head feeling racked and clean, her face scrubbed and sparkling. She hoped that Sebastian would be impressed, for he had stayed away several hours after they had argued, goodness knew where he had gone - and since then he had been quite subdued.

"I'm sorry for calling you a wuss," she had said, "I think what made me so defensive was knowing you were right. I'm just so horribly jumpy at everything." He had said it was all OK, but that he wished she could react like the Connie he had come to know and care about and that Demelza was too special a girl to bring her down. Connie had come away from this feeling disquieted – she had hoped an apology would clear the air completely, but she wished, too, that he had apologised too for being a little melodramatic himself, instead of merely discussing her present inconsistence in moods.

Connie stopped musing as Poppy scuttled into the room holding out the pictures that she had drawn on the bright shiny paper:

"I've done a card for Demelza and a picture of Tramp for you – See? He's on his back with his paws in the air – Sophia says the proportions are a bit wonky, but they aren't, are they?" She looked up brightly for a reassuring answer to her rhetorical question and then looked again:

"Oh! my God!" She clapped a hand across her mouth both at her blasphemous outburst and at what she saw before her: "Wow! Why've you done that?" Connie leapt up from the bed and crossed the maze of brightly coloured rugs across the oaken floor to Sebastian's newly acquired cheval mirror and gasped.

"Does Madam approve?" asked the beautician, rather too quickly. Connie swallowed, unusually lost for words. Sophia heard Poppy's exclamation and came into the bedroom: her eyes widened in disbelief and she laughed uncertainly:

"Oo – why have you done that to your hair?"

"I thought a little more pepper and less salt," said Connie wearily: "I had rather hoped it *wouldn't* be noticeable."

"If you didn't want it to be noticeable what would have been the point of doing it?" asked Poppy logically. Ella was with them by now:

"Wow, Mum; wild! What a wicked colour – can I have mine done too?"

"Trust you to turn it to you – this is Mummy's surprise! I can't wait to hear what they say when they see her at school... Miss Spanner will *so* disapprove!" laughed Sophia. The colour had actually come as a shock to the lady in white, who was wondering hurriedly whether to take the bull by the horns and apologise, offering further free treatments to make up, or whether to attempt to reassure her client that flame colour was all the rage and actually quite close to the original chestnut. The situation was taken satisfactorily out of her hands, since no one seemed to have considered blaming her; although she now realised that she had not mis-matched the colour, as she had first thought, but left it on for twice the time that she should have – as she could now plainly see on the instructions.

Connie was simply staring at herself, clearly in a state of shock for every day that she had seen herself in the mirror, absently, her hair had been the same – and, if she was honest, quite a number of people had said nice things about it over the years, unruly though it was. She had taken her natural colour for granted and perhaps it was vanity from this that had made her balk at allowing nature to make its natural changes over the passage of time.

"Well!" she said at last. "I suppose the colour will fade away?"

"In about six weeks it should all be gone – if you don't like it," answered the lady.

"We love you whatever colour your hair is!" piped Poppy loyally *She's trying to say that she doesn't want me to have it dyed again,* thought Connie, *which is easy enough!* A voice in her ear spoke to her and Connie found herself echoing it aloud:

"*We say bring on the grey!*" she said and the children all looked at her sharply, each thinking the same:

"That sounded exactly like Demelza!" said Sophia.

"Well I think she's right too!" smiled Connie.

"I think it's cool to have a make-over, but that Boho skirt you're wearing is going to have to go – it's just not punk!" put in Ella.

"Who says I'm punky?"

"With hair that colour: me and just about everyone else out there!" The voice sounded in Connie's ear again:

"Just because *I* don't choose to wear a skirt that looks like gone wrong pants!" retorted Connie to her own surprise – and then, as Ella heaved at the hem of her micro skirt and looked offended she added: "I'm sorry Ella – that was Demelza getting in the way again – I actually think you are one of the few people who *can* wear a skirt that length and get away with it... But I think I'm going to have to go to the hospital this minute and have a chat with your sister!"

No one disagreed with Connie – they all felt disquieted by the snatched, mischievous hilarity of the remarks which had passed from Connie's lips and which were so unlike her.

"I'll come with you," said Ella, unusually quick at being mollified, "But first I want to see Sebastian's face when he sees what you've done!"

The lady in white was reading and re-reading the instructions on her discarded packet of dye, deciding to slip it into her bag rather than risk a waste-paper basket for it, where the instructions, and her mistake, could possibly be discovered. She was relieved that no one had thought to blame or quiz her about the product and, while the going was good, she decided to withdraw. She hastily replaced all the grooming items in her bag and announced that she really must be somewhere else. Connie seemed to have forgotten her existence, but looked up quickly to thank her and say that her face and nails felt a million dollars.

No mention of her hair, thought the lady, but actually that was understandable – you couldn't always have successes; the occasional failure put the successes and the amount of skill necessary for them in perspective. She hurried out, passing a fit looking Caesar-number-one cut on the stairs. The owner of the haircut had winked at her:

"Thought I'd stay well clear – have you managed to make her even more ravishing?" and without waiting for an answer he had bounded on up the stairs and the lady had scurried down the hall to find an exit.

"OK, you can come in now!" chorused the voices behind the door, and Sebastian pushed the door open to find Connie sitting on the bed looking radiant, twiddling very pink and white nails with a towel on her head.

"My goodness your skin looks like peaches – and I'd thought the brown was a tan!" he said with a twinkle. "Now let's see the hair – is it not quite dry?" It was completely unlike Connie to be coy, but it was quite pleasant to play along to. At his words they had all burst out laughing:

"Oh it's dry alright: just prepare yourself for a shock! Hide your eyes and we'll take the towel off!" encouraged Ella and as he did so, she flicked the towel off her mother's head and Connie looked at him, feeling very silly and girlish. Sebastian took in the sight of his beloved with the normally wild outrageous hair, sitting demurely before him looking tamed and frightful; her eyes full of hope that he wouldn't show revulsion or disappointment. He focussed on those unchanged, green and glorious eyes, and looked into these only, swallowing hard:

"Of course – well – a change! Everyone likes a change now and then, don't they? Why not indeed?" Connie threw herself at him, knocking him onto the bed and they were all laughing, jostling and smiling:

"However!" Sebastian continued, "I do hope you won't find it necessary to make it again. Ever! Promise?" Connie cuffed him gently in his softening middle, saying that the promise was entirely dependent on his non-wuss behaviour, and therefore quite out of her control.

~

Still in a light hearted mood, the family clambered into the ancient Discovery and rumbled off to the hospital, despite the rather late hour.

"We'll just pop in, have a little word in her ear and go. There are times when it just feels right to see her," Connie explained, rather inadequately, since she was having difficulty explaining it to herself, running her hand self-consciously through her new glossy candyfloss for the umpteenth time.

As they arrived at the hospital, they were met by a stream of cars containing those who were leaving; visiting hour being now officially over. For the Sharlands, since Demelza's case was a severe one, the visiting rules did not apply and, after the first few days when Connie could barely be peeled away, they were told they could visit when they needed to. Evening visits allowed Connie to supply teach during the day, and she was thankful that she was under no contract, so that she could refuse work at any time that she felt Demelza's strong sleeping presence draw her, like a magnet, to her bedside.

The steps to Intensive Care were worn by the tread of anxious families, each housing their own hopes and dreads. Connie could have reached the room blindfolded, she thought, as she strode down the over-lit corridors, her hand in Sebastian's on one side and Poppy's on the other. As they arrived, a senior house officer greeted them:

"This is a very opportune visit," he said, "I was on the point of phoning you."

Connie exchanged an anxious glance with Sebastian before asking, her mouth suddenly dry, what the matter was.

"Please don't worry – if anything this is good news – or it could be nothing, so don't get your hopes up, but her blood pressure's coming up – and we think she's beginning to respond to stimuli... one of the nurses is convinced she saw Demelza moving her fingers this evening when she turned her."

Connie's eyes misted with hope:

"Does this mean she's waking up?" Not a breath was taken until the answer was complete – as always it was guarded, for fear of false hope and subsequent recrimination:

"We can't be sure, but the signs are good: it could very well be!"

"And excuse me!" put in Sebastian excitedly, "But if she's moving her fingers then she can't be paralysed, can she?" They could barely contain themselves, but the answer Sebastian received was again measured:

"Well certainly, if her fingers are moving then her hands are not paralysed – but that does not include the whole of the body necessarily." Everyone was exchanging expressions of hope. A hope which had held for so long, but until today had received no confirmation of bearing fruit. They burst into the little room to see Demelza, who was lying as still as ever, her music switched off because it was night-time – although in the world she was inhabiting it was forever night, the curtains permanently closed.

"Can I go first?" called Poppy as she seized one of Demelza's cool hands, gently rubbing and chafing it:

"Come on Demelza – we know you can hear us – wake up!" she commanded. Ella smiled generously at her:

"Well it worked for Jesus, didn't it?" protested Poppy defensively.

"I know! Let's put on some of her music. How about *Plastic Max's* 'I Feel Dangerous'!" suggested Sophia.

"How about 'We Will Rock You?' put in Connie: "It's gentler for this time of night."

"But it's her favourite and it's kind of stirring: it's much more likely to get her moving," supported Ella.

"You're right there: OK, but not too loud, or we'll wake everyone up."

"Everyone except Demelza!" Ella put on the screeching vocal of Baz Tard, but at a lower volume than they were used to.

"She's going to tell you to turn it up any minute now!" the unshakeable faith of Sophia's voice was heard over the din. Ella had begun to jig around to the music, even though she had always professed to loath it for it was *so,* like, not cool and immature!

Each person, in turn sat beside Demelza, holding her hand and encouraging her to squeeze their hands if she could hear them:

"Perhaps the nurse was mistaken?" Connie said flatly, "I know I've sometimes thought –"

"But her blood pressure – don't forget her blood pressure," Sebastian interjected, "it all ties in."

"If we could will her to wake up, believe me we'd have done it by now," answered Connie despondently. She and Sebastian were sitting on either side of the bed, while the others were fidgeting and intoning to the music, which had moved on to…

We feel so Deflated
We're bang under-rated!

"I saw her!" Poppy shouted suddenly,

"Saw what?" they chorused.

"Her eyes! They sort of flickered!"

"But they're closed: they can't have."

"Well her eye *lids* did – I swear!" Everyone looked from the protesting Poppy to the supine Demelza in disbelief. No movement was visible.

"It's easy to imagine," Connie said gently, "I've found myself seeing all sorts of stuff – it's to do with the mind playing tricks." The sheets surrounding Demelza's still form stirred:

"H'o Sebbo!" said a faint voice beside Sebastian, as Demelza's beautiful grey eyes flickered open, focussed on him for a second and then fell closed again. Poppy, Ella and Sophia whooped, Connie wailed and Sebastian burst into sobs and the senior house officer emerged from nowhere to check on the commotion. They all attempted to explain at once, but he could see from their faces what had happened. He began to question them, but Sebastian was still utterly overcome and Connie had to repeat what they had all plainly seen and heard. After this they all began to urge Demelza for a repeat performance to show the delighted house officer:

"Do it *again,* Demelza, do it again!" called Sophia and Poppy.

"Sing your din to the music!" Ella was urging.

"Darling, well done!" Connie repeated over and over. Sebastian had begun to blow his nose, both nostrils at once, tumultuously, his chocolate brown eyes still streaming; at last he managed to utter something intelligible:

"She called me Sebbo! There can't be anything wrong with her brain: she's the only person ever to call me Sebbo," he spluttered at the houseman.

"She even rhymed: she said 'Ho Sebb O' – that rhymes!" beamed a round-eyed Poppy, nodding her head profoundly, which made the ringlets that had escaped from her scrunchy, dance in emphasis.

"I think that 'Ho' was short for 'hello'," Sophia explained solemnly.

The house officer had only been made Senior House Officer recently, and his tender years and inexperience contributed to making it hard to discipline this family, whom he had watched through so much pain and exhaustion. At this point he knew that Demelza needed no more encouragement but rest. She would gradually make her way back to the here and now in her own time. If this sort of noise continued, the consultant might overhear, and then he would be for it!

"Everyone!" he called, over some rather unpleasant garage music that they had put on – not the most soothing for a patient either; but none of them seemed to notice or pay attention to him. He must take command: but it wasn't working. He strode over to the CD player and searched for the stop button, which he eventually located and pressed - everyone became poised in a split moment of celebration and looked towards him, expectantly. This was it:

"I know you're all really excited – and so am I," he began, "I think we may say that Demelza, after a sustained absence, has returned to you." They began to whoop again and he held up his hand for silence (just like the teachers used to do in the school playground, not so long ago). "But her journey to recovery will be swifter if we can just give her space to come to in her own time. She does not need noise."

"Wa's happened to your hair, Mum?" asked Demelza, her gaze on Connie for a full moment, before her eyelids gave up the struggle to stay open again. There was a burst of laughter from everyone except the house officer, who hadn't been able to miss the fact that Mrs Sharland's hair certainly looked oddly coloured.

"She's had a bad hair day!" answered Ella "And by the way you won the bet: I said you'd never be able to do that move on the trampoline and you did, but I so wish you hadn't and I'm sorry."

It was unlikely that Demelza heard, but Ella had rehearsed saying this so often and with it she felt the weighty cloak of responsibility shrug itself from her shoulders. They were all talking and laughing again – and Connie was especially pleased to have been noticed, not caring in the slightest that it was with reference to her disastrous hair colour.

At last Sebastian seemed to have pulled himself together and, wiping his eyes, he pointed out that he thought that this kind gentleman was trying to extract them – and he *had* said it would be in Demelza's best interest.

"I just want to see her say something else!" wailed Poppy, "Do you think she knows we're all here?"

"Without a doubt!" answered Connie happily, "But now I think we'd all better let her get some rest."

"But she's been resting for months and there's so much to say!"

"It's strange that she needs some more, isn't it?" answered Connie, "but there'll be more tomorrow – and the next day."

"And the next and the next and …" They each kissed Demelza, promising to return tomorrow, and told her to sleep well, which was a change from urging her to wake up. The relieved house officer closed the door behind them as they clattered out, before preparing for a series of tests on Demelza: what a privilege it had been for all that to happen on his duty – and the signs looked encouraging at last. Somewhat taken aback, he found himself hastily wiping a tear from his own eye.

Chapter Twenty-five

Connie refused two offers for supply teaching the next day and hastily rang Stuart with the glad news of Demelza's 'return'. He promised to visit her himself later, explaining that he hadn't visited much before this time, since there seemed little point when Demelza was unable to see him herself – and anyway, Sue had needed his support what with Fifi, night feeds and so on. *If he's getting up in the night that will be a first,* scoffed Connie to herself; but then again perhaps he really *had* turned over a new leaf regarding commitment to his new family. If this were the case, she was delighted for Sue, but she couldn't help feeling just a little piqued that the change of heart had not transpired one or two babies earlier!

When Connie arrived at the hospital after the school run, Stuart was already there. He wanted to 'fit Demelza in' before the office, he said. Connie searched for any tell-tale traces of baby sick on his lapels, but there were none, and he looked remarkably well on his late nights: his eyes were clear, his freshly shaven cheeks glowing with health and happiness! He took one look at Connie and clapped his hand across his mouth in a way very similar to that of his daughter, Poppy:

"Oh my God: what *have* they done to your hair?" Connie was unable to summon any dignity and admitted with a shrug that she'd 'had it done'.

"No! I assumed the children had done it!"

"Something like Red Nose Day?"

"Well," he smiled awkwardly, "you must admit it does rather resemble that sort of catastrophe. But why did you do it?"

"To hide the grey."

"Was there any grey? I never noticed any!"

"Is that a thing I would be likely to invent? And anyway, I was shown a handful of evidence." Stuart pondered the notion of women going grey for a moment or two, but gave it up:

"When will it go away? That is, I assume you're not keeping it like that?"

"Why not? I thought it was rather fetching! Actually, I've been told six weeks and I'm praying it will have sort of dimmed a bit before Boo's wedding."

"Oh yes, to the frightful Ken. He doesn't age gracefully either, does he? We saw him cavorting around on the telly doing that Connie song of his – *so* embarrassing for you!"

"Actually, I must confess it makes me feel rather special... and Boo doesn't care, so why should I?"

"Oh well. Raather you than me! Anyway..." He searched around for an improving phrase: "You know I think your hair will always be lovely the way it was!" This gallantry had cost considerable ingenuity in ambiguity and he felt pleased that he had handled the disastrous situation with aplomb. At the same time he experienced relief that Sue would not reach a similar middle-age crisis for many years to come – however, considering she had dyed her hair consistently since he had known her, the thing should not have to arise, which was a mercy. He resolved to examine his own hairline closely as soon as a private minute emerged, for surely this meant that he would not be immune – horrific thought – to greyness himself!

~

James, their friend and doctor, was already at Demelza's bedside, struggling with a feeling of awkwardness at seeing Connie with Stuart, whom he had not clapped eyes upon since they had been a couple. It wasn't that he didn't like Stuart exactly – more that he gravitated towards the sort of things Connie had continued to do, while Stuart had veered away from that life to pastures new. Perhaps it might have been kind to lift the phone and suggest a visit to the pub, or a game of golf; but it had never occurred to him. Stuart's first sentence, which did not begin with 'Hello' or anything similar, served to make him feel less sub-standard with regard to his inadequacies as a friend, however:

"But Connie, you said she was awake and talking!"

"She was, Stuart – she was. But it doesn't mean she'll never sleep again! We were told to expect a good deal of dozing." James hastily intervened:

"She's right. What Connie saw last night was just the beginning of a waking up process from deep layers of unconsciousness, out of which she may take some time to come to. It doesn't always happen all at once but bit by bit: some of the night staff reported eyelid flickers again early this morning so she's making very real progress, believe me."

"I see, I see. It's just such a bugger –– I was so looking forward to talking to her and telling her about Fifi and everything and I've got a meeting at ten. Because of Sue being off, we're short staffed in Accounts and I have to be everywhere at once."

"Very annoying for you Stuart. I am sorry," put in Connie unconvincingly and James had to hide a chuckle. Stuart advanced to the bed and kissed his daughter gently on the cheek, his eyes pleading some reaction, but she didn't stir. He hovered undecidedly for a moment longer:

"Look – sorry – I've got shed-loads to do and there's not much point my staying here if she's not – er…"

"Talking to you?"

"Well yes actually. So – whenever she comes to, please send her a hug from me and tell her I was here and I'll be back soon."

"That's fine Stuart: very sensible. I'm sure she'll be more *compos mentis* for you next time." Connie called out 'goodbye' at his retreating form and he returned over his shoulder what lovely news it all was, trying to mask the strange feeling of disappointment for himself and resentment towards Connie: time always seemed to be her ally where the children were concerned, but he had a business that wouldn't run itself.

Connie and James exchanged a glance of mutual understanding before James gave further details of Demelza's progress: she was beginning to respond to stimuli and – they both saw her eyes flicker half open as she murmured:

"Stuart?" Connie ran to the door and not bothering to wait for the lift, tore after Stuart. As she reached the vast double doors of the exit, she saw Stuart's car accelerating away. Producing her mobile she jabbed his number into it:

"Stuart, Stuart – she's awake – she asked for you!"

"What – actually asked?"

"Well she said your name: she must have heard you in her subconscious."

"Well that's marvellous! I should have hung around after all."

"But aren't you going to come back?" asked Connie, her

astonishment goading a number of people who loitered outside the entrance smoking, to stare in her direction.

"Can't – that's the bugger of it – it'll take me another age to park and get one of those ridiculous tickets, by which time I'll be late for my meeting."

"Right – goodbye." Connie snapped her mobile shut in disbelief – but she wasn't going to miss another second of Demelza being awake and she sprinted back through the doors, up the many flights of stairs until, completely out of breath, she reached Demelza again.

"Stuart sends his love. He really wanted to see you, but there's a meeting he can't be late for." James lifted his eyes, unprofessionally, to the ceiling before completing his examination. Demelza looked dazed and confused and asked, this time, how Tramp was. Connie gently reminded her daughter:

"He died peacefully – remember? And he's gone to the happy hunting ground. We gave him a great send off, didn't we? And now we keep his grave all neat and the crocuses and daffodils that we planted seem to have come up really well. Poppy and Sophia re-write his headstone regularly 'Best friend and confidant' was Sophia's last contribution – and I'd thought the confidences were exclusively mine."

"He probably makes great compost for those flowers!" Connie's face lit up: this kind of irreverence had been missing for a long time in their household – and although the subject was a delicate one for her, she felt a surge of amusement and excitement that her daughter, after so much trauma, was essentially unchanged. Demelza's eyelids began to droop and she was losing focus:

"Sorr Mum – so sleepy."

"It's OK, it's OK," Connie answered: "Now I know you're back with us it's all OK." As Demelza settled back into her dreams, Connie put her head gently on the pillow beside her and a moment later, still smiling, she too was asleep.

~

Connie and Demelza drifted in and out of consciousness together all day. Connie had felt exhausted before, but rarely able to allow herself the luxury of giving in to a solid night's sleep – much as she would have liked to: the nagging worry of Demelza blotting out the kind depths of slumber. Now, at last, she was able to give in to her tiredness, and the slumber she was experiencing felt as though it was all caught up in her happiness that Demelza was coming back – that she *would* recover.

The nursing staff were kind and understanding, bringing her tea and sandwiches in the moments she was awake. James had told her, before he left for his other calls, that as yet Demelza seemed unable to lift her limbs or 'twiddle her digits', but this was natural because her muscles had wasted from lying still. Gradually, he said, she should regain movement, but they must expect only one thing at a time. Right now they must simply rejoice in the fact that she could wake and talk and that there was evidently no permanent brain damage. Connie had lifted her head from Demelza's pillow as he said this, but sunk down as soon as he had finished into another contented doze.

Somehow the children were fetched (Sebastian, of course) and joined her and Demelza for a short time before the registrar on duty had firmly told them to take Connie home, for she was as tired as her daughter. At this, all of the celebrating family had become a little subdued and left unusually quickly and quietly, each privately appreciating for the first time quite how affected their mother had been by the whole episode. On reaching home, Connie was unable to manage the delicious feast that the delicatessen had helped Sebastian to choose, for she said she would have a quick lie down while he prepared it – but she had then slept the clock round! Sebastian had told the children not to awaken her, and they merely removed her shoes and pulled the duvet around her, kissing her gently in much the same way as they had become used to when leaving their sleeping sister.

"Do you think Mummy's alright?" the younger children had wanted to know.

"She's *Alright Now*," Sebastian had answered happily, to the tune of Jim Morrison's epic, which none of them knew, but the gist was good enough. "She's more alright than she's been for the past few months," he continued unnecessarily, for each of them had absorbed and felt it, warm and reassuring, like porridge on a cold day.

Chapter Twenty-six

The days fused into a heady happiness associated with early Summer, as Demelza's health – and Connie's – began gradually to renew itself. Demelza resided amongst a daily barrage of Get Well cards from the most unlikely assortment of people, some of whom she barely knew! There was some old gent called Joe from the village, whom her mother had met in the graveyard and who was responsible for keeping her little room in the hospital bright with fresh flowers, delivered regularly and always anonymously: however, Connie said she knew they were from him. Then there were bags full of cards and wishes from Connie's various classes: she had been unable to resist setting the task of drawing a picture for someone who has never been outside for five months, resulting in the brightest and most garish of artistic endeavours. Propped up on pillows, Demelza had begun to eat proper food and dispense with her drip. She was painfully thin and she and Ella had actually laughed at the awkward memory of Ella calling her fat! Leticia had been tireless in her efforts to bring Charlie to visit Demelza for ten minutes, for that was all she was allowed, most days, and Charlie had caught Demelza up on the gossip at school. Demelza was not allowed to use her ipod in the hospital, but Charlie smuggled in her own and they had an earplug apiece, on which they listened intently to the strains of the latest heavy metal charts, exchanging rapturous glances. She underwent daily sessions of physiotherapy, which left her feeling stretched and exhausted; but the reward was the progress she was greedy for; and while she could not sit up unaided, she began to flex her fingers and lift her thin arms from the elbow.

On one after school visit, Ella asked her if there was anything she remembered from when she was unconscious and Demelza answered that she had sometimes felt she was aware of them – and of strange, scary and 'scrapey' dreams:

"That would be the operations – you were lucky you didn't have to see the bolts in your neck: you looked *so* Sci-fi!"

"Gee thanks – and there were some weird bits and pieces – I dreamt Mum tried on some new trousers and wet them!" Everyone had laughed at the absurdity of this, but when the laughter had finished Connie spoke up in a foiled attempt at frosty dignity:

"Actually the substance of what you heard was correct, which is interesting." There was a shout of laughter at this admission, to which Connie explained over the hubbub: "I simply sneezed unexpectedly: only a teaspoon full. Of course I had to buy the trousers – and they didn't even fit! Come to think of it," she went on, "Now I've lost all this weight…"

Stuart made another visit and rang before-hand, asking if Demelza might take a snooze for a couple of hours prior to this, for there was someone very special who wanted to be introduced. Demelza followed the instruction, for she was still finding much difficulty in staying awake for any length of time and her visits, much as she thrived on them, made her tire easily. She had guessed that the new acquaintance was Fifi and was not disappointed: Stuart had pushed his way backwards through the swing doors and turned to reveal a little dark mop, halo-ing a round, red, shiny face, peeping out of a zipped pink sleeping bag. Demelza squealed with delight:

"My baby sister! Oh she's gorgeous – I'm going to be your number one baby-sitter and I will sing you Nursery rhymes, à la Plastic Max, and I'll teach you everything I know!" She gazed at the little face:

"I think she wants a tissue – her nose needs a blow. Do you think I can blow it for her?" Stuart was frightened of releasing his hold on his precious burden even slightly, but managed well in not showing his anxiety as Demelza slowly, painfully, stretched for a tissue from the rubble of cards on her bedside table, extracted it with what was clearly an effort, and gently wiped and squeezed the tiny button nose, which their father was exposing from the folds of Fifi's covers. Demelza dropped her hand, drained from the effort but delighted at her achievement:

"See! We managed that alright – but *Fifi!* What a name! Can't we do better than that?"

"We thought it was rather good," answered her father, a little disgruntled: "Sue likes it a lot: she had a favourite cat called Fifi, and you know how she adores cats."

"That's what I mean – I'm not sure it's really *her!* Never mind," a mischievous look spread across the pale face: "I'll think of something."

"But Demelza, she's already had her name registered and it's official – we like it!" he repeated defiantly, the old feeling of exasperation with this daughter at, he searched for a reason, not quite being in command; overwhelmed him momentarily, before he found himself actually smiling! He had been surprised at being *quite* so strung up when the accident happened to this daughter, and it had churned over feelings of which he had been unaware. He had wanted another chance to get things 'more right' with Demelza's indomitable spirit – why should he care if she didn't like his baby's name?

"Tom, Dick, Harry: you can call her what you like, but she'll always be Fifi for Sue and me," he finished mildly, placing Fifi across Demelza, his own arms still encircling the precious bundle.

"Fifi, Fie fie, foe foe, fumfum! Maybe I'll call her Fum - Fumbelina!" replied Demelza, quite unruffled, but rather sleepily: "I'm sorry Stuart – I'm going all snoozy again and I'm afraid of Fum slipping. Could you take her and help me down a bit? Your very big sister is conking out now, give her a blobby kiss." Stuart smiled indulgently, brushing Fifi's smooth, shiny little face over against Demelza's before easing the pillows flatter for Demelza and kissing the tip of her nose as he used to do when she, too, had been tiny.

"Thanks," she called after him as, exhausted from her meagre efforts with her baby sister, sleep overtook her again.

Connie had begun to take part in the minutae of life once more, returning to the telephone for lengthy gossips with her friends, and arranging to attend band practices and gigs. She was looking forward to meeting the new keyboard player and singer about whom she had heard much, and wondered if he had filled the gap so well that she would no longer have a niche in the band. The band members had taken the unprecedented step of advising her not to bother to attend a second audition for the final choice, because there didn't need to be one: the musician that they had found was simply without rival – and they couldn't believe their luck at his finding him!

Connie had filled out a little since Demelza's improvement and her skin had lost the sallow look, being replaced by a hint of honey, equivalent to the amount of time she spent outside. Resuming the delights of her aimless strolls, she was surprised to find that the garden was not as neglected as she would have expected. Here again, she suspected, the anonymous local village fairies must have been at work, for instead of the chaos of weeds she envisaged, there were broad beans and the feathery green fringes of carrot leaves appearing above the soil, while last year's brassicas had been carefully weeded and nurtured. Connie fetched a fork and began the laborious task of digging over the heavy soil, but she found that she soon lost her stamina and drove the fork back into the grass, ready for a further foray another day. She decided she deserved a quick visit to the ducks and hens, for the purpose of sheer admiration, and watched the little brown call-ducks scurry to the pond in the expectation of scraps; their excitement made clear by the raucous, scraping screeching sounds they omitted, the attraction of which must have been exclusive to members of their species. The shambling, soundless Muscovays flew to their 'pondipad', as Connie called it, landing with webbed feet braced, braking against the water. Next it was time to watch the collection of hens, as they shuffled around in the dirt, fussing and vying for scraps, their hot red combs flopping absurdly over their heads. Bustle, the strawberry hen was there, but she didn't seem much interested in the scraps, and paced crossly up and down, her comb still short and brown, indicating that she wasn't laying at present. She seemed to have lost condition, but this could have been due to a moult; however suddenly Connie remembered Sebastian's ministrations to the netting over the gate, through which she had always flown for her sojourn on the other side; to scratch about, settle into her nest under the yew trees, lay her small freckled egg and return back over the netting – all within a short stretch of time. Without thinking further, she fetched some wire cutters from the stable and set about removing Bustle's incarcerating torment.

The job was simple and the feeling was pleasant: Free, Free: Set Them Free! Connie heard herself singing, realising that the sound of her own voice had been something she had done without for a while. Having done her best justice for *Sting,* she proceeded with *Denise Williams'* version: I Just Want to be Free, followed by *Ella Fitzgerald's* Freedom! and marvelled at the way certain words, such as Freedom, Hallelujah and Britannia leant themselves to uplift a stonking melody throughout all bounds of music. She ambled off to the orchard for a moment, the glorious lyrics unleashing fountains of good songs, and on her return noticed, with satisfaction, that Bustle had already absconded!

On entering the kitchen for a reviving mug of coffee before retrieving the washing from the line, Connie could hear Sebastian's voice in the back hall nearby.

"Well I was pretty sure it was *that* William III piece, but I never got time to really examine it – the phone went and it was an emergency. Just one of those things, so near yet so far. Well it sounds like the end of the road for the piece if it's *definitely* been bought privately - pity, but thanks for telling me anyway. Bye." Sebastian entered the kitchen looking pre-occupied and smiled absently at Connie, who was standing in her favourite position with her back against the Aga while the kettle boiled:

"Was that *your* William III?" she asked,

"Seems it was – I asked my scout to keep an eye out for it, but apparently it's definitely been bought privately by a little old lady in Worcester, so that's the end of that pipe dream: I might as well get rid of my end of the pair: it's a pain, but win some lose some."

"The portrait figure you were after on the day Demelza had the accident? But you told me it was the *wrong* William!"

"Well I didn't want to burden you with my stuff just when Demelza was life or death."

"So you lied to me." Connie answered flatly.

"Well yes, I suppose I did," Sebastian replied comfortably: "It was to save you bothering about it."

"So, because it was an inconvenient moment you took it upon yourself that it was best to lie?"

"Something like that," Sebastian mumbled, beginning to look uneasy.

"So whether you choose to tell the truth to me or not depends on how I'm going to take it?"

"Well – at that moment in time…" Connie's heart had dropped like a stone. She had been here before with others she had trusted – but Sebastian had seemed so much more solid and dependable than any of them. *Here we go again,* her inner voice sang, warningly.

"No – wait – Connie: that's unfair. You're taking this out of all proportion! I was simply so sorry for you – for Demelza – that I didn't want to upset you more: I didn't even want to talk about it." Sebastian was beginning to protest, now that he saw how earnest Connie was, and she felt winded by his misplaced display of protection.

"Alright – so the quickest way to fob me off was a lie! That means I can't trust you."

"Don't be absurd; of course you can – why would I…"

"Of course I can," she interrupted, "until the timing happens to be inconvenient or I might be upset! So, to take an analogy, suppose you go out with someone else, I would be upset about that, wouldn't I? So you would lie."

"But I haven't – I wouldn't want to!"

"That's not the point. The point is that it will always be a possibility and I would have to live with that knowledge."

"Connie, look at me! These past few months I've been here for you all I could: I've cooked, taken the children to school, to the hospital, tried to cover a million jobs that need doing around the place – *and* keep my business afloat: I wouldn't have done all that if I wasn't totally committed to you and the life that you carry around." At the mention of what Sebastian had done for all the family Connie began to waver; for she had leant on and trusted him like nobody she had known: but didn't that make the lie the more distressing – or *was* she taking it out of proportion? She thought for a moment more. Perhaps this, then, was an opportunity to clear the air – and there were things to say:

"I do appreciate enormously everything you did – but you really didn't need to do so much."

"What's that supposed to mean? Did I drive too much, eat too much, take too much care of the other childrens' feelings when you were away?"

"Away with Demelza who needed me more!" Now it was Connie who was on the defensive: was this a deliberate neat manoeuvre?

"Alright, but they needed you and I was there to help – and of course it was only what I wanted to do: for them, for you. So what did I do that was 'too much'?"

"Well, for example, you put netting up around the top of the hen pen, so Bustle couldn't get out."

"Oh excuse me. So I'm wrong for making the hens safe?"

"Well, actually yes – and if you'd asked me about it, instead of charging off to do it because you thought I had it wrong – you having lived in the country all of two minutes, then I would have explained that there is only one hen who escapes that way and she needs to and she always comes back herself."

"*Needs?*"

"Yes, to lay her egg outside and be happy," Connie answered rather lamely, hearing herself sounding like what Demelza would describe as a 'lentil loving hippy', "If she hadn't needed to, I wouldn't have had to open it up again for her."

"You did *what?*"

"I had to open it up again so that she could get out. She wasn't happy – but you would be so pleased with yourself, you wouldn't have seen that!"

"And did you never think to ask *me* to reverse the job I'd so stupidly botched – a hen's needs not having been sufficiently paramount? You say I should have asked: perhaps you should have explained! I wouldn't have minded, but no! You and your hen had to be all martyred and keep it all in and then you had to creep off and change things behind my back as though I had intended harm! When actually – obviously – I was only trying to help!"

"I know you were, but you asked for an illustration and I gave you one," she answered, thinking that she had perhaps underestimated Sebastian's male ego.

"Ah! So *you* don't tell me when you think I could be hurt by an explanation, but when I try to save you a tiny bit in the midst of an enormous crisis I'm branded a liar!"

"I didn't lie," Connie answered simply "I just didn't *say* – there's a qualitative difference. Actually I do tend not to say when things bother me – I internalise. It's part of my pattern and I suppose why I'm so scratchy with you is because I didn't think *you* were like that. You are trustworthy." she stated, trying to soften the situation, which she realised had gone too deep, but without going back on her main thrust.

"You mean I *was* trustworthy, but now you realise I'm a low down charlatan and you've been duped!"

"No – not that bad – I just hate any kind of lie and I found you making one – all be it a small one. Which I know was meant to be *kind!*" she added, trying to be conciliatory now, for she saw the hurt on his large features and with this she lost all her own remaining resentment and wanted to make everything good again with a hug; but by now it was too late.

"I'm sorry to be such a disappointment: you are clearly better off on your own getting things right!" he announced as he slammed the kitchen door behind him and trounced out of the house.

Connie was paralysed for a moment, realising the enormity of what she had done and then she sped after him – but already his car was speeding away, the furniture in the back jumping painfully with the depth of the potholes.

∼

As Connie perched foetally on the stairs, missing Tramp's soft warmth and rocking backwards and forwards, Sebastian was driving at full tilt, having cranked Gluck's Jai perdu mon Euridice to full volume as he wailed the lyrics tunelessly with all his heart:

"What happened?" they both wondered in dismay.

"Surely he'll come back – he did before…" thought Connie as she began to wish she had put things differently.

"She won't want me back now," thought Sebastian miserably, wishing he had picked up the olive branch which, surely, she had falteringly offered – and he had refused so haughtily.

Chapter Twenty-seven

Some days passed, during which time Connie hoped that Sebastian would breeze back in as he had done before, and that she would not have to mention anything to the children, who assumed he was working in London that week. However, after more time elapsed, Connie felt compelled to climb up to the loft over the stables where he kept his tools and polishes, and saw what she had dreaded: a few unessential tins of oil and chair legs remained, but the bulk of his working kit had gone, and the floor was swept clean from the normal array of rags, wooden pegs and glues. She returned to the little dressing room beside theirs where he kept his clothes, to find bare drawers and a number of empty coat hangers. It was only now that Connie knew with a certainty that Sebastian did not mean to come back and had indeed evidently been at pains to retrieve his things while all the family were out; rather than undergo further confrontation with Connie or an explanation to the children. This seemed both considerate and cowardly, and Connie was gripped by a feeling parallel to icy water being tipped down her back. She had hoped that if he *had* decided to move and fetch his things then this might have been the chance, with time for reflection, for them to see the situation objectively as resolvable – and she might have managed to persuade him to stay...

To compound everything, Poppy returned from collecting the eggs, so distraught that she cracked the glass on the French windows as she barged through: in her hands was a mangled collection of feathers from a strawberry-coloured hen. They were unmistakeably Bustle's. Connie tried, inadequately, to comfort her:

"Bustle loved her freedom to lay her eggs outside the run – the fox was almost bound to catch her one day; and think what a lovely long life she had!"

"Longer if we'd kept her in!"

"Longer, but less happy perhaps..." Neither of them mentioned Sebastian's thwarted efforts to prolong dear Bustle's life.

"How's Sebbo?" Demelza had demanded that evening, after she had demonstrated her latest feat of lifting each limb in turn, clean off the bed and winding them in three circles, solemnly and painfully, before carefully replacing them. It was as if each member were detached from the rest of her body and required personal concentration.

"He's alright, I think."

"What do you mean 'you think'? Haven't you called him?" Demelza asked in her straight forward way.

"Because I *don't* know – we're not really talking."

"Why? Where is he?"

"I don't actually know, but I assume London."

"What happened?"

"We had the most stupid argument about nothing really worthwhile – but perhaps we're just better off without each other," she answered lamely and somehow ashamed.

"What? So you've split up? I can't believe it."

"Yes, I suppose we have." These two words were ones Connie had deliberately not accepted as relevant to their case and it was a shock having to accept their appropriateness.

"How could you both be so stupid?" Demelza protested: "You were perfect for each other; he was equally mad as you and we all liked him – unlike your ex, Psycho! What's more, I liked his bike – all my friends did. Now you've spoilt that too!" she added peevishly, and she turned over carefully – her newest accomplishment – and closed her eyes in apparent sleep. "Thanks for your support," retorted Connie, but after waiting five minutes, she realised there was going to be no further exchange with her daughter: she was delighted with the progress Demelza was making, but Sebastian's departure had taken the edge off the exultation. She decided to adopt her Scarlet O'Hara protective maxim, virtually unused since the advent of Sebastian, and not to think about this today, but to think about it tomorrow. Therefore, leaving it aside and focussing back on her daughter, she lifted her pointed chin and left the ward. She looked forward to briefing Demelza's sisters about her road towards recovery, for surely it couldn't be too long before she could come home and they could begin to return to normal – what ever normal now was.

Boo telephoned in a level of high octane excitement, even by her standards. The song, 'Connie's Elegy', had moved three more places up the charts – not a rapid enough escalation for a number one (though you never knew!) but at least it was still climbing, with the result that Ken was being offered yet more prestigious work and at a higher fee: this could be the start of his going out as a soloist, which was something he had never envisaged. If this was the case, Boo would need a course from Connie on harmonies for backing vocals, for Boo was determined to be a proper part of the band:

"For all I admire Linda McCartney, she really wasn't much of a singer and I'm far better than that, so if she could do it..."

"Should I be saying one thing at a time and haven't we got a wedding outfit to be considering, etcetera?"

"No. Definitely second place!"

"Good: I'm miles better at backing vocals!"

"Well they can still have a habit of falling apart," put in Boo, mischievously: "talking of which: how is the wonderful, marvellous Sebastian and before you ask: no! We cannot have a double wedding because I want all the limelight for myself!"

"I don't think you should worry about any sort of threat like that – like I'd *want* to share a wedding with you anyway! Let's get back to vocals: you'd need to start with something really simple and just sing a third above the melody. You could hold the line easily – and then the fun will start, and you can get a whole lot more inventive – but Ken will show you."

"*Connie?*" Boo sounded annoyingly like her Aunt, Connie's mother: "Is there something you should be telling me? I asked you about Sebastian and you started gabbling stuff about which I don't understand: tell me everything *is* alright?"

"Not," Connie faltered," As you might say, 'swimmingly'."

"If not swimmingly, then how?" Connie tried again.

"Very well: not very well, thank you for your concern, and can we talk about something else?"

"He was dotty about you – what have you done?"

"And I too – I don't know really. Anyway, what do you mean by 'what have *I done*?' Why does everyone assume it's me? We had an argument and *he's* the one who's left – and I can't cope with someone who runs off every time there's a problem because I, after all, have to stay here, so it's really uneven and unbalanced and unfair and anyway, actually, I have come to the decision that I'm way better off being accountable just to myself and being as single as the day is long!"

"You know I can't decide whether you're a complete prat or whether there isn't a tiny part of me that doesn't fully sympathise with both of you: I'm hard enough for Ken to take on, when I have only two 'ghastlies', and they're both packed away at boarding school, soon to become dazzling adult citizens, but *you!* You have double my numbers, plus they're younger *and* you dote on them so much that when one of them gets ill, you become a total moron to all who care about you. The heroic Sebastian must have experienced an understandable sense of inadequacy!" Connie tried to look at this objectively:

"Actually, I have to say, in his defence, that he never actually showed that I was wearing him down – so probably I took advantage of that and leaned all the more! When I think about it, he did just about everything: school runs, cooking, caring for them – OK, the place may have looked a bit of a tip."

"No change there then."

"Hmm well – it seems that you *have* been a bit of a prat, doesn't it?"

"That's what I was going to say."

"So – about these wedding plans..."

~

Connie arrived at the band practice out of breath, due to parking difficulties and every other thing at home sliding her further into lateness. The band had already begun and were jamming, to fill in time and to aid concentration on the more serious music they were due to cover after Connie's arrival. She heard their music from above ground as a dull thud, but as she ventured down the dark back stairs leading to the little room under the station, it became more distinct and she paused, listening to the new addition of the keyboards and realising that the band certainly had discovered someone with marked talent. In fact, the sound was so complete, she wondered again if perhaps this newcomer might prove sufficient and the others would not welcome her return. After all, they would make less money with an extra player – and if she didn't enhance the sound? Realising that she had seen *herself* as the extra, rather than this new unknown quantity, she shrugged and heaved at the door, which was damp and unwieldy. The players stopped as she entered and, with a shout, rushed forward to welcome her. Only the keyboard player hung back, which was natural, since they had not yet met. Connie advanced to greet him where he sat behind his keyboards, comprising a conventional semi-acoustic piano and a range of synthesisers, and noticed a pair of crutches propped up beside him. Glancing involuntarily downwards, expecting to see a limb in plaster, she saw that his legs were very thin and withered, compared to his robust and muscular top half, and realised that he was disabled. Her smile instantly flicked back to his face, which was grinning broadly through a thick curtain of shoulder-length dark hair, while his eyes danced in perceived merriment at the surprise Connie had striven to hide; for he was evidently much used to similar confused reactions. He was wearing a short black T-shirt, which emphasised his physique of broad shoulders, bulging biceps (down which a dragon tattoo snaked its way from the edge of one sleeve), and what she imagined must have been a definite six pack; for leanness and muscles bunched in all directions. He held out a hand:

"I'm Martin and you must be Connie, about whom I've heard loads." She shook the proffered hand and said she had heard enough to hope he wasn't about to oust her from the band, but he returned the compliment smoothly by saying that he could say the same.

"And how's your daughter getting on?"

"She was a bit slow for a while and she still keeps falling asleep; but she's going to get a wheelchair soon, so she can become mobile, which is really important to her." She faltered, wondering if she had just been tactless, but Martin was naturally accustomed to these situations:

"Don't over-emphasise the mobility," he quipped, "She'll suddenly have to start doing things for herself, and that could be a pain!" he went on kindly. "You may not be aware of just how much you can do from a wheelchair: I was never confined to one, but when I was at secondary school we all used them to play football in: I promise you we were lethal! No biped would have stood a chance with all these over-sexed, undersized teenage paraplegics wheeling around!" He laughed at the memory, revealing a set of very white even teeth with what appeared to be a diamond fixed into one of the incisors. Connie was fascinated at the idea of football on wheels, but decided she shouldn't become personal with her questions too quickly; even though he had begun the discourse. Instead she said that she had taken up enough of their time being late, so how about launching right into the set. Andy, Nigel and Cake resumed their places around the room and took up their instruments and, with four beats tapped in the air by Cake's drum sticks, they were into the first number.

For Connie, returning to playing music after a longer lapse than she had ever had was like releasing a valve: she felt her shoulders sag under the lapse of tension as the other dimension – that of music – reclaimed her, and the rest of her world micromorphed itself into insignificance. Her playing was not technically at its best after her absence, but her voice soared, powerful and true; blending effortlessly with Martin's husky vocal, as each watched the other for the mutual understanding over when to take the melody and where to harmonise.

When a point was reached for each to take a solo, they unanimously nodded at Martin who, realising that particular attention was being paid, launched into a remarkably dexterous break, his long, lean fingers glancing so swiftly over the keys of his *Fender Rhodes* piano. Next, his left hand filled in the bass while his right flew dizzy musical patterns over a synthesiser. Connie looked up, to join the others in exchanging glances conveying their high regard for Martin's abilities: certainly nothing needed to be discussed as to his suitability, for their feeling of awe was unanimous. He finished and caught their expressions.

"OK?" he asked, unnecessarily, to which Andy responded.

"Shit hot!" while Cake spoke simultaneously.

"So cool!"

"So I'm in then?"

"Don't be daft: you're so far in, that we won't let you out!" Connie responded, while Nigel, true to type, sat quietly smiling his approval which did not necessitate words.

They had begun to tackle *Razorlight's* America, a favourite which they saved for towards the end of the set, and Connie was attempting to weave an additional flute melody into the lengthy acoustic guitar introduction, when the door was shoved open again and a willowy looking woman with bright cornflower eyes and sun-bleached hair walked in, apologising for the disturbance. She crossed the room to Martin who kissed her and introduced her as Peggy, their ease with one another making it clear that she was his girlfriend.

"Otherwise known as 'Dog's body'," she laughed: "I carry his gear: he only plays keyboards because they're the most cumbersome instruments and weigh half a ton!" Andy was obviously taken with Peggy's Scandinavian looks and muttered gallantly:

"I would make you a coffee if we had the facilities," to which Cake replied:

"Since when have you ever made anyone a coffee!"

"Well I would if I could – but how about a beer instead?"

"Ah now you're talking - it's about that time and mine's a pint!" returned Cake, whose evasion for buying rounds, due to the frugality imposed by living on benefits, was legendary.

"I was actually talking to Peggy and Martin," replied Andy, a little coldly, embarrassed at his own transparency with women. Peggy was already helping Martin to stow his piano into its case and fold up the piano-stool in what was clearly a well practised procedure: she lugged the front end of the piano by it's heavy-duty handles on the side, while Martin somehow slid his hand through the handle at the other end, using his 'sticks', as he called them (crutches were far more afflicting and came right up to the elbow instead of the hip), to support and manipulate his legs. Andy offered to take one end but was told that they were fine.

"Be careful of those stairs!" he called after them.

"Probably not!" was Peggy's answer: "Martin's for ever falling over."

"Thanks!" replied Martin "I'll try not to let you down." So saying he feigned a slip on the top stair, fooling everyone except Peggy, who asked them if they had built 'These boots *aren't* made for walking', into their set yet.

Once at the bar, Martin bought the first round, easily establishing himself at the centre of the conversation. Peggy perched on a barstool, thus matching Martin's height as he leaned on his sticks. He rapidly drew Connie out, asking her more about Demelza, and she felt completely comfortable talking to him because his questions seemed to stem from informed interest, rather than embarrassed politeness, which was the norm. He was soon fascinating her with tales of his own history of becoming mobile:

"I was born like this – totally spastic – so in those days it was just assumed that it wasn't really worth trying for a progression, but once I was about eighteen months I began to be able to kind of pull myself along, like a monkey – and on my fifth birthday I was given this little toy push along car, and once I was inside it, I could move it about, not just with my arms, but a bit with my legs! Wow! After that was discovered, I lost a lot of power over siblings! It was all 'Oh, get it yourself!' and before I knew it, I was whisked off to 'special school', where they eventually got me walking with these!" He waved a stick at her and Connie was struck again by the enormity of his shoulders in comparison to the rest of him, and a sudden unbidden thought of Sebastian's vast chest ("So nuzzle-worthy!" she had always said), loomed icily into her mind, before she shrugged it off and returned to concentrate on what Martin was saying.

"Once she's mobile they'll be pleased to free up the bed at the hospital and you'll really have your hands full."

"Well I can't wait to have my hands full then," replied Connie, happy at his optimism and his daring to talk of Demelza's home coming as a definite occurrence.

"Of course you'll have to be around her all day to start with: is there a Mr Connie lurking to help out?" Peggy remonstrated at his nosiness,

"What's wrong? You don't mind, do you? Anyway, I bet there is!"

"Actually – sadly – not." Connie heard herself answer, the realisation at the truth of this striking her painfully. Immediately Andy made it clear that he had been listening by chipping in:

"Yes I had heard. Didn't like to say anything – but I'm sorry about Sebastian. Running out when you most needed him – really hard, but better to know he could be like that than get further involved." Connie wheeled round at him:

"We *were* involved – very really and he didn't 'run out' as you put it. We just didn't *work* out. In fact – I rather drove him away!" Andy coloured: spending his days regularly renewing the box of tissues on his desk, used by his potential divorcees, had not furnished him with the tact that should have been instinct:

"Sorry – obviously touched a nerve. That is I just assumed…"

"Andy: never assume!" answered Connie "And as a matter of fact,

I don't know how we'd have got through the first part of Demelza's accident without him." Andy, remembering this time the need for sensitivity, swallowed the retort that 'Demelza's Demise' might be a worthy title for a song and Martin cut in smoothly:

"You must have lost a lot of work – and you'll lose still more when she's home: how about we do a benefit concert for her?" Connie beamed at him:

"She'd absolutely love that. Mind you! What she really likes is garage rock and Heavy Metal. She just tolerates what we do – but I know she'd still love it if we could." Nigel was at her elbow, smiling his enthusiasm and Andy was wishing he had thought of this himself:

"I could run off some fliers and posters at work." Andy offered. "All we need is a date and a venue."

"Maybe our paddock?" answered Connie tentatively, "That would keep it small enough not to bother about security, so we could restrict tickets to strictly friends and 'friends of'. As for the money – if you guys are good enough to do it for nothing, *I* certainly wouldn't want to benefit, but maybe we could give the proceeds to the hospital."

"For the spineless!" suggested Martin, who, they were quickly coming to realise, seemed to use his disability to make outrageous utterances that would sit badly with others.

By the time the landlord called 'last orders' the benefit gig was pretty much in the bag, in the minds of those concerned, and Connie sped home in the hopes that at least Ella might be awake so that she might tell her the news. She had become used to Sebastian, an adult, being there for her to discuss things with at her own level, just as she had counted on Tramp's welcome as she ascended the stairs: but soon there would be Demelza in a wheelchair! That would also take some adjusting to – Connie was beginning to wonder just how many more alterations she would have to accommodate into her concertina'd lifestyle. *This is beginning to feel like juggling with jelly!* she thought.

Chapter Twenty-eight

Connie took her turn in the shower, singing It's Such a Perfect Day, for it *was* a perfect day for a wedding, and the race was on for them all – all except Demelza – to be ready spruced before the tedious journey to the little village outside Ramsgate, where Boo lived. They wore everyday clothes, carrying their carefully selected wedding glad-rags in bags in the 'doggie compartment' at the back of the car. (It had to be admitted that the absence of Tramp on this occasion made everything far easier!) Ella and Connie had new dresses and Sophia and Poppy had barely used hand-me-downs. Without Demelza, no one felt strongly enough to point out the obvious advantage that Ella, being the eldest, held over them; in terms of always being the one with the new clothes!

Eventually, everyone was sparkling clean and ready, even at this ungodly hour, for they had elected to do the journey 'on the day', instead of staying with Boo's family the night before. That would have been fun, but it was turned down unanimously, in favour of being able to maximise the time spent with Demelza beforehand; since she was going to miss the wedding. Connie felt strangely unsettled at leaving the close environs of Brigstow, since she had not ventured beyond since the accident, but the news from the hospital had heartened them all, for they said she would be ready to come home soon; as long as her daily physiotherapy was adhered to. Stuart had agreed to drop in on her on the day of the wedding, with Fifi and Sue; so Demelza had something to look forward to and should feel less left out.

The journey was as dull, slow and uneventful as expected and after a few brief games of *Spot the yellow car* and *I Spy,* played by Sophia and Poppy, followed by *Spot the geek,* played by Ella, who quietly missed Demelza's noisy and revelatory contributions; the children fell into the torpor created by the motion of transport, caused, apparently, by the speed at which the landscape passed the eye.

The sleepy little Kent village to which they eventually arrived, contrasted with Boo's greeting: she steamed out of the cottage, glass of champagne in hand, wearing a bright, multi-coloured Japanese silk dressing gown with trainers:

"At last you're here – we couldn't wait, so Samantha has very kindly poured out a pick-me-up to steady my nerves! Come in, come in, grab a glass. Pour it *slowly*, Samantha, or the froth will – oops *told* you…! There it goes – well, cheers anyway! Here's to – *me!*" She upended her glass, "*and* you!" she countered.

"You and *I*, Mummy," put in Jules, in a weary voice as she winked at her young cousins and began to pour two more glasses for herself and Ella.

"I say Jules: what are you doing? Only *one* glass each – it wouldn't do to be squiffy before the wedding… *Mind you, I seem to be doing a pretty good job!*" she whispered in an undertone to Connie, as she tipped the frothing liquid carelessly down her throat and added "Well *squitty* actually – I'm so overwrought. I know you couldn't come last night, but it might have been better for my health if you had!"

"Worse for mine!" answered Connie, pulling the glass from Boo's hand and drinking it herself, "Now I think one of the best woman's jobs is to deliver the bride to the church relatively sober – even if it means sacrificing herself," she added, taking another short swig before attempting to take command of the situation:

"Right girls: clothes from the car, and isn't it the turn of the ravishing young bridesmaids to have the bathroom first and then strut their stuff, while the bride and I vacate to the bedroom? Sophia: why not put the kettle on for a sobering cup of coffee?"

"Hang on I'm starving and we've made some delicious canapés to munch as we dress," called Boo, scuttling through to the kitchen and delving in the fridge, from whence she emerged triumphantly, carrying some smoked trout open sandwiches.

"Should work as blotting paper, don't you think?" she asked, as she tore hungrily at the soft brown bread and jigged around the kitchen excitedly, twirling before the mirror to see how well the 'non-surgical face lift' had taken, on her (in any case invisible) crows' feet. Samantha had managed to pour herself a glass of champagne during her mother's caper and she and Jules shot a quick significant glance for their cousins to follow them with their dresses and a handful of sandwiches.

The next two hours consisted of squeals of fun and delight, as each admired one another's dresses, as they twirled and pirouetted to the greatest advantage. Boo had intended to have Connie's dress especially made for her, but since Connie had been unable to visit the dress-maker Boo had instructed Connie that anything in indigo would suit her own colour scheme, which consisted of a brilliant orange that only Boo could have carried off, with her creamy English-rose complexion. The hairdresser had experienced difficulty in matching the exact shade on Boo's spiky locks, but it was done to her satisfaction and gleamed in the June sunshine.

"You look like a May Queen," remarked Poppy.

"Only twice as pretty!" added Boo.

"Yes – I *think* so." Poppy went on thoughtfully, unable to comprehend the laughter that so many of her serious remarks seemed to incur. Jules and Samantha, Boo's unquenchable bridesmaids, were wearing orange too, but in rather paler shades:

"I couldn't afford them upstaging me!" confided Boo, but Connie replied that there was not a chance and became swamped by an overwhelming feeling of affection for her staunch cousin. She kissed her carefully on the cheek, so as not to spoil the make-up and announced that it was time to get to the church on time.

"Of course we're married already," Boo said carelessly as everyone gaped: "Yesterday at the register office, but we are taking no advantage of it, if you know what I mean, until after the Blessing, which is now." Connie let out a sigh of understanding as she looked admiringly at the line of girls, their hair gleamingly groomed, and their faces radiating fresh youth and verve. It was especially thrilling for her to see Poppy in a *dress*: perhaps because none of the older girls seemed to dislike putting them on, Poppy had put her own on without the usual moans (although she had confided to Sophia that she wasn't sure what all the fuss was about, when, after all, lady pheasants were far prettier than *any* of their dresses, and lady pheasants were basically brown).

It had been the shoes that posed the problem. Connie had forgotten these until two days before the wedding and they had all invaded a small shop in Brigstow *en masse* and hastily purchased bright little slippers in brocade, dotted with sequins to match their dresses. Poppy had been forced to go through Sophia's rather meagre wardrobe to find a dress suitable for herself: no one had taken a lot of notice at her choice, so she had stuffed an unremarkable denim pinafore dress which had fitted her, into a bag and simply got on with it. She was doing more of that these days – being unremarkable, she thought, because no one noticed her any more, due to the Demelza topic, and it was something for which she was really quite glad. She looked at her mother in her indigo silk from *Monsoon*, and thought that, in fact, if she wasn't her mother she would actually be quite nice looking as things went. Her mother's hair, the flame red dye having paled somewhat now, was brushed sleekly from her forehead and she wore a matching pearl pendant and earrings, set off by the pale honey colour of her bare arms. She stood awkwardly and, with a sudden flash of intuition beyond her years, she wondered if her mother didn't feel as out of place in all this garb, and without Demelza, as she did?

Two white cars had arrived at the cottage gates, adorned with orange ribbons, one containing Boo's mother, looking resplendent in navy, topped by a huge hat which sported a peacock's feather. Poppy became caught up in the excitement, tempered with her secret sadness that Sebastian was not there to admire them and make them feel 'right'. She watched her cousins' obvious joy at the sight of their grandmother and wished that her own grandmother had been with her sister, grinning and laughing and admiring them all. She decided to visualise her, sitting on a soft bouncy cloud, wearing pearls and watching all the proceedings.

"I bet even *she's* fed up that Mummy messed up with Sebastian," she thought sadly. Sophia, standing shyly beside Poppy, poised for kissing her great-aunt, heard Poppy's involuntary sigh and interpreted it correctly. She squeezed her sister's hand very quickly while no one was looking and whispered fiercely:

"*Don't let it show: it's going to be better soon,*" she was unspecific about what she meant, but somehow an intuitive brightness warmed them both as they climbed into the back of the large car, lifting their skirts high off the floor to reveal the twinkling shoes, and becoming once more infected by the high spirits all around them.

Ken sat in his pew, his long dark hair so gleaming that it reflected the colours of the stained glass window. He wore a cream suit and shoes, which Boo had picked out because she said she wanted him to look every inch a retro-rock star and to give all her friends everything they had hoped to gawp at and more! He had demurred at her suggestion of a large pair of reflective Bono sunglasses, however, but agreed reluctantly to a splendid, swirly silk handkerchief for his welted breast pocket. He still found himself slightly dazed at his change in attitude towards commitment and marriage; for it was something he found himself looking forward to as nothing before. He had certainly enjoyed the carefree hedonism that his music had facilitated thus far: it was simply that it just didn't interest him as a way of life any more. He heard a commotion in the porch and Boo's unmistakeable pealing laughter and felt his stomach turn over. The wedding march began in a somewhat freer style than would have been expected (the organ being played by a mate who owed him a favour), and this made everyone smile in surprise. He turned to see Boo, looking more stunning than anyone could imagine, clutching a posy of orange roses and wearing the flounciest of tiered apricot, grinning cheesily all the while!

After the frolics and register signing in the vestry, the organ thundered a florid interpretation of Handel's Hallelujah chorus, and Ken caught Connie's eye for the first time:

"Where'd you get him?" she asked, referring to the organist,

"Isn't he so shit hot? We played together at the Apollo, a couple of months ago," laughed Ken, and Boo's mother recoiled, tapping Ken on the nose:

"Now, Sonny: we'll have none of that sort of language in church," she said reprovingly, but with a hint of a twinkle as she waggled a finger at him. As yet Ken wasn't entirely sure how to take his new mother-in-law's humour and quickly apologised, as his father gallantly proffered his arm. She took it with a demure inclination of the head and a hint of coquetry, as each couple lined up to file out. The best man was a drummer, Alan, whom Connie had met briefly when Ken had toured with him. Connie took his arm, thrilling at the tumultuous music (for the organ was swelled on full throttle!), and the tangible exultance, experienced by two of her favourite people. However, suddenly the tune had changed and three long-haired men, dressed in distinguished pale grey morning suits, stood up, as did the organist:

"Ba-ba-ba-ba boo!" they sang, in 'do-wap' accompaniment to the organist, who began the main vocal line of 'Crazy Little Thing called Love'. Connie looked more carefully at the excellent backing trio and then did a double take as she noticed *Bryan Ferry* was one of the singers. Connie had last seen him on stage in Worcester, where Ken was sessioning with him in a concert: although she had met Ken backstage, she had never managed to clap a close eye on Bryan, which had been galling to say the least. However, here another chance had been presented, and she promised herself a closer inspection this time – possibly a conversation even – at the reception. She wouldn't introduce herself – that would be far too crass and she would probably trip up or stammer – but perhaps Boo…? (A spot of Dutch courage would be needed of course: easily arranged!) Meanwhile Boo and Ken were dancing down the aisle to the music, swooping and sweeping like a pair of peacocks!

As Connie followed their lead, she glanced happily to right and left, taking in familiar faces and winking proudly at her decorous daughters in their pew near the front. She suddenly noticed another familiar face – this time one whom she knew personally – and she gaped in disbelief. The face responded with a delighted grin: it was Pete, her ex before Sebastian and known as *Psycho* to her children – not without reason. It was only a moment and then she was past him, grateful now for the absence of Demelza who would have been loudly cheeky; but fearful for Ella, whom he had enticed with alcohol and spliffs, in order to get news of her mother's activities and whereabouts after they had split up. This had been a strict secret which had somehow outed itself during Demelza's incarceration, to become common knowledge amongst the children.

Outside the little church, the bells were pealing and confetti, in the form of orange rose petals, floated through the air in lazy response to frenzied hurling by well-wishers. Cameras clicked and flashed and Ken had for some reason lifted Boo right off the ground and whirled her for the photographers, some of whom were paparazzi, seduced by the current interest in 'Connie's Elegy'. Connie felt oddly detached from the joyous throng, her plastic smile determinedly fixed to her face: what she wanted to do was to ask Boo how Pete came to be there; but now was definitely not the time. She wondered at what point Ella would see him and how she would react, for as far as they knew he had gone to the Far East and would not be hurrying back, but then – when had Pete ever stuck to anything he said he was going to do?

More and more people spilled outside into the watery sunshine, and with them Pete. Connie watched, as shutters continued to flash and as her daughters, from the front of the church, filed out last. They were looking around delightedly at the spectacle of Boo horsing around and their mother being photographed. She waved at them and, as if in slow motion, saw Poppy's wave stop mid air and her mouth form the word 'Pete' as she pointed and hustled her way over to him, tapping him on the arm. He smiled that flashy smile, exposing even, white teeth, set off by gold fillings, and bent down to her level to talk to her. Connie caught Ella's eye and lifted her own to the skies in a gesture of disbelief, but at this point, mercifully, the crowd had begun to move; for the wedding cars had inched forward to take bride, groom and their closest entourage to the reception. Connie gestured to her scattered children to go to the car, in doing so again catching the eye of Pete, who flashed his engaging smile again as Connie grimaced one back in acknowledgement.

Once in the car, the mayhem ceased momentarily as Ken and Boo sat in the centre kissing and admiring one another. Boo began to explain about the line-up when they arrived at the reception, and to discuss the turns the children must take in making sure that their Great-Great Aunt Agatha was plied with everything: she was deaf, and preferred to watch the goings on from a distance. She didn't want to attempt to join in, she had instructed, because she wouldn't understand a word anyone said, which would prove embarrassing for *them* not for her, because she was used to it. She was a game old lady and wouldn't miss a family occasion for anything: always making it abundantly clear when she had had enough, by falling asleep in her chair, head nodding, ill-fitting teeth gaping and loud snores escaping. Someone would be dispatched to cover the frail old lady with a warm rug until she awoke with a snort, saying loudly that she hoped she hadn't missed anything.

Ella muttered to Connie:

"Seen who's here?" and Connie nodded, replying in the same undertone that she was sorry.

"Why? Did you know he was coming?"

"Certainly not!" Connie replied, appalled at the notion that she would have kept such a thing from Ella.

"Mum – it was so long ago. I've grown a lot since then. Do me a favour and stop looking at me as though it *so* matters." To Connie it seemed like the proverbial yesterday; but Ella's life had moved on a year, which represented so much more to a child and she was right that she *had* grown up a lot: what with one thing and another it could almost be said to be too much. Thus the whole 'Pete episode' was just a disagreeable chapter in her childhood which she would prefer to be forgotten. Connie was relieved beyond measure by this, as she listened with half an ear to the rest of the chatter.

Standing in the line-up, in turn shaking hands with those to whom she was introduced and kissing those she knew, she noticed her Aunt Belinda and Uncle Gerald, who were weaving their way towards her. Uncle Gerald had somehow already made friends with one of the waiters whom he called over immediately to replenish Connie's empty glass. Aunt Belinda was wearing a tasteful lilac affair and the family amethysts, which set her gown off splendidly, while Uncle Gerald wore a many coloured silk waistcoat beneath his morning dress. They hugged everyone and asked after Demelza, offering to stay and look after her and the house so that Connie could take a break. Connie replied that it would be lovely if they could stay, but that they really didn't want a break.

"We knew you'd say that, you know, but I wish you would because you look very pretty of course, darling, but *peaky,* if you don't mind my saying. *Doesn't* she look peaky, Gerald?"

"Oh yes of course – splendid!" answered Uncle Gerald promptly, as some particularly appetising canapés caught his eye and he smiled engagingly at his waiter to bring them right over.

"Gerald – you're not listening to me – I said that Connie seemed a little *peaky.*"

"Oh dear me yes – you do, now you mention it: splendid, but definitely a little peaky. I think you'd better try one of these, my dear – that'll peak you up!"

"Why thank you both of you!" responded Connie, fondly amused rather than concerned, "and Demelza said particularly to ask how the Morgan is bowling, because she thinks that when she's better you will give her a ride!"

"Well she's in fine fettle, a little thirsty on the way of course – so many ups and downs – but she's tuned to a tee and we had an extraordinarily good run. Where's Great-Aunt Agatha, by the way?

Has anybody fed her? D'you think I'd better busy my nice waiter to seek her out?"

"She's all sorted: the children are taking it in turns to attend her with champagne and fodder until she finds a snooze coming on."

"And you've got a rug for the old girl? You have? First rate organisation! We must remember to slip her a bottle of the Parsnip: we've had such a good year for parsnip wine!" Uncle Gerald enthused, "And if the champagne runs dry, you'll have to come down to the car with us for a little snifter – in fact Connie should have a bottle, shouldn't she, Belinda old thing? That'll stop the peaky thing."

"Really, I don't feel especially peaky – just a bit tired sometimes – but the hospital is discharging Demelza soon, and then I know I'll sleep more easily, in spite of wheelchair problems."

"Where's that nice young man you told us about?" asked Belinda, gazing around her. "We need to be introduced – he may like the parsnip too." Aunt Belinda knew her mistake at the sight of Connie's face and before she could answer:

"Oh, my dear I'm so sorry. Couldn't he come?"

"I'm afraid it's actually worse than that – we sort of, didn't work out."

"Oh too dreadful, just when you particularly needed someone: better to get it sorted out early on though, I suppose," Aunt Belinda ventured a motherly arm around Connie's slim shoulders: "My goodness! You're all skin and bone! The child must eat: Gerald! More of those... yes these here! Thank you, Waiter, if you would kindly leave the plate just here near my niece? Much obliged, so kind!" Over the next few minutes, caviar on cream cheese in a puff pastry case melted down their throats, after which Boo and Ken had swooped on Connie:

"Are you having a wonderful time?"

"I should be asking *you* that, but the answer's obvious: what a hunky couple you make!" Boo giggled.

"D'you know that's practically word for word what *Hello* magazine said!"

"Well it's what we told them to say – and it was 'funky'," laughed Ken.

"And they're here all because of your flaming *Elegy*!" said Boo, in mock anger at Connie.

"But I didn't write it, record it *or* have much to do with it," protested Connie, remembering fondly her quick fling with Ken, from which it had resulted: "It was really just waiting for *you*, but for the name! Maybe I do have the edge over that – 'Boo' wouldn't have quite the same ring somehow!" she teased.

"Anyway, without *Hello* this shindig might have taken place in a hut," countered Ken.

"Did you see Bryan Ferry?" asked Boo, *sotto voce*.

"I should think I did – you know I'm an enormous fan."

"I'm going to introduce you!"

"That's what I was hoping – I can't believe I'm going to be able to eyeball the singer of Avalon and Love's a Drug!" Boo looked across to where a knot of people surrounded what seemed to be him and prepared to interrupt, as only the Bride could, and Connie panicked:

"But wait, Boo... I'm not quite ready yet – I think I may need just one more of these," she indicated to her glass, "before I dare even *look!* But just for now I'll settle for looking at you two: I really don't think I've ever seen you look more lovely – or *happy!*" She hugged her cousin and friend delightedly, an arm around each.

"You know what? I wouldn't expect to ever feel this, but I would've married Ken in a veritable yurt!" trilled Boo. Connie replied that marriage to Ken had changed Boo's outlook already, while Ken cooed that actually he would be quite prepared to marry Boo in the bath, to which Boo responded that she couldn't have all those gorgeous women seeing all his bits, for they were all hers; and Connie said she was going to be in need of a sick bucket if she were to hear any more. Boo stopped suddenly:

"Are you OK though?" Connie wondered if she should hedge, but this would take longer because Boo would get it out of her in the end.

"I was a bit taken aback at seeing Pete," she explained, "but of course it's up to you who you invite." There was a pause, during which Connie wished she had at least *attempted* hedging.

"Ken ran into him at a place he was playing – well more exactly Pete ran into Ken. He came around the back and introduced himself as a 'fellow ex-suitor', actually, which kind of annoyed me – but you know Pete. Anyway, Ken didn't know the extent of the story – thought Pete looked a bit on the dejected side and asked him – verbally, mind: he didn't get an invitation – to the wedding."

"Boo told me later, when I happened to mention it to her, and I'm sorry; but by then the damage was done."

"It's OK," Connie said, in a noble attempt to make this sound true, "really I was more bothered about Ella, but she says she doesn't mind. It was just a bit of a shock, that's all."

"You're thinking I might have told you," interpreted Boo correctly, and as Connie began to protest she went on, "and I should have. But everything's been so crap for you, I didn't want to load on any dread about today: I hoped, once you saw him, you'd just get over it and it would be average OK," she said lamely. Connie made a big effort:

"And you know what? It is OK. It's all in the past and I expect we'll have a good chat when I've had a few more of these," she gestured to her glass, which was empty again. "I'm having such a good time seeing you two, the family – everyone – that nothing's going to get in my way! One more of these and I'll be ready for my introduction to Bryan F."

"And if he *does* try to hassle you, you just let me know," said Ken, completely failing to look menacing and they all laughed.

Connie allowed her glass to be refilled and tottered gently from one group of family and friends to the next and inevitably, before too long, Pete was at her elbow:

"Connie!" he said loudly, as if in surprise: "Fancy seeing you!"

"You took the words right out of my mouth," she answered ironically. "How was Sri Lanka and how long are you here for?" Pete shook his floppy baby hair across his dreadfully handsome features and laughed:

"Not trying to get rid of me already I hope!" Connie winced a smile: "Actually it turned out to be Singapore – never even got to Sri Lanka – didn't need to – got some amazing stuff – watches in particular – *what* a deal!" he tapped the side of his nose significantly, and Connie saw from the size of his irises that there was something more than champagne that was buoying him up.

"Anyway," he went on easily, "poor old you! What a rough time you've been having by all accounts. When I heard about Demelza I very nearly sent a card, but I thought you might still be cross with me. You're not though, are you?" He was wearing his 'little boy lost' expression that was so comical it was hard to resist. He saw its effect and quickly pressed his advantage: "Because you know I'd really like to put all that behind me."

"Me too," answered Connie, eager not to have to refer to it.

"And I heard you had another man and he left too!"

"It wasn't quite like that," defended Connie,

"Yes but how awful, when you were so upset already – I would never have done such a thing!"

"It *wasn't* quite like that!" Connie repeated, with more emphasis. Pete held up a hand:

"Peace, peace – I come in peace," he said, "but I do need you to know that – well if I can be of any help – any at all – I'll be there like greased lightening!"

"Thank goodness!" Connie laughed at the absurdity of his offer, but even in her own tipsy state, she needed her message to be clear: "but really we're doing fine and we have all the help we need. Thanks though," she added as she witnessed his face fall. The thanking was a mistake, for they represented a straw and Pete snatched at it hastily:

"Care for a spliff?" he asked suddenly, hitching back the lining of his morning dress to reveal a veritable army of ready-mades.

"Definitely not," answered Connie, "and don't let anyone see you with that lot either!" This was another mistake.

"Ah – I see you do still care! You see I could sort of move nearby and help out with the children –" Connie heard his words through the mist of alcohol and flared at him:

"Never. Ever. Have you got that? Never, ever come near my children again: we can put the whole thing behind us but I'm sorry – I will never forget and I'll always want you to stay away!" People close to them turned at the sound of vehemence in her voice and Pete tried to shrug it off:

"OK, OK: I only offered that's all." Connie felt another sudden yen for Sebastian's solid presence – had he been here, as previously planned, Pete would never have thought in his all-be-it well intentioned way, to re-open the wound. She mustn't feel the need of a man, she told herself sternly, each time she got herself out of her depth, and turning she shook Pete's hand:

"Look, it's been good to talk to you again and I'm glad things are going well, but please let's not discuss *that* ever again, OK?" Pete was just about to repeat that actually this did show that she couldn't help caring and that maybe one day, if not today – but he had learned one or two things from this experience and he closed his mouth again, instead suggesting that actually, perhaps, she might prefer a cup of tea? The swing around took Connie by surprise, as did the delightfulness of the idea, and she almost laughed as she accepted and saw Pete's figure disappear hastily from view in search of a nice cup of tea for her, via, no doubt, a quick visit to the Gents to do away with another member of the army!

The afternoon drifted speedily into evening and, when Connie felt properly ready for her musical conversation with Bryan Ferry, she discovered, on enquiry, that he had slipped quietly and inconspicuously away – probably while she had been talking with Pete!

"Foiled Again!" she moaned, "But perhaps I should have made a fool of myself and had to live with and regret it for ever... at least now I can go on dreaming about tomorrow!" An odd feeling of relief overcame her as she allowed her glass another re-fill: now she didn't need to save any coherence for Bryan, and instead became absorbed by the band, with which Ken could not resist joining for a quick jam! Boo stood swaying directly in front of him and Connie was unsure if the swaying was to the music or the alcohol. She put her arm around her cousin's comfortable shoulders, as photographers from *Hello!* snaked around them, vying for the photograph most worthy of stealing mass appeal.

"Don't wake me up," said Boo. "I know this can't last for ever – real live happiness sort of dips in and dips out, doesn't it? And if I went on fancying him to this intensity I'd be frazzled in a year or so!"

"Hang on to it; hang on for ever and ever."

"Amen!... I mean – you know when I call my children *ghastlies* it's only a form of endearment because I can't – I can't really express how much I actually adore them," she confided, wrinkling her nose in her efforts to find the right words, in spite of – or perhaps because of the alcohol she had imbibed – and then out came the truth of the matter: "They've all been so brilliant: I love them all so much and I'm so *hap - py*!" This final triumphant word was trumpeted in true Boo style and tears sprang from eyes as she whooped and grabbed Connie's hands, spinning her around and lifting her orange flouncy skirt in the manner of an Irish jig. Ken's eyes were focused adoringly on her and a historic moment took place, for he carefully propped the guitar he had been playing against the speaker stack and left the band mid-song to encircle Boo's waist and join her dance.

Jules, Samantha and Ella had managed to consume enough champagne to make them very giggly as they watched the antics on the dance floor: Jules and Samantha's grandmother managing a brisk foxtrot with a dapper old fellow, distinguished by silvery-blue hair; the swallow tail of his jacket billowing out behind his knees as he whisked her spryly through a variety of impressive manoeuvres. Uncle Gerald and Aunt Belinda were jigging jollily to the band, though they privately wondered why the music had to be *quite* so loud when there was no evidence that anyone in the band was hard of hearing. Great Aunt Agatha, however, was dozing comfortably through it all, the rug fitted snugly over the old lady's knees, her glass and a plate of tempting goodies on a table within reach, for when she re-awoke.

Pete was dancing alone and had been given a necessarily wide berth, since he was limbo-ing dangerously backwards under an imaginary line – real perhaps to him – while doing his special manoeuvre, where he depicted concentric circles in the air with his fingers, each hand propelled in the opposite direction. Ella and Jules were having an animated, somewhat squealed, discussion, resulting at last in their shoving Samantha in the direction of Pete. She looked back at the other two for reassurance and they squealed some more and gestured for her to go on. Pete looked at her in surprise and began to dance with yet more energy, thinking that she wished to join him; but gradually he realised that Samantha was asking him something. He bent exaggeratedly low to discover what she was saying, putting a helpful hand to his ear. She giggled and looked at the others again, who mouthed '*Go on!*'

"Hm, I wondered," Samantha spluttered, as Pete moved his other hand to join the first beside his right ear, "I wondered have you got any *crack?*" she asked as innocently as she could, while her sister and cousin, realising she had done it by his expression, doubled up laughing at her daring.

"I'm afraid I haven't got any of *that,* young lady," he answered, his face a picture of regret, but I –"

"No cracked wheat? Because I really like it – on my cereal with milk and sugar," sparkled the mischievous Samantha. Pete's mouth formed a gaping 'O' as he struggled to take in this one. In his euphoric state he was unsure how much of a *faux pas* he had made, so he smiled benignly and said that he, too, of a morning, occasionally rather enjoyed the odd bowlful himself. Samantha could hold herself together no longer and blew an undignified and explosive raspberry, mixed with the champagne she had just taken into her mouth; thus performing what was known at home as 'the elephant trick', as she hastened back to the others.

"You did it, you did it!" they cried.

"Oh – it's all going down my nose!" was Samantha's reply, as they shook with hysterical giggles. Pete looked after Samantha and saw that she was with Ella, to whom he had behaved so badly in that other life that he preferred to put behind him. He shrugged: *I suppose that was fair karma,* he said to himself, before deciding he deserved another visit to the Gents. He deftly picked up a glass of champagne as he passed a table and, taking a generous swig, looked once again in the direction of the hysterical gaggle of teenagers:

"Even stevens!" he called amiably and continued on his way.

$$\sim$$

In the small hours, after the ecstatic Boo had pointedly hurled her bouquet at Connie as she and Ken swept from the front of the Georgian manor house amidst gales of good wishes, and after Connie had dropped it; the family and Boo's daughters returned to Boo's cottage to snatch a few hours sleep before the arduous journey homewards.

Connie lay in Boo's bed, strewn still with the chaos of the morning and dotted with champagne flutes, some still half full, while Poppy was already flat out beside her. Boo's cat lay contentedly curled up in the folds of Boo's florescent Japanese dressing-gown, near where Connie had tossed her own dress. An impulse moved her to reach for her mobile, which had remained hidden within the folds of the dress just in case of an emergency. Sure enough, the little window winked the icon of a text, and it was from Demelza: all tiredness left her as she fumbled with tiny scroll keys for her Inbox, imagining a set-back, a fall – or worse – a relapse!

Coolest news ever! They r letting me home Tues! So oh! happy! Cant w8. How weddin? C U 2 moz
Luv u, D. XXXXXXXX

Wow! Can't take it in! All ecstatic. C U 2day! Yahoo! Weddin 1derful but missed u so! Can't sleep now! Only 3 more days! Loveumore, Mum

Connie lay there musing and beaming, as she observed the pink dancing lights of dawn steal through the chiffon curtains: this *had* turned out to be an almost perfect day.

Chapter Twenty-nine

Everyone refused to go to school, for they all wanted to be there: Connie had decked the hall with early summer flowers, the fragrance of which should be extra sensuous after the anti-septic smells of hospital. They had heaved Demelza's bed down the two flights of stairs into the playroom, which had received a face-lift, involving paint and the removal of a variety of old plastic toys, redundant for years, from where they had been stowed beneath the piano. CDs had been brought down and some of Demelza's favourite books; and they had swapped the current table for one more suitable for school work, for latterly Demelza had surprised everyone by putting in much time and effort into this, which was in turn marked and returned by her teachers. At first she had not been interested in catching up and considered her confinement a great excuse to lie and listen to music all day. Then suddenly, as with her determination with the physiotherapy, she had begun to work. The reason was not intrinsic interest in any subject, but a determination not to have to stay down a year at school and be separated from all her friends. That, she reasoned, would also result in her having to spend an extra year in school: not a thing she relished at all. The piano remained, for there was nowhere to which it could be shifted, and so did the familiar, tattered armchairs, which had acted as host to the family and hoards of friends over the years. The family had become so carried away that even the windows were cleaned, for they felt Demelza would need as much light as possible, and as they scraped away the murk of recent years it became clear that this job was necessary everywhere because it made such a difference:

"I am not going to wash the curtains: that would be taking things too far," protested Connie; but she discovered them in the next wash, the work of a triumphant Sophia aided by a step ladder.

The next thing they turned themselves to, on the evening before Demelza was due, was welcoming food: strictly party fodder which, they reasoned, was all fat and carbohydrate and just what was required to put flesh back on Demelza's wasted limbs. The children asked if they could go to the delicatessen (to which they had not returned since the departure of Sebastian, because it was so much more expensive). There they chose many of the foods he would bring home by the arm-full, consisting of seafood pâtés, sun-dried tomato dips, crusty brown loaves, banana bread, chocolate brownies and little tiny jars of locally made jams and jellies of extraordinary mixtures, involving elderflowers and rosehips, made by *Cranfield's*. Finally, Connie and Ella had set about making an enormous cake, and Poppy and Sophia had iced it with the words 'Welcome Home D,' there being no further room for her full name.

"And we should have egg sandwiches!" announced Connie, "Because she won't have had proper home eggs in all that time."

Thus, the day was spent in fuss, preparation and rising excitement for the family, while Demelza – the object of their labours – fiddled and exercised, too on edge to read or even settle to listening to her music. The physiotherapist came with final instructions and several sheets of paper with regard to the exercises and the frequency in which to do them:

"You haven't got rid of me, you know," she said, "because I shall be coming out three times a week to check on your progress and make sure everything is working as it should be." There were several visits from consultants and housemen, who each checked over the same areas and asked identical questions. Demelza felt they were almost reluctant to see her go and she felt very odd, for this had been her lair – she couldn't exactly think of it as 'home' – for over half a year and, longing as she was to return to her family, she was secretly almost afraid of leaving the routine: the cups of tea (she had never drunk tea before coming here and now she was addicted to the stuff), her wash while the bed was made, the banter with the nurses, the consultants' frowns, the excitement of selecting her meals from a menu and pouring over the dietetic value of each item, and her visiting times with friends and family. She had become so close to some of the staff, who had shown interest not simply in her physical welfare, but in herself too. She was actually going to miss some of this in a funny kind of way, and she felt strangely disorientated.

At last she could hear her family coming clattering up the stairs and she felt suddenly shy – they did not know the individual who had lived apart from them, who had cried for the time she had lost, sleeping in a coma from which people had feared she would never awaken. She had cried from fear and frustration when she had awoken and not been able to lift her hand from the sheet. She had cried useless, feeble tears at seeing her sisters leave here with her mother to go to her home, and being unable to be there too. She had even cried for her rabbit and for the fact that Poppy was probably looking after him so much better than she ever did, so that he would now love Poppy better than herself. This was all her private secret life that she hadn't shared with her family – and now they were here, overjoyed to bring her back again as one of them; and they were seeing her cry when they were so happy – Demelza, who never cried: how could she explain what she didn't understand herself?

"I'm sorry – I don't know why I'm doing this," she wailed, as her mother thrust bunches of flowers into her hands to give to her favourite nurses and consultant.

"It's OK, it's OK – we're crying too," blubbed her mother, and Demelza looked up to see that this was true in varying degrees, for all of them; even Ella, who had missed her company probably most of all her sisters. So they all understood, or thought they did, and it was going to be all right. She gave the flowers to the nurses, who also looked tearful and said they would miss her and her music. One of them gave her a life-sized plastic head of *Baz Tard*, who was wearing a transparent bath hat, such as they gave you at hotels, and had for some reason blacked out one of his teeth, so that he looked cooler than ever.

Finally, Demelza put the brake on her wheelchair and levered herself into it. Each of her family instinctively sprang, ready to help, and then remembered what they had been told by the liaison lady, who had emphasised how important it was that they let Demelza do things on her own at her own pace "or you'll be making rods for all your backs, especially Demelza's." She had taken much time getting into the going home clothes that she had selected, horrified at how loose and baggy her old favourites had become. Her mother had put it that she had grown, which was true, and that therefore they would need to buy replacements. *No mention of my wearing Ella's stuff then,* Demelza had thought gratefully: *she knows that I'd float in them – and that would upset Ella, as well as me!*

They all squashed into the lift with Demelza, no one wanting to be separated from her even for a moment, and soon they were actually outside, and the air was moving and fresh and was a different temperature. There was as well an indefinable 'outside' smell, a mix of cars and earth, and the old Discovery, homely in its accustomed muddiness, was parked outside. It was a long way up into the front seat, with a nurse and her mother hovering beside her wheelchair ready to help; and it had in fact required every grain of strength in her wasted arms to drag herself up there, but she had done it: the wheel-chair was folded up and placed in the back, and they were off on the familiar winding road across bridges straddling gushing, trout-filled streams, over rolling hills, past dense woods and verdant cattle strewn pastures, home!

Demelza commented eagerly on everything: how the grass in the middle of the road seemed longer – it would, because it was mid-winter when she left – and on the rash of Public Footpath signs, which had sprouted in her absence also.

When the old car rumbled around the last bend in the drive (surely shorter, to her memory?) her eyes fixed on the tissue paper roses dangling from the wisteria branches about the porch, and a huge paper chain, bearing the words WELCOME HOME! each letter decorated on an individual piece of A4 paper. Demelza felt overwhelmed and almost awkward, but she carried it off, as Poppy and Sophia explained how they had made everything and what ages it had taken.

As she approached the front door she noticed a bouquet of many coloured old-fashioned tea roses entwined into the knocker. A quick question to her mother had Connie answering that the flowers were not actually from her – but she had a good idea from whom they could be. When she took them down to put into water she saw a card, written laboriously in copper plate: *for the Maiden,* it read, so there was no doubt that somehow Joe had got to know, through the redoubtable village grapevine, and had left another of his anonymous gifts. At the back door a huge cauliflower resided in an oily bag, which was no doubt intended for their supper, for what would a welcome home be without a cauliflower?

They realised that the side door would be the simplest for the wheelchair, because it didn't have a step, so Ella went in through the front door, racing around the house at top speed to unbolt the side one and hold it open ceremoniously. Demelza commented that the house looked especially clean, but the damp, toasty, churchy smell she would know anywhere as that of her home lingered faithfully on.

Demelza guided her wheelchair over the uneven mosaic tiles of the main hall in pursuit of the others, who wanted to show her the temporary room they had rigged up as her bedroom. They kept turning back to see her progress and to be sure she was still following. Demelza felt uneasily like a guest in her own home and privately looked forward to the moment she was taken for granted again. However, when they threw open the pitched-pine door with a flourish, to reveal new looking curtains (surely they hadn't been that colour before?) and more welcoming bunting across them, she saw her books and CDs in the re-arranged shelves of the old playroom, and the ancient familiar swirly black patterned quilt, covering her bed, which had been jammed in right next to the grand piano. Now she became infected with their excitement and felt humbled at all the time and effort they had put in just for her – and it wasn't as though she had always been nice to them! She felt the dangerous prick of the humiliating tears again as she resolved to give everyone *less* of a hard time with her teasing; and glided the wheelchair over the polished oak boards of the playroom – her new bedroom. The loo and an ancient Butler's Pantry were next door, into which a towel and her wash things had been placed. Connie left the children to find their own equilibrium without her, as she disappeared to the kitchen to put on the kettle and see to the planned feast, however, before she had reached the larder door, the old house was awoken by the throbbing bass of Demelza's favourite: I Feel Dangerous! – and instead of a grimace, she smiled at the proof of a return to normality and unconsciously hummed along happily to what existed of the tune.

As the four sisters graduated to the kitchen, their nostrils were assailed by the rich smell of baking:

"I smell cake! Are we having cake?" asked Demelza expectantly.

"Yes and I made it!" beamed Ella. Demelza did not return with a swift put down regarding Ella's baking skills – instead she enthused.

"You *iced* it," corrected Sophia.

"And you licked out the bowl!" added Ella: "Let's have it now; I'm starving."

"Hang on! Feast first – cake second," put in Connie, as she began to produce heaped plates of the goodies they had selected and prepared for Demelza. At first she had seemed like a guest, but as the easy banter began to run and the number in the house returned to its even pattern, everyone began to thaw and relax, settling down to indulge in the delectable fare and fill Demelza in on all the minutiae of occurrences at home and school that had occurred in her prolonged absence. Half way through, Poppy insisted on bringing in her own surprise, which were a clutch of wriggling baby rabbits, delivered, to everyone's amazement, by Demelza's rabbit, Punk.

"You must have let her out of her run!" said Demelza, both accusing and delighted by Poppy's mistake.

"I never did!" she answered indignantly: "You see what happened is she came into season and stuffed her bottom up against the chicken wire of the run. A wild man rabbit came by and sniffed her and then he mated her through the wire!"

"He never!" scoffed Demelza, but Connie, through her laughter assured her that this was in fact precisely the case, and that she had doubled the wire to prevent such an event recurring.

"Naughty old Punk. I think I've just thought of a rhyming name for her husband," but Connie had anticipated this one at the same time and shook her head in the direction of the little ones:

"They know quite enough words already."

Appreciating the return of Demelza's insatiable humour, their eyes met and sparked with private amusement.

"Well *I* think that we should change Punk's name to Mary, because it was a sort of emaciated conception," returned Sophia primly, surprised and pleased at the guffaws that her helpful suggestion had rendered.

"Then *one* of these boys must be Jesus!" continued Demelza, "and I have to thank you, Poppy for looking after Punky Mary and her disciples, so carefully. And for all this," she added, more quietly, momentarily abashed again at the sudden choke she felt in her voice. She made the most of it, however, by clearing her throat loudly:

"And this is my toast – well the one Mum and Grandma were always saying to each other when they overdid the sherry!"

"*Would* we!" interposed Connie, knowing again what was about to be said and steeling herself against showing the emotion she felt.

"*Oi looks towards you!*" Connie raised her glass of elderflower cordial:

"*Oi bows accordin',*" she answered and continued in the Devon brogue "*Yur'z to us!*"

"*None like us!*" answered the assembled company and Connie was touched and surprised that they had all remembered, as she raised her glass to her absent mother and restored daughter.

Chapter Thirty

The house began to swing and reverberate once more as a form of normality, as the family knew it, was restored. Demelza received visits from the physiotherapist and carried out her exercises with such zeal that she had to be actually urged not to over-do them. Her tutor from school continued to send resources and worksheets for her to complete and return, in order to remain on track – and the teachers, too, were amazed at the steadfast zeal, hitherto unknown, that Demelza appeared to be throwing into her education. Connie spent much of her time with Demelza, going to work only occasionally, and at these times Stuart took Demelza to the office or home to Sue and Fifi.

Sue was learning to cope well with little Fifi, but she was almost frightened by the exhaustion she was experiencing from the interrupted nights and found herself increasingly irritated by Stuart's ability to sleep through the most piercing of wails, while she changed and fed the little scrap again and again. She now felt unreasonably annoyed at the sight of Stuart's fresh complexion and clear, bag free eyes, while she saw herself looking forever more pale and wasted. Her figure hadn't returned the way it was supposed to do, sterilising bottles was taking for ever, and when Stuart had patiently explained that probably Connie had coped so much better only because she had breast fed, it was the final straw and Sue had screamed her frustration at the comparison.

"I didn't mean it the way you're taking it," Stuart had answered, much too patiently: "It's just that I think Connie was far too lazy to be bothered with all that sterilising and hard work that you put in. That's why she breast fed – and it made her get horribly thin," he added, an inspirational put down on Connie that he thought would restore Sue instantly. He was not at all prepared, therefore, for the sterilising unit when it came hurtling towards him! Fortunately her aim was not too true and it only succeeded in grazing his elbow as it whistled past, leaking its contents and splintering into a thousand plastic fragments on the floor. Following this, Sue had burst into loud tears, which had awoken the baby and made her sob the more hysterically:

"I'm sorry, I'm sorry, I'm *sorry*!"

"Don't worry, Shoogy: I'll get another one –"

"Not about the unit, just about," she faltered, "I'm so tired... I'm good at accounts, aren't I? But I can't do this: I'm so, so tired, fed up, tired. Tired and fat!" At last Stuart had put an arm around her (the other was holding the sodden and squealing Fifi).

This dramatic outburst had unleashed something strangely akin to admiration in Stuart, and he determined to reward the demonstration of feisty exasperation with the action it deserved: but what was to be done?

"Don't tell Connie, will you?" Sue had snuffled anxiously: "She was so kind to me when I had Fifi –" and the tears began afresh at being such an obvious failure on all counts; only they were gentle this time. Stuart hushed and reassured her: *Why would I tell Connie?* he thought, *we had enough spills of our own and I don't want her to know it's starting again! They'll be seeing me as the weakest parental link next – and what if they're right?*

It was this that had prompted him to do a little lateral thinking of his own, as he hurried to the chemist in search of a new sterilising unit, and he came up with the ultimate plan, which might actually, amazingly, please both his ex and his present partner at the same time! He reasoned that Demelza was taking up a huge amount of Connie's time and preventing her from work, which – never let it be underestimated – brought in money. Sue, on the other hand, was unused to the *sort* of time she was now spending at home and was exhausted. Demelza would be a free baby-minder: she would be able to bond with her little sister and benefit from the responsibility and a change of scenery. Sue would be on hand if there was anything that Demelza couldn't manage, but she might be able to catch up on some of the sleep she had lost at night. This, in turn, would restore Sue to her former adoring graciousness by allowing her to recapture her looks, her figure and her sense of proportion.

The arrangement worked well, allowing Demelza to feel as though she were being useful to someone else. It also produced a genuine affection for her little sister. After the initial awkwardness of having her partner's teenager breathing down her neck, calling her baby 'Fumfum' for some unfathomable reason; and crooning nothing resembling nursery songs into her ear, Sue began to look forward to the break in what she secretly found to be something approaching tedium – which no other parent seemed to feel apart from her! Fifi seemed to respond amazingly to her big sister's caterwauling and she smiled and crowed delightedly, very often filling her nappy in her enthusiasm, which resulted in Demelza making comical disgusted faces, and sounds such as were really inappropriate, but which resulted in Fifi chortling all the more. Indeed, they got on so well that Sue began to feel ridiculously jealous, wondering what it was that this wheelchair bound girl possessed that she didn't. However, Sue soon started to appreciate the peace and the fun that Demelza seemed to inject into things, which allowed her to leave them to their own resources while she curled up on the bed to steal delicious deep, restoring slumber; from which she would awaken gently, in her own time, and then wallow in a relaxing bath and a bit of a make-over before Stuart came to fetch the magical teenager home again. As for Stuart, he experienced a sense of well-being, fuelled from meeting the needs of his three most important females and thereby achieving a rare sense of altruism. He resolved to become yet more 'hands-on useful' in the future!

When Demelza heard about the proposed benefit concert in her honour, she became manically excited by the prospect: she called Charlie over, and the pair made plans to invite their heroes, *Plastic Max,* to make a guest appearance. They wanted their invitation to engender just the right appeal, first so that he would select and read it from his fan mail, and second for him to decide it would be worth appearing in a small paddock to a maximum audience of two hundred, which, after much debate, was the sealing limit that Connie had put on numbers.

Very dear Plastic Max, was how they elected to begin, having eschewed more passionate endearments as 'tacky and teenage'.
We have long been amongst the coolest of your greatest and – dare we say –'wildest' fans. Sadly, however, the wildness has been

only in our hearts and eyes, when we watch your DVD, 'Wasted', due to the fact that one of us has incurred an accident to the neck. (We will not tell you how this occurred, but will leave you to wonder!) They felt that not giving the details would prevent the embarrassment of being seen as childish – and they hoped it might also serve to intrigue. *This resulted in paralysis for some time which now, we are happy to say, is becoming ever less prevalent; although head banging and moshing is still sadly temporarily off the limits... Getting better has been largely thanks to your so-oh! cool music, which kept me from mind-numbing dingbattism in the hospital, especially the brilliant track 'I Feel Dangerous', which in the end all the doctors and nurses were headbanging to. (So your fan base may have become bigger in an as yet untapped quarter, thanks to me – and you!) Ahem – this is where we ask you the big question and you say 'Yes!' My Mum's rock band is doing a benefit concert for more hospital equipment in the ward I was in, (the money was going to her because she lost so much of it looking out for me, but she's refused for some reason), and we would LOVE YOU to make a guest appearance for as long as you want. We're afraid there won't be enough to pay you anything more than expenses, but think of all those little brats who will get better treatment because of your playing here and them giving a big donation and becoming greater fans?*

We hope we may have persuaded you, but in case you're in any doubt we think you're amazing anyway and sizzlingly sensual. Even if you can't come we will feel this for ever.

With more affection than you've ever had yet!

Demelza, and Charlie (Demelza's staunchest friend.)
XXXXXXXXXXXXXXXXXXXXXXXXXXXXX

After this they gave details of the date and venue, describing it as a playing field, 'because, after all, it sort of is'.

Charlie and Demelza continued to craft and graft their letter until they felt it to be completely irresistible, after which they signed it in red ink that looked like blood and Charlie put it carefully into her schoolbag to post on the way home.

These days, Leticia elected to stay while Charlie was visiting, instead of disappearing in a cloud of dust. She seemed, to the girls' surprise, to derive pleasure from Connie's company and was even to be seen teetering behind her while the hens were being fed, wearing her inimitable patent stilettos complemented by a pair of pink marigolds.. Connie gave Leticia some eggs to take home which, having scrubbed them vigorously, she seemed pleased to use for breakfast, explaining shamefacedly to Neville that 'eggs for breakfast rather reminded her of home', and when Neville had looked up sharply at the reference to home, she admitted apologetically that she had meant the cottage at Torrington. This had startled him somewhat, since there existed a certain tacit agreement that the place she had referred to was not mentioned – and she had just done it! Charlie had added to the discomfort of the situation by adding, when Leticia could have sworn she couldn't have heard their conversation through that iPod thing:

"Yes – how are Grandma and Granddad? You never take us to see them: why don't we see them? After all, they're only just down the road." Leticia would normally have fobbed her off with something withering, but a tiny spark of rebellion had flickered for some time now and as Neville cleared his throat and explained patiently that her parents actually preferred to keep themselves to themselves, she heard herself butt in with:

"Actually, you know they just *might* rather appreciate seeing you – if you're sure you'd like to come with me: I always show them photos of your gymnastics events and so on and they do always comment on how much you've grown, so they *are* in fact interested." Neville had been contradicted and Charlie was impressed, supporting her mother by saying that she would actually love to join her. Thus plans were made, although after this minor victory, Leticia felt a crippling desire to visit the newly stocked sideboard!

As soon as she decently could, she stealthily popped a bottle of vodka into the bottom of a shopping bag and covered it quickly with a swirly-patterned *pashmina,* which she topped with a bottle of wine. She then returned to the drawing room and announced to a surprised Charlie that she had promised to deliver a bottle of wine to Connie in thanks for the many eggs. She invited Charlie to join her, to which she eagerly agreed and they were off, a rare mixture of conspiracy and harmony pervading.

Neville put down his newspaper and stared after the disappearing car in disbelief: she had not even asked if he minded! He began again to be dimly aware that his wife was less – well, controllable these days. One minute she seemed animated, the next withdrawn. He knew she wouldn't have the guts or inclination to have a 'thing' for anyone else – she loved him too much, obviously, but something made him sit up and take quick stock. Pre-empting anything Leticia would have had time to do, he took the unprecedented step of phoning her parents and brothers first, and inviting them to 'a little soirée – just us', at home. He would pick them up, he insisted, and it would be absolutely no trouble. He settled back in his chair, feeling surprisingly comfortable with himself, half amused and wondering what had brought that on? He found himself looking forward to the effect that this startling, out of the blue invitation would have on his wife, and deep down felt a certain unease with himself at the great pleasure she would derive from such a small and hitherto unknown gesture. It would demonstrate that he cared, and hopefully banish any further sense of independence of thought such as she had been displaying.

Leticia's visits seemed to have a remarkably reviving effect on Connie, Demelza noticed, who would stop what she was doing to share mugs of what must presumably have been tea, although she was never seen to go near the kettle – and afterwards the contents of the peanut-butter jar would be visibly lower too!

~

Plastic Max fan club,
Streatham.

Dear Demelza and Charlie,

Plastic Max wants you to know that they were very touched by your letter. They say that if Baz Tard had been free they would assuredly have come to play at your playing field; however, their commitments run right into next year and beyond. They say they hope you get better soon.
To make up for any disappointment, please find enclosed passes to next year's show at Wembley, which is to promote the new album

'Snort Fare'.

Thanks for your interest,

Sally Fanshaw, (pp Plastic Max)

When Demelza and Charlie received this, *Snort Fare* was the topic of every conversation: Demelza had now moved on to crutches, and she could crawl up the stairs by dint of a mixture of determination and the banisters. They sat in her den of a bedroom in the attic, cradling the letter:

"I never really thought he'd write back."

"Nor me – but I suppose he hasn't *actually* –"

"But what about 'Plastic Max wants you to know'! They *want us to know* – that means they read our letter and *talked* about us – which means they must have wanted us to have the free passes… Hey: d'you think this means Baz Tard'd like us to visit him back stage?" A wild yelp of glee answered this remark:

"Yup, yup, yup – he must do! Well he will when he sees us coming through the door: can I borrow those tall black boots you've got? The ones with the heels – or will you wear them?"

"No, you can have them. I think I'll be in my pink jelly moonies. How will we make them let us go though: my dad's a toe rag – and you can't walk!" A look of concern flitted across Demelza's face momentarily, followed by the old resolve:

"Just let him try to stop us! We've got a whole six months to work on him and now that our mum's get on, they'll help him see sense – as for me: do you doubt that I'll be walking perfectly in six months' time – 'specially with this to look forward to?" Charlie smiled loyally: everything was becoming so cool, she could barely dare touch the sides! Her house was more of a home these days, with her dad actually talking to her mum and laughing sometimes at the things she said. Even her spots were beginning to recede – perhaps because of the reduction in stress levels: each day was better than the last and now there was a personal invitation from Plastic Max to Wembley!

"You didn't really think they'd come to our benefit, did you?" she asked, suddenly fearful.

"Plastic? Naaa – but we did have to ask them, didn't we, like just in case. It's kind of better this way because by the time I see Baz I'll be really well fit!"

"Not as fit as me."

"Fitter, Honey!" and Demelza began screeching along loudly and raucously to:

You think I'm wwww Wasted!

Per-pet-u-ally on my face-sted!

And this efficiently drowned her friend's protests!

Chapter Thirty-one

The day of the benefit concert had arrived and everyone was talking incessantly about the weather: would the low grey blanket of cloud that enveloped the sky, fold away and allow the sun to filter through? Or did it signify the onset of rain? Cake and Nigel had spent the preceeding week putting a block stage together over a motley number of feed bags, and they had rigged an awning over the top. A long mess of leads spaghettied from the house, having been plugged in and tested with much trepidation; but so far nothing had fused, and the trip-switch in the larder remained unmoved. They believed that they could probably play safely if there was a *modicum* of rain, but if it were to settle in, as rain from the West was well known to do, then they would have to call the whole thing off and reimburse all the 'fans', as Demelza insisted on calling the audience. The speed at which the tickets had sold had surprised even the children; for no sooner was it known that there was to be a festival of sorts in such a remote region of Devon, than everyone who did live in the area had wanted to attend and see for themselves. There were also all the children in Demelza and Ella's classes; not to mention staff and representatives from the hospital.

It had been decided that to provide food would be too troublesome, so the concert goers were encouraged to bring their own picnics and drinks. It was being held in the afternoon, partly to deter too much drinking; and since it was a private event there would be no policing. A local farmer had kindly offered neighbouring fallow fields for parking and Sophia and Poppy and friends were in charge of ushering the cars to park as economically as possible. Meanwhile Demelza, Ella, Charlie and Susanna had rigged up a table by the gate, from which to take tickets as people entered the paddock, which had been freshly mown down to a short stubble. In the interests of comfort, they had suggested that people should come equipped with rugs; and they contributed an untidy heap of their own for those who lacked them. All guinea pigs, hamsters and rabbits had been moved inside, while the hens were put into an ark and transported to the farthest end of the orchard, in the hopes of minimum disturbance from the noise.

Lurking behind a gaggle of teenagers at the make-shift entrance, Charlie spotted Pete and nudged Demelza, stage-whispering the familiar warning:

"*Uh oh: Psycho!*" Ella took command of the situation:

*"*What are you doing here?" she asked abruptly.

"I heard about your pop fest and it sounded so over-poweringly cool that, forgive me, I simply couldn't resist!" he answered, as unquenchable as ever, "And before you suggest anything unpleasant, please peruse the contents of this envelope." Demelza had grabbed it rather hastily and several fifty pound notes fluttered to the ground:

"That's my contribution for my ticket – if you'll allow me in," he said smoothly,

"Wow!" she couldn't help uttering; but then looked doubtfully at the others for their views: each was impressed by the size of contribution; but loyalty prevented their acceptance. Pete took in their confusion and pressed his advantage:

"Here's a further fifty if I promise to skulk at the back," he said, flipping out another note from the pocket of his Barbour.

"Even-stevens, remember?" he wheedled,

"I thought we were supposed to be forgetting!" answered Ella coldly. The girls looked questioningly at one another.

"Can we really turn down as much as that?" wavered Demelza to Ella, to whom, in this particular situation, she for once deferred.

"I s'pose if you really do stay at the back out of everyone's way – and if you promise to be first out...?" Ella had taken over the initiative.

"First out I promise." Pete answered eagerly, adding: "Scout's honour!" as he raised three fingers in salute.

"OK then – don't make us regret this," threatened Demelza.

"I won't – and neither will you. Think of all that wonderful hospital equipment," he gabbled as he ambled hastily off in the direction of the front.

"No you don't!" Demelza called loudly after him: "You agreed to go to the back: it's over there." she indicated with her index finger, unable to help smiling as Pete made a dramatic 'about turn', followed by a mock bow and proceeded to the back of the paddock, saying affably:

"Of course – absolutely – fair cop!" as he felt in his top pocket for his usual ward against stressful situations.

Rowan had arrived with a pile of sandwiches, to lend an extra hand – partly in the hopes that she might have a chance at improving her acquaintance with 'the divine and enigmatic Nigel', and to be able at the very least to gaze at him from afar. Clara, another close friend, had agreed to come early to offer moral support also. She had plummeted herself in the rocking chair in the kitchen with only the feet of her small baby showing beneath a shapeless (but somehow elegant because *she* was wearing it), cornflower mohair sweater. She had previously ignored the baby's demands to be fed, as she hastily made some tea for the three of them, for she had noticed, with the intuition of friendship, that Connie was beginning to panic and she needed pacifying.

"I can't think why I ever agreed to this," Connie was confiding to them over the rim of the welcome steaming mug, "It seemed a great idea at the time, but..." Connie continued: "but you remember the state I was in – I wasn't thinking straight! And you can stop *posing* like that!" she told Rowan "Nigel hates to be watched – or seen for that matter – you're going to have to adopt a far more subtle approach!"

"Well how come he performs in front of people if he's so shy?" Rowan pouted, pulling herself away from the window reluctantly.

"When he's playing he's in another space and he's not thinking about his audience."

"What a crying shame – and *you* must stop worrying: this is a brilliant idea! I could have wished you'd chosen to donate the proceeds to the antenatal unit, but maybe next time. The whole thing is unfolding and all the hard part of planning has been done – largely without you – so where exactly is your problem?"

"Problem? Don't you see – first there's what to do if it rains."

"You've already said: cancel!"

"Easier said than done with so many involved and after all this effort that the children have put in – but also I'm nervous as hell!"

"But why? You're used to performing and this is your back yard,"

"That's exactly it: I am *not* used to performing in my back yard!

It's home – and it's so pretentious – I should never have agreed to it. I was off my head." Clara had remained apparently quietly absorbed in her infant, but she now demonstrated the maternal capacity for lateral listening:

"Listen: those tickets went in a flash, didn't they? And no one had to be persuaded to buy them, did they? No: they bought them because they wanted to and maybe – just maybe of course – this wasn't about you at all, but about Demelza! They'd seen that overactive adolescent go through hell, come out the other side in a wheelchair and then organise a concert! Just *maybe* there are a few people coming who'll be there simply because they admire her – or even because they're glad it didn't happen to *them*… And perhaps they think *you're* amazing to put this on for her as a sort of treat, after all you've been through. I very much doubt you've given them time to see the pretentious side!" Connie shook herself at Clara's calm clarity, for of course this had been all about Demelza – a gesture born from a need to do something, no matter how futile, simply *because* no one felt capable of being able to do anything constructive at all. Now that Demelza was improving in huge strides, she had already allowed herself to put the feelings that had driven her to put up with this present invasion away. She had felt the benefit of moving on so profoundly that she had lost the impetus for the concert along with it:

"OK," she said slowly, "I'll just have to get out there then – and Martin, our new keyboard player, is going to do a solo spot. You wait till you hear him: I don't think we'll be able to keep him long; he's simply too good and someone will see it… and *then* I've got a surprise laid on which you mustn't make me tell!" After these words Connie was fallen upon by Clara and Rowan, and Connie couldn't help but whisper her secret!

"And now – I think Nigel must really be in need of a sandwich," Rowan announced as she picked out a selection, "And you are both to stay away!"

"Then you won't want me to tell you that he's a veggie unless he killed it himself!" Connie called after her and Rowan spun around, discarding chicken for marmite and lettuce:

"Now, girls, just watch and learn: I may be gone a while!" she said as she slid for the door again, giving her bottom a little wiggle for their benefit, to peals of laughter. She turned fiercely and told them to 'shhh!' before continuing determinedly, invoking fresh mirth:

"I do hope she's not back too soon," said Connie anxiously.

"You've warned her enough – she must know she's climbing for a fall. I wonder why she does this sort of thing to herself," retorted Clara.

"I don't know… perhaps she just gets off on a lust for rejection," answered Connie as they stood at the French windows, craning their heads for a view.

As it turned out, the rain held off, it was not warm, but everyone had arrived in thick clothes, equipped with blankets and umbrellas – except for the teenage contingent, whose bare midriffs seemed uncannily immune to the temperature without. In spite of it being an afternoon event, plenty of alcohol was arriving; the adults providing bottles of wine to go with their picnics and the teenagers clutching bulging, colourful, hessian bags, from which tumbled cans and bottles of vodka and to which Connie turned a blind eye, saying they had at least done their best – just as she noticed Demelza, leaning on her crutches and expertly upending something in a can.

"Looks like a glorified Sports Day from here!" observed Clara, who was deftly changing her baby on the kitchen table next to the sandwiches, while pouring out a glass of chardonnay for Rowan, who was not looking in the best of sorts.

"We *won't ask*," Clara and Connie had agreed, as they had seen Rowan striding away from Nigel and they had sprung back from their vantage point: "But aren't we dying to know?" Connie had added and Clara nodded vigorously.

Rowan was saved explanations, for outside a car had drawn up, in spite of notices indicating that this was not to take place, out of which bounced not only Leticia, but Neville too.

"Oh my God – she's going to hate this," sighed Clara, reaching hastily for the wet wipes.

"Actually, give her a chance, she can grow on you," answered Connie, as Rowan and Clara wrinkled their noses in distaste and Leticia strode in with a very new looking hamper, followed by a bemused Neville, who was bowed slightly under the weight of a union jack emblazoned cooler box, containing half a case of champagne from the wine society.

"I *knew* you wouldn't mind our driving up: I thought – that is *we* thought, didn't we, Neville? that you could all do with a jolly good snifter. Now Neville, let's pop a bottle!" Neville listened to his wife being demonstrative amongst all these clearly liberated women, with a strange touch of pride and efficiently did as he had been bid. He wasn't a complete fool: he had become aware that his wife did seem to enjoy the odd tipple, which he now recognised to have occurred on the occasions when her breath smelt strongly of peppermint. It was odd, he reflected uncomfortably, how the more she had cowered in the past, the more he had thrown his weight around. He had stopped her family from contact with the children because he *could,* yet he had known inside himself that this must have caused her discomfort. When, therefore, her parents and brothers had come around for tea, Leticia had suggested a couple of drinks pre-arrival, as she put it 'to calm the nerves' – which was a bit weird when you considered they were only her family with whom she had grown up. He had looked upon this idea with his customary frozen distain, but when she had timidly pushed a glass into his hand and he had seen hers shake as she said bravely: 'down the hatches', tossing the liquid down her throat, he became oddly touched by her vulnerability and the over-riding courage she was attempting to display. He saw, too, that she could really handle her drink – in a way that he had been unaware. He swallowed his measure too and, resisting the urge to gasp, for fear of losing face, had suggested another one. At this, she had glanced at him quickly to check he wasn't sneering at her in some way, and then agreed with childish alacrity, resulting in his experiencing a surge of desire for the feistiness that he had almost managed to extinguish in this lovely woman: his wife.

This was the beginning of Neville's loosening up: they both began to care about how others perceived them a little less, and instead looked forward to the sun being over the yard-arm when he got home; when they would enjoy the company of one another a little *more.* Neville also realised that there were times when she seemed to have a head start on him; but now that their drinking was shared, Leticia felt less need to sneak in a quick bevy before he got home – because it was more fun with two! Thus, here they were in the kitchen of that woman whom they had both despised whole heartedly, and attempted so often to put their daughters off their evident devotion to this kind of chaos. Now, however, he found himself in the throws of a double-take, on realising that the figure of the woman changing a honking nappy amongst the sandwiches was his accountant! Clara smiled and held out a hand:

"Mr Leason! Lovely to see you – how's biz – or shouldn't I ask?"

"Neville," he had answered firmly – and he had given her only a brief résumé of the meeting he was due to have with her on Monday. Glasses were held out for the frothing champagne and Connie was saying she wanted half a glass only or she would forget the words of her songs.

"Come on: let's see what you've got in that hamper," Connie had demanded and Leticia was answering that she simply 'could never *resist* a spot of Fortnum and Mason' when she saw one, and Clara and Rowan had exchanged glances.

The hamper had been couriered down and contained the finest pots of seafood creations, bottled fruits in exotic liqueurs, sliced *Wiltshire ham*, *Cranfield's* Balsamic jelly, Shropshire blue cheeses, Gamekeeper's fruitcake and Demerara shortcake; complete with half bottles of port and claret.

"Come on hand it over," called Connie: "We can offer you a swap for lettuce and marmite sandwiches," and Neville found himself agreeing with Clara the accountant that actually, what ever the posh nosh, a marmite and lettuce was better than anything!

"I'm simply *dying* to tell you all about that girl in Charlotte and Demelza's class" Leticia enthused excitedly, "Coriander, the one that looks as though she's going on twenty-one, with the very dubious looking boyfriend with an eyebrow piercing? Well she had a tattoo done right across her stomach saying – would you believe it – *Plastic Max!*"

"Oh I would," put in Connie, "Demelza's potty about him – she'd probably do it too if she thought she could get away with it!"

"But listen to this: the poor gal had a grumbling appendix and the surgeon had to whip it out quick, before it erupted."

"Ruptured." Rowan couldn't help correcting, which would have floored the old Leticia, but she went on unabashed:

"But he didn't take much notice of the tattoo – or perhaps he didn't have time. Anyway, *half* the tattoo was taken out with the

incision and now she's got '*Stic Max*' emblazoned across her instead!"
All of them, Neville included, fell into squeals of mirth at this,
agreeing with Leticia that it really was 'too, too killing!' and Leticia
revelled in the delight her story had brought.

The French windows flew open to the assault of one of Martin's
sticks, expertly aimed onto the painted wood at the side. He swung
himself deftly through and called Connie for a final sound check.
They were planning on starting shortly, provided everything was
working properly; but they were uncertain as to how much they would
need to hear through the fold-back system. Connie thrust her
champagne glass guiltily at Martin, who downed it swiftly while she
searched in the fridge for a bottle of water to take out with her and
hastily followed him, only to be hit properly for the first time by the
sight and humming sound of their paddock, brimming with picnickers.
They reached the makeshift stage via the pond, which saved them
from having to be delayed by meeting so many familiar and expectant
faces.

Connie's whole family shared a feeling of excitement and
nervousness at hosting anything quite so ambitious; but each also
knew that the event would not possibly have taken place without the
(joint) co-operation of so many, and the passion they had all
experienced throughout Demelza's incarceration in hospital.

Andy and Nigel hoisted Martin onto the stage behind his set of
keyboards. Not expecting him to be so light, they almost thrust him
over the top of his piano.

"Steady, lads," was all Martin had to say: "Dangerous load, you
know," and he whizzed off a number of arpeggios from bass to treble
on each keyboard, checking tone and vibrancy. They had volunteered
to play first, out of generosity to the other local bands; for the later the
spot, the more warmed up the audience should be. Connie was
privately glad to get it over however, for once she had got her own
music out of the way she could properly appreciate the evening.

The band left the stage and signalled their readiness to the
children, whose cue it was to begin the clapping as they clambered
back onto it, where Martin remained, unfazed. They were taken aback
by the roar from the crowd of friends, many of whom were there more
to wish all involved in the concert well; their interest in the music
coming second. The audience's enthusiasm helped still the nerves of
the band members and Cake clapped his drumsticks together and they

were off. At the end of each number the applause increased in volume and verve, led by the teenage contingent doing what they could do best. Connie had felt self-conscious at singing her songs in front of so many familiar faces and she began by looking through the crowd into the middle distance of the vegetable garden; but once she had picked up her flute, she thawed into the swaying rhythms, and felt herself gratefully transported into that wider world, where Music swamped and tugged her along in its current. At the end of her solo her shoulders were relaxed and she joined the audience in their excitement at being a part of this extraordinary event. After their last number, she looked for the first time into the crowd, and at the back she saw Demelza, supported on either side by Charlie and Bindy, waving her crutches crazily in the air, her mouth wide open in a prolonged and raucous whoop. The ear splitting smile that Connie wore, mirrored that of her daughter and she knew from the lump in her throat that, in spite of riotous clamours for an encore, she couldn't have sung another note. Bowing to the daughter she feared she might have lost, she jumped down off the stage and for her, there was at that moment only two people present in the paddock – and the rest of the jumping, rollicking revellers had disappeared.

Last minute advice was hastily given from one band to the next as, one after another, each heaved themselves carefully onto the 'very unhealthy and safety-free' structure which served as the stage.

The applause continued to swell in equal proportion to the wine consumed and the sheer joy in being present. The rain held off, although the clouds continued to threaten, but the audience had ceased to be concerned. The final band was now expected and Connie and Boo (who had contrived to arrive with less noise than was normally her due) held onto either end of a pair of faded, sagging velvet curtains, which they were suspending over the stage manually before the arrival of the surprise top act. With a nod to one another they flipped the curtains up as a thunderous chord rent the air! All the teenagers and their parents were familiar with that particular series of dissonant notes, and with a shout of "*Plastic,*" they surged at the stage, pogo-ing energetically into the air. Onto the stage rushed a tall figure, manically hammering his guitar, clad in black plastic from head to toe and screeching the lyrics to *Snort Fare.*

Closer scrutiny of the cavorting figure revealed, to the more discerning of *Plastic Max's* fans, that while he shared both gender and clothing with *the* Baz Tard, his stature and features gave away that he was not in fact the genuine character, but extraordinarily similar. Demelza had been amongst the charge to the stage front, having been precariously but carefully transported to it by her loyal friends. She knew immediately that it was an imitation, but she was happy with that. She realised, too, that her mother was in on it, saw mischievous cousin Boo – and guessed the rest. He was speaking now about a very special kid, who 'rocked and kicked ass', and went on further to ask that kid – 'his most favourite fan' – if she would do him the honour of joining him in one of his songs. Amidst the exultant haze, she felt herself being hoisted up, up, onto the makeshift stage. Part of her froze with embarrassment, while the other glowed with pride and excitement at this much *adulation* (which was how she afterwards described the motley crowd of screaming well-wishers). With the aplomb that those who had carefully arranged all this knew she would display, she smiled beatifically as Ken (for he of course was the masquerader!) He adjusted a microphone to her level as she leaned lightly on her crutches and spoke the ubiquitous words she had on so many occasions heard her mother repeat in the sound check:

"One-two, one-two – tickle test?" and to the crowd's reaction she went on:

"Why thank you all of you: you all *rock!*" At this Ken thrummed the infamously discordant lick, introducing what had just about become her theme song and she screamed out with Ken, in tuneless abandon with:

I feel dangerous!
I feel sssss so alive!

The afternoon was rounded off by bringing the mood down with an acoustic set from Ken, now divested of the Baz Tard disguise, including, of course, Connie's Elegy, which had by now disappeared off the charts; hopefully soon to be replaced by his next classic, for which many were already enthusiastically waiting. Boo and some of the teenagers remained swaying and gently dancing at the front, while Connie's band joined him for his last number. This was typically generous of Ken, for it meant they all shared the final moments of rapturous applause. He took alternate verses with Connie through

REM's heart-rending: Everybody Hurts Sometimes, and the audience sang along, barely conscious of the fact that they were; for this was a natural response to the warmth and gladness that the afternoon had generated:

Sometimes – some times – some times.

Demelza looked across the audience of friends and relations, her eyes not the only ones misted with tears. She saw her father and Sue, quite far back with little 'Fumfum' in his lap, clapping and swaying, and looking as though somehow not only he, but the three of them belonged amongst them all here again, as a wider extension of her family home. Pete was just discernable, positioned near the back, as promised, his arm around a beaming Rowan, as he gyrated expertly. At last even he appeared to be amongst the harmony that was weaving its magical way around everyone. (He was later to be glimpsed actually heading the procession of leavers, his hand fixed in Rowan's, who shared his glassy grin), and could that be the stuffy Neville, standing on what appeared to be an upturned bucket? (Actually it was an ice bucket and therefore, of course, crucial to the proceedings.) He appeared to be conducting with a champagne bottle and Leticia, *barefoot* (those stilettos had sunk into the ground when she had stood up to dance, and Neville had suggested she removed them!) was beside him, seemingly similarly the worse for wear and clearly experiencing the happiest of abandonment.

'*Sometimes – some times' – some times'* they continued to chant, each wishing the song and the vibration it brought with it, should go on for *all* time.

Chapter Thirty-two

By Christmas time the household had returned to its original shambolic routine: Demelza continued with her physiotherapy and check-ups, but she had gleefully returned her crutches to the hospital. Her gait had changed, for it was slow, careful and deliberate. Martin had professed to be all envy but had taught her his own techniques, with the aid of banisters, for getting upstairs, which he purported to be quicker and more economical in movement than the moves the hospital had shown. She helped to decorate the tree, as always vulgarly over-laden with every bauble and school-made object, necessarily escalating in number every year. Ella, who now topped Connie in height, was chosen as the obvious one to place Sophia's fairy that she had made in Year Two, precariously on the top most branch; while the finishing touches, consisting of a combination strangely at odds with one another, of swathes of gaudy tinsel and proper candles, were wrapped around its burgeoning branches. The ancient vinyl record was then ceremoniously laid on the turn-table, which Connie's parents had donated on her twenty-first birthday and it scratched and lisped through a number of tortuous carols while they lit the candles – each one tipping precariously at angles to another and dripping wax into the tree and onto the old tablecloth that hid the pot from view below. Then it was time to turn the record over for *Slade's* Merry Christmas Everybody and the *Beach Boys'* Little Saint Nick. There was the usual mulled wine for the older children, mixed with much noise and laughter.

Last Christmas had been tricky because it was the first without Grandma, but successive Christmases would prove easier, not that they missed her less but they accepted her absence more; thus the memories now brought nostalgia in place of pain. Last Christmas Uncle Jeremy had contributed the tickets for this Christmas to be spent with his family in Australia, yet this Christmas, due to Demelza's treatment and her inability to travel such a distance, they were remaining here. Last Christmas Sebastian had readily agreed to come with them to Australia, yet now he was no longer a part of the family and hadn't been seen since the summer: such was the turbulence of life; the main focus being that Demelza was here with them and becoming ever stronger; her *own* particular aim focused on being strong enough to see *Plastic Max* at Wembley in a further few months.

This Christmas morning Poppy was the first to wake. Before she opened her eyes, she wriggled her feet, one to each side of the bed, finding, to her satisfaction, what she had been waiting for: the weight of a present-filled pillow case, referred to as a stocking. Connie had been up late the night before painstakingly wrapping each individual item, which she had been collecting gradually in a drawer in the spare room since October, continually counting them on behalf of each of the four girls to make sure the number of articles was even. The paper was recycled from past birthday presents, being ready crinkled and easier to wrap, and she flew at the task, ripping at the Sellotape and snipping the paper into shape in her haste to finish this task and get on to others. It had been observed in the past that Mother Christmas was either a rather untidy person or a lousy wrapper and Connie had felt qualified to confirm that she was probably both! Now Poppy hooked her feet around her 'stocking'; brought it to the top of the bed but still beneath the quilt for the next tactile examination: this time crinkling at the contents with her fingers. She felt around the series of bumpy parcels, squeezing and poking to try to discover consistency, but kept to her own self-inflicted rule of still no peeping. She had only recently officially learned the identity of Mother Christmas, and why they had so named her. Being the youngest, she was the last to know, but this Christmas was special too because now there was her new *little* half sister, Fifi, from whom Poppy resolved to keep the secret with her life. It felt good that the buck no longer wholly stopped with her being the youngest, and she could look forward to superior 'big sister' status. She lay beneath the covers, eyes tight shut, exulting in the knowledge of the day ahead and the fun it would bring and then she rolled out of bed and tottered up the attic stairs to Demelza's room, surprised to find her sister already awake and staring at the ceiling.

"This Christmas is going to be *so* extra mega," said Demelza mysteriously, as Poppy hopped under the quilt with her for a moment to warm her frozen toes and to dump Demelza's surprisingly untouched stocking within easy reach. Poppy was relieved that her sister felt like this, for she had feared she might be feeling bad because, but for her, they would be in Australia right now. However, Demelza evidently shared the view that anyway they could still look forward to the journey the following Christmas. Next, they clambered down to visit their other sisters, who joined forces to spring into their mother's room with excited cries of '*Happy Christmas*' as Ella deftly slid a stocking under the covers at the end of Connie's bed. Connie feigned surprise at finding it there, and in truth – the first year that Stuart had left, she had been touched and amazed that a stocking had been organised between the three older girls, consisting of soaps they had found, bath beads and gewgaws bought with their combined pocket money, and pretty toys that they had grown out of which she still appeared to like! This year Poppy's pocket money and offerings had been included into the equation, now that she knew the identity of Mother Christmas and they didn't have to pretend. Somehow they all managed to fit into the bed and Connie felt squashed and loved as she joined in the turns to open presents and exclaim at their smell, their taste, their beauty! Gradually, the piles of opened presents grew, the ceiling became adorned with sticky 'silly string,' shot from party poppers and the like, and the quilt was a mass of discarded scraps of paper, eagerly torn from their confines.

Once 'stocking time' was done and chocolates and tangerines eaten and smeared around the bedclothes, it was time for the wild ducks to be placed in the Aga to roast for lunch. These had been shot and reverently placed at the porch by Joe, who had himself discovered a bottle of whisky with his milk that morning. Once the ducks were in, it was time for church.

"You know the last time we went to church it was because of you," Ella confided to Demelza, to which Demelza demanded an explanation:

"We had to pray for you – so you see you getting better was an answer to prayer!" Poppy explained reverently.

"The Lord works in mysterious ways," put in Sophia, not quite knowing what she meant by this remark and wondering at the quick smile which had played at her mother's mouth: it was irritating that so often the apparently funniest things that she said were not jokes.

Church seemed to last for an eternity, for the rector was in full swing, due to the unusually swollen congregation because of it being Christmas. He was determined to instil the joy of Christmas spirit in every being and for this reason his sermon was particularly long, with a number of visual aids, questions for the youngsters to keep them busy, and requests for volunteers to hold up the visual aids and parade them around the church for all to see. It took a long wait each time a volunteer was summoned, and engendered a fierce exchange between Ella and Poppy:

"Answer his questions and carry that donkey like he's asking."

"Don't want to."

"'Present time' will come quicker if you do and we'll all get out faster - "

"*You* do it if you're so keen!"

"I'm far too old – make Sophia do it then,"

"*Shhhhhhhh!*"

Connie's own thoughts were interspersed with thoughts veering between the ducks on the pond, which they had not yet fed and the ducks in the oven, which they were going to be fed *by*; while distantly experiencing the mystery and excitement that the carols had always engendered – especially singing the final verse of Oh! Come all ye Faithful, reserved for Christmas day: *Yea, Lord, we greet thee, Born this happy morning!* She looked down their bulging pew: it bulged because no one had wanted to sit in the pew in front next to Gordon Sellick, who was pronounced a geek. Connie was rammed in on the inside, so could set no example by placing herself next to him and his father, who was perched uncomfortably, his neck becoming red and chafed where the too tight, stiff Sunday shirt collar cut into it.

They had driven to church, although it was only a short distance over a field, because of Demelza's limitations and had paused at Grandma's grave to place a holly wreath that Sophia had made, on top of the shiny new headstone. The feeling had been good, for by this gesture she felt that somehow her mother was, as always, an inclusive part of the gathering. The yellowing lichened gravestones were redolent with similar adornments from friends and relatives, and the little yard seemed to have lost some of its sobriety, looking as though it was offering its own bright display as part of Nature's playground. Once, in her lowest, most secret moments between three and five in the morning, when the wakeful mind plays its cruellest tricks, Connie had imagined this Christmas, where Demelza's presence would have been marked out there beside her grandmother, never again to share their family life. She had prayed fervently during those frightened times, and now, filled with thankfulness and warmth from the closeness of all her daughters', pressed up hard against her in the pew, she forgot the ducks – both the pet and the food varieties – and, her eyelids squeezed together, she sent up a mute shout of grateful exultation.

~

Once they had returned home, presents were exchanged and exclaimed over, vegetables were prepared and the pudding put on to steam. The house echoed with noise and twinkled in the light given out by fires in the downstairs rooms and a myriad of candles. The old oak dining table had been heaved out from its place in the hall and moved into the playroom, which reverted just for this time into its original use as a dining room (Demelza's effects having been restored into the chaos of her bedroom). The table had been dusted and polished until the ancient patina gave out its own dull, waxy shine; its surface crammed with mats, dishes and shining cutlery, crackers and more party-poppers. The bookshelves adjacent to the table were adorned with tangerines, walnuts from their tree, dates and pots of Devonshire cream, ready for the pudding. Connie had put a final log on a roaring fire and pulled her head back carefully, so as not to hit it on the low, heavy beam that protruded across, and from which hung an array of Christmas decorations, in smaller proportion to those which were draped over the beams above, where Demelza's trumpet hung, drunkenly draped in ribbon and mistletoe. Stretching herself up to full height she felt she heard, above the general tumult, a strange rumbling sound, which appeared to be getting increasingly louder.

Suddenly she was alone in the paper littered room. Where the children had before been hastening in and out, their hands full of things for the table, a swift exit for the front door had been occasioned. They had left it swinging open, in spite of the cold from outside. Connie stumbled out after them as the thrumming stopped and a tall, portly figure, clad entirely in black leather was being set upon by her daughters as he attempted to lift off his helmet. His large brown eyes swivelled quizzically towards Connie, their uncertainty showing plainly. Connie stood transfixed, as her mouth broadened into a delighted grin:

"*Sebastian!* What…?"

She walked slowly towards him as he continued to struggle with the releasing strap on his helmet and the children anxiously watched their mother's reaction.

"I invited him – on all our behalves – you *did* want him to come, didn't you?" Demelza was saying, rather too hastily, aware of the enormity of the risk in her undertaking.

"I – I hadn't actually thought..." Connie replied, before she realised that she was lying. She *had* actually thought, wistfully, a number of times – but had swept the feeling away 'to think about tomorrow' in her time honoured Scarlet O' Hara tradition. Everyone was looking at her beaming face, which belied any words to the contrary. At last, the wretched strap was free and Sebastian was able to distract himself with levering off the helmet and giving his big shaved head a little shake from its confines. It was his turn to speak:

"I've just brought some presents – I can go after." The adults were not doing very well, for the ellipses in their speech gaped wide and Connie's response was a muttered 'Oo' sound, of polite interest. He looked into her face, so full of poorly suppressed joy, and dared to say:

"I'm so glad to see you," and then *she* dared to stand on tiptoe and extend her arms to hug him as she answered:

"Me too: I've missed you so much." Demelza and Ella were winking conspiratorially and ushering the others inside, while Poppy was to be heard complaining bitterly that Sebbo had only just got here.

"You can carry in his presents," Demelza had answered kindly.

∼

Connie had entirely lost the ability to sort out the final, crucial coming together of the Christmas dinner: Sebastian had disappeared briefly to the barn, bringing back with him a box which he dumped, unceremoniously into her lap. The box was open and the contents visible: she gave a cry of delight and gently lifted out a tiny, fat, fluffy mongrel puppy; who whined and wiggled at everyone, snuggling and snuffing into arms, licking and lapping at their fingers. Connie felt overwhelmed as she pulled Tramp's old water bowl from the debris at the back of the kitchen cupboard and placed it beside the box in the far corner of the kitchen, where his basket used to be. They covered the area with newspaper, but the puppy was barely out of anyone's arms. Connie looked wonderingly at the little warm bundle of soft fur with its wiggling tail and then at Sebastian:

"He's just so perfect: oo I'm simply so happy – and I haven't got you anything!"

"That is a matter of opinion," he answered and he tried, unsuccessfully, to resist hugging her again, trying not to overdo it in front of the children. However, he need not have worried, for they all piled around and on top of him and Connie, joining them; while the puppy yelped and peed for attention!

The dinner, somehow, materialised amongst a melée of eager helping hands, and was scrumptiously edible, against all odds. The pressure-cooker screamed for attention as they were scraping the final mouthful, bringing Connie temporarily out of her reverie from this glorious day, which had swamped her. She raced out to the kitchen to turn out her pudding, which was stuffed full of home walnuts and drowned in brandy. In family tradition, she held out a spoon-full of brandy while the children and Sebastian scraped at numerous matches, which they lit and held under the spoon until the glorious moment when its contents burned blue and gold and were poured over the sizzling pudding, filling the room with the intoxicating aroma of Christmas.

After the crackers had been pulled (the puppy becoming over-excited with the bangs and letting out one of its own on the hearth rug!) the clotted cream-filled dates passed around, accompanied by glasses of Nigel's present of sloe gin, the family collapsed onto sofas around the dwindling fire. Carrying the sloe gin and two glasses, Connie beckoned to Sebastian, who quietly rose from his seat and followed her into the Snug.

"I've been wanting to speak to you on your own since you arrived," said Connie quickly, before they had properly sat down or kicked the fire into life; "I wanted to say that I know I treated you horribly, when actually you had been a complete rock to us all – during that awful time."

"Connie, you didn't treat me badly. It was me, filled with the usual 'me me' self-importance, expecting attention where I had no right! I was so ashamed of myself and I've been hiding away, determined – unsuccessfully – never to be reminded of what a prat I've been. I simply haven't been able to deal with it at all."

"I couldn't stop being horrible: it was like watching myself from the wrong end of a telescope – posturing and carping. I wasn't in control of anything I did or said – and the worst of it all was I was so swamped that I really didn't care! You had absolutely every reason to leave and I would have too, if you'd treated me so ungratefully after everything… I don't really deserve the chance to say this, but I'm so sorry – and I didn't contact you because I felt I didn't deserve you." Sebastian was in the armchair and Connie was sitting, rather primly and carefully, on the arm. She was determined to use the chance to say all the things that had lurked inside her, in the place which she reserved to 'think about tomorrow, for tomorrow was another day' – but this time she would face them today!

"Are you beginning to notice that our excuses for staying out of contact are about as daft as one another's?" Sebastian asked, looking at her for the first time, since prior to this, when he had been confessing his inadequacies, he hadn't felt equal to her gaze and might have balked.

"Perhaps we have Demelza to thank for splitting us up and Demelza to thank for –" she returned his gaze shyly, still unsure if she should voice this. His large brown eyes, that she had once described as *Minstrels* chocolates, looked back at her, unwavering. "And Demelza to thank for getting us back together?" she said in a rush. Sebastian smiled happily and drew her close into the chair, which was ridiculously small for two of any size – let alone his large frame. He kissed her gently and went on:

"We can't give all the credit to Demelza, you know – there was someone else." Connie froze, misinterpreting his meaning, her heart thudding in her ribs, the blood singing in her ears: she might have guessed: it served her right. This was what happened. Of course he had met someone else: why wouldn't he and where was she? Why was he here? She made an attempt at composure, trying to struggle up from the tight confines of the armchair and hoping she could manage a casual inflection to her voice as she asked:

"Who?"

"Your Aunt Belinda."

"What? But you don't know her!"

"Oh I do now." Sebastian was enjoying her incredulity as he explained:

"You remember my quest after the William III portrait figure? The one that had its own number but no substance and which I almost tracked down when –"

"When you rushed off because of Demelza: could I forget? And I was so vile about you saving my feelings by not telling me about it. I think I called you a liar!"

"You did – more than once as I recall!"

"Oh I'm sure only once!"

"Only once?" Sebastian teased.

"Well once too many anyway. But come on, nice as it was to revisit that shameful episode: what has a portrait figure got to do with Aunt Belinda and Uncle Gerald?" Connie gobbled, immeasurably relieved to hear the mystery woman was an octogenarian.

"Well I sort of threw myself into finding out about the other figure, really just to keep me from thinking... and this missing figure had, it turned out, been snaffled up by a lady in Worcester. With a bit of delving I managed to get hold of her address – invasive, I know – and persuade her to let me see the piece, so that I could verify if it was genuine and legitimise its existence." He paused, and Connie, still much confused, begged him to continue quickly.

"She really shouldn't make herself so readily available to every hum-dinging hawker that springs up from nowhere, you know: she and your uncle asked me to drop in on them and opened the door to me just like that!"

"They would – and don't tell me – the homemade wine was ready."

"Almost as I got my foot in the door in fact! Anyway, they invited me in and just as we were about to sit down, and your aunt had gone to fetch the piece, I saw a picture of you and the children on the piano. It shook me sideways and I went all goosepimply!"

"You're making me go goosepimply just talking about it – I can't *believe* this – go on!" Connie urged impatiently.

"Well I said something a bit daft like 'Where did you get that picture?' And your uncle said it was his niece and great nieces. I just kind of gawped at the whole unlikeliness of the thing – and then, of course, I had to explain. And your Aunt Belinda called us both a thing or two and said that you were 'still pining', as she so kindly put it. She said we should have our heads knocked together and such, while your uncle administered the wine copiously (my God! but that was heady stuff – they seemed to cope with it a whole lot better than me and I had to get back to London)."

"Was it the parsnip?"

"No, the *rhubarb* I believe."

"Anyway, at the point when she said that it was obvious you still *held a candle* for me (again, so kind), I wanted to pluck up courage and speak to you. I was still sort of *plucking* when Demelza called, and she said *if* I happened to be thinking of furnishing you lot with any presents, then Christmas Day would be ideal! She was so positive as well – and that helped me get my nerve up to call; but I can tell you I could barely get off the bike, I was quaking so much! First I walked across the fields from the village, where I bought the puppy, and put it into the barn (which was Demelza's idea), and then I couldn't delay any longer because we couldn't leave it in the box for long – the rest is history." Connie drew a long breath, trying to order the extraordinary chain of events:

"But what about the portrait figure? Was it the right William III?"

"Oh yes – and now it's properly catalogued."

"And what's happened to it?"

"Last seen, both reunited and living happily together next to a bottle of nettle wine." Connie still looked puzzled, but Sebastian continued: "I was very glad to give her mine and I hope they (William and William) live happily ever after." Connie was delighted and touched, knowing more than anyone how much the figure and the quest for it had meant to Sebastian – and therefore the enormity of his gift; but he shrugged these considerations aside.

"Maybe we should take a bit of a leaf out of their – the Williams III's – book," he began mysteriously.

"Are you saying you *would* come back then, like William III?" asked Connie slowly, hoping but barely believing she had caught his allusion.

"*Would* you be prepared to at least give it another go?" Connie, for a moment lost for words, nodded her head and squeezed him tighter.

"Then I'm dancing!" pronounced Sebastian happily. At this point the door shot open, battering into the back of their chair and Ella burst in with a noisy remonstrance that Demelza had 'Stuck the puppy on her' just at the point when he was going to do a whoopsy; and it was *all* down her new Christmas top and Demelza had *done it on purpose!* Shouts of laughter from the others confirmed that this was probably the case, while Demelza protested:

"Like I could possibly know when it was about to do that!"

"Because you saw he'd already started!"

"Yeah right!"

"We all *so* saw you – he sort of started grunting and you bunged him at me and I couldn't *not* take him." Connie attempted to jump swiftly from the confines of the armchair she was sharing and landed in a bundle upon the floor, telling Ella as she tumbled, to run her top under the tap, for puppy poop wouldn't stain. Ella was then mollified by the further suggestion of changing into a somewhat coveted top of *Demelza's* – just to make it fair.

This exchange actually served to make Sebastian feel at home again and he noted that no one had batted an eyelid at his sharing the armchair with their mother after so short a re-acquaintance. He suggested that the puppy probably needed a bit of a walk and felt gently pleased that everyone seemed to want to accompany him; thus the warmth of the fireside was abandoned for a while, during which time they dragged suitable coverings from the hooks in the hall and trooped out into the half light of late afternoon, carrying tempting scraps, consisting of stuffing and congealed vegetables, for the ducks and hens; while the puppy cavorted backwards and forwards from one adoring new mistress to the next.

The ducks tore greedily at the scraps, shaking and worrying each morsel; after which the family continued on their way up the paddock towards the hen run, passing, as they did so, the trampoline. Sebastian stopped:

"Remember last Christmas Eve, when we spent all those hours trying to put that thing together?" he asked, and they all stared at the object that they had treated with distain ever since the fateful day of Demelza's accident; for no one had felt like revisiting the scene since then, and the joy derived from the equipment had turned on its head. Many times of course they had passed the path to it, which had turned into a mere stain on the grass, looking more as though it signified ancient earthworks. Some people had even *stood* on it at the benefit concert, to improve their view – but this had not included any of the family. Now they turned involuntarily to look at it, with eyes that remembered the pain of past times. No one spoke, each busy with thoughts united over one moment – and how that moment had shattered their lives.

Slowly, very slowly, Demelza moved away from the group and limped purposefully towards the trampoline as they watched in silence. When she reached it she put her hands up behind her, arms strengthened by the use of crutches, and heaved herself up to a sitting position on it, facing them defiantly: each heart beat more rapidly at the sight. Connie tensed further as Ella, too, splintered off from the group and walked purposefully towards her sister, following her example and pulling herself up beside her. After Ella it seemed to be Sophia and Poppy's turn, and they struggled and heaved one another into place. Sebastian was watching Connie, who looked strained and pale, in contrast to how she had seemed earlier. Gently he held out his hand and she grasped it tightly, as together they crossed the short distance to the trampoline, Sebastian hoisting Connie up before clambering after her. Without awareness, hands became joined and the circle was emotionally and physically complete. Solemnly and slowly, very slowly, they began to jig very gently up and down, their faces beginning to lose their restraint, with the unison of the pulsating movement. Gradually they began to share a grin, began to laugh, began to sing, began to shout as one:

I feel dangerous! I feel ssss so alive! while the puppy yapped and pogoed its own tattoo at the joyous, new world it had begun to inhabit.

BIBLIOGRAPHY

Antonia Fraser (1976) *Lives of Kings and Queens of England.*
Weidenfield & Nicholson

Leslie Wenn (1976) *Restoring Antique Furniture*
Barrie & Johnson

Michael Doussy (1977) *Antiques, Professional Secrets for the Amateur*
Souvenir Press Ltd

Dr Maxine Long (1998) *Encyclopaedia of Medicine and Health*
Robinson Publishing

P D Gordon Pugh (1987) *Staffordshire Portrait Figures and Allied Subjects of the Victorian Era*
Barrie & Jenkins Ltd